The LIFE of

Martin

LIFE: Book 1

By Alec Managhan

3rd Edition
ISBN#: 978-0-9960126-8-3

For the immense support and unending encouragement, I am indebted to my dear friends and my family. Your names grace the pages of this book. Special thanks to Olivia Taylen, Jack Lehl, and Zach Floyd, for without your enthusiasm and hard work, this would never have come to be.

Thank you!

Contents

Chapter 1
Who am I?

Memories are strange. Some can be bright and joyous, while others cover you in darkness and despair. Memories can also be lost. The loss of memory can be caused by injury to the brain. This condition is called amnesia. Often, this injury takes only the victim's memories, nothing else. In many cases, a person who has amnesia can read, write, and talk just as they could before. Learned skills and muscle memory often remain with the victim, although memory of how they were obtained does not remain.

This was the life to which I awoke. Not one instance of my life before was left for me. I was not even permitted to know what I had done to lose it all. New memories would have to take the place of the old. This was the new beginning of my life.

Rain pelted down on me as thunder boomed, lightning illuminating the small boat in which I sat. These simple details constructed the scenery of my first memory. The startling environment drowned out all other details with shock and awe. I sat up, confused, and looked around. Drenched head to toe, I realized the boat was flooded with water.

A brilliant flash and loud boom caused me to jump, splashing some of the pooling water into the air. Another flash of lightning revealed more in the distance. Barely, I could see an outline on the horizon in front of me. I was about a mile out from the mainland. Coming to my senses, I started bailing the rainwater with a baseball cap I had found floating on the surface of the pooled water of the boat.

My mind drifting from the non-stimulating action of bailing water, I contemplated about who I might be. I examined myself to the best of my ability in the darkness, and I determined that I wore a jumpsuit and tennis shoes. Sitting straighter, I measured the distance from my shoulders to the seat of the boat with my eyes. I stretched out my long legs as well to guess at their length. I was tall, taller than the average male, and my shoulders were quite broad. I ran my fingers over my face. The prickly origins of a beard could be felt, perhaps a couple days old. My hair was matted down atop my head, straight but thick. These small things were all I knew about myself.

I turned my attention back to what I was wearing. Even though it was dark, I could see that the jumpsuit looked as if it had belonged to some kind of manual laborer. The material was slightly rough, probably rougher when dry. A certain odor remained on this soaked garment that I could not have mistaken for anything other than the smell of seafood. I guessed that I was a fisherman, hopefully a good one.

I continued to bail the water. I dunked the hat in and then quickly flung the water into the sea. This boat had little depth to it, so it did not take much water to fill the boat to a dangerous level. I worked diligently, having only a single task assigned to me.

Minutes feeling like hours, the water was brought to a much more manageable level. My task complete, I sat back and inspected the boat. Nothing of interest was here. Nothing but the baseball cap that I had found remained in the boat, not even oars.

My presence in a lifeboat only raised more questions in my mind. Where was the main ship to which this lifeboat belonged? How had I come to be out here? Had we wrecked? Where was the rest of the crew then? For the time being, I did not have any answers. I looked eagerly ahead for the time when I might receive them.

Moving closer to the shore, I could make out a makeshift dock jutting out into the sea, lit barely by the distant moon that was blocked mostly by storm clouds. It was short and looked as if it had been ravaged by the angry sea, but it was a dock. The unsettled waves were rocking a small rowboat violently into the wooden supports, causing a banging noise that slowly increased in volume as I impatiently came closer.

Drifting only several yards from the dock, I saw that a lone figure was coming to the dock with a flashlight. I had no idea who this man might be. I did not know if he would already know me from the past or if he would be someone new. I only knew that I knew nothing of him.

His footsteps sounding on the wet and rotted wood, he turned the flashlight to the rowboat. He seemed to be checking to see if it had been torn from the dock in the storm and drifted away. Satisfied that the boat was there, he turned from it and, doing so, turned the flashlight on the sea. The beam of light hit my eyes, and I shielded myself from it. The man shouted in surprise, and he turned the light from my eyes. He ran to the edge of the dock and waited for me to drift to him.

The boat nearing the rotting boards that were saturated with seawater, he offered me his hand and pulled me in to the dock. His hand was calloused and cracked, much different than my own.

With mystified curiosity, he looked down and asked, "Are you shipwrecked?"

Hearing this question, I became momentarily frustrated. "How should I know?!" I shouted at him, the words weak due to my hoarse voice from being out on the water so long. I could tell he did not hear me, for he tilted his head down toward me and lifted his hand to his ear. I shook my head to indicate I was not going to repeat what I had just said. It would be unfair to lash out at the man, for circumstance was my enemy, not he. There was no need for me to attack him.

As I climbed out of the small lifeboat with his help, the boat moved in the opposite direction. It rocked and swayed and then settled back to the rhythm of the waves. I noticed that the ship to which it belonged was evidently called the *Annabelle*. The name was printed in big, bold letters, which must have been painted on with great pride, on the side of the lifeboat.

I stood, legs wobbling momentarily and then adjusting. I was now free from the tiny sea vessel, and my eyes drifted down to inspect this individual. The man was about medium size and had wide shoulders. He must have been about his late 30's, and he had on old, worn clothes. The hair on his head was brownish-blonde, and it continued with his beard. By the state of the clothes, the man was most likely living in poverty. Despite the weathered look, the man had noticeably kind eyes that had a certain brightness to them.

"Do you know me?" I asked, fighting the soreness of my throat.

"What?!" he yelled over the noise of the storm, his hand cupping around his ear.

"Do you know me?!" I yelled, moving closer to the man and speaking into his cupped hand. He looked at me in confusion as if he had not heard me correctly a second time.

"Know you? Sir, I've only just met you!" he said.

At least, I knew that both of us had no recollection of the other. He was no enemy to me. Hopefully, he was a new friend. A person like myself could always use another friend. As far as I knew, this was my first one.

"So…are you shipwrecked?" the man asked again.

"I'm not sure. I can't remember," I said to him, shaking my head.

"What do you mean you can't remember?" he asked, just as puzzled as I was.

"I just... I just don't know."

His confusion was replaced with concern, and a new look of duty was on his face. He took a couple steps back and shined his light on a tiny house not far away.

"You must be freezing out here in the cold. Come, you can dry off in my home."

He led me to his house which became apparently smaller as we came nearer. Rain was pouring off the roof in buckets, coming down the nearly bare walls. The walls of the abode were stripped of almost all the white paint that had been applied many years ago. There was also a noticeable slant to the whole building. I was beginning to grow concerned that a storm such as this one might knock down this humble estate.

When we reached the door, he opened it for me, and I was assured that this man was a fisherman because of the terrible smell of fish that emanated from within. Stepping inside, I barely noticed the difference from the outside, as water dripped from the ceiling and into cups and buckets scattered throughout the house. I noted the time on entering the house: 6:23 am.

The man closed the door behind himself and me. A woman sitting in a chair positioned by a card table spoke to the man without looking up from a magazine she was reading.

"Is the boat okay, honey?" she asked the man.

The man chuckled and gave an affirmation. Then, the woman looked up and was surprised by my presence. She was about to ask the man about me, but then two children entered the room from a smaller room to my left. One let out a yawn, and the other child was rubbing her eyes. Then, both noticed me. The two ran to me, awakened by excitement, and gazed up into my soaked visage. They were both very curious of me, and the girl asked the same question as her father had, "Are you shipwrecked?"

I replied, "Indeed, I am." I saw the man, knowing that I knew not myself, smile at the poke of fun at the children who I assumed were his kids.

The woman, who I guessed was his wife, set down her magazine, stood up from her chair, and came to me. She shook my hand and introduced herself as Mia Callison. She was also medium-sized and donned the same worn apparel. Her hair was long and brown, and, even though you could see that she had suffered through much, she had a smile that lit up the humble room.

"I wish I could tell you my name," I said, "but I can't seem to remember it."

She laughed and said, "Well, *Martin*, maybe you should check your shirt."

I looked down, and, now that I was in the light, I could see that "Martin" was stitched into my jumpsuit.

"Can I assume that's your name?" she asked with a smile.

I started to respond when I felt a tug on my leg. It was the man's daughter.

"Martin, what happened to your boat?" the young girl asked me.

She seemed to be perhaps nine years old but was somewhat short for her age. Long blond hair flowed from her head, and she resembled her father. She shared the same kind eyes as her father as well.

"You know, I'm not entirely sure. In fact, I have no clue," I answered. It truly was the best answer I could give her.

The father looked concerned.

"Martin, what do you remember?"

I answered the question to the best of my ability. "Nothing," I said. "I can't remember anything.."

They provided me with both food and clothing. These people, who looked as if they barely had enough, were giving me their possessions. I felt quite guilty, but, understanding the situation in which I was, I politely thanked them and ate a large fish breakfast.

The clothes were slightly baggy and quite ragged. Holes were plentiful in the them, and it was evident that they had been passed down as work clothes. Still, I wore them with much gratitude, for they were much better than the fisherman's jumpsuit. It felt good to be in drier, more comfortable clothing.

The fish breakfast mostly consisted of cod. It was a good-tasting fish, and I did not have any problem with it since it was my first meal in memory. I sat at the table with the four of them. The two kids were on my left side, the wife was on my right side, and the man was across from me. Of course, we might as well just have been bunched in a circle, for the dining table was only a card table. Mia's legs were crowding mine, but the boy's were not, being withdrawn so that they would not accidentally bump mine.

The man's name was Jonah. His children were Alyssa, the inquisitive girl, and the younger and quieter boy was Cody. I had not yet heard the boy talk, and I wondered what he was like.

I glanced back at Cody. He had the dark brown hair of his mother which curled slightly because of its length. Looking in his deep blue eyes, I saw curiosity. The youth looked naturally strong and full of energy. He was a boy looking for an adventure.

The children were very well-behaved, but I could see that they were dying to ask me questions. Unfortunately, I knew that, if they were to ask me anything, I would not have answers. They ate their breakfast and would occasionally sneak looks at me.

Jonah had the same feeling and finally asked me, "What do you think happened that made you lose your memory, Martin?"

Swallowing, I looked up and met eyes with Jonah. I then turned them away, embarrassed that I lacked knowledge of what really happened to me. "Maybe I hit my head when the ship was sinking or something," I responded, shaking my head in uncertainty. It was a plausible reason to lose one's memory, but the answer was not fulfilling to me.

"Well, if you need any help with anything, you can ask anything from us," Mia said, her eyes leaving her food to meet mine.

If the remark had ever been made that poverty turned people towards cruelty, I believed it to be proven false here. This family was undeniably great to me. They treated me as if I were their own. I received a kindness from them most reserve for guests of the highest honor. I was glad I had run into these people first. They were the nicest people I could have met.

"No, thank you. You've been so good to me. I couldn't take anymore from you. But thank you! Truly. These clothes should be enough."

Mia did not seem to believe me.

"Are you sure?" she asked. She was very persistent, "I mean, you have nothing but the clothes, that we gave you, on your back."

The remark brought about a wince of embarrassment from me. She was right. I did not want to take more from this family, but I really needed something to help me find my memory. "Well...perhaps you could take me to wherever most fishing boats dock so that I could find the boat that brought me here. It is possible that it didn't sink." The boat would be my best chance at finding some fragment of my past.

She considered what I had suggested. I guess I had asked for more than she was expecting. The children's eyes darted between their mother and me. A drop of water fell from the ceiling and struck Alyssa on the head. She flinched slightly, and a small smirk appeared on Cody's face. Mia turned to her husband.

"We've got to help him," she pleaded with him.

"I know, but we can't afford the gas money or the time away from my fishing or your work," he said, lowering his voice as if he were embarrassed by what he was saying, but I could tell he really wanted to help me.

"Jonah, now is not the time to be selfish! This boy needs our help! We will make it through somehow, and we need to help him! We've always made it through. Why not him? Have a little hope!" she insisted in a more demanding way.

Jonah thought about it more. He was struggling with the idea of leaving their work, since they did not have much reserve money. He sighed deeply. Jonah's bright eyes settled on me. A lot must have been going through that man's mind. His eyes moved down, and a smirk graced his face. He decided to take a chance.

"Okay, let's go. Pack your bags, son. We're gonna get your memory back!"

Chapter 2
Ride of Contemplation

As the sun rose over the horizon, we all packed into the family's station wagon. Scooting into position in the middle seat, I could feel no cushion left in the torn up interior. There was no seat belt where I sat, and my head was close to hitting the roof. The two children took their places on either side of me, still mystified by my presence. Jonah and his wife sat up front.

Everyone in their place, Jonah turned the key to start the car as well as the journey forward into the mystery that had become unsolved in my brain. The car sputtered and struggled but would not turn all the way over. He pulled the key back and then turned it again, but he failed once more. Over and over, he tried to start the vehicle, but was unsuccessful in his efforts. After seven attempts, he grumbled and looked over at his wife. Mia gave Jonah a look of encouragement and that bright smile of hers. For the eighth time, Jonah turned the key, and, to the surprise of everyone but Mia, the car started immediately. The kids shouted in rejoice, and Jonah shook his head and chuckled. He shifted the car into drive, and we were on our way, a new beginning ahead of us.

I was quite glad that the comment about "packing my bags" was just a joke about my lack of bags because there would have been no room for them. Not having any possessions actually benefited me. This irony was in my favor.

The children to my immediate left and right were sitting quite still, staring. Feeling a discomfort from their undying gaze, I finally spoke up. "What do you guys think happened to my boat?" This question would release me from their silent eyes.

"Maybe you were attacked by the evil sea monster!" Alyssa said excitedly.

Finding her choice of words interesting, I laughed and turned to the boy for his reaction. I saw that the boy disregarded the very idea of a sea monster without hesitation. "I bet it was just some engine failure or something," I said. Alyssa seemed rather annoyed that I so easily dismissed her amazing idea.

"I think that someone did something to the ship that caused you to have to escape in the lifeboat," Cody said.

This was the first thing the boy had said to me. He seemed rather mature for his age, which looked, I estimated, to be seven years old. The way he spoke was very odd. It was as if he were an intellectual addressing the ramblings of a fool. Yet, he remained a young boy.

"Why would someone do that, Cody?" his sister responded coldly.

"I don't know, but it seems more likely than a sea monster."

Alyssa seemed very surprised that her brother, who was maybe around two years younger than she, had a very good response to her insult. I, too, was surprised. There was more to Cody than I had initially noticed.

"Where exactly are we going?" I asked the adults up front.

"We're going to a larger fishing town called Alemande. If you came from a big boat way out there in the ocean, then odds are you came from Alemande," he paused, thinking before completing the thought. "I was also hoping to get a better job there. Working anywhere on the docks in Alemande would be a huge step up from what I'm doing now, but I'd hate to take the kids away from their school and friends."

"No, no, no, no, no! No way we're moving! No way!" both the children screamed from the backseat.

"Don't worry. I don't think I'd be able to get the job, anyway," Jonah said, looking somberly at his wife.

"How long until we get to Alemande?" I asked, full of questions.

"It should only be an hour or so, Martin. Not too long of a wait," Jonah said.

An hour or so?! How could I wait that long in this cramped car? I wanted answers, and I currently was lacking the patience necessary for such a long car ride. To have to wait now felt like torture. I only had about an hour of memory so far; I did not need to fill my head with another hour of a dull car ride.

Accepting my fate, I invested my time in the children and their parents. The kids told me about their school, which was in a very small town that was a mile walk from their house. Mia and Jonah discussed their jobs with me with commentary from the children.

The town's name was Jordanston, and its population was slightly over 400. Jordanston Elementary was, from what the kids told me, a mockery of the education system. Rules were unbelievably restrictive due to constant delinquent behavior. This behavior was not unique to the students, though. Alyssa spoke of her fourth grade teacher's bottle in a paper bag from which she drank often. Sadly, this school was the closest and only option for Jonah and Mia to send their kids.

Mia worked as an employee of the local grocery store. She was paid minimum wage, $15.65, and faced conditions that should only be faced by those meant to combat crime. While I felt she should be paid more for the danger in which she was put, Mia disregarded it as she considered it as part of the job.

I did not feel that our society's condition should be treated as commonplace. From what had been explained to me, foreign relations had destabilized the global marketplace, damaging our country's economy badly. Desperate times fell upon many, many people, and these desperate times led to a significant rise in crime. From there, society had only continued descending into deeper darkness, unable to break its cycle of pain begetting pain, desperation forcing others into that same desperation. This was a hard world in which to survive, let alone thrive. Yet somehow, this family was just barely scraping by.

Jonah did not have a paying job. He supplied the family with food, specifically cod. He went out every day with his rowboat and his fishing pole and brought back as much fish as he could. He was out there from dawn to dusk, but he was limited by his dinky boat and cheap pole. For the man's effort, he should have brought in two boatfuls of fish.

Life was unfair to this family. To its two bright children, it gave a poor learning environment. To its dedicated mother, it gave a paycheck that was more an insult than a way to pay the bills. To its hard-working father, it gave half as much as it took. What would this same life give to me?

As we neared the end of the trip, we passed a building that looked vaguely familiar to me. The building spelled out L.I.F.E. in capital letters above the main doors. It towered above the sea from atop the cliff that we had been ascending in the car. It looked outstanding at this pinnacle, away from any sign of life besides the humble road that lay right outside its walls.

It looked as if it were home to modern kings and knights, a certain similarity to a castle portrayed by the dark gray, towering fortress before me. The blacked out windows dotted all over its face appeared as sinister, beady eyes, sending a chill down my spine. The way the sun hit the letters and produced shadows over the stubbornly motionless doors positioned directly in the center of the building was undeniably familiar. I had amnesia, though. Why did I feel as if I had seen this before?

"What is that building over there?" I asked Jonah.

"I don't really know much about it, but I believe it's called the L.I.F.E. building. Some kind of government facility, I think. Do you know anything about it, honey?" he said, turning to his wife.

"I don't have much of a clue as to what exactly it is, even though I pass by it quite often. Why do you ask, Martin? Just looking for something to talk about?"

"No, it's just that it... It just looks so…familiar."

"We'll be there in no time, so sit back and relax a little. You only have about 20 minutes until we get there."

Jonah said this to comfort me, but I was uncomfortable with it. It felt wrong to ignore what my mind was trying to tell me. Why was this familiar? I wanted to know why I recognized it. I needed to know.

If this building were actually a part of my past, why would a fisherman like me have any connections to this place? Though, I was never really sure if I even was a fisherman. The only clues were the boat and my uniform. Was I connected to this building? Was I a fisherman? I had so many questions.

"Do either of you know anyone who works in that building?" I asked the adults, determined to learn something about this mysterious structure.

"No, Martin, and you'd be hard pressed to find anyone in this area who might know someone who works there. The folks in Alemande have a real dislike of that place from what I've heard," Jonah answered me.

"Why is that?"

"Lots of dark rumors about that L.I.F.E. building. People say kids have come running back to town freaked out and with all kinds of stories about what goes on in there after having snuck around a bit. I think they're mostly ghost stories, but they've had an effect on the town. That and the people of Alemande are pretty conservative. They don't like the government blowing huge amounts of tax dollars on expensive facilities which only seem to negatively affect their community."

"But no one actually knows what they do?"

"Not specifically. They're a government organization. That's all we really know."

I sat back and considered what could be going on inside those walls. L.I.F.E. had to be some kind of acronym. The Leading Incorporation in Frying Eggs? The Living Interest-Free Economy? I did not know for what it might stand, and I could not come up with a good solution. It stood for something, and I desired to know what.

I also wondered why all the windows were blacked out. Why all the secrecy? What were they up to in there? The acronym reminded me of such government agencies as the C.I.A. and the F.B.I. What kind of government business would go on in this building? I had a lot of questions, but no answers. It was like my memories.

And what could I have been doing out on the sea that night? A fisherman had a good enough reason for being out there: fishing. Though, a fisherman does not tend to fish so late at night. Of course, the boat could have spent days at sea and fished for possibly weeks at a time. That would explain being out at night.

My thoughts shifted towards the uniform. The uniform was just a plain tan jumpsuit. I remembered feeling as if I had worn it for a long time. The way it rubbed against my skin felt familiar. It was possible that I had owned a few jumpsuits, possibly just two, and had switched when I needed to wash the one being worn. The uniform had smelled heavily of both salt and fish. With these points brought up, I felt quite sure that the boat had been at sea for some time and that I had worked aboard it.

Thought turned back again to the L.I.F.E. building. If I was so sure that I had worked on the boat for quite a while, how did I know this building? A plausible explanation came with the fact that I had possibly lived close to here. If I had lived by this structure, I would have seen it many times.

Again, the boat was meant to stay at sea for long periods of time. This being the case, I would have lived on the boat. If I had lived on this boat, why would I have much need for a house? Also, why would I remember the building so well? Being on the boat so much would have meant that I probably would have stayed within the confines of Alemande. It left no reason to come out all this way. How did I know that place?

Sitting here in the car, I had not made a sound for a long while. The kids on either side of me babbled about many topics to each other. Jonah and Mia seemed to be talking about the chance for Jonah to get a job in Alemande. I then chose not to listen to these conversations and fell back into my own mind.

Amnesia had definitely set me back. With no memories, I forced myself to play detective with the few clues with which I had come here. Of course, with no memories, I could be sure of nothing at all. Simple mysteries became infinitely more mysterious in my situation.

I closed my eyes and searched desperately for a memory. Nothing came to me. I could find nothing within my broken brain. I would have to go through this the hard way. Perhaps with time, doctors, and therapists, I would regain the past I had lost.

I awoke from my daydreams to a call for which I had impatiently awaited.

"We're here, Martin!"

Chapter 3
Welcome to Alemande

Alemande was a community that had many more people than you would expect, since it was just a simple, fishing-based town. I watched the stereo clock turn over to eight o'clock, and we soon were caught in the masses of Alemande who were scattering to their workplaces. Contrary to the fact that the town was packed with people, our car was the only one in sight. I soon understood why.

People crowded the streets as we tried to drive to the docks. The pedestrians had lost respect for those driving vehicles that could have ended their lives if operated carelessly enough, and now they wandered into the street whenever they pleased. It became quite difficult to move even ten feet before once again being blocked. A few people even approached the car and tried to solicit us. Carpet salesmen, "used" jewelry salesmen, and other peddlers incessantly knocked on the windows of the car. We tried to ignore them, but it got to be too much for us. We were not making much ground.

Giving up this fight, we managed to find a parking lot and decided to walk from there. Parking was easy here with only two other cars, leaving 12 for us to choose. We drove into the first spot and parked.

The doors of the car were flung opened, and the family and I piled out of the vehicle. Mia and Jonah brought the kids under their arms and instructed them to stay close. Cody and Alyssa pried themselves free of their parents, but they promised to not run off. Jonah and Mia led the group out of the parking lot and into the bustling town. The kids strolled in front of me, their eyes huge and darting about the scenery of their new environment. I brought up the rear of the group.

Even more people decided to approach us when we were on foot, somehow figuring out that we were new, even with the crowd surrounding us. We decided that it would be better to go through the alleys to avoid as many people as possible. Breaking from the crowd, we retreated between the two-story, decrepit buildings of downtown Alemande. We were disappointed to find somebody traveling in the alleys just as we were. His eyes were locked on us, and I could tell he had something to ask us. I stepped up to the front of the group to put myself between him and the kids.

When he came up on us, he asked, "Hey, do you know where the 8:15 bus to West City is? 'Cuz my car was stolen, and I need to get to my sister who is giving birth in West City. You gotta help me out, guys."

I found it strange that he did not recognize that we were new to town as he was. I also found it strange that a bus would attempt to drive through the city.

I turned back to ask the family if they knew anything that could help this man. An overwhelming expression of terror appeared on their faces. I turned around only to have a pistol shoved into my gut.

"Hand over your money and the car keys," the man threatened, stepping back from me but keeping the gun pointed at my gut.

"Whoa, just take it easy, man. We don't have money or a car. Hey, look at my clothes! We're just as bad off as you are, okay?" I said, trying to trick him.

"I saw you peoples trying to drive through the city in that car. I had pretended to be a salesman and got a good look at you peoples. You wouldn't buy something from a stinkin' peddler like me, now would ya? You wouldn't let me speaks a word to ya! Now, I'm in control. Now, I get my chance. Finally, I get a chance... And you getta take my place. This is my time!"

The man stood about six foot and appeared to weigh approximately 200 pounds. His hair was scraggly and brown but was covered by a baseball cap, on which "Bishop Transportation" was written in bold letters. He also wore a large leather jacket, a dirty T-shirt, and dark black jeans. The gun was held solidly in his right hand. He seemed experienced in his criminal profession, but still he panted lightly in anticipation of any action I might take against him.

I knew there was no tricking him, even though the poor grammar alluded to it. That being said, I was not about to surrender anything to this man. I comforted the family with a smile and reached for my pocket. This act surprised the mugger a bit and he backed up. Then, as quickly as I could, I lunged at the man, grabbed the gun, and pointed it upwards. He fired into the sky, and then I delivered a punch to the man's ribs, feeling a cracking sensation as my fist plunged inward. When he bent over in pain, I kneed him in the chin. He stumbled backwards and hit the pavement with the back and his head, the pistol tumbling out of his hands and under a dumpster. The man moaned and then blacked out.

I was surprised by the sudden burst of speed and strength that had taken this man down. Yet, it felt natural to have strength over an adversary. And it felt good, too. I approached him slowly to check his condition. I pushed on his chest and felt that I had broken this mugger's ribs. Then, I looked at his mouth, which was full of blood and broken teeth. I turned to the family. They looked very fearful of me.

"How did I do that?" I questioned them, a similar look in my own eyes.

"I...I don't k-know," Jonah stammered, shocked at what I had done.

"You beat that guy up!" exclaimed Alyssa, both excited and appalled by what she had witnessed.

"Is he going to be okay? He's not moving," said Cody, his mouth agape.

"I guess we should take this man to the police station," Mia suggested sensibly, recovering slightly.

"Good idea," I responded, lifting the man onto my shoulder.

We exited the alley and went back out into the masses. I carried him through crowds of very curious streetwalkers of the small town. Strange looks were exchanged with me often. With the strange looks came the ability of these people to finally move out of our way. I could see a building far away that appeared to be a police station. We made our way there.

Surprisingly, the man barely weighed anything even with his overweight appearance. This merely added to the confusion that came with the event that occurred in the alley. I surely felt strong and capable, but this seemed to surpass that greatly.

Our group's footsteps sounded on the pavement of the station's reserved parking. Two police cruisers sat outside currently, and I guessed that they were the only two owned by the station. Cars were not popular in this town, but the vehicles remained nonetheless, a tool to be utilized by a force meant to be superior to the masses it protected.

As we entered the police station, the officer behind the desk stood up and practically ran to us, his hand over the holstered weapon at his hip. He smiled as he looked upon the man we had brought in. I held the mugger in front of me for him to examine.

The officer seemed amazed and intrigued. He ran his fingers through the tiny bristles of blonde hair on his head and stared for a second, unable to say anything. His quick eyes failed to miss a single detail as he ran them over the mugger's body. He chuckled slightly and came back to his senses.

"So the bad guys don't always get away, huh, Liam?" the officer poked the man in the chest with a satisfied air to himself.

The mugger, Liam apparently, groaned in anguish. The officer pulled back his finger, embarrassed to have caused pain to the criminal unnecessarily.

"Whoa! You broke his ribs...and his teeth!"

The officer called back to the rest of the station. His eyes shot back to me, and I could tell he felt bad for taking such satisfaction in seeing Liam incapacitated in my arms. Two men came through the door and then ran to the bleeding mugger.

"Wow, nice job...uh...kid."

The officer was quite confused by the fact that a "kid" like me could hold this full grown man with no trouble. His thoughts were also probably on how this mugger was so severely injured. The look on his face gave me certain pride, and it felt good to be respected, or even possibly feared, by this man of the law.

"I'm Officer Turnbull. These are Officers Chase Thompson and Heath Thompson," said the first officer, while Jonah and Mia shook all of their hands.

"Oh, so you two are brothers?" I asked the other two.

"Yes, we are. How could you tell?" Chase responded with a joking smirk.

The resemblance was too easy to spot. Even without knowledge of their last names, I would have been able to tell that they were brothers. They shared the same dark hair and joyful smirk. Their shoulders could not be more even. Even their facial features looked almost like mirror images. They looked as if they were twins! Though, Heath's nose jutted slightly to the left, possibly from being broken. This feature gave him away.

"Well, nice to meet all of you, but where do I set this guy?" I asked, wishing to be free of the bloody and moaning man.

"I'll take him," Heath said, then took him to the back of the station to lock the culprit/victim in a cell.

When he came back, he called the hospital.

"There is a reward on that man's head, you know? Do you want it?" asked Officer Turnbull, more as a formality than a real question.

The rest of my party were too humble to speak up, but this was my chance to repay them for their kindness. I said, "Sure, how much?"

He laughed and went over to his desk. Punching some keys on a cash register sitting on the desk, he got the drawer open and grabbed out some money. He then turned back to us with the $500.

"What is your name?" Officer Turnbull asked me, his eyes squinting slightly.

"It's Martin, sir."

"This is yours, Martin," he said as put the bills in my open hands.

The crisp clean feel of these five one-hundred dollar bills was definitely new to me. Their weight was close to nothing, but I could feel the enormous power behind them. The feel of money was one that I would learn to respect.

"The police department of Alemande thanks you for your service to this city. Without citizens like yourself stepping out and fighting back against those who would spread terror in our streets, we might never take back Alemande and return it to its once peaceful state. Thank you, Martin," Officer Turnbull said to me, shaking my hand.

"Thank you, sir." I handed the $500 to the family behind me. "You guys deserve this money, truly. Thank you so much for your help. You didn't have to, but you did."

"T-thank you, Martin," Jonah stammered and accepted the money with slightly trembling hands as if it were ten times as much.

Officer Turnbull smiled and said goodbye as we were leaving the station. This man's heart displayed itself on the outside, and I could feel it. He was a man who fought for justice wherever he could find it. This warm smile was the product of the joy in finding it.

"That was fun," Alyssa said as the door closed behind us.

I smiled and said, "Well, at least that will fund this trip." Jonah nodded happily, and I could tell that the emotion was shared by Mia. It made me quite happy to return some of the family's generosity.

The streets mostly clear of the once obnoxious crowds, I walked with my chest puffed out, boldly in the middle of the road, proud at what I had done. Jonah and Mia were arm in arm and they hugged the kids on either side of them. I was happy they were happy.

As we finally headed to the docks, I wondered how my speed, strength, and ability were related to my lost past. Was I an athlete who was well-conditioned daily? Maybe I was some kind of secret agent or something. Although, neither was all that likely. Perhaps being a fisherman had given me some handy perks.

I thought about how rowdy fishermen could be. I must have picked up all kinds of fighting tricks on that boat. Strength came naturally with hard work on a boat, and my reflexes probably were brought on by the fear of one of my shipmates beating me up.

These explanations made sense, but punching so hard that I could crack a man's ribs? This did not make sense to me. The mugger, Liam, maybe did not have much calcium. With lack of money comes lack of food which could explain weak bones. With an explanation like that, I did not feel very convinced. I might have been somewhat muscular, but not that much, and I doubted that a lack of milk was the bane of this man's existence. No explanation was in sight for this one either.

The boats in the distance became more and more visible as we neared the docks. I could hardly wait to get there, awaiting the slightest opportunity to clear up the terrible mess within my brain. Maybe the pieces would start to fit together and make sense for once. I was tired of playing this mind game. Answers were down there at the docks, and they were so close.

I then tried to clear my mind. With all the answers I needed not far away, I just relaxed and got ready to know what I needed to know. There was no more need to worry about it. It was coming. The truth would be here so soon.

As we came closer and closer, I could feel it all throughout my body. My heart pounded fiercely in my chest. Adrenaline surged throughout my body. Sweat was forming on my brow. A shiver went down my spine.

"Yes, this place is definitely familiar."

Chapter 4
Brawl at the Docks

The smell, the look, the people, the atmosphere, the boats. They all carried with them a sensation with which I knew I must have at one point been acquainted. I must have been here before. There was a wetness in the air that made my skin feel normal again. I had smelled the salty sea smell that wafted among the burly men of this place so many times before. Could the answer be that I was once a fisherman here? My heart pounded and demanded an answer.

"The fishermen here should know something," Jonah said. "Come on, Martin."

A few boats had just come in from the sea, and the docks were flourishing with burly men and distant profanity. I looked throughout the crowds at the many fishermen gathered here. Did I once know these people? I hoped that maybe one would recognize me and tell me what was going on. As we went through the crowds, the fishermen could not even spare a glance at me. It was the treatment one gives to those who he feels are of little importance to him. I fell out of hope and into doubt.

Traversing the crowds of foul-smelling, profane fishermen, we reached one that seemed to be keeping an eye on everyone. Yes, just an eye. He had only one eye, and it was busy darting through the crowds. The other, his left, was covered with a dark black patch. He was perched on a barrel, and his heavy brown boots rhythmically tapped the metal side. The man had very thick brown hair, which continued with his excessive mustache and beard. His blue jeans looked stiff as if he had worn them for over a week out at sea, and the sleeves were cut off from his jacket. He stood about as tall as myself. This man would hopefully be the one with the answers about my past.

"Hello, I'd like to ask you some questions," Jonah asked the large, one-eyed man.

"You cops?" he asked us.

He was kidding, but we answered him truthfully. "No, we need to know about a man named Martin," I spoke up.

"Don't know nothing 'bout no Martin," he mumbled, attempting to dismiss us, but I would not give up so easily.

"Look, man, it's important! Just tell us which boat he would be on!" I frantically responded to the man. I did not realize how panicky I had become. Anxiety in the face of being so close to the smallest portion of truth brought about a shakiness in me.

"No need to get all mad, Hoss," the man laughed, looking about to see who of the others had caught his humorous remark.

"Hey, my name is Martin," I said to him, angered by his unwillingness to cooperate and the disrespect he was showing me.

"So you're so confused you're asking questions about yourself?!" he laughed and got about ten people to join in, some by force.

"I have amnesia."

He still persisted in making fun of me, "I'm sure they have a cream for that!"

This time it seemed the whole place was laughing at me. My face flushed, and I could feel their words piercing my pride. This was my first experience with humiliation.

The fisherman would not let up. Insult after insult came my way. I tried to return them, but I could not fight the whole crowd with my words. Besides, these men were trained for this very type of attack in all their downtime. Profanity and insult sat on the tips of their tongues all day, waiting for their chance to be unleashed.

"Martin..." Mia's voice came from behind me, her hand perching on my shoulder.

"Let me handle this," I responded, and she recoiled slightly.

The family stood awkwardly by as the crowd tore me apart with their words. Glancing back, I saw the look of helplessness on their faces once again. Jonah and Mia both had their hands over their kids' ears, blocking out the language that was so carelessly tossed about in this place. I was tired of people putting us in this position. These kind souls had helped me so much, and I kept walking them into trouble. I knew I had to get us out of this mess, but I was not about to leave without getting my answers.

I decided that the only way to fight this man was with my strength. Perhaps being somewhat rash in my decision, I threw myself at the cyclops and knocked him off his barrel. Without thinking, I started punching him repeatedly in the face. He, not one to take a beating lying down, pushed me off him and rose to his feet. Even though he previously seemed fat and lazy, after he had risen, I could not miss the size of the muscles bursting forth from where his sleeves should have been on his jacket. The fishermen formed a poorly made circle around me and the man. Jonah and his family were pushed out of the group.

Everyone was cheering, "Fight, fight, fight!!!"

I smiled at them. Something was urging me to fight this man. Not just fight, but hurt, wound, maim, injure. He would suffer by my own hands. I knew I was stronger. And he needed to learn that. "Okay then. Let me give you something to laugh about, Cyclops!"

He laughed and replied, "Me being taken down by a... How old are you? 14? Yeah, good luck with that, kiddo!"

The fishermen laughed again. I had no response to this because I still had no idea what I even looked like, let alone how old I might be. Perhaps I really was only 14 years old, but it seemed unlikely that I could be that young.

The cyclops rushed at me with a burning desire to put me in my place. I, too, rushed forward, determination to destroy him a roaring flame within me. Both our fires were hot, but mine yielded better than his. I stood toe-to-toe with a grown man, a born fighter, and I was winning the fight.

The insults flew even between the blows, but now I was giving them. I told him how sad it was that "a 14-year-old" could drill him so hard. He had nothing to say to me since my performance was amazing for my age. The statement surely made his comrades chuckle, though.

On the balls of my feet, I danced around the lumbering man with the elegance of a seasoned boxer. My moves were so much more nimble than his, but I hit with the same force as he. I could feel the momentum of the fight, and I flowed with it freely. My body surged with energy, and I could not imagine ever growing tired of doing this. Adrenaline pumping, I could not help thinking how much fun this was!

A flurry of questions passed through my mind as I fought this man. Chief among them was the perplexing question as to how I was doing this at all. How could I fight like this? The power I could feel welling up within me, was it real? Did I have what it took to finish my foe? And if so, who was I before this amnesia?

I parried every punch and kick. When his big foot swung upwards, I rolled beneath it and flipped him with it. When his fist flew towards my head, another duck and repeated punches to his gut followed. Surely, it would have been easier if he had just rolled into a ball and hidden. He was not fit to fight the likes of me.

I fought like a martial arts master. My punches were precise, and I analyzed his every move. I saw what he was doing before he could complete the action. My brain picked up everything on this man. Once I had gained that advantage, there was no chance this man could beat me. This fight would end in my victory and his defeat. There was nothing he could do to stop me from breaking him.

Winning, I began to take the fight less seriously and have a little fun. My punches were packed with less power and more insult. I struck strategically and humorously, fear of losing no longer within me. Frustration built on his face with every humiliating attack that he could not return.

Frustration overtaking him, he thought he would try to end the fight in a single punch. He thrust his fist at me with all the strength he had within him. I grabbed the brute's fist and used his terrific momentum to chuck him into the crowd. Luckily, they all scattered away before he crashed to the concrete.

The cyclops let out a grunt from his position in the dust before me. Not willing to let me beat him, he forced himself to his feet once more. Angered, he charged at me and attempted to grab me. Sleekly, I dove between his pumping legs and then flipped around, jumped on the brute's back, and began choking him. Within a few seconds, he had his hands on me and ripped me from his back. He proceeded to chuck me along the concrete as it had been done to him.

The fishermen cheered even louder, but they were surprised when I got back up faster than their home player.

I reengaged my foe. He punched at me again, and I ducked under it to deliver blow after blow into his pudgy stomach. Infuriated, he tried to kick at me. I grabbed his leg and tipped him over. I jumped on top of him, holding down his shoulders with my knees, and threw some punches into his face. I hit him not with force, but with intent to insult and humiliate.

His buddies stood in astonishment. How did this kid just beat up the scariest man at the docks? They were stunned and did not move as I repeatedly punched him in the face. What had caused me to win? They surely did not know.

Neither did I know how I had done this. I had flowed throughout the battle, and he had just flopped. I had known exactly what I was doing, but I did not know how I had known. There was yet another mystery to solve.

Again, I was thinking. Even as my punches connected with this brute's face, I wondered about all of this. This was crazy. Whatever was happening, I hoped that all would be revealed soon. Not even halfway through my first day, I was fed up with the enigma that was my past.

His buddies quickly decided to help their fallen comrade. Five of them charged at me from all sides. I rose to face them. I took out the first one with a knockout punch, the second I shoved into the third, and I was just about to finish the fourth, but then I took a barrel to the head given by the fifth and was knocked out myself.

I hit the concrete and my head bounced off the ground. As the cheering faded and everything turned black, I knew I had won. I passed out with a smile on my lips.

When I woke up, I was looking up at the overconfident man who had thought he could beat me. He helped me up and smiled at me in a strange way that was perhaps very new to him. In proving my physical prowess, I had gained his respect. Everything that had brought us to blows before was forgotten and forgiven. We were just two men with a mutual interest and shared experience.

"You have bested me, friend," his smiling continued, and he offered his hand to me. I took it, and he introduced himself to me, saying, "My name is Andrew."

A fitting name for a large man like him. The great sea-faring Andrew, strong and determined under any circumstance. Of course, he could not even beat up a teenager.

"My name is Martin," I told my new friend.

"Sorry about the fight... Good job, by the way. But isn't there something that you needed to ask me?" Andrew asked, patting my shoulder with his great big hand.

Chapter 5
Donovan

"Yes, I have heard of you, Martin," Andrew said, sitting himself upon his barrel. "But I know just about nothing about you. I can't say I know which boat you would be on. Can't say I know anything that might help ya."

Disappointment flooded my face. "Well, that's okay. I'll get this figured out," I said, but still, my hope was fading away.

"And also, you were kinda a legend. I've only heard about you from my fellow workers. They said you were some kind of super kid. Like, never had they seen a kid work so hard in all their lives," Andrew told me, chuckling.

A murmur rose up from those surrounding us that seemed to confirm what Andrew had said. No one came forward with anything more tangible, though.

"Well, maybe that explains why I was able to demolish you," I joked with him.

"Ha, I sure hope so! I hate to be beat up by a kid like you... How old are you, anyway?" he asked, concerned that he had really been beaten up by a 14-year-old.

That is when I explained to the entire group that I did not truly know my age because I had amnesia. I told them about how I woke up and then how I got to the docks here in Alemande. When I had finished my story, they all looked shocked. They seemed to pity me, and Andrew seemed as if he felt guilty for fighting with me. They all offered their assistance immediately.

"Here, take a look at this," a fisherman said.

He offered me a broken mirror which he had found on the ground. Finally, I gave myself a thorough analyzing. My eyes first caught themselves, and I gazed into my own hazel circles. Dark brown hair sat upon my head, and a lighter variety went around my mouth and up my jawline, which looked stronger and wider than one might expect of a child. My prior thoughts proved to be quite accurate. I estimated my age at about 18.

There was a lull in the conversation as I examined myself in the mirror. Jonah took advantage of it and made his way to where Andrew was sitting on his barrel.

"Hey, uh…I was just wondering if maybe I could get a job here," Jonah asked shyly, almost whispering.

"As a fisherman? All the boats around here are at max capacity in terms of crew. And most of this area is covered in boats already. Sorry, bucko, but employment is limited here at the docks," Andrew said.

"Where are you from, anyways?" another fisherman asked.

"I live in a cottage about one and a half hours out that way," Jonah answered the man, pointing to the north.

"We do have a small fishing boat that you could fix up while you're here. We used to have a guy who would head out by that area all the time. He's long gone now, so I don't think he'd mind you taking the boat he's been neglecting forever. And you could fish out that area and bring the fish back here to sell them. A lot of the crew around here don't care to go out that far."

Jonah thought about the idea. I looked up from my mirror and into his eyes. I could see the wheels turning. This was his big chance. All he had to do was say yes and get the boat fixed up, and this job would be his. Success was so close.

"We could always use more fish to bring to market, and practically no one fishes over in that area. To tell you the truth, it's because some of our guys are a bit superstitious about that area. We don't really trust those L.I.F.E. folk and all their experiments. But you look like a guy that ain't scared of that kind of talk, especially with Martin around. And that boat is fast enough to get you here to there in about 30 minutes. Of course, you would have to take only a small crew with you. The boat can't hold too many," Andrew said.

I could see the euphoria dance on his face. Everything was working out. Everything was going to be okay. Hope had been found in this little fishing town.

"Okay, I'll do it!" Jonah decided.

With a massive smile and a nod of his head, Andrew spoke loudly to the crowd, "Listen up! We've got another brother here at the docks of good ol' Alemande! Give him our welcome, would ya?!"

Many of the fishermen let out a series of hollers, and everyone clapped for him. They celebrated the arrival of another of their kind. They were pleased to add one more to their beloved team. So, they celebrated, but their celebration could not come close to the exuberance that was inside Jonah.

Mia hugged her husband tightly as he stood there awestruck. The love and joy between them was so pure and obvious. I was glad that I had seen this. This was fortunately one of my first memories.

"All right then," Andrew laughed. "I think it would be wise for you and your family to stay at the Ale Inn while you fix it up. The rent isn't much, and the bed bugs in this town appreciate a good man and his loved ones, haha!"

"That sounds great! Let's go check-in, guys!" Jonah said excitedly to us, his arm around Mia and a hand on my shoulder, the kids gripping each of his legs tightly.

We walked to the inn with a big crowd of fishermen wanting to talk to us. Apparently, they thought that an extremely strong, 18-year-old fighter and an up-and-coming fisherman were quite interesting. They talked to us the whole way, asking questions like "When did you get so tough?" and "How's the fishing out your way?". We answered all their questions to the best of our ability. The questions asked to me were not answered as well as Jonah's questions, of course.

When we got to the Ale Inn, the fishermen departed because they could see we were tired and needed a rest. Coming inside, I looked around at the sparsely furnished lobby. Before me was the check-in desk, and behind it was a girl. We walked up to the desk, and the girl behind it greeted us with an anticipating smile.

"Hello, folks! Welcome to the Ale Inn. My name is Amber, and I would be happy to get you settled in with us. Can I get you set up with a couple rooms today?"

"Yeah, we'll take two rooms, please." Jonah turned to me and asked, "Or would you want your own room without the kids? We do owe you for getting us the job and reward money."

I appreciated that they were thinking of me, but I turned down the offer. "No, I will bunk with Cody and Alyssa. And it is I who owe you for taking me here."

"Okay, two rooms under the name Jonah Callison," he said to Amber.

"Perfect, two rooms. All right, Jonah, here are your keys."

Jonah took his key, and I took mine. Then, we headed to our rooms. Jonah and Mia's was up one floor from us because of a plumbing incident that made several rooms unusable and because of a general lack of rooms. We separated, and I led the kids to our room.

As we walked to our room, I found myself analyzing everything. 16 doors passed, 24 lights, 4 signs concerning hotel policy, and color scheme of green, tan, and brown. I thought about the girl who checked us in. Amber from what she told us, Amber Brown from what I read on her name tag. I remembered all her characteristics. Long brown hair, somewhat short, wore glasses, and she seemed to be almost a little excitable. As we walked, I noticed everything.

When I got to my room, Alyssa wanted to open the door with the key. "Okay, okay. Here you go, Alyssa." I handed her the key, and, immediately, she took off through the halls. Giggling, she rounded the corner and was gone. I looked to Cody for assistance.

He just shrugged and said, "Get her."

Left with no other option, I ran down the halls to chase her down.

Even though this was just a small game, I took it as a big annoyance. All I needed right now was to lie down and think more about what had happened. As soon as she ran, a brief feeling of desperation filled me, but was drowned out quickly by the need for the key.

Running through the halls, I could not find her. She was nowhere in sight. I ran through every hall looking for her. Where could she have gone? Although this was frustrating, I found a small bit of fun in this game. Strange how, even though I was about 18, I still had some interest in this childish game.

Finally, I found her. She was on the ground crying at the end of a hall. "What happened?" I asked her, kneeing when I came to her.

Through the sobs I could only make out, "Man…he…he took it!"

I saw Cody behind me. Worry filled me as I knew where the crook was going.

"Weren't you supposed to be guarding the door?" I shouted without thinking.

"You didn't say that," Cody responded, avoiding the blame that was rightfully mine.

"You're right. I'm sorry, dude. That wasn't your job," I said, lightly putting my hand on his shoulder in apology. My own inadequacy in taking care of these kids weighed upon my own shoulders, but the job was still mine for now.

I told the children to follow me, and we went back to the room. This ordeal was becoming more and more inconvenient. When we got there, I saw a shadow under the door. "He's in our room."

"Maybe…we can go talk to the hotel people," sobbed Alyssa.

Even though that was the intelligent decision, I wanted to settle this myself. This crook thought he could steal from me and get away with it. No, he could not. I would not let him win. This was between me and my thief, and I would settle this without outside help because I needed to prove to him that I could.

"I got this," I said. I noticed that she had a hairpin in her hair. I took it out and bent its shape to best fit its new use. Satisfied with the tool, I put it into the lock.

As I put the hairpin into the lock, I could feel the little parts moving in the doorknob. I closed my eyes and used the small vibrations to create some kind of sonar image in my mind. I soon found how easy it was to unlock the door. "A little move here and…got it!" The door unlocked, and I pushed it open.

I entered the room. The man was sitting on the bed watching TV when I walked in. He looked as tired as I and twice as dirty.

He got up and frightfully shouted, "What's going on here?!"

I grabbed him by the throat and asked him where the key was. He shakingly pointed to a table. I threw him onto the bed and grabbed the key. With what was mine once again in my hand, I looked at him, about to yell in anger, when I noticed he was crying.

"What are you doing?" I asked him, still hostile.

"I'm so pathetic that I had to steal a key from a little kid just to get some shelter! And I stole some of the rolls at the hotel food court!" he confessed.

I pitied the man, but it was hard to do so since he had stolen from me. Also, I wondered why he confessed stealing the rolls. Even with my feeling of pity, I was not going to show any mercy to him. "I'm sorry, but I can't help you now. Get out. And don't you dare come back," I said to him as I pushed him out the door. I watched him walk down the hall, out of my life.

With that ordeal over and the man gone, the kids came into the room and sat down on the bed. I changed the channel to a kid's cartoon, and, soon, Alyssa stopped crying. Both sat and watched the television while I pondered what had happened today.

A little while later Jonah and Mia came to the room.

"How you guys holding up in here?" Jonah asked us.

Alyssa started to speak up, but my glance informed her that she had better keep quiet. She looked down at the floor instead. Although probably quite unwise to not let the family know what had happened, I did not want to fall out of the good grace of Mia and Jonah right at the moment.

"We're doing fine," Cody said.

"Good. Do you think you can help with the boat later, Martin?" he asked me.

"Sure, that would be no problem," I replied.

"Good! But first, let's get a bite to eat. It's free for hotel guests. Isn't that great?"

The thought of food brought great emotions back into me. We left immediately to fill our empty stomachs.

The food served was lasagna, and I made sure to eat as much as possible, for it had been only the second meal I could remember. The whole time, I kept an eye on the kids so that they did not say anything to their parents about the strange man who had stolen our key. They did not even speak a word.

After we had eaten for perhaps half an hour, Jonah leaned back and exhaled deeply.

"I'm full. You good yet, Martin?" Jonah asked me.

"I'm good. Let's go fix that boat," I answered with a smile. I was ready to help him get his life on a great new road. Success would be in this man's future.

Before I got up, I heard a slight whimper from Cody. I looked over and saw the man who had stolen our key by the buffet. I could see he was again stealing food, stuffing it into pockets inside his large overcoat. Another thought of pity came to me, but something in me blocked it out.

"Hey, you!" I yelled at the man. He immediately recognized me and took off. I flew from the table and pursued the thief. Although he was quick, my long legs gave me a speed greater than his. I caught him in only seconds. My hand grabbed onto his arm like a vice. "What are you doing back here?! Do you not remember what I said?!"

"Please, I'm sorry! Don't hurt me!" he cried, sinking to the floor.

"Martin, what's going on?!" Jonah said as he came up behind me.

"This man was stealing food!" I explained, shaking the crook.

"Well, there is no need to beat up on him!" Jonah said, putting his hand on my arm and releasing the man from my hold.

I thought that Jonah was crazy for releasing him at first, but then I realized that Jonah was right to show mercy to this man. Jonah's mind was clear about the situation. He was objective, and I could trust him to make the right choice.

"What is your name?" Jonah asked the crook.

"It's Donovan," he answered.

"Donovan, would you like to help me fix up a boat? I could pay you a little bit of cash," Jonah offered.

"I would like that a lot! Thank you, sir!"

Jonah, someone who could barely afford to be here, was now employing this thief. I wondered if it was because he was so ecstatic about his new job or if it was because he understood that through which Donovan was going. Either way, I had a deep feeling that he had made the right choice, a choice I was incapable of making.

The kids departed to their room, and Jonah, Donovan, and I all left to fix up the boat. It was good to have another hand to help, but I did not wholly trust this man. I would have to learn to trust him. Truly, he was only trying to keep himself safe, and I knew he was sorry.

Again, the analyzing started and, this time, towards the new man. He stood about as tall as Jonah who was at his side, but I could tell that Donovan was significantly skinnier. His clothes were as ragged as mine, and his hair had similar disarray to it. It was dark brown and quite long. He was young, though, perhaps in his early twenties. I noticed that he slouched and he had a quiet nature to him. He trusted us as much as I trusted him.

I knew this man was of no threat to me and probably none to Jonah, but all I wanted was to attack him for what he appeared to be. I knew he was a thief, and a thief belonged in jail. Perhaps another reward awaited me for turning him in. Jonah did not believe that this man had done anything really wrong and would be very upset if I tried to turn him in. The end decision was to just trust and hopefully become friends with this man. I would go with Jonah's judgment, not my own.

We began to approach the docks. We made our way there and even we were walking in the middle of the road. It was such a waste to have such nice paved roads with none but a few cars every day to drive on them.

With the few cars every day was one taxi cab. Jonah had told me that it stayed by the Ale Inn only and it never seemed to make any rounds around the town. It obviously just stayed there to pick up anyone who departed the hotel. I felt it was unfair that instances such as these were so clear but my past was always a cloudy mess. I saw things and could almost automatically know their purpose. Whenever I tried to remember something, fuzziness overtook me.

At the docks, there was a workshop that the fishermen used to fix up their boats. It was usually used for small jobs, but we intended to fix up a boat that had been devastated on the waves. It would not be a quick, one-day job but, instead, a week of hard labor.

Entering the workshop, I saw our boat. It was lifted off the floor, which would have been flooded with water if the gate to the ocean would have been open. The boat itself looked in poor condition. Two, no, three holes were in the hull! The mast looked bent and the motor was nowhere to be seen. Also, it looked quite pitiful as it was only taking up about a fourth of the work space that was provided for the larger vessels. It truly was a disaster.

Jonah smiled upon the boat. He walked up close to it, and Donovan followed. He put his hand in the giant holes.

"What a bargain! Can you believe they are just giving this to us! For free! And they're letting us use this shop! I can't believe this is happening!" Jonah exclaimed.

He ran over to me and hugged me. His grip was tight, and I had nowhere to go. I hugged him back and stepped back with an awkward smirk.

"You've saved us, Martin! You have saved us! Thank you so much! I can't believe it!" Jonah told me as he danced around a little.

"And you have spared me, Martin. For that, I am eternally grateful," Donovan said, and I could see a tear roll down his cheek to the floor.

"Wow! This is so amazing! What are we waiting for? Let's get to work," Jonah said and motioned for us to follow.

Jonah showed us all he knew about the boat. He described everything in elaborate detail, gesturing with his hands in grandiose motions. He then showed us the tools with which we would be working and how to use them. I caught on quickly and was assisting in fixing the boat in no time.

There I was with two men I had just met today, fixing up my new friend's dream. I had made great strides today. I knew I could find my memory with such progress as this. I knew I had the skill to go out and learn about my past, whatever it was. I was ready to go on that journey. My hope was returning.

After many hours of work, the mast had been straightened, and Jonah had made some progress with the motor he had found in the back of the shop. We left our work and returned to the hotel for some rest.

Dinner was served, and the main course was chili. Not a bad dinner in comparison to all the other dinners I could remember. We all ate our fill while Jonah, Donovan, and I discussed the work on the boat with Mia and the kids.

Later, I went back to my room along with the kids. Donovan decided to stay in Mia and Jonah's room. Sleeping on the floor of a hotel room was much better than he had gotten in the recent past. I, too, would sleep on the floor. I did not mind; I just wanted the kids to have some kind of comfort.

I lay on the floor with a pillow and a blanket. Cody and Alyssa asked more questions throughout the night, all of which I had difficulty answering. With their continuing interrogation came an anxiousness to find my past. I was even more curious than these two children. I could not wait to find my boat and return to my old, normal life once again.

The questions coming from the kids ceased as they grew groggier and then fell asleep, but the questions coming from my mind never ceased. Even as my eyes slowly closed that first night, my mind still burst with curiosity.

I woke up to the laughter of children. They were jumping on the bed. This was not something of which I had any prior knowledge, but I was quite sure that this was not found acceptable by their parents. Urging them to stop in fear of their parents' suddenly entering the room, I ended their fun.

Not much later, Jonah was knocking at the door. Quickly cleaning up the room, I made my way over to the door. I unlocked, opened it, and let him in.

"What are you kids watching?" he asked Cody and Alyssa.

"Isaac, the Space King!" they both shouted to their dad.

He chuckled, looked at me, and said, "They love that show! They are always telling me about it when they come back from a friend's house."

Donovan appeared in the doorway behind Jonah.

"Are we ready?" he asked.

Jonah turned and looked at me.

"Yeah, I'd say we're ready," I answered.

We left the room and went to the hotel's dining area where Mia joined us. The food this morning was greatly varied. Cereals, waffles, fruit, and a lot more were lining the buffet. Not wanting to miss out on anything, I took a plate and filled it with every kind of food. I found that I enjoyed all of it, but I enjoyed the bacon most. I sensed that in large amounts, this would not be healthy for me. I concluded the same for the other foods as well and decided to get even more bacon.

Arriving at the table and setting my food down, I noticed the concerned look on Mia's face. Sitting in my chair, I waited for her to address, which she had no issue doing.

"Martin, you seem pretty hungry. Isn't that a bit too much bacon, though?" she asked me, the correct answer to that question inescapable.

"Uh... yeah, you're probably right about that. I don't have to eat it all."

"I'm not saying that, haha! You make sure to eat it all, Martin. Let's just make sure to get some better balance with what you're putting into your body next time, okay?" her tone leaving me with no other option.

"Yes, ma'am!" I responded, and that room-warming smile came upon her lips.

When breakfast was over, we decided to return to our work on the boat. We left the hotel and walked down the same road as yesterday. Donovan was no longer shy with either of us. Had he become so comfortable because of Jonah's unbelievable compassion for him? He talked endlessly about his life and what had led him here.

He had grown up in Jordanston, the tiny town near where Jonah's family lived, and had gone to the same school Alyssa and Cody were currently attending. His parents were teachers there. Around the age of 17, Donovan had become very rebellious, and he dropped out of school and ran away to Alemande, seeking work. All he could find for work was to be one of the salesmen that often flooded these streets. Donovan explained that the competition was fierce, to the point of salesmen attacking and sabotaging each other frequently. One night on his way back to the homeless shelter, he was mugged and beaten severely with a baseball bat. He had lost everything. After spending a few weeks in the hospital, he tried to return to his family, but they would not take him back. He had been trying to survive in the streets of Alemande ever since then.

I looked at the man differently now. Yes, there was what I saw before, a man who had made mistakes and was going down an incorrect path, but now I saw him through a new lens. I saw him with empathy, knowing what it was like to feel abandoned and what it was like to desperately need help. Who knows what I might be doing if Jonah had not taken me in when I came to him?

As we continued walking to the workshop, I felt a tug on my heart that told me there was more to people than I thought before. Some part of me felt it was necessary to put people into groups and to look no further than that. I had done so with Liam the Mugger, and I had done it with the fishermen, and now I was doing it with Donovan. There had to be more to people than what I was seeing on the surface. I knew there was more to me than what others could plainly see. These thoughts bounced around inside my confusing mind even as we arrived and began to work on the boat once more.

Work on the boat went on for about three hours. At that point, I heard Jonah's stomach growl, and Donovan's and my stomach soon joined in. We all decided it was time for a lunch break.

We returned to the buffet in the hotel and met with Mia and the kids. They told us of their plans for the day, and we told them of ours.

"I think I might take a look around the store here in Alemande. We haven't had cash on hand in quite some time, and I think that an occasion like this deserves a little shopping," Mia told us.

"Isaac, the Space King comes on at three o'clock. We are staying here!" Alyssa said, speaking for her brother.

"Well, we have to put in hours now so that I can work hours later on. We need to have this boat finished pretty soon, so we are definitely going to put in the hours. That's what we'll be up to," Jonah said.

With everyone's plans accounted for, Mia left for the store and the kids left for the room. The three of us remaining decided to get seconds.

After filling up and feeling good, we accepted the fact that it was time to get back to work. We left our table and went towards the lobby to exit the hotel.

As we were leaving the hotel, Amber, who always seemed to be working the front desk, said, "Good luck, guys!"

I nodded to her as did Jonah and Donovan.

Again, we walked the familiar streets, and I truly felt good. I liked it when things felt familiar. When everything is perpetually new and strange to you, it is nice to have something familiar. I hoped for even more familiarity. I walked with a bit of a skip to my step as we approached the docks.

When we got there, we did not actually fix up the boat. Instead, we went to investigate a large crowd of more than just the fishermen. Everyone was gathered around the water and fixated on it. What had happened here?

I walked up to a man who seemed to know what was happening and who was speaking to the crowd. I quickly analyzed him. The man was dressed in a professional-looking dark black suit with a pure white dress shirt beneath. Brown curly hair was all grew neatly on top of his head. He was clean shaven, and he appeared to be very well-employed.

He was telling some people about what had happened when I came up to him and tapped him on the shoulder. He looked back at me. "What did you say happened here? What is this?" I asked him. The man studied me heavily before answering.

"Looks like a boat blew up out in the ocean. Completely destroyed it, blew it to pieces! You can tell from the burns on the debris. Those engines can sometimes explode if not maintained properly, and there's not much evidence as to how this one went. Engine most likely overheated." He sighed and continued, "It would have been completely unexpected. There will be no survivors…"

Chapter 6
Loss of Hope

As I looked upon the wreckage, I felt overwhelmed by a dark despair. This boat had been the only clue that could have possibly taught me anything about my past. No survivors, nobody to tell me what I was doing out at sea. There was nobody to help me find my past. My only hope of ever regaining my memory was gone. This ship was my past, and it had just exploded out at sea.

The well-dressed man continued addressing the crowd. I no longer needed to hear what he had to say. The fact that the boat was destroyed, taking the lives of all who could have helped me, was enough to let me know that there were no answers here.

Jonah approached me with pity in those kind eyes.

"Martin, are you okay?"

I could not even respond.

"He said it was a sudden explosion, that nobody would have known it was going to blow. How do you think you got off of that boat?" he asked me.

That was something I had not considered. How could anyone escape such a sudden and unexpected explosion? There was no way I could have been blasted into the lifeboat in which I had floated to Jonah's cottage. "I...don't know...how I could have possibly escaped an exploding engine. It makes no sense," I told Jonah, lost in thought.

He gave me a smile, but it failed to make his countenance any less pitiful. Jonah wrapped his arms around me and held me tightly. When his hug was finished, he pulled away and looked into my eyes.

"Well, maybe it was just a miracle."

I smiled at Jonah, loving his optimism but not really believing him. I no longer had the hope for life that he did.

My only chance was that I had been on another boat. Just as this thought passed through my mind, the man in charge of investigating the debris made a statement to the people gathered around him.

"What we have figured out here is that this boat, the *Annabelle*, had some kind of engine failure, most likely due to a lack of maintenance, and then blew up, destroying the boat," the man said to the people.

I remained in sorrow to learn that the boat was indeed mine. I remembered climbing out of the lifeboat and seeing "Annabelle" on the side of it. My boat was gone, and so was all hope for finding my past.

I walked closer to the official, even though I did not expect any answers. "Is it possible that someone could have been blown into a lifeboat and survived the blast?" I asked him. He looked at me with an expression that made me feel crazy.

"Sir, we are quite sure that the blast would have completely fried anyone on board as well as throwing them hundreds of feet away. It would not just throw them into a lifeboat. To tell you the truth, the notion that anyone on that boat could have survived is completely ridiculous. They would have to have already been in the lifeboat on the water quite a ways away," he said to me. "Oh, and all the lifeboats have been accounted for except for one. I guess that it might be possible that someone survived by leaving the boat before it exploded. But, more likely, we might just not have found it yet. The whole thing was blown to hell."

What that told me was that no one else survived except for me. There was nothing else for me to learn. All that I had learned was that my boat blew up and that no one could help me get my memory back.

I digested the information and tried to think of a question to ask the official, but before I did, he got a phone call. He looked at the phone and quickly looked back at the crowd, their eyes glued to him, anticipating a response.

"I have to take this. My apologies."

He then walked quickly away and answered the phone. Another man dressed the same as the last took his place, assuring the crowd of their safety on the waters and inland. It did not matter, though. I had no more questions for these investigators.

There was nothing left for me here. I wanted to help Jonah and Donovan with the boat, but a terrible resignation within me was dragging me away. Giving up fighting it, I began the long walk back to the Ale Inn. Jonah and Donovan did not try to stop me. They knew what I was going through, and they had no desire to hold me to my previous commitment. They instead went over to the workshop where Jonah's boat was being kept. They would finish the job without me.

I might not have been fried by the explosion, but my mind surely felt like it. I walked in a daze, barely ever looking up from the ground. I kept trying to remember. I hoped that the amnesia might fade and that I might remember something. It never did.

As I entered the inn, I felt such confusion. What was I doing on the boat? Was I a fisherman just like everyone else on the boat? How did I escape the fiery end to the ship? It all did not make any sense. I so desperately wished I could get my memory back.

I walked back to my room. As I did, a new thought entered my mind. What if I was sent there to destroy the boat? It would explain the fact that I had escaped the blast and that there had been no survivors. What if I was a killer who had murdered all the people aboard? Why would I do it, though? Perhaps I was on a rival fishing boat. They could not take the competition, so they sent me to end the feud by destroying their main rival's boat. An action such as that was not at all out of place with all the violence and crime I had been witnessing lately.

Even if that was the truth, it left so many blank spots. Why did I have these strange fighting abilities? How did I lose my memory? Maybe one of the crew on the boat fought back and hit me on the head when I was escaping. I finished the job, but was knocked out, and, when I woke up, I had no memories.

I did not know what to think. So many ideas, but none made much sense. How could I solve this mystery with my main lead gone? Whom could I ask? Where could I go? Was there any logical action I could take that would move me towards the truth?

Out of all these questions, I struggled with one more than the rest. Where would I go next? No boat, nothing but stories from the fishermen, and no family that I knew. I had no leads, and finding my past seemed like a dead end.

I did not have another place to go, and that was the truth. With no past to find, the future was the only time I could seek. I knew that a life with Jonah's family was not for me. They would take care of me. They would love me dearly, but I needed to learn about the world I had forgotten. I needed to find my own way. I did not want to be given the world; I wanted to take it for myself. I decided that I would leave Alemande and the kind family. I would instead go to West City.

I had made the choice of West City solely because it was the only other place of which I had ever heard besides Alemande and the small, destitute town of Jordanston. Liam the Mugger had said something about it right before he had tried to attack. Since he had mentioned a possible bus route to West City, I imagined that it could not be too far away.

When I got to my room, I knocked on the door, and Cody answered the door with a smile and a cheer, happy to see me. I smiled back, but it was weak.

Walking into the room, I listened to Alyssa and Cody excitedly blather on about the TV show they had been watching. I did not know how to tell them that I was leaving. They looked up to me and thought that I was a great mystery. I thought that I was a great mystery, too, but I had already given up hope of solving myself. They would hate it if I left. Perhaps they would hate me.

I sat on the bed and Cody followed me and sat next to me. Alyssa got up from in front of the TV and leaned on the bedpost next to me, smiling, which made what I had to tell them even harder.

I looked down, away from their faces, and said, "My boat just washed up at the docks. Pieces of it, anyway." Raising my eyes, I saw that they were mystified.

"Was it attacked by a sea monster like I said?" Alyssa asked me.

"No," I responded somberly. "Engine failure like I had said."

"Yeah, I didn't really think it was a sea monster," Cody said.

"Lucky guess," Alyssa said coldly.

"But the thing is that…there's nothing left for me here," I said to them. I watched their expressions change.

"But we're here…" Alyssa said.

It was hard, but I persisted. I had to do this. Looking away, I began again.

"I just can't be here because I have to go find a life for myself. If I can't ever find out who I was, then I'm going to go out and prove who I am. I have to leave to do that," I told them.

There was a discomforting silence that made my heart ache. I looked to them again. They looked as crushed as I did when I found out that there was nothing I could do to find my memory, which made it ten times harder because I felt like I was putting the same pain on them.

Cody started to tear up a little.

"Will we see you again? You're gonna come back, right?" he asked, quivering.

"Maybe." I knew that I had to leave soon or they would try harder to get me to stay. "Tell your parents goodbye for me. And thanks for everything."

I grabbed Cody, who sat next to me, and hugged him. I put my chin on his head, and he sobbed into my dirty jacket. Alyssa came to my left, and

I hugged her as well. She cried harder than her brother and dampened my jacket considerably more. I ended the embrace and stood. I took three steps and stood in the open doorway. I turned back and said, "I will really miss you guys. Goodbye, Alyssa. Goodbye, Cody."

I walked out the door and did not look back. So odd how these random strangers had made themselves such friends to me and that I was just as much a friend to them. I had only met these people one day ago. We had both helped each other so much, and they desperately did not want to lose that bond. I did not either, but I felt it necessary.

I started for West City, only knowing the name because of Liam the Mugger. Coming to the lobby, I ran into Mia on my way out. I was going to avoid this if at all possible, but I felt it appropriate that I should say goodbye to her in person. She had done much for me, and I was very grateful.

"Oh, hello, Martin," she said with a cheerful look in her eyes.

I looked at her sadly. "Mia, I'm sorry, but I have to leave."

"What do you mean?" she asked, teetering on the brink of realization.

"I'm leaving Alemande. I'm going to make a future for myself."

She looked shocked.

"And why would you do something like that?" she said, angered.

"We found my boat, but…well…it was just the burnt debris of the boat."

"And you think that because you have no chance of finding your memory that you can leave this family?!"

Her desperation to make me stay was projected through hostility which was very much out of character for her. This rapid transformation due to impending loss frightened even me. Yet, she was more frightened by what I was saying than I was of how she was acting. My exit was having more of an effect on them than I had thought it was going to have.

"I'm going to West City," I told her.

"Ha! You don't even know what it is like over there! There are more muggers than the police could ever pay you for if they were all brought in! You are *not* going over there, Martin."

I just averted my eyes and started to walk away.

"Where are you going?!" she said in fear.

"I'm going to West City. You can't stop me," I told her, expecting another hurtful response to try to keep me there. Instead, she slowly reached into her new purse and grabbed five twenty dollar bills and a hundred dollar bill.

"Wait, Martin. This will get you there," she said, holding the money out to me.

She had given up all hope in my staying. Her hostility faded, and I could see the guilt of what she had said on her shoulders.

"Head down to the subway. An intercity train can take you where you want to go. This money will cover the fare. And make sure to buy yourself some food," she said apologetically.

"Mia, I gave you this money. Why..."

"And I'm giving it back to you," she cut me off, thrusting out the money even closer to me, almost putting it into my hand.

I saw that she was having a very hard time with this. I took the 100 dollars from her hand. "Thank you for everything, Mia." Her humble smile returned.

"Please come and visit sometime. I mean that, Martin. Please."

I nodded with a weak smile on my lips. She gave me a hug and then gestured for me to go. I looked away and then back at her. "Goodbye," I barely got out, a tear forming in my eye that I did not want her to see.

Then, I took off for the subway. I passed a lot of people as I walked there. An overly fat woman, two pairs of twins, six people on cell phones, a father with a crying baby in his arms, and a man that I noticed at a distance away, pretending to read the newspaper. He kept an eye on me the whole time I was in sight. I thought it to be strange, but ignored it. It was not as if the two pairs of twins were not strange as well.

At the entrance down to the subway, I saw a familiar face. It was Officer Turnbull. "How are you doing, Officer Turnbull?" I asked him cordially.

"Oh, I'm just dandy. And you know, you can just call me Nick," Officer Nick Turnbull said, putting out his hand for me to shake.

"Um, okay. Whatever you say, Nick," I said and shook his hand.

"So, where are you headed...uh... Martin was it?"

"Yeah, it is. I'm going to West City."

He laughed and responded, "Going to finish off the crime over there now, huh?"

"I did look at that as a job opportunity while I'll be over there. But what I need is to go somewhere without the...fish smell."

"Haha! I wish they would send me to West City. I know my guys and I could do a hell of a lot of good over there. And we would be working in the regional station, so I could still come back here. Man! That would be nice!"

"Don't worry, I'll take care of things over there for you," I joked.

"Yeah, good luck! The crime over there is crazy! They have all kinds of gangs and a real life mafia, too! But bounty hunting is profitable, and it does the city well. I'd love to help you out over there!" Nick laughed.

"I don't think it will be too much trouble for me!"

He smiled and said, "Well, I won't keep you."

"Goodbye, Nick."

"Goodbye, Martin."

I turned away from the officer and made my way down the stairs to the station.

Entering the subway station, my mind raced. So many people and so much information. My analytical brain rushed to meet this challenge. Within seconds of standing, staring at the station before me, I knew where every person was and what they were doing. I located all the exits and identified any threats. I picked up on anything out of the ordinary and found the best places to stand should there be an emergency. Nothing here escaped me.

I paid, went through the turnstiles, and waited for my train. After several minutes of sitting, I no longer had to wait. The train slowed to a stop, and I got on it. Sitting again, I watched a couple dozen people storm the train. Some came in and sat by me. Other people made their way to the back.

Right before we took off, I saw Jonah run into the station. He frantically talked to the main booth. The woman told him something, and then his eyes turned and locked on mine. Filled with a sudden urgency, he jumped over the turnstiles and raced to the train, but the doors shut before he could make it to me. He was too late. I waved goodbye to him as the train took off. I would not see Jonah for a long time after that.

Chapter 7
The Vaillancourt

The ride on the subway train was full of regret. As soon as the decision was carried out, it felt wrong. Why did I leave them? They were the closest thing to family I had. I felt that I had made a great mistake, but I would have to live with it. Maybe, it would give me something better in my life. I just had to have hope that everything would work out. Hopefully, I could prove to myself that I was capable with this new life.

I had to focus on my goal: facing this new world and every challenge it could throw at me. West City sounded like a hard place to live, and I was going to thrive there. I did not want to take the easy road, so I could not stay with my dear family by the sea. Only a few days into this life, and I had already run away from everything familiar.

Looking around the train, I began analyzing again. There was a pattern to the arrangement of the seats. A line of seven seats were bolted to the wall of the train, and, in between them and the next seven, was a bar on to which one might hold if the seats were taken. Also, fifteen men and sixteen women had boarded this train when I had. In this car, there were only four men and two women. Though, these bits of data were really of no purpose but to occupy my mind.

I continued my inspection of the train. I noticed that most people had not sat right in front of the door as I had. One man was to my immediate left and two more were farther right. The remaining man and two women were to the left in the back of the train. I had never been on a subway that I could remember, and I did not know if this spot I had chosen was undesirable.

The apparent lack of anyone familiar on the train brought my mind back to my situation, and the gloom came upon me again. I felt lonely now that I knew no friends would greet me where I was going. I wondered what I was going to do. Would I really fight crime to pay for my needs? It sounded like a cheerless life, but it might be my only choice. Society seemed to highly encourage such employment, anyway.

The person next to me must have noticed my grief because he asked if I knew the man who jumped the turnstiles. "Yes," I answered him sorrowfully. "He was like a father to me. And I probably shouldn't have gotten on this train. I just felt like I needed to prove myself by leaving and starting my own life."

"Don't worry about it. There are lots of opportunities in West City. I'm sure you will do great there. My name is Jimmy Hanson," he said, offering his hand. "What's yours?"

For a moment, I just looked at his outstretched hand. Who even was this man? Seeing someone trying to make friends on a subway train was a very rare event. He had a certain charisma to him, though. Deciding to forsake my distrust of the man, I reached out my hand, too.

"My name is Martin," I said and shook his hand.

His grin grew all of a sudden, and he reached into his pocket. He pulled out his wallet. The wallet was quite fat, and I assumed it was full of a lot of cash. It was also made of a higher quality black leather and had a silver clasp that held it shut. Flipping up the clasp and opening the wallet, he looked inside. His eyes then turned back to me expectantly.

"Would you like to see some pictures of my family?" he asked me cheerfully.

"Sure," I replied, for loneliness had overtaken me.

He reached into his wallet and suddenly pulled out a switchblade. He flipped it out and lunged at me. In my surprise, my instincts kicked in, and I grabbed the man and threw him to the ground. He jumped back up and showed his knife. Some people in the train screamed and backed away from him. Jimmy slashed at me with the knife. Then, I saw his pupils dilate, and he lunged out to stab me. I grabbed his wrist with my right hand and, exerting immense pressure with my left on his elbow, snapped his arm in half. He dropped the knife and screamed. I threw him away from me.

I turned around, and two men in suits were standing, ready to attack me. "It was his knife!" I yelled at them, thinking that they were some kind of police. Much to my disadvantage, they were not police.

The first one lunged at me, trying to restrain me. Instinctively, my hand shot out and two of my fingers dug deeply into the man's sockets. With an awful shriek of pain, my enemy was temporarily blinded, and I used this to dodge behind him. From there, I grabbed for his head and, without hesitation, twisted. With a horrifying, wet, snapping sound, his neck spun around, and the man was dead.

The second one pulled a gun and tried to shoot me. I ducked behind the cadaver, and his body took a bullet instead of mine. I shoved him into my adversary, but he just pushed the dead body of his partner to the ground and took aim at me again. I hit the gun out of his hands in time to save my life and then punched the man in the throat. He slowly choked and fell to the floor beside his comrade.

I heard a scream from behind me. When I turned around, Jimmy thrust the knife into my chest. I felt the blade slide between my ribs, but I did not care. I tore the knife from my chest and, in one fatal move, slit open Jimmy's throat. The crimson liquid splattered around the train. Trembling violently, he tumbled to the floor of the train, dead.

I looked upon the crowd in the subway train. Everyone stared at me, believing I was the real monster. I saw a police officer in another car of the train coming for me. He was yelling into his radio as his eyes locked on mine. Fortunately, the train jolted and quickly began decelerating. The officer was knocked to the ground by the sudden movement, and, when the train came to a complete stop, the doors opened. We had arrived in West City, and not a second too late, either.

The officer stood and raced forward toward me. I ran out the door and through the station, jumping the turnstiles and racing towards the stairs. My speed made getting away from the officer even easier. No one could catch up to me as I sprinted through the station and up the stairs to the surface.

I ran out into West City and was immediately stunned by the bright sun gleaming off the windows of the skyscrapers that towered over me. Remembering my plight, I ran to an alley and threw myself behind a dumpster. I caught my breath and tried to think of what had happened only a minute ago.

What was going on? Three people just randomly attack me in a subway train? More confusion than ever before ran through my head. Why was I targeted? Who were those men? There were no obvious answers. Apparently, there was even more to the mystery that could not be solved, the mystery I thought I had given up.

The police ran past my hiding place. I heard them yell something about the likelihood of my being armed. I decided to wait here a little bit longer. The cops would not be able to search the entire city and find me. They had already concluded that I had gone farther into the city, anyway.

I looked down at my shirt. It was torn, now more than before, and blood was stained all around it. I remembered the switchblade entering my chest. I had felt no pain then, and, even now, there was no pain. I examined the wound. What I saw surprised me. There was no cut in my chest. A gnarled scab covered the wound now. There was only a small amount of blood around the area where the wound should have been. It made little sense how I could endure a stab like that, but to heal from it in a few minutes made completely no sense.

Extreme strength, lightning fast reflexes, the speed of a cheetah, rapid healing, and complete understanding on how to defeat my adversaries. These skills that I possessed were extraordinary. Things did not make any sense. I doubted I would ever make sense of my life.

I took a quick look out of my hiding spot. Seeing no police officers, I came out slowly. I could hear the sirens quite a ways in the distance. I knew I was safe for now. Coming out of my hiding spot, I observed the numerous buildings and the countless people. Structures stretched to the sky, and planes soared overhead. A cacophony of voices filled the stale air, and cars honked demandingly in impatience. This city was much larger than Alemande was.

There was a restaurant across from where I was, so I decided to spend the money Mia had given me there. It was just a little pizza place, but I could not remember the taste of pizza, and, once again, I found myself hungry. It seemed to be the obvious choice.

Upon entering the pizzeria, I immediately made my way to the bathroom. I quickly cleaned the shirt and my hands with ice cold water from the sink. I wrung out the shirt and replaced it on my torso. Looking in the mirror, I saw that I did not look suspicious anymore. No blood was on me, and I looked clean. I returned to the restaurant with a confidence that I would not be found out.

I ate a large pepperoni pizza. It was some of the best food I had eaten. It had been a very long day for me, so this was exactly what I needed. Finishing up the pizza, I was not satisfied. With fair amount of money remaining in my hands, I ordered another pizza and a pop.

My life had been quite eventful so far. I woke up on a lifeboat from a sunken ship. I was saved by a common fisherman. His kind family gave me breakfast and new clothes. Then, they took me to Alemande. I beat up a wanted mugger and turned him in for reward money. I ate hotel food for the first time in my memory. I began fixing up a boat. After that, I discovered that my ship was destroyed. I lost all hope for finding my memories. I rode on the subway. I was attacked by three goons who wanted me dead. I ran from the police. To finish it all, I ate this delicious pizza.

This life had started out strangely, and I was still going to need a place to live. I asked the cashier where I could find a place to stay. He suggested a hotel a few blocks away from where the restaurant was. He did mention it was very expensive, but I decided that it was the best place to go. I finished my pizza and left.

As I walked out, a police officer walked in. Hit with sudden panic, I refused to act suspicious. I walked to the door and through it as nonchalantly as possible. He looked at me just for a second and then ignored me. Apparently as well as luckily, he did not recognize me.

I continued to the hotel. It came into sight immediately. It was massive! This was the Vaillancourt Hotel. Finely trimmed shrubbery winded up the sides of the hotel, and exotic trees and bushes precisely spotted the pathway leading up to the majestic doors. The building literally glowed from its own brilliance. It appeared as if it were made of gold or of a material even richer. The architecture was bewildering and strangely pleasing to the eye, featuring curves and twists that made the structure appear as if it were dancing. A cobblestone path guided me in through the doors.

I was astounded upon entering this masterpiece. Beautifully intricate glass chandeliers hung from a mirror ceiling that only multiplied the glory beneath it. Designer sofas and chairs that looked both eccentric and comfortable spread out from the entrance in a symmetrical and efficient fashion. This must have been one of the most amazing hotels in the world. The place was covered in the most expensive furniture and art. The pure regality of the room weakened my knees. I came to a sparkling check-in desk.

The clerk behind the desk was impeccably dressed. Stern features were juxtaposed by an afro bursting outward from his head in all directions. Behind his giant hair was a poster advertising something called the Fight Arena. The poster mentioned a prize of $500 and a free stay for a week if one could defeat the Vaillancourt's hired fighter in a cage match. It was an odd concept, but perhaps a good way to earn a stay in the hotel and some spending cash.

The clerk cleared his throat to get my attention.

"Sorry... I'd like a room, please," I asked the fancily dressed man behind the desk.

"Okay, sir. We have several rooms open. Would you like a deluxe room...or would you prefer one of our cheaper ones?" the man said, eyeing my torn clothing.

I knew that I probably could not afford an expensive room, so I decided on a cheaper room. Anyway, I only had about 150 dollars left. "I'll take the cheapest you have."

He looked down at his computer before saying, "That will be $2000 a night, sir."

The price practically knocked me down. How could I ever pay $2000 a night?! "Oh, never mind," I told him. He scoffed at me and returned his gaze to the computer screen. Though I wanted to address his rudeness, I stopped myself before causing a scene.

I dropped into an expensive couch not far from there. Even though I could not afford a room here, I could bask in the luxury for as long as I wanted.

"Jaymen!!!" I heard someone yell. "Check-ins are down 20 percent, and I just lost our fighter for tonight! You know how hard they are to replace!"

A noticeably wealthy and important man was yelling at the snooty check-in clerk. His long, blonde hair was slicked back, and his mustache was finely trimmed. His purple 3-piece suit was both edgy and classy, and swayed on his body in a way that showed its exact tailoring. Shininess emanated from the man due to a multitude of jewelry that hung about his person. Apart from the power of wealth he commanded, there seemed to be great authority that emanated out of his inner being. It was clear this man caused trepidation in those beneath him, for he wore an undeniable confidence that bordered on offensive arrogance. As he approached the desk, even I felt intimidation from his constitution alone.

"No, Mr. Vaillancourt, I swear, I am not driving anyone off," said the clerk, whom I now knew as Jaymen, as if he had said it many times before.

"How about him then?!" Mr. Vaillancourt said, gesturing towards me. "Why didn't he check in?! What is your excuse this time!"

"I…I do not know, sir," Jaymen cowered.

"You *do not know*?!"

"Perhaps it is because…"

"Why didn't you check in, sir?" Mr. Vaillancourt addressed me.

I did not have much of an answer, but I decided it was best to just agree with Mr. Vaillancourt. "He seemed kinda…snooty. I really didn't want to check in with him. But don't worry, I was about to leave. Can't stand people like that," I told him, dishing out revenge as well. A sigh exited Mr. Vaillancourt's mouth. Jaymen shuddered in anticipation of what came next.

"JAYMEN!!!" the magnificent man roared.

"Y-Y-Yes, sir?" Jaymen cowered even more.

"You are FIRED!!!"

Jaymen was frozen in horror. It took about ten seconds for him to lower his head in shame and answer.

"Yes, sir."

Mr. Vaillancourt straightened his suit and watched his former employee leave.

"A fighter and now a check-in clerk," Vaillancourt muttered.

I made my way to him. "Mr. Vaillancourt?" I respectfully addressed him.

"Yes?" he responded, looking curiously at me.

"I think I could help solve your problem," I said, attempting to seize this opportunity for a new life. I could not let an opportunity like this get away.

"How so?" he asked, lifting an eyebrow.

"I could fill in at the desk. I've never done it before, but, with some training, I could be great. Also, I'm an excellent fighter and could fight at your fight shows. No one would ever beat me. I swear!" He looked at me briefly, studying me, and then burst out laughing.

"*You* help *me*?"

He laughed again. Whatever it was about me, he could not believe that someone like myself could ever help someone like him. I aimed to show him that he was incorrect.

I knew this was my only chance to show him I had what it took. I walked over to a couch and picked it up above my head. He stopped laughing. He just stared at me. He knew it had to weigh at least 300 pounds, for it was quite long. His head tilted in perplexity. Believing I had satisfied my objective, I set the couch down.

"H-how old are you?" he asked me, astonished.

It took me a second to remember what my supposed age was. I told him I was 18. He stared at me for another couple seconds. Then, he shook his head and addressed me.

"What's your name?"

"My name is Martin, sir."

"All right, Martin. The job is yours! Welcome to the Vaillancourt!"

Chapter 8
Fight for a New Life

"My name is Miles Vaillancourt, but you will always address me as Mr. Vaillancourt. And I mean that. None of this 'dude', 'man', or even 'Miles' crap."

The man demanded respect, but I guess he deserved it, owning a hotel like this. The man truly was quite powerful. I did not have any problem with showing respect to a man like this.

He handed me a uniform. It was essentially a purple tuxedo. Jaymen had been wearing one earlier, but I had not guessed that these were company issued. This place was eccentric, fitting the personality of its owner well.

"This is the only thing you wear when in my hotel. No bracelets, hats, necklaces, or any of that other stuff," Mr. Vaillancourt said, gesturing always. "You treat anyone who talks to you with absolute respect. I don't want anyone to not check in because you're a jerk."

He had a lot of rules and regulations, but that is how you run a business as successful as this one. He had order and discipline. He had made it very far with those traits, and he was not going to abandon those values now.

"Every day after work and before your fights, you will take your uniform to the cleaners in our hotel. You will pick it up the next day when you come in to work. Oh, and you get one hour of break time whenever and however you want to spend it," he continued as we walked through the majestic halls. "You will want to take that break every day because I want you to be rested up for your fights."

I wondered what kind of fight it would be and with what types of age groups. Would it be with just men or with women as well? Were weapons allowed? What decided the winner? Whatever happened, I knew I could handle it with my enhanced abilities. If anyone was qualified for this job, it had to be me.

"Ah, yes, I almost forgot. One last thing before we talk about your fights. If anyone comes in here and asks for the usual and flashes a ring, you take the package from under the desk, give it to them, and say, 'Thank you from Miles.' Is that clear?" he said with that sternness that can bring a chill down any man's spine.

"Don't you mean, 'Thank you from Mr. Vaillancourt?'" I joked with him, but he did not seem amused.

"If you don't do it just like that, you will be fired. You got that?"

It seemed pretty clear to me. I nodded my head and said, "Yes, Mr. Vaillancourt." He seemed rather pleased.

"Come on now. We must show you where you will be fighting."

If someone was to come in and flash a ring, I was to give them a package. I already knew that crime had gotten out of control here in this city. The flashing of the ring most likely was a sign that the ring wearer was in the local gang. I assumed that this hotel was forced to pay protection money.

We walked through the halls, and, all the way, Mr. Vaillancourt checked and made sure none of the staff were messing around. Again, I was analyzing the place. 15 maids, 6 of them messing around, and a 60 percent work average among the maids. I could not stop myself from thinking about everything.

When we got to where I was going to be fighting, I was surprised. There were elevated bleachers all around the center, and in the center was a large platform with a chain-link fence around it. Unlike the rest of the hotel, this room was devoid of class. A heavy sense of brutality and dread descended on me as we entered.

"This is where you will be fighting, Martin," he said to me. "You will fight anyone who wants to challenge the main fighter. For anyone that beats you, they will earn 500 dollars and free stay for a week. That is just throwing away money, so understand that losing is not an option. Though, when you lifted that couch, I highly doubted anyone could beat you. It costs 20 dollars for a try to fight you, and it is 20 dollars for anyone to come watch. This is a good profit margin...if I can get you for a good price."

Mr. Vaillancourt's cheerful demeanor quickly left him and his sternness returned. He stood up a bit taller and puffed out his chest slightly. His eyes dropped down to my feet and then slowly traveled all the way up to my eyes where they stayed locked. He was attempting to intimidate me, but I was not that easily frightened.

"How much do you want for a fight? And it has to be less than 30 dollars."

Ignoring the almost illegal nature of his low, low offer of 30 dollars per fight, I thought about how expensive his rooms were and how I did not really need to get a hefty paycheck. My money would just go to food and shelter, anyway. This was a hotel, albeit a very expensive one. Why could I not get those things here?

"How about this? If I fight for you and work the check-in desk for you, can I just have a free room and free food with no paycheck?" I asked him hopefully. He looked at me as if I were crazy.

"Do you know how much the food and rooms cost here?" he asked me, gesturing furiously. "And that's not even touching the legal issues that will arise."

"I know they don't cost half as much as you charge, and it's not like I'm going to lose a fight. That way, you will have a constant profit. And you don't have to sign a contract with me. I'll volunteer my time here, and you can offer to board and feed me for free. No contracts, no legal issues," I told him with a cocky smile on my face that assured him of my confidence in myself.

He pondered the offer for a while.

"Okay…" he sighed. "Technically, that's still against labor laws, but law enforcement have bigger fish to fry these days. And I won't make too much of a profit, but I will make a profit. But there's one condition."

I made eye contact and said, "I shall follow your conditions whatever they are."

He smiled and said, "If you lose a match, you lose our deal. Deal?"

He thrust out his hand. I took it and shook. "Deal."

This was an important step in my life. My first job, a place to stay, and free food. These things were a great start to my new life. I had stepped out of the desolation of my past and into the new hope of my future.

How had I just obtained all of this? Mr. Vaillancourt had simply chosen me to work for him. Had it really been that easy to get a job? Perhaps this new life would be less difficult than expected.

The rest of that day was spent training for my new job. After a quick tutorial of how everything at a station worked, I was thrown behind a desk. Within my first hour, I was already checking people in. Occasionally, I would grab and eat a mint quickly so that no one would notice. Mr. Vaillancourt had strict rules concerning even the mints.

The job was easy and boring. A high-tech computerized system did all the work for me. I was just there for a more personal interaction, which I did not have to facilitate all that often. I would get about one group of customers every half hour or so. It seemed as if most customers were avoiding me and going to another employee to check in. Was I really all that intimidating?

It was a very tedious job, but I hung in there because this was my chance to actually start a life for myself. I was always very polite to all customers. People were shocked almost every time by the high prices. I would make something up about the amazing service and the all-you-can-eat buffet, and they would check in happy. Albeit with lies, I was becoming quite the salesman.

After a while, it was getting late, and I had an hour and a half before I had to do my fights. Flipping the sign on the desk so that it read "Closed", I took my break and lounged about in the lounge. When my hour was up, it was 9:30 pm. It was a half hour before my fighting began.

As I retook the desk to resume my work, Miles walked up to me.

"I just wanted to check on my big fighter. How are you doing? Ready to go? Ready to crush somebody?" he asked me, the excitement emanating from him.

"Yes, I am, sir." He was very glad.

"Hell, why don't you take off work early? I want you to be relaxed for the fight. I still haven't told you all the rules. And everything else, haha!"

I went with him into the Fight Arena. All the way there, he yammered on about how terrific this was going to be. He continually told me about how cool these fights were. He did not stop until I asked him to fill me in on the rules.

"First off, anything goes. The only thing we don't like is weapons. We will screen them before they get in the arena with you, so there is no need to worry about anyone trying to stab you. After that, all you have to do is K.O. the guy or make him cry uncle."

Miles seemed very confident of me. I saw pure joy in his eyes. This man was very greedy, and I was his jackpot.

"I'm sure you will have no trouble," he assured me. "Just watch out for the girls that come in here. They will go right for the nuts, and there is nothing you can do about it. 500 bucks and a week here is a lot of money for some people."

His warning worried me a little bit, but I was sure I could handle anyone that came into the ring. I had handled everything up to this point with the greatest of ease.

"Why don't you go drop off your uniform and then come back here to stretch and warm-up for your fights? I never really worried about the last guy, and I bet he was not even as strong as you. Older, too."

The encouragement helped with my nerves a little bit, and so I went to go drop off my uniform at the hotel's laundromat.

I found the laundromat and went in to give them my uniform. When I gave it to them, they recognized me as the new fighter.

"It gets a bit rough in there sometimes. Never give up, dude. This is a big part of funding the hotel," one of the workers said to me.

"Just give it all you got. You're gonna be great!" another worker said, shadow boxing in front of me.

I thanked them and went back to the Fight Arena.

On entering the Fight Arena, I once again noted the odd difference in this place compared to the whole. While the Vaillancourt shined with regality, this place was dark and felt a lot like a dungeon. The air was heavy here, and I felt the severity of this room fall on me when I walked back through the doors.

I saw that, even though it was not time for the fight, about half of the bleachers were already filled. Miles, the opportunist he was, had surely advertised that a new fighter was premiering tonight. I knew the turn out would be good because everyone wanted to see the new kid. I was glad to be the new kid and was going to show them that this was where I was meant to be.

I walked into the ring and heard the crowd cheer. It was awesome to have some fans, even if they truly did not know me. I was glad that, even if I could not find my past, I could build an amazing future. I started stretching, and someone I did not recognize came to the ring to give me some water.

"It's ice cold spring water, sir," said the unknown man.

"Thanks," I said. "Who are you?" The man looked up at me and smiled.

"I am the fight manager, I am just supposed to make sure you have what it takes to win. Hydration's the first step in that."

"All right. Thanks! My name is Martin."

"Creighton."

Creighton was a short, stocky kind of guy, and I was happy to have him helping me. He had an air about him that assured everyone that he knew what he was doing. His age was shown clearly by his wrinkles and gray hair, but it surely would not hold him back. With his experience backing me up, I knew I would win.

"Nice to meet you, Creighton."

"Now, the match will start in 15 minutes. Is there anything else you need? Nothing's off limits, sir."

I thought for a second, but nothing came to mind. "No thanks, Creighton."

He looked at my ragged clothes.

"If you need, we could get you some real nice fighting clothes. Much better than those rags. Wouldn't be here 'til tomorrow, but we could get them for ya," he said.

"With these, I've done my best work. I think I will be fine dressed like this," I chuckled. He nodded but did not fully believe me. He walked away from the ring to go talk to Miles.

I did not know whom I could possibly be fighting, but I knew that if I could take down three goons that wanted me dead, I should be able to take down one person who was fighting for money and a week at a nice hotel. I had no real worry and was ready for the fight. I took off my old leather jacket and set it on a chair just outside the ring. I stretched for the next 10 minutes and then sat down to rest and prepare myself.

Then, I saw Miles walk into the middle of the ring, and he waved me over. When I got to the center, the lights were lowered.

"You ready, kid?" he asked me.

"Of course," I answered confidently.

A microphone dropped from the ceiling and a spotlight hit Miles.

He grabbed the microphone and announced, "Welcome to the Fight Arena! It's 10 o'clock, so you know what that means! It's time to see some blood on the mat! And tonight, we have a new fighter for you!"

The whole crowd, which I noticed was full now, cheered as loudly as possible.

"He stands 6' 4" and will really pack a punch! It's…. Martin!!!"

The crowd went wild. There was whistling and people cheering my name all over the bleachers. This applause made me feel powerful. Yes, I could feed off their approval of me. I was ready for a fight.

"That's right, ladies and gentlemen. You paid to see the best, and now you get the best!" Miles yelled and gestured to me.

The spotlights shined on me, and everyone cheered again. When the cheering began to die down, all the lights above the bleachers came on.

"Who shall be our first contender to take on the mighty Martin?"

Miles was a fine announcer, and he was making me look like a god. I saw about half of the crowd jumping up and down asking for a chance to fight the mighty Martin.

"Well, I don't really know who to pick…" announced Miles, feeding their frenzy.

His eyes darted quickly through the crowd. I knew for what he was looking: someone he knew I could beat. He did not yet trust me, and something about that frustrated me. He should have known I could handle anyone. Had I not shown him my strength. I knew I could handle myself; he should have known, too.

"How about you, sir?" Miles said, pointing to a man high up in the bleachers.

"Yes! Yes! Yes!" the man shouted, dancing out of his seat.

The man made his way down through the bleachers and down some stairs. I heard groans throughout the crowd as he whooped on his way down. This was the lucky guy.

He approached the ring, paid 20 dollars, and two men at the gate quickly patted down the guy. They decided he was clear and opened the gate.

"What's your name, sir?" Miles questioned the man, allowing him use of the microphone.

"My name's Cain! And I am willing and ABLE! Haha!" the man said.

I believed he had made some kind of joke, but I did not understand it. Whatever the joke was, the audience did not get it either, and the smile disappeared from Cain's face. He replaced it with some fake enthusiasm and whooped again to encourage it.

"All right, folks! You ready to see a fight?!" Miles yelled through the microphone.

Cheers erupted from the crowd. A giant grin was on Miles' face. He nodded to me and left the ring. The gate was locked behind him.

I examined the man as I was prone to doing. Long, shiny blond hair fell past his shoulders. A huge smile was plastered on his face by a cocky attitude. He was about six feet tall and was only slightly muscular. His only real strength seemed to emanate from his enlarged ego. This would be too easy.

"AAAAAAAND...FIGHT!!!" Miles announced from outside the ring.

Without hesitation, Cain launched his fist right for my jaw. My reflexes easily captured the fist. I followed up with the same move, except my fist was not caught. The punch connected with his jaw, his head snapped to the side, and he fell over.

I dropped his now limp arm and stared at the comatose body. One punch? Was that all it was going to take? This job might be easier than I ever thought!

I heard the bell ring, and Miles ran in. The crowd did not cheer, for they were absolutely stunned. Miles grabbed my arm and raised it high. The crowd slowly caught on and applause was given to me.

"Your winner…MARTIN!!!" Miles announced.

An eruption of cheers attempted to deafen me. A grin appeared on my face that was just as big as Miles'. I had won. This was my life now, and it was glorious!

Five more fights were won that night, and all were claimed by me. I was amazed at this power I had, and so was Miles. He knew that he truly had something here. Indeed, I was his jackpot.

When we were finished for the night, Miles raved to the audience about my strength. They cheered for me once more before they all departed. I did it! I had made an amazing future for myself.

Miles handed a room key card to me.

"You have definitely earned this, man! I can recognize something that will last from miles away, haha!" Miles said to me.

"Thank you, Mr. Vaillancourt."

His grin inflated, and he left to go to his house. I left for my room, which was on the fifth floor.

I swiped the card and entered the room. For something that would have cost me $2000 a night, I was not impressed. It was a very nice room, but it was surely not a $2000 room.

I flung myself onto the bed. I began thinking about how much I had accomplished. There was no doubt that I had done well today. The job of a lifetime was mine. I knew I could do it! My future was secured.

Then, I began to think about the family I left for this. The main question was: Was it right to leave them so soon? I did not know if I had done the right thing. I knew that it would be cheaper for them to not have to take care of me, but I also knew that they really wanted to take care of me. It was a hard decision, but I thought I had made the right choice.

Lying in that bed, which was much more comfortable than the floor, I quickly drifted off to sleep. All night, I beat challengers into submission in my dreams.

A knock at my door woke me up. I got up and ran to the door. I opened it and peered outside. It was my boss.

"How are you this morning, Martin? Sore at all?" he asked me, intrigue shining in those greedy eyes of his.

"No, not at all. I feel great!" I responded. The giant grin showed itself again.

"Well, just thought I should check on you. Your shift begins in about 3 hours, by the way."

"No problem. I'll be there in uniform right on time."

"Great, great. I'll let you get back to whatever you were doing," Miles said and nodded before walking away.

I closed the door and walked back over to the bed. Glancing back at the alarm clock on my night stand beside the bed, I noted that I still had two hours before it would go off. Content with getting some more sleep, I quickly returned to slumber.

The job I had during the day bored me immensely. The whole day, I was ready to get in that ring and beat up more and more challengers. Now that I knew I could do it, it was all I wanted to do. It felt as if it was what I was meant to do.

The hours stretched on forever. I felt like I was checking in people for thousands of days. At last, 9 o'clock came, and I took my break then. This meant I could go straight into my preparation for the fights.

I dropped off my uniform at the cleaners, and the workers there wished me luck. I thanked them once again and left for the Fight Arena just like yesterday.

I was earlier today, and no one was in the bleachers yet. I went into the ring and began visualizing the fights I had fought yesterday. I remembered knocking out that cocky fighter with one punch. I remembered kicking the legs out from under one woman and then violently kicking her in the stomach until she gave up. I remembered one huge man who everyone thought had a chance against me. He even got a few hits on me, but I did not care. I put him in a headlock for about 20 seconds, and he was done.

"Excuse me. Martin?" I heard a voice from outside the ring say.

I flipped around, surprised that this man had snuck up on me.

"Yes, that's me," I said.

"I was hoping for a quick picture and an interview from you. I'm Kolton Hensleigh with the Westerly Herald," the man said, a camera around his neck and a briefcase in his left hand.

"Sure, sure. No problem at all," I responded happily.

I posed for a picture and answered some short questions for the reporter. They were easy questions: How are you feeling about tonight's fights? What is your favorite part about fighting? How does it feel to win? These questions I could answer, and that only assured me that I was back on the right track. No more questions without answers.

"Thank you so much, Mr. Martin! This will be in tomorrow's Westerly Herald. Check it out if you will," the reporter said.

"I definitely will," I assured him.

He left the ring, climbed the stairs, and went into the bleachers. The bleachers were quite full by now, for it was nearing 10 o'clock. I waved to the crowd, and some whoops rang out from it.

Creighton opened the gate and entered the ring. He handed me a bottle of ice cold spring water. He looked happy to see me.

"If there is anything you need, Martin, just ask me," he said.

"This is all I need. Thank you, Creighton."

He left, and Miles soon showed up. He came into the ring as Creighton had, and he put his hand on my shoulder.

"I'm really, really excited! Are you ready for this?" he asked me.

"Of course I am! When do we start?"

"Any second now. Oh, man! This is going to be fantastic!"

The lights were lowered and the microphone dropped from the ceiling. The spotlight once again hit Miles, and he snatched the microphone from the air.

"Welcome to the Fight Arena! It's 10 o'clock, so you know what that means! It's time to see some blood on the mat! Tonight, he returns to the ring!"

The crowd erupted. I felt a huge grin forming on my face.

"He stands at 6' 4" and will really pack a punch! It's…. Martin!!!"

The crowd burst into applause once more. There it was, my true happiness. This was my future, and it looked beautiful!

"That's right, ladies and gentlemen. You paid to see the best, and now you get the best!" Miles announced and enthusiastically gestured towards me again.

The spotlights shined on me, and everyone cheered again. Then, when the cheering began to die down, all the lights above the bleachers came on.

"Who shall be our first contender to take on the mighty Martin?" Miles announced, just as he had yesterday.

I noticed all the similarities between today and yesterday. Both these days had been quite alike. It was pleasant, feeling this normality and familiarity. If every day was going to be like this, I knew I would always be happy.

"How do I pick? There are so many!" Miles announced.

A lone figure jumped from the bleachers, which had about a ten foot drop to the main floor below. He walked up to the ring.

"Pick me," he said in a deep, threatening voice.

"How about you then, sir?" Miles said to him and opened the door for him after he paid and was quickly screened.

He walked to the middle of the ring.

"Tell us your name, man!"

The man snatched the microphone from Miles.

"My name is Jack Lamb. You will not win, Martin."

The grin he gave me seemed as if it were going to an old friend, but he was no friend to me. He gave the microphone back to Miles.

"Okay then, folks. You ready to see a fight?!"

They cheered wildly. Miles left the ring, and the gate was locked.

I studied the man. He was taller than I was at about 6' 7", and he looked as if he was in his late 50's. Despite his years, muscles burst from all over his body. He looked like an aged tank. I had my worries when I saw him, but I knew I could take him down since he was just an ordinary man with big muscles.

I would soon learn that I was not as strong as I had thought.

Chapter 9
Jack Lamb

"AAAAAAAND… FIGHT!!!" Miles announced from outside the ring.

The fight began. The entire crowd was on their feet, cheering.

Jack Lamb simply stood there. I could tell that he was studying me, preparing for any tricks I might have up my sleeve. If I waited too long, he would know me too well. Acting quickly, I ran to him and tried to punch him in the gut. My blow was blocked by his quick hand, and he followed up by throwing a punch at my face. I quickly dodged under his fist, which was exactly as he planned because, right then, his knee connected with my nose. The blow sent me flying into the opposite side of the ring. I lay against the barrier for a second.

There was a wetness under my nose, and I lifted my fingers to it. My fingers were a dark red color. Jack Lamb had made me bleed. This man was something else. How could he plan a move like that so quickly, forming it to my attack?

I ran at him to see his response so I could plan around it. With precise motions adjusted to my motion circling him, he punched, then kicked, then kicked. Then, I came back around him, dodged his last move, and landed an uppercut. He was not stunned in the least. He effortlessly grabbed me by the shoulders and chucked me against the chain-link barrier.

I was so confused. Doing that move on any of the other people I had fought would have snapped their jaw, but it did not even affect this giant man. Jack stood there laughing as I realized my chances of beating him were slim. I had to try to win whatever it took. My new life depended on it.

Looking for a new angle, I climbed up on the chain-link barrier and ran along the top of it. Jack watched me carefully. The crowd cheered at the interesting development to this already exciting fight. I jumped off the barrier and onto the man. I came down with a punch which was successful at first but proved fruitless. He was not even affected and grabbed my other punch as it came. He slammed me to the ground. Then, he started repeatedly kicking me in the ribs.

I felt true pain for the first time. Even the knife stabbing into me was nowhere near this pain. I felt my ribs stressed under each kick. My mind became fuzzy with pain. I rolled away from him and got back to my feet, but Jack was still smiling at me, mocking me. What was with this guy?

I had not even put a dent in this man. Even having landed a couple solid hits, my efforts had proven to be of no consequence to Jack Lamb. His breath was slow and steady, his heart rate not elevated in the slightest. This monster of a man held power much greater than I had ever seen.

The crowd booed me, thinking that I was a fake. Jack Lamb's mind-blowing strength dwarfed mine to a microscopic level. He made me look like a normal kid with no abilities, but I knew I was different. I was better than this! Why could I not prove it? What had happened to me between now and yesterday?

I then wondered if I had been wrong all this time. My strength, was it all fake? Had I lost it somehow? When I needed this strength dearly, it no longer came to my aid. Yet, I felt no different. What had changed?

I looked him over for some kind of weakness. His neck was thick, so I could not attack his throat or his head too well. His belly was fat and muscular, so I could not attack there either. His legs, though, seemed a bit less muscular than his arms, and so I thought maybe I could use the momentum from his punches and trip him to somehow beat him. It was a risky plan because I had to let him punch at me and somehow use those punches to throw him into the hard chain-link barriers, but it seemed to be my only choice.

I approached him, jumping side to side. My jumps got slower, encouraging him to try to strike me. Unsatisfied with the speed of the fight, Jack tried to K.O. me in one punch. The punch barely missed me, and I grabbed his arm and threw him into the barriers. He went face-first into the chain-link.

He got up, slightly amused. He thought it was a good trick, but that I would not win. I begged to differ.

Jack Lamb approached me again. He wound up for another strong punch. He threw it, and I did the same thing as last time. He crashed into the opposite side of the ring. He rose to his feet again, his determination unswayed. He wound up, same as the last times. He threw the punch, and I dodged it and grabbed his hand, but there was no momentum this time. I had been tricked! I was caught facing away from him, trying to throw him once again. He put his foot on my back and pushed me to the ground. He was in perfect position for his victory.

"Say uncle, Martin," Jack whispered into my ear, twisting my arm like a bully.

"Never," I said and wrapped my legs around his one leg that was not on my back. I pulled it to the side, and he tumbled over. I seized this opportunity and flew to my feet. I started kicking him in the face.

There was great satisfaction in seeing his head knocked back by my foot. I knew I had won. The crowd cheered louder for every kick. I felt my power returning and my ego enlarging. That is when he grabbed my leg and yanked me down to the ground. I hit the ground with extreme force. Then, he jumped up and wound up his leg for a kick.

Just before his foot hit my face, that same feeling at the docks with the destroyed boat returned: despair. Again, I lost all hope. Symbolically, his foot was the exploded boat. It came at my head just like the debris came to the docks, only this came so much more quickly and violently. Here was my despair now.

As the kick connected, I felt my head snap to the side and blood pour out my mouth. The crowd's cheering faded away. My vision blurred, and I slowly blacked out. The last thing I remembered was that haunting grin looking down on me.

The deal was now off. Was my future now as lost as my past? With Mr. Vaillancourt's deal off, I had no home and no food. Despair was surely what I felt. Hope had abandoned me. It was all over.

I woke up later. Creighton was standing over me as was Miles. Creighton helped me up, and I sat down in a chair they had out. Miles stood with his back away from me, refusing to look my direction.

I looked at Creighton. "What happened?" I asked, shaking my head.

"He kicked you in the head. You suffered a lot of trauma which caused the blood to flow from your mouth. That last kick to the head straight up ended you. You were in bad shape, bud," he said.

I knew he spoke from his experience with the other fighters.

Miles turned and glared at me with agonizing disappointment.

"You're fired."

He held out his hand commandingly. I knew exactly what he wanted. Oh, how I did not want to give it to him! Sadly, I set the key card to my room in his hand. He just walked away. Yes, the despair was falling heavier and heavier on me as the seconds progressed.

"You did a good job, but… There just wasn't much you could do against a tank like him. Guy was a beast. Total monster," Creighton told me.

"What time is it?" I asked him. He looked at his watch.

"It is 11:23 pm."

I had been there knocked out for about an hour and a half. I lost my future. I had no past and no future. I had nothing. Nothing remained.

"How was he able to sustain those hits I gave him?" I asked Creighton. He sighed deeply.

"I have no idea. And there's no question whether or not he really did sustain those blows. He did! He didn't even look hurt when he grabbed his prize and left."

Not even hurt. It made no sense. How could someone take a blow to the chin and not be hurt, especially a blow from me? It made no sense, much like the rest of my life. I began to think that maybe I was in some bizarre and horrible nightmare. Was that my life? So dark and doomed to only be explained as a fevered dream of a tortured, insane man?

"I have to go, bud. I'm not being paid for this, and I've got to go home to my family," Creighton said, zipping up his jacket.

He had to go back to his family. He had a family. He had a place to go. He had love. He had shelter. I was without all of these. My only option was to somehow convince Mr. Vaillancourt to give me another chance.

I ran out to the lobby. "Where's Mr. Vaillancourt?" I asked a woman at one of the check-in desks.

"You just missed him, Martin. He went out those doors only a second ago," she said, pointing to the front doors.

I thanked her, and then I ran outside. Miles was treading on the last of the cobblestone path that led to the sidewalk.

"Mr. Vaillancourt!" I yelled to him.

He completely disregarded me. Not willing to let him go, I ran up and intersected his path, forcing him to acknowledge me.

"Please, sir, give me another chance!"

"And why should I?" he asked. "We had a deal, and you failed on your part, so you don't get my part. That's how the business world works, kiddo."

"Is there nothing I can do? Please!"

"You can leave."

He turned his back on me coldly. His expensive, shiny black shoes sounded loudly off the cobblestone and then the concrete. The sound probably kept him from hearing my knees hit his walkway. He would not have cared, anyway. He continued on, heading to his welcoming home to sleep in his warm bed.

I knelt there, not knowing what to say. There was nothing to say. I had failed. There was only sleep for me now. I walked back to where I had hidden from the cops across from the awesome pizzeria. I found a refrigerator box and climbed inside. I lay down and went to sleep, miserable.

Chapter 10
New Occupation

I woke to a rat licking the dried blood off my face. I slapped it away. It hit the alley wall hard, and it died. Why could I not exert that kind of force on Jack Lamb, the man who humiliated me and made me lose my future?

I lay in the box for a while longer, not knowing what to do. It was not long before my stomach growled fiercely at me. I remembered that I had skipped dinner and lunch yesterday in wild anticipation and excitement for last night's fights. Now, I saw the grand error in that. What a fool I was to think it could last!

My mind was made up, and I decided to get some breakfast. I left the box as well as the alley. The sun was rising as I wiped the sleep from my eyes. There was not another soul for many blocks. I wandered around the lonely streets for a long time before I found a little cafe which had just opened and had some breakfast food. I walked in.

There were only a handful of other people in there besides me. I did not order, but instead I sat down and read a newspaper that someone had left there. I flipped through the paper, reading about the recent findings on the *Annabelle* and other big topics. I came to the comics and decided to read them. The comics page was short and only had about ten different comics in it. It was also strangely in the sports section.

I flipped to the front cover of the sports section. "New Kid Downed on Second Night" was the main story. The picture featured my bloodied face with Jack Lamb's giant foot swinging past. I threw the paper to the ground. A few people glanced at me, but no one cared enough to say anything.

I stared at the crumbs on the table. Was my life to be as insignificant as these forgotten morsels of an eight dollar burger? Where was the meaning in my life? Where was my purpose? I did not understand why I had been condemned to suffer. I did not want this life, but it was mine. I would have to deal with the terrible ups and downs that came with it.

I was furious that the fans I had gained so quickly had just as quickly turned their backs on me. They only knew what they had seen the night before, and, for all they knew, the people I fought were all weaklings or actors. They all thought I was the liar. They did not know the truth. Their affections for me were fickle and sickened me.

I looked around the room out of boredom and my constant urge to analyze. There were nine tables arranged in a three by three pattern. Three of these tables were occupied, but in no order, just randomly. I occupied the closest table to the door. Behind me was the door and to my right of it were large glass windows that went floor to ceiling. Two potted plants were on either side of the door, and an exit sign was above it. To the left of me was the counter with the cash register and the cashier, immediately to the side of the door. On the right was nothing but a large flat-screen TV, which was currently off, on a blank white wall. In front of me, the white wall continued, but was broken by an opening that led to the bathrooms and a clock to the left of the opening.

I looked at the clock. It was 7:16 am. It was early, but not as early as the day I had woken up on the boat at about 5:45 am. Not that I had rested well, but, even if I had, it would have been to no satisfaction. I had nothing on which to spend that energy. With nothing else to do, I finally decided to order some breakfast.

I walked up to the counter. I took my time to look over the board behind the cashier and decided to get the Basic Breakfast. The man in front of me finished ordering and turned around.

"Whoa!" he said. "You're the guy who totally failed yesterday!"

I glared at the man with hidden rage. I desired to punch him, but such behavior would not be taken so lightly. I would cause more trouble for myself.

"I'm right, right?" he asked me with a mocking smile.

I pushed past him and ordered the Basic Breakfast. The man walked back to his group at the table in the back, and they all started laughing.

I gave the lady 14 bucks and walked back to my seat. Now, almost everyone in the cafe was looking at me. I stared angrily at the insignificant crumbs on the table until I finally heard my order number. I walked up to the counter, grabbed my meal, and walked back to my seat. Everyone was still sneaking looks at me. I slammed down my food onto the table. They all looked away, perhaps embarrassed slightly.

I ate the food as if I had experienced a great famine. There were bacon, eggs, hash browns, sausage, and orange juice. I ate it all in about ten minutes, threw away the garbage, and left for the door as fast as possible.

As I was opening the door, a police officer came in. He looked at me as if he recognized me, but then ignored the fact that he actually should have recognized me. This had now happened twice. Were these officers truly so poorly trained?

I was going to leave, but then I considered what might have happened if the officer had recognized me. I would have been thrown in jail and would have probably stayed there for the rest of my life. Free food and shelter did not sound too bad, but the lack of freedom was usually the deal breaker. This time, though, did I care about my freedom? I was going nowhere and had no plan. Prison sounded like a fine place for someone like me. I did not have anywhere to go and did not have to hide from the cops anymore, so I walked over and tapped the cop on the shoulder as he was about to get in line.

He turned around and said, "Yes, sir? Can I do something for you?"

He still did not recognize me. "Don't you recognize me?" I asked him.

"Um...can't say I do," he answered, scratching his head.

"Really?" I asked him. He looked at me harder.

"Oh, wait," he chuckled. "You're the guy that got his butt kicked at the fight last night. That one was a real blowout!"

I heard the man from earlier as well as his group laughing in the back of the cafe.

Apparently, they did not go through any kind of training for these police officers. This foolish man could not identify the only suspect for the subway killings. They most likely even had pictures of me! His stupidity was making my blood boil.

"Even though that is correct, there is a more correct answer for which I was looking."

He looked at me and asked, "Uh...you got me beat. Who are you?" he asked, glancing back at the group to give a sly smile.

"I'm the man who killed three men in the subway two days ago."

My small audience showed sudden surprise and fear. The officer jumped back and clumsily pulled out his pistol.

"S-stop!" he squeaked out.

He pointed the gun at me, and I nonchalantly put my hands above my head. He told me to turn around, and I did. He then pulled my arms back and handcuffed me.

The people in the cafe clapped as he pushed me out the door as if he were some kind of hero. The officer had a dumb smile as the people cheered for him. He pushed me into the back of his car and slammed the door closed. I saw him do a little dance after he closed the door, and it caused me to laugh a little bit, despite my current situation.

He climbed into the driver's seat, turned back, and told me, "You are my first arrest! When we get to the station, I'm going to be a hero!"

He seemed very excited for a police officer who arrests people for a living. "How long have you been an officer?" I asked him.

"Two years!" the officer responded, still thrilled by his accomplishment.

He drove me to the police station. The whole drive, he told me how much praise he would get for this arrest. When he stopped the car and climbed out, he did the same dance all the way around the car. I stopped myself from laughing too hard. He opened the door and pulled me out. I almost considered escaping only to ruin this man's mood. I let him push me into the station instead.

The station was much larger than the one in Alemande. Looking closer, I noticed that this station was a regional police station. It was a strange concept to have a number of stations all working together to cover an area instead of only a city. One good thing might come of this: larger and better cells. Perhaps better offices were in here as well. I knew that would make Officer Turnbull happy.

As we approached the station door, I thought back on all I could remember. I was shipwrecked and found by a great family, which then I abandoned so that I could try and fail to find a better future. Now, I was being arrested. I now thought how my life with Jonah's family would be. I felt like a fool.

When we entered the station, three officers were lounging about the main office. When they looked up and saw me, all three of them jumped into the air and then ran to congratulate the officer who had brought me in.

"I told you so," he whispered into my ear.

The three men ran into the back to go get some help with me. They pulled me into the back of the station just as the officers had done with the mugger I had brought in. We traversed the halls of the station, and I analyzed for an escape route. With many windows throughout the station, escape could be quite easy if I needed it. They threw me into a cell and locked the door.

"Not so tough now, huh, scum?!" one of the officers said to me.

The officer who had brought me in was probably trying to sell the fact that he was a great police officer. He was not a great police officer. Officers like Nick, Heath, and Chase were the great officers. Or at least, better than these ones. That was quite obvious after a single meeting with them.

I waited in the cell, wondering what prison would be like. Being the natural fighter I was, I would fit in just fine, perhaps even make a name for myself there. Ambition would lead me to climbing up the ranks until no man stood above me. All the lowly criminals would bow to my power and authority. Going to prison did not actually sound that bad. It was part of the reason I got myself arrested. The other part was that I was feeling bored. Free food and shelter did not sound bad at all. Of course, it would not be as good as the Vaillancourt, but I could settle.

Within the hour, an officer came to the cell.

"Your bail has been paid," he said.

I was incredibly confused. I had been arrested less than an hour ago, and somebody had already paid my bail? Who would pay my bail? The officer unlocked the cell and led me out. I did not even know I had a bail. Why would they give bail to a murderer? I did not understand the system well, but I knew this was not how it worked.

When we got out to the main office again, I saw two men talking to an officer.

"You're cool with us now, little piggy," the taller man said.

He patted the officer on the shoulder, and the officer looked terrified. Then, he grinned and looked my way. His eyes locked onto me and would not leave me.

"Ah, yes, he does look like a fighter. And a killer."

Quickly judging by the expensive and stereotypical clothing of the two men and the language of the taller, I guessed that these men were with the West City Mafia.

The taller man had a bit of his white hair left, and that which was left was mostly covered by his custom mafia-styled fedora. He had thick glasses on his wrinkled face. His face bore a solemnity that no one could miss. He looked very experienced as well.

The shorter one looked much younger, perhaps around 20. He had thick red hair and wore a fedora that was similar to his companion's. He looked to be about 5' 5", and every inch was well-dressed. There was an eager and somewhat manic look in his eyes. With his clean shaven face, I could see every bit of his greedy grin. He wanted me.

Now, my anxiety got intense. The mafia of West City had bought me to make me a killer for them. The smaller man walked up to me and pulled me over to the other one.

"The name's Glen," the taller one said. "But you will call me Mr. T. This here is Little Ty."

I looked at Little Ty. He gave me a look that one should only have to witness in an asylum. I turned back to Mr. T in fear. There was just the shortest smile on Mr. T's face, one that was both nostalgic and fresh.

"You will be working for us now, kid."

I started breathing harder, and he could tell.

"Well, don't be 'fraid now, kid. We're gonna take great care of you."

He smiled at me creepily.

I left the station with them. We walked to the car, which was parked in the spot reserved for the police chief. I got into the back, and they got in the front. When I was in the car, there was already someone next to me. I closed the door and observed the man. This man was dressed even more impressively than the others.

"Well, hello there, my friend," he said to me. "As you may know, I am the leader of the West City Mafia, Keir Sanzano."

The man looked big and dangerous. The car took off, and I wondered exactly what they wanted with me. Whatever it was, it could not be good.

I studied the man. Very expensive clothing, clean haircut, and a big, shiny ring on his finger. His piercing eyes stared evilly at me. This man thought that I was a cold-blooded killer, just as he was. I did not want to work for him at all.

"You are going to be our new cash collector," Keir told me. "You will go around with the other cash collector and collect our protection money from the different businesses we provide protection for."

The job would not involve hurting people if I could collect their money without problem. Maybe this would not be as bad as I thought. Perhaps this would turn out well.

"Now, if they decide to not let you collect the money, well…that's when their little family get drowned and their homes get burnt down to the ground."

Now, I was worried again. I would have to convince everyone from whom I collected to give me the money then, instead of later. If there was any dispute over this, then I might be forced to hurt them. I feared I might not be able to receive such results.

"Why did you pick me, Don Sanzano?" I asked him carefully, keeping in mind that he was the mafia leader.

"We picked you because you are a fighter and a killer," he answered with a grin.

"But I lost that fight at the hotel."

He did not seem to care about that at all. He waved his hands in a matter that suggested that what I had said was not important in the slightest.

"Look, kid. If you can kill three men like that and get stabbed and not care, I want you on the team."

He knew of the subway incident. That was why he recruited me, not because of the hotel fights. He must have had a mole in the police station that informed him of a killer being brought in. It was only a matter of time before he arrived to pick me up. I could not say I was glad to be on the team, but it was better than living in either a cardboard or concrete box.

"All you have to do is enter each establishment, get the money, and get out. Anything you need to do to get it is up to you. And to make sure you are up to the challenge, you're going solo your first time," the don said.

"When do I begin?" I asked him.

He grinned and said, "Now."

The car stopped, and I looked out my window. We were at the cafe where I had eaten breakfast just about an hour ago.

"Oh, and one more thing, kid," Don Sanzano said and handed me a ring. "You will need this to let them know you are in the mafia. It was made especially for you. Now, you are doing this mission solo, so you need to show them that you mean business," Keir told me. "Now, get in there and get us our 2000 bucks."

I looked down at the ring he had given to me. The ring was made of silver and it had gold around the ruby in the center. Inscribed above the ruby in the gold was my name: Martin. I could see that below the ruby was another place for a person's last name, but neither they nor I knew my last name. I put on the ring, and it strangely fit perfectly. I did not question this, for I had a job to do. I opened the door and got out.

The plan seemed simple. Walk into the cafe, flash my ring, and collect 2000 dollars. It was incredibly simple, but, every so often, people like to cause you difficulty and mess everything up. This would be one of those times.

I walked into the cafe. A few people looked at me and recognized me. One of them walked up to me to talk about my loss. I knew I had to put on a show for the mafia.

"Hey, dude! I was just wondering how you could…" the man started to say, but I interrupted with a swing of my arm.

I punched him in the face and knocked him into a table. The table fell over, and its glass top shattered. Short screams rung out from the back of the cafe. My large mafia ring left a large mark on the man's face. He groaned and spat out some teeth.

I walked up to the counter nonchalantly and asked for the money, flashing the ring.

"I-I can't get the m-money today. I-I'm s-sorry," the lady behind the counter stuttered in fear.

Something clicked within me, and I felt a strength within my veins. This woman was so afraid of me. She could see my power. I could so easily demonstrate it in this place. All of them could see my strength, my superiority. I would show them my true self.

"Sorry? Sorry. I can believe that you're sorry. But it doesn't change a thing. Where is my money?" I asked her again.

"I can't give you the money right now," she said, shaking terribly.

"*Can't give me the money right now*?" I laughed. "When can you give me the money? Because it better be soon!"

I looked over towards the car, and the mafia men were still watching me. I looked at the girl and then ripped the cash register from the counter and threw it at a table at which a person was sitting. It smashed through the glass top and knocked the man out of his seat.

"I think the cafe is closed!" I yelled at the stunned people trying to eat their breakfasts. "OUT!" I yelled again. They all quickly departed, their eyes glued to me as they side-stepped out the door, not willing to show me their backs.

"Now, give me my money!" I yelled at her again.

"Please, have mercy. We don't have enough money to give you right now. I will pay you. I swear! I *swear* I will pay you! I just can't right now," she pleaded with me.

I was not convinced. I slammed my fist down on the counter. "Who the hell do you think I am?! And who the hell do you think you are?! You are weak. I could kill you without a care in the world. Is that what you want? Or do you want to live?"

"Please! Please, don't! I don't have the money! I swear!" she cried.

Now was not the time for mercy. I picked up a table and smashed a window with it. "YOU HAVE MY MONEY NOW?!!!" Tears were pouring down her face.

"Please!" she pleaded.

I smashed another window. "How about now?!" Her crying continued. I threw the table out the large front window, almost hitting the mafia's car. I turned back to her and returned to the counter. Reaching across, I grabbed the woman by her collar and lifted her off the floor. I glared at the other employees behind her and warned them with my eyes that they should not intervene.

"Now, if I don't get your money... excuse me... *my* money by tomorrow, I will tie you to a table and torch this place!"

I dropped her, and she fell to the floor, weeping uncontrollably. Looking down on her, I felt an exhilaration greater than anything I had experienced previously. This was better than any drug a man could take. This was power, and it was in my possession.

I walked out of the building, making sure to kick anything in my way as I left. I opened the car door and jumped back in with my new partners.

"Nice show, kid!" Don Sanzano told me. "I don't think we will even have to send a team with you!" he laughed. "Good job in there. She is terrified, and there is no way she will ever miss another payment. Man, that was hilarious!"

I evaluated my performance also. Somehow, yelling and smashing things was so easy for me. I felt it was instinct. Even though I knew that I was doing this to show off for the mafia, something inside me wanted to do it...badly.

We proceeded to the next destination. I felt guilt for what I did to that woman, but I thought it was better to break her stuff and threaten her than to have to hurt her. I had chosen the best option afforded me.

We drove to eleven other businesses. I did not have to get too hard on anyone. Not like I did with the cafe lady, that is. I broke their stuff, yelled at them, and threatened them. I got all but two payments, and Don Sanzano loved my work. He would give me an evil grin and say, "Good job," after every stop, even if I did not bring back money.

Finally, we went to the last stop.

"Are you ready for your final job of the day?" he asked me.

"Of course," I answered. He nodded at the door, and I opened it. Outside was the towering Vaillancourt Hotel. I looked back at Keir, and he nodded for me to continue.

My feet hit the cobblestone, and soon I was at the grand doors of the hotel. I walked inside, feeling as if I had much more purpose here than the first time I had entered. I went straight up to my old check-in desk.

The guy at the desk was new. I asked for the usual and flashed my ring. The clerk was confused.

"The what?" he asked me, tilting his head slightly.

"Just give me the money, man," I told him, losing patience. His expression remained blank for a second before turning into realization.

"Help!" he yelled, backing up to the wall. "Robber!"

Frustration quickly consumed me. He had alarmed everyone in the lobby. Ten people ran out of the building. Three people called the cops.

I picked him up and threw him into the center of the lobby. "Where's the money?!" I yelled at him. One man tried to intervene by punching me in the face. It did not work. I grabbed his fist, broke his hand, and kicked him into an expensive table. Everyone stared at me in terror.

"Please, stop!" I heard a man say.

I turned around. It was Miles Vaillancourt. He had the packet full of money in his hand. His hand was outstretched to me, and his expression was distraught. He wanted badly for me to leave his hotel.

"Just take it, Martin," Miles said, holding it out to me.

I took the packet from him and said, "Now, I'm your boss…" I paused, "…and you're fired."

As I said this, I knocked over a table, and candles fell and ignited very expensive furniture. Miles and his employees quickly moved to extinguish the fire. The money in hand, I marched proudly out the doors, grinning. With the Vaillancourt at my back, I felt as if I owned the place.

I opened the door of the car and gave the money to Don Sanzano.

He grinned and said, "Good job, kid."

We then went back to his mansion. This was his base of operations. It was a large house that probably had over fifty rooms. All these rooms were most likely stocked with weapons, money, and possibly drugs.

When we got there, Mr. T got out and opened the don's door. Then, Little Ty opened my door. We got out and then walked inside. I noticed that when the don got inside, a man was waiting to take his coat. He had a well-run organization.

"You did good today, kid. Our family could really use someone like you," my boss said to me.

I did not know it right then, but I had just become one of the three caporegimes. This title, also shared by Mr. T and Little Ty, meant that I was captain over many of the soldiers in this mob. I had gained power so quickly.

With the boss's praise came a monetary reward as well. He handed me five crisp, clean 100 dollar bills. It reminded me of when I turned in the mugger for 500 bucks. Except this time, I was on the other side of the law. I might have been doing wrong, but it paid the same as doing right.

"Now, kid," he said. "If you want to stay at someplace nice, we like to stay at the Vaillancourt Hotel. Since we own it, we can get free rooms there."

I was glad that my plan to live in the Vaillancourt was actually going to work. The don deposited his money at his house, gave orders to some of the men there, and then the four of us got back in the car. His management of operations complete, we drove back to the hotel.

When we entered, all the people in the lobby either left for a different part of the hotel or acted as if they could not see us. I saw that a small portion of the lobby was covered in black soot. I chuckled at my revenge.

We walked up to a check-in desk. The new guy was still there. He was a little bruised from when I threw him, and he was shaking a lot more than the first time.

"We'll take four of your best rooms," Keir said.

"S-sure, guys," the clerk stuttered.

He gave us our key cards, and we went up to our rooms. I was on the tenth floor this time. Before, I had been on the first floor. Things were looking up once again.

The don got the best room, I got the next best, Mr. T got the next best, and Little Ty got the next best. I was near the top of the food chain for once, and it felt great.

On our way up to our rooms, I saw Jack Lamb.

"Shepherds better watch their sheep!" he said to me.

He grinned at me, and, when we were a distance away, he started to laugh loudly. I did not understand his joke, but still it made me furious. I boiled with rage and wondered if there was anything I could do about him with my new mafia powers, but I decided to let him be.

Jack Lamb thought he was better than I, but he was not. If I desired to do so, I could kill him so easily. He would be dead if I just said the word, but he would be a waste of my now so valuable time. He was still in the little leagues. I was the superior one now. I would not waste my breath on him.

We all split up and went to our rooms. My room had a nice street view, a king-sized bed, a refrigerator full of free food, and a 50" TV with a Game Box plugged-in. It was a great room. I now knew why the rooms cost so much. A room like this one would have cost me 18,000 bucks a night, which I considered to be a lot of money.

I knew that the mafia was where I was supposed to be. I did not want to take things from people, but it was where I was. I did it well enough to not destroy any businesses and not to hurt any people. I also thought that now that people had seen my power, they would not dare miss a payment. That meant that I would not have to hurt anyone anymore. It was a good deal for me and for the people under me. I had finally found my place, the mafia. I hoped that I could prevent anything from happening to the innocent. If anyone in the mafia was going to do it, it would be I.

Another thought came to mind. Did I truly enjoy attacking the people and destroying what they had? I could feel it back there in the cafe, a passion springing forth out of violence. I never thought I would want to hurt people, but some evil thirst for it was deep within me. I was supposed to be the good guy, but I was now pulled straight towards the evil. Did I genuinely desire to hurt those people?

I disregarded my thoughts and relaxed in my room which the thirst had given me.

Chapter 11
The Robbery

The time I had in the hotel was fantastic. I ordered room service whenever I felt like it. Flashing my ring made it free for me, which was the best part. I tried all kinds of new foods that I could not remember eating. I experimented with the Game Box. I watched TV for a while. I drank the pop in the refrigerator. I even took my first bath, lying in the bubbly water for hours. The life of a mafia member was one of great luxury.

My life had changed so much. No longer did I wear the old, weathered clothes of the fishermen, but instead I donned an expensive suit of the highest quality. The life of poverty was left behind. I had taken my rightful position on top of the world. I was truly on top of everything.

I loved not having any rules, save the respect given to my leader, Keir Sanzano. He was a good leader, and he must have thought I was a good follower. He gave me the best of everything that he did not keep for himself. I even received respect from my fellow members.

My life was good now. I had fixed the problem caused at this hotel's Fight Arena. My future was once again safe. I had no need to worry about what I was going to do next. My life had turned completely around from yesterday.

Yesterday, I had woken up with certain expectations for the day. I had believed that I was invincible, but someone named Jack Lamb was ready to disprove that. I fell asleep in a box in an alley.

Today, though, I had greatness thrust upon me. I had gained everything. I had unlimited resources on hand. I now owned the police. Also, tonight, I would sleep on a huge, expensive bed. The past was forgotten, and my future was beautiful.

I would no longer be held down by the curiosity of my past. I no longer wanted to learn about my time as a lowly fisherman. To hell with the mystery that plagued me before! This life I had now was clear and bright, not foggy and dim. Having gained an extraordinary place in the West City Mafia, I would devote myself to it.

As I lay on my bed, I dreamed about what was going to be. I would live here in West City for the rest of my life most likely. Might I climb the ranks, eventually take over the mafia when Don Sanzano died? The thought of my name becoming famous in this city made my heart soar! They would know my name, and they would know that I had what it took.

I had created something great for myself with which I barely had to work to achieve greatness. All I had to do was collect money every once and a while. If I did not receive the money, I would just have to threaten the people and destroy their property. Unknown to me before, working for the mafia was actually a dream job, and I had it. Everything was changing, finally in my favor!

I turned my head to look at my expensive clock on the table. 10:35 pm was digitally displayed on it. I decided it was best to go to sleep now. I tucked myself into my enormous bed. With a clap of my hands, the lights turned off. I left the TV on and went to sleep.

In my dreams, I saw over and over again a friend left behind. Jonah ran to the train and banged on the door as it slowly started to move. Frustration was in his eyes as all I did was wave goodbye. All that was good was lost to the speed of the train. Then, Jimmy and his goons attacked me, and I heartlessly killed all three without a second of contemplation. I stood in a pool of blood while three lifeless corpses lay motionless on the floor. This dream repeated throughout the night.

I awoke to the knocking on my door. I looked at the clock and noted that the time was 8:15 am. I found myself to be extremely tired, although it was not too early a time for me to be waking up. I found it very hard to get out of bed. It was a very nice bed, and it enveloped me perfectly, requesting I stay within it for only another five minutes. I wanted more sleep, but, when the knocking continued, I decided to get up.

I put on my clothes and walked to the door. Behind the door was my boss, Don Sanzano. He looked rather annoyed, having to wait about two minutes for me to get the door.

"We have a job for you, kid," he said without showing his frustration.

Throughout yesterday, I had not heard him use my name very much, and I believed that he was trying to nickname me "kid". The name made sense, but I did not wanted to seem limited because of my youth. I was stronger than men twice my age.

"What's the job?" I asked him, becoming distracted by a loose thread on my sleeve.

"We need you to rob one of the West City banks for us," he said nonchalantly.

I almost ripped the thread from my jacket upon the completion of his sentence. This was a job that I did not want to do. I did not want to hurt anyone or take a lot of their stuff. I was okay with the protection money, but I thought that the bank robbing went too far. If I was to be who I thought I should be, I could not go through with this.

"Why can't you get someone else to do it?" I questioned, looking for an escape.

"Because they will screw it up. I need someone with brute strength and cunning to take this money, kid. That's you. I'd suggest you stop questioning my decisions..."

Again, he called me kid. I did not know what to say. He was my boss, and, if I disobeyed him, I would either be fired or killed. I had shown him enough resistance already. There was no other choice.

"Okay then, Boss. Consider the bank robbed." His evil grin appeared once more.

"Good," he said. "I will send Mr. T and Little Ty with you to help you carry the money out. You guys will make a good team. Trust me."

"What is the plan?" I asked him as he started walking away.

He scoffed and gave me a confused look.

"The plan's simple. Just walk in and shoot some people and take the money."

The plan was simple, but I did not want to hurt anyone. I would not allow them to cause anyone pain. I would have to make some adjustments to the plan.

The mob was always doing things to gain more power over the city. They would rob the city's banks, kill off rival gangs, and desecrate something if it meant bringing more respect to them. Respect is sometimes best gained through fear.

The mob also had connections. Running the city, they had the ability to get practically anything they wanted. Also, only the toughest and smartest people could enter the mafia and be a part of it. That is why they had picked me. They had every resource they needed to get the money from that bank. There was no way that I could back out on these people. The safest way was to just go with their plans and try to not get anyone hurt. I would fix this potential issue from the inside.

As I followed the don to Mr. T's and Little Ty's rooms, I rehearsed the robbery in my mind. We enter, shoot into the ceiling, people duck down, have someone watch the hostages, move to the back with a partner, take out guards, leave with money from the vault. That was all we had to do.

This plan I had made also seemed simple, but I feared that either Mr. T or Little Ty would not go along with it. If I did not step in, they would kill many. I guess it was a good thing the don called on me to help.

Both Mr. T and Little Ty exited their rooms much faster than I. They most likely respected and feared Don Sanzano more than I did. I had not known him for long and did not know his reactions. Seeing their response, I had learned something.

The team assembled, the three of us headed downstairs and back to the don's car. We departed the Vaillancourt, leaving Don Sanzano behind. I watched him through the rear window, his eyes glowing and his hand waving at us goodbye.

Mr. T handed me back a pistol while he drove. I looked it over. It was a nice weapon. It seemed this weapon was borderline average to pistols of the time. I pulled out the clip. It was full of 16 bullets. This was a good amount of shots, but I did not intend to shoot anyone. It was indeed a nice weapon, but I would not be using it in the heist.

Mr. T had a shotgun, and Little Ty had an Uzi. I was worried about the fact that these weapons were in the hands of murderers, but if I pulled it off for them, they would not have to use them.

We pulled into the parking lot of the bank, and the two of them prepared themselves for the heist. I watched them both quickly inspecting their weapons, and another thought came to mind. Why did Keir choose the three of us to do the robbery? I had figured that we three were highest ranking, but there was a reason we were above the others and a reason we were supposed to stay above the others. It gave the boss plausible deniability in case something went wrong. Perhaps the don trusted us so much that this did not worry him. Or maybe he felt that the legal system could never take him down. Whatever his reasoning, I still did not like how unorthodox the don was being.

"Okay, here's the plan, everyone," Little Ty said. "We will walk into the bank, and I will spray the place with my Uzi. Today's a Tuesday, so there shouldn't be too many people there. Anyone left alive will be killed by Mr. and Mrs. T."

I was suddenly confused about who Mrs. T was, but then I looked at Mr. T. He motioned to his shotgun. When I inspected the shotgun, I noticed that Mrs. T was carved into the side. I thought it was strange that someone would name their shotgun as if it were their own wife, but I did not know Mr. T that well.

"Then, you," Little Ty said, motioning to me. "You will take all the money from the vault, killing anyone who gets in your way."

This was worse than I was expecting. His plan involved killing everyone in the whole bank, and I could not let them do that. The prospect of changing their minds put a huge lump in my throat, though.

"Hey, guys," I choked out. "Why don't we not kill everyone there?"

They looked at me as if I were insane. Of course, I was not helping my own case very much. I would have to sell it better than I currently was.

"Why would we want to do that?" Mr. T questioned me.

I thought for a second. "Well, if we left some people there, they could spread the word of how powerful we are. That fear builds our reputation and makes jobs in the future a bit easier for us."

"Yeah, but these people we're not killing could really get in the way and try to kill us," Little Ty said to me as if I were a child.

"That's why we put some bullets in the ceiling to scare them to the floor. Then, I will take down the guards and grab the money. One of you guys can help take out the money while the people are being held hostage," I responded, talking to Little Ty as if he were a child.

They both looked at me and then at each other.

"You know, kid…that is a pretty good way to do this. That way, people are even more afraid of us, especially the people that were in the bank and their families. We would be even more feared than we already are. And we wouldn't have to waste a bunch of ammo," Mr. T told me.

Little Ty nodded, reluctantly, in agreement.

"Then, that's the new plan," Mr. T said.

I smiled. I had found a way to rob the bank and not hurt anyone. The murderers in the car even thought it was a great idea. It was perfect, except for the fact that I was still bringing fear to the streets and stealing people's money. It was the best I could do, though.

"Okay, guys," I said. "When we enter the bank, I will put three bullets in the ceiling and will yell that we're robbing the place. That's when you guys point your guns at anyone who dares to try and stop us."

"Kid, we don't need an explanation for everything. We might have done this a few times, you know?" Little Ty said to me.

"Ty's right. We're just robbing some bank. It's not a big deal," Mr. T affirmed.

"Listen. I just don't want anything to go wrong. That's all. And I've never done this before. We should talk about this a little before we actually do it."

"Seriously, kid, don't worry about it. We got this one," Little Ty assured me.

"Okay, okay. Why don't you stay and guard the hostages, Little Ty?" I asked him.

"What? Wait! Why?" he asked, insult burning in his eyes.

"Well, you seem scarier with that Uzi than Mr. T. No offense, Mr. T."

Little Ty was happy with the option I had given to him along with the compliment. Mr. T seemed somewhat irritated by my comment, though.

"Not that you aren't menacing, Mr. T. It just seems like the people would think that Little Ty would snap easier than you. You, on the other hand, seem more like you know what's going on and are ready to snap someone's legs instead," I told him.

"Thanks for the clarification. I'm good with the plan," Mr. T said.

"Me, too. I'll guard the hostages, but I'm sure as hell not going to make it boring," Little Ty said.

They both seemed satisfied.

"Let's do this," said Mr. T.

We left the car. Walking into the bank, we showed our weapons. I saw the horror in the eyes of the innocent citizens in the bank. I walked into the center of the bank's main lobby. I fired three shots into the ceiling.

"Listen up! This is a robbery! If I were you guys, I would drop to the floor right now," I yelled at the people. Almost everyone dropped to the floor. I saw a bank teller grab a shotgun from under the desk. I was about to threaten him when Little Ty put about 15 rounds into the man's chest.

"All right! Now, we don't want any funny business. We are going to take the money here, and no one else here has to die. But you can if you want to!" Little Ty exclaimed and then started shooting like mad into the ceiling.

The rest of the bank tellers knew he meant business and stayed under the desks where they were hiding. Mr. T walked over to the brutalized bank teller. He grabbed the bloody shotgun from the desk the man had fallen behind. He threw it over to Little Ty.

"Hahahaha! Now, I have double the killing power! Woohoo!" Little Ty exclaimed.

Everyone on the ground hid themselves from him with their arms. I was not exactly sure if he was acting the part or if he was actually insane, but it did not matter at the time. I had a job to do.

Mr. T motioned towards where the vault was. "Now, my friends, Mr. T and I will kindly steal...uh...I mean borrow everything from your vault. I hope we will have no problems because I would like as many of you to stay alive as possible. But do understand and keep in mind, we are *so* willing to end anyone's life who would like to inconvenience us in even the smallest of ways," I said to the crowd. Mr. T and I headed back to the vault.

When we got back to the vault, there were three men ready to kill us. Mr. T lifted his shotgun to kill the first, but I would not let him. I ran up and crushed the first guard's ribs with a punch and threw him into the next. Then, I ran to the third and knocked away his gun and slammed his face into the wall. He was knocked out. I kicked the guns away from the two others and kicked them both in the face, merely knocking them out. Mr. T looked surprised.

"Well, I guess that's why we recruited you," he stated bluntly.

I smiled at him and walked to the vault. Mr. T came over to the vault to help me open it, but, with my immense strength, I opened it with ease. Again, he seemed surprised. Then, he helped me clear out the vault. He had brought a few garbage bags in which to carry out the money. We stuffed the garbage bags until they were almost bursting with cash. I grabbed two of the bags, and he took the other. We walked out into the lobby again.

Little Ty was having fun terrorizing the horrified hostages. I threw a bag to him. It dropped to the ground in front of him.

"One sec, kid," he said, unloaded the shotgun, and threw the gun away from the bank hostages.

He then grabbed the bag. "Give me another bag, Mr. T," I said. He handed me another empty bag.

I walked over to the desks and lifted the man at the end into the air. "You want to empty the desks for me, man?" I asked him loudly.

"Sure, sure. Of course, I would," he said with a slight tremor.

I set his feet back on the floor. I then gave him the bag, and he went through the desks, emptying out the cash. When we got to the end, which was far away from the two other mobsters, I said to him, "Listen. When I take this bag to my friends over there, I'm going to take a shot at you." His eyes widened. "Don't worry. I will miss you. But when I do, you must act like you have been hit and killed. Deal?" I asked him. He nodded his head with confusion still on his face.

I led him over to where he was initially. "Stay!" I yelled at him. I then walked over to my counterparts.

"Well, we only had to kill the one," Mr. T told me with an approving look.

"You mean two," I said, secretly knowing the truth.

"What? Did you kill one of the guards?" he asked.

"No, but I still think you are miscounting," I told him.

"Nope, just the one, kid," Little Ty said to me.

"Really?" I asked. Then, I turned around and shot at the banker who had agreed to help me. The bullet skimmed his suit, but he fell to the ground, seemingly killed.

"Okay then!" Little Ty laughed hysterically. "I like you, kid!"

I grinned the evil grin back at him even though the thought of this crazy murderer liking me made me feel gross inside. That being so, it was good to know my partner in crime liked me and was not completely distrusting of me anymore.

"Well, that's all for us, folks! We have been the best of the best from the West City Mafia, and you have been the helpless victims. Thank you for playing your part so very well, and we do hope you continue playing your part for us in the days to come. Your cooperation is what keeps fine establishments such as this from being burnt to the ground. And we would just hate to have to pay any personal visits to any one of you wonderful people. With that all said, we're outta here! Have a pleasant afternoon, citizens of West City!" I announced to the cowering masses still face-down on the floor.

We walked out of the bank with our chests puffed out.

"Mission complete!" said Little Ty, slapping both of us on the back.

We got into the car and drove off to the Vaillancourt Hotel. It definitely was a mission completed, and completed well. I only let one person be killed, and there was no way they were not going to kill him. I felt bad for letting this one man die, but being in the mafia had changed my way of thinking. I was quite glad there was only one casualty. I also felt that there was nothing wrong with taking the money from the bank. It was all part of staying alive for me. If this was what I would have to do, I would do it. This was my life now.

Chapter 12
Life in the Mafia

When we returned to the hotel and talked to the don, he was very pleased.

"And to think you only had to kill two people! I bet the rest will be scared straight into our trap! Our plans can finally reach fruition! That was brilliant!" Don Sanzano shouted excitedly, giving me that huge grin.

"Plans?" I asked.

"Yes, plans. You see, Martin, we are planning to capture this whole city so we can expand to other cities. Right now, we only have about two-thirds of West City under our influence. We plan to strike fear into the hearts of all our protection money customers. This will, in theory, make us our customers' number one choice instead of our competitors. Then, our competitors will lose out on money and have less equipment and ammunition. In the end, we will crush them using this advantage. We will then drive them out of the city and take over the place. Eventually, we will take other cities and expand our mafia empire. We're months away, but, soon enough, all will be under our feet," he said, his eyes glowing with greed.

He seemed to be very proud of his plan, and with good reason. His plan did seem quite foolproof. Fear was our strongest weapon, and I was the king of such fear.

"Thank you for leaving the rest of them to lie in their houses in terror. Our rivals will not know what hit them!" Keir Sanzano said excitedly.

The don was power-hungry, obviously so. Nothing would get in the way of his conquering the whole city, or even the whole state. I felt that he might be taking his rule too far. I did not want this man to have control over a whole state. Of course, it would all go to me when he died, for I was positioning myself to be next in command.

"I'm very glad we were able to get you, kid. You're the key to the whole plan."

A wave of guilt fell over me upon hearing my thoughts leave his mouth. I was the strongest force causing terror and villainy to cover the whole city and even further. His plans, in the long run, if I could not do anything to stop them, would cover the city in darkness. I did not want this to happen, but somehow my mind convinced me that this was the only way I could have a life. My twisted perspective convinced me that there was nothing wrong with letting these people conquer this region as long as I got compensated with the glorious life that the wealth gave me.

Anyway, I had no idea how I could possibly back out of this situation now. If I did, I would have the entire mafia out to get me and I could never rest. In this situation, though, I could rest in peace with the wonderful life of wealth. I was completely torn, but in the end decided to go with the more comfortable choice of life in the mafia.

"Well, tell me if any more jobs come up," I said, flashing an uneasy smile.

"I definitely will, kid. But for now, you should go rest."

Returning to the hotel granted me a safe space away from the guilt and weight of my decisions. All my worries melted away as I did as I liked. Everything was open to me. Even if I wanted to go swimming, I could go down to the pool and wave my ring in people's faces, and they would scatter. The Vaillancourt was my personal paradise.

I loved my new power. It was better than being crammed into the back of a destitute fisherman's car and driving for hours. I felt as if I were in complete control of my life. I had what I wanted all along: power. I had no need to find anything else. I had control of anyone but the don, and there was no need to control him. He gave me anything I wanted.

I no longer wondered where I would sleep or what I would eat. I no longer worried about what I had lost. All I really cared about was what I had gained. Nothing was out of my grasp. No one ever got in my way. I loved it.

To be on top these days was of utmost importance. As I watched society crumbling around me, I did not have to fear the effects of such a collapse. Truly, it only would drag down the weak; I had nothing about which to worry. As prices skyrocketed and crime became unstoppable, I would only benefit. The police, however much they offered in bounties, could not stop my reign. This was my time, and I would rule it for the rest of my life.

I relaxed on my huge, comfortable bed and thought about what I had gained. It was great having wealth that brought me my power and power that brought me my wealth. The mafia was not so bad after all. They had given me the best life I could imagine. Nothing could take this from me. I threw away any thought of the consequences of this city being run over by crime. As long as I had a life that was high above my other life, I would fight to slow the darkness. If it meant killing the rival gangs and anyone who got in the way, I would slaughter them all.

I lay on my bed and enjoyed the rest of my break.

***   ***   ***   ***   ***   ***

Ten months passed for me with my new life in the mafia. I continued to collect protection money and became increasingly proficient at the job, never missing payments. I was many times scarier and more violent than I normally would have been. This was to follow the don's plan of domination, of course. Yes, I tortured, maimed, destroyed, and even killed, and they feared me for it. I became a nightmare to the citizens of West City.

My compassion had disappeared for these people now. My focus now dwelt solely on increasing in power and reputation. I did whatever it took to lift myself higher. To do this, all I had to do was impress the boss, and he was always impressed with me. We went to about fifteen businesses a week, and every one of them bowed to us. We were as monarchs among peasants. I noticed that every place to which I went, the people there could not look me in the eye. They trembled and handed over what was mine to take. The plan was working perfectly.

Outside of every store, I left a fire in front of the door to show that I had been there, a sign I had taken up since overturning candles at the Vaillancourt. Citizens of West City had given me the title of the Beast of Flame. I wore the title well and was pleased with my reputation. I had become that which no force could stop and towards which none could contemplate compassion. I was a monster among these weaklings, and I led a team that sought to control them.

We committed multiple crimes each week. Muggings, bank-robbings, selling of illegal arms, and all kinds of evil were our daily activities. The citizens' fright grew and grew, and we knew that the city was ripe for the picking. Soon, we would seize it all.

I was too glad that the plan was to be a success. In the past, I would not have cared for conquest such as this, but now the thirst within me left me terribly unsatisfied with what I had. The West City Mafia needed to take this place. If we owned the whole city, there would be no luxury that I would not have. Life would be perfect.

I started noticing more changes in myself other than the overwhelming confidence I had gained. I looked much more mature now. I was only eighteen years old, but this occupation had hardened me, and I looked as if I were now in my twenties. My appearance was that of a man, and that was exactly how I felt.

Life was simple for those ten months after the robbery. I just collected protection money, did some random crime, and then lounged in my expensive room at the Vaillancourt. This was the easy life I had, and I had no regrets about living it anymore.

I had gained many friends or, as the don referred to them, brothers during my time in this great mob. I had not become too close to hardly anyone, but we all looked out for each other, and everyone was treated like family. The truth was, they were like brothers to me. I felt as if I had been adopted into a family of misfits who all understood each other's plight perfectly well. They understood me, too.

Strangely, though, I never had any sisters here. It seemed to the don that the opposite sex was much weaker and not necessary in his mafia. He even had rules against their presence. He had stated that they were distractions and they only messed with our heads. It seemed that many of my brothers had wives and girlfriends, but I was never permitted to meet them, nor was I permitted to pursue that kind of relationship.

Even with our numbers of about 70 strong, I grew closest to only two of the members: Mr. T and Little Ty. They were fellow caporegimes with me and shared my power, so I spent the most time with them. I had a special bond with these two better than that of any of my other brothers. They were like an actual father and brother to me. This bond strengthened me more than anything I had ever known. No one wanted to come face-to-face with the three of us.

I received excessive amounts of cash each week from the don, but I never really seemed to use it. I appeared to be confined to the limits of West City by order of Don Sanzano. Since I never left this city that I controlled, I had no use for cash. The only time I used it was to gain more of it in poker games with the mob.

These games had been played in the mansion. I found it strange that Keir often decided to sleep at the Vaillancourt rather than at his own house. I guessed that the mansion was more his base of operations and the hotel was his home. It made sense to want to separate his work and his home.

Downtime was spent in the hotel for me as well. I loved going to the Fight Arena to beat someone up. Although I was there a large amount of the time, I never did see Jack Lamb. Not that he mattered at all. I had become the more dominant. He was but a flea on a dog's corpse compared to me now.

Soon, a time came when I could feel the atmosphere changing. The boss seemed to be preparing something, and it was going to be big. Whatever he was cooking up, I knew he would inform me when the time was right.

After I had put ten months of work into the don's plan, it was time.

"Kid, the end of our plan of conquest is nearing. I believe now that we shall finally be rid of our rivals. You will be the one leading the charge," Keir told me one night, after pulling me away from a poker game.

Don Sanzano was going to send us to kill off our main rivals, the Pirates. They had earned this name by attacking people's cars and stealing everything inside them, sometimes, even the car itself. This gang was the second largest compared to us, and the don's thoughts were that, if we took these guys out, the other gangs would back down. West City would be ours.

The Pirates were well-supplied. They had to be to take down people's cars as they passed by. They had all kinds of bombs and firearms. They had multiple weapons and tools to help defend against and attack their enemies. Though, now, they were most likely experiencing a hit to their supplies since we had cut off their intake from their protection money. Now would be the time to strike.

"When do we start?" I asked Don Sanzano.

"We go tomorrow. I'm sending 30 men with you to go and finish off those foolish Pirates. Don't worry, though. You will be well-armed. Very well-armed. Not that you will need it, kid," he said, patting me on the back.

30 of my brothers and I were going to kill this rival gang. It seemed to be just another easy mission. The Pirates were probably 40 strong at the most and would have lacking resources. I would be there, so victory was assured. I was happy because, when we killed these people, there would be no one else to try to stop us. Conquest would be ours to seize.

The Pirates worked out of the east side of the city and would take protection money from the businesses around there as well as steal from cars. They were spread throughout one-sixth of the city. When we finished them off, we would have practically the whole city. The only resistance left would be one smaller gang that was north of the Pirates. They would most likely surrender and flee the city when they found out that we had killed off the Pirates. Then, we would claim that land and control the entirety of West City.

The don was actually going to do it. His ten month plan behind us now, it was time to take what was ours. Don Sanzano was to be the new authority over the weak citizens of this crumbling city. I had no problem serving under this man. The power given to me was the only confirmation I needed. He was mine to work as a puppet, anyway. The don trusted me deeply, and I doubted he would ever catch on to my small remarks and slight shifts that so easily guided the man to the choices I needed him to make.

"Now, everyone, listen to my words and know. In this mansion, we have all the weapons you could ever need. There's enough for everyone to destroy the statue of liberty…six times. You don't have to take them all because I don't want you wasting all the ammo, but take what you need," Don Sanzano announced to the team in the main foyer of his mansion.

There was no doubt that we would crush these Pirates. I nodded in agreement with him as did my brothers. Don Sanzano then led us to the room with the weapons.

There, laid out on several tables in a room near the west wing, was an assortment of about 100 weapons. The don had received these from different contacts and had made the rest. I had not known that the don was also a skilled weapons maker. He had more talent than for which I had given him credit.

He had nail bombs, C4, grenades, and RPGs. He also had automatic shotguns, all kinds of assault rifles, semi-automatics, and all kinds of pistols. He had tomahawks, baseball bats, chainsaws, and knives. He was very prepared.

"Kid, you will be our star player. You will need some C4, this automatic shotgun, this Uzi, and this grenade vest. Oh, and you can also take this tomahawk," he said, packing some of the weapons into a backpack and handing it to me.

The weapons were the best he had. He wanted me to be well-armed because I was the only one he trusted for power. There was no doubt that I would supply that power.

With these weapons in my hands, I felt an unbelievable surge of strength and, for a brief second, I contemplated killing everyone in the room. I could eradicate the cause of terror in this city with barely any effort. Then, I could go alone and kill the Pirates and any other gangs. Yes, they would all be dead, and I could rule alone. The violent impulse was clouding my ability to reason, but then I thought about my friends in the mafia and the loss of my great life. I decided against it in that split second. I just looked at the weapons and grinned at the don. He returned the evil grin. He moved on and distributed the weapons to the rest of the group.

I did not understand from where this strange impulse had come. I had lived with these men for almost a year, and yet I came close to deciding to murder them all. I knew that I could single-handedly kill every one of these mobsters before they could respond, but, living in the mafia, there was no way I would turn on my brothers. I put the backpack on and forgot the idea.

Don Sanzano gave Mr. T an LMG and two nail bombs, and Mr. T grabbed his shotgun, Mrs. T. Little Ty got some grenades, two pistols, and an assault rifle. They were bursting with excitement. This was their favorite part of the job. I returned the thrilled expression. They smiled to see me as excited as they were.

Excited to take lives. Was this why they were excited? Only seconds ago, I had contemplated mass-murder myself. How had I come to this? I had left the normalcy of life with a family behind that day when my boat was discovered. I had traded a happy life for a life of death. This life had been good to me, but I was starting to see no quality in it. I was having second thoughts about living for death.

The don was assigning weapons and tasks to my brothers. Mr. T, Little Ty, and I were first because we were the don's favorites and he wanted to give us the best. For sure, I knew we deserved to be given the best. We were the strongest here without contest.

I looked back at the weapons. I had two very destructive automatic weapons and some very dangerous explosives. I also had the tomahawk for any close encounter with the Pirates, even though it was made for throwing. I was ready for a fight.

The don had then finished arming our team. He walked to the center of the room, in between the tables on which the mass assortment of weapons had been placed. We all lifted our eyes when we saw that he was about to speak.

"You will show them no mercy and kill every single one of them! The Pirates will be sunk! The West City Mafia shall reign forever!" he cried.

Everyone in the room cheered. This is for what they were waiting: more power. This was the cry of the mafia. Every mafia wanted more wealth and power. Most often, they would fall out of power and crumble, but I did not see that in our future. I would kill every single one of these Pirates. I, too, wanted what every mafia member wanted. I thirsted for power.

A sense of exhilaration came over me as well. I remembered how I had liked terrifying the people of this city. I remembered how I enjoyed slashing Jimmy's throat in the subway. I remembered beating up the guards in the bank. How I had loved the violence! How I so deeply desired it!

No drug I had taken had ever matched this upwelling of euphoria. Seeing my fellow man bowed beneath me, either limp as a corpse or trembling and rigid, gave me satisfaction like no other thing could. It felt as if I were born to stamp down and subdue, that it was my rightful place. No place felt more like home to me than this.

I forgot all about the life of peace I had left behind and all the second thoughts of this life I had felt. As my brothers cheered, anticipating conquest, I cheered as well. In this life, there were no consequences. In this life, I was the strongest, and no man stood above me. Who cared if I was a murderer? A murderer was what I was.

There was evil within me. I did not know what it was, but something within me desired the killing and the terror. I fed off fear and pain. A part of me still wanted to be the good guy and save the world, but I was irrevocably drawn to this evil. My mind craved the feeling of making others hurt.

With this inside me, there was no way I could do any good work here. I could not and would not fight it. The Pirates would see the culmination of my darkest side this day.

Chapter 13
Sink the Pirates

Outside the mansion, there were ten armored vehicles waiting for us. A heavy machine gun was mounted to each of the roofs. For some reason, the don had thought it necessary to cover them in a green camouflage paint, even though we were in the city. Preventing my analysis of the inside of the vehicles were black tinted windows. The perfect form of transportation had been put before us. In these, we would storm the Pirates.

I strapped the shotgun to my back and held the Uzi in front of me. I was given three extra clips for the two guns. I wore my grenade vest that had six grenades on it. In my backpack was my C4, and my tomahawk was harnessed to my hip. My grenade and clip vest tripled as a bullet-proof vest. I wore steel-toed boots as well. I was very well-suited for this battle.

I climbed into the driver's seat of an armored car. Mr. T got in beside me, and Little Ty climbed up on top of the car to take the machine gun. With us as a team, I knew nothing could go wrong.

The lead car honked its horn, and the men erupted in a short cheer. Then, we took off through the streets of West City. In seeing our convoy, the citizens of the city ran behind their cars or into their homes. They did not want to get in our way. They knew that something was going down.

We drove for about 20 minutes. I drove the third car back, which was nice because my mind slipped away from driving often to analyze and hypothesize. While driving, I contemplated the process of learning to drive ten months ago. The don let me take his car for a spin, and that was the first time I remember driving. The controls came so easily to me. It was like riding a bike as they say, even though I had never ridden a bike either.

The convoy turned right, and we were then headed down a narrow, two-lane street. We drove in a separated pattern, alternating lanes to make sure no one could drive past us. On either side of us were apartment buildings, the sight becoming an almost never-ending repetitive image that stretched out quite far. It was not too exciting to say the least, but we continued on.

Suddenly, the car in front of me came to a halt, and I slammed on the break to avoid colliding with it. I opened my door and peeked my head out to see what had happened in front of us. There was a small group of about six people in front of our vehicles. The Pirates knew we were coming for them. It did not matter, though, because we were prepared to take on any challenge.

This was their chance to slow us down. One of them pulled out a bottle. Another one lit it, and, before anyone could react, the bottle was thrown. It burst on the first car's windshield, and an inferno blocked the driver's sight. Little Ty and the two other gunners opened fire on these Pirates. They ran to cover, but we had taken three of them.

It was such a bold strategy to just walk up to our convoy and attack. I wondered what the reasoning behind this was. They could have struck with a simple surprise attack, but instead they faced us straight on. That took a lot of bravery. The Pirates fought with great pride.

The fire was put out, and our cars moved forward again. Out of nowhere, there was a bang to my left. I looked out the window, and one of the three remaining was hitting my window with a sledgehammer. The window burst open and glass flew everywhere. I opened the door with force, knocking the man down. I pulled out my tomahawk and put it through his head. With a scream, he died, and I cleaned off the axe on his shirt. Without another thought on the matter, I returned my axe to its harness and got back into my car.

Another bold strategy. I found it strange that the man was concerned with killing only one, me. Again, I thought of the different ways that the man could have attacked that would have done more damage. I started to wonder if the Pirates had ever defended against a group assault before.

We still did not know where the other two were. Through my shattered window, I yelled to Little Ty, "Do you see anything, Ty?"

"No, nothing up out here. They are like ghosts," he responded.

They seemed to be catching on. They could not intimidate us with a head-on strike. There were too many of us, and we were all armed quite heavily. They now stuck to the shadows and watched, adapting because it was the only way to fight.

For a while, nothing happened. We kept driving to the Pirate base. I thought I saw something out of the corner of my eye. I looked closely at my surroundings.

"Did you see…?" Mr. T began, but then the car in front of us exploded.

Little Ty and the other gunners fired into the windows.

I remembered seeing something out of the corner of my eye. It was to the right of us. "Little Ty, fire to the right, next to the mailbox," I yelled to him. He fired into the door that was behind the mailbox. He stopped firing, and I saw the downed Pirate. He was exactly where I thought he was. The last one must have escaped.

He fled. Not knowing how to continue fighting against such force, he ran to the safety of his gang. He would warn them of what they would face, and they would prepare in all new ways. I now could see all the tactics of battle. All this new information seeped in. I felt stronger knowing it. I felt even deadlier than before.

Jerking the steering wheel to the left, I pulled around the exploded car, and we continued without the lead car or those who were in it. I wished to grieve for my comrades, but this was war.

A three-story office building appeared before us, and our convoy stopped in front of it. We were there, the Pirate hideout. Nothing was significant about it, except for the fact that it held our deadly foes. Our cars blocked the roads leading away from the building. There was no way a car could get past us. They were trapped, and we would finish the job.

All the gunners fired into the building. The walls were torn apart, and the windows and doors smashed. The building was quite large, and it took a lot of bullets to destroy the front of it.

When everyone was satisfied, the two in the first car got out. They both had RPGs. When they had loaded and prepared their weapons, they fired into the building's first floor. Dust and debris burst out of the windows. Next, they went for the second floor. That time, when the debris burst out of the windows, people shot out with them. Three people flew out the window and crashed to the ground dead. They reloaded and shot into the last floor, the third floor. Dust and two more people flew out.

The death count so far was ten. We were expecting 40 of them. We ourselves had only 31, including myself. We had lost three in the car explosion. We had 28 of us left in this war. Only about 30 of them remained.

I did the math in my head and calculated what we should do next. I got out of the car as did Mr. T. I walked up, Uzi at the ready, and kicked in the destroyed door. Nobody was there. I turned around and summoned the rest of my crew.

There is a sense that everyone has felt when another person creeps up on them. The hairs on your neck stand up when you have that feeling. The hairs on the back of my neck jumped up so suddenly.

I turned back, and there was a Pirate before me. I jumped away, but she still managed to shoot me in the leg with what seemed to be an AK-47. I tumbled to the pavement and grabbed my leg in pain. Little Ty put a bullet right between her eyes, and she fell dead.

I clutched the bullet wound, and blood flowed around my fingers. Mr. T ran up to me and knelt down to help. He felt my wound. I had two bullets in my leg, about three inches apart. He put his fingers deep into the wounds and snatched out the bullets. It was strange, but my interest was on this odd surgery and not on my pain. My leg went cold.

The team surrounded me and went on alert. They protected me with their lives, for they knew that I was their only hope. This was the best team for which I could have hoped. They were the kind of men you could count on in a crisis.

"Put some pressure on that leg," one of the men advised me.

I did so. Then, the coldness went away, and my leg felt much better. The blood flow slowed. The spot was numb, but I felt a hundred times better.

"Do you think you can go on?" Mr. T asked me, concern in his voice.

"Sure," I said and stood up with no problem.

My crew was astonished. They looked at me in awe. Mr. T inspected my wound again.

"T-the...the wound...it...closed," he stammered, pushing around on my skin where the two holes used to be.

Two scabs covered their respective places, just like when I had been stabbed on the subway. Everyone looked at me in bewilderment.

I remembered back to that time I was stabbed and had recovered within a minute. This was exactly the same. I did not understand what had happened. I had not understood what had happened back then either, but it did not matter right now. I did not have time for mysteries.

"Let's move on, men," I said to my troops.

I split the group into two teams of 14 each. One of the groups went around back, and my group was going in front.

Going through the door and into danger, I was slightly distracted by my thoughts. Again, I was wondering how I had healed so fast. Again, I was wondering about my past and my power. It had been so long since I had.

I led them into the hostile territory. Mr. T and Little Ty followed closely behind me. We slowly secured the first floor. All the rooms were clear, and the second group met us to confirm. I knew it had to be some kind of trap. I walked up to the bottom of the stairs that led up to the second floor.

I stopped the team and inspected the stairway. Looking closely, I saw a claymore was set up to explode about halfway up the stairs. I told the team to back up and I shot at the explosive. It blew and destroyed part of the stairs.

They now no longer had such a head-on approach to this fight. They were hiding, ready to strike when we let our guard down. This was exactly what they should have done at the beginning.

Barely a second after the explosion, one of the Pirates jumped off the railing of the second floor and tackled Little Ty. The Pirate went straight for his throat, but Little Ty was too quick. He grabbed his knife and put it through the Pirate's eye. He then stabbed it through the other eye. The Pirate screamed and rolled off of him. Little Ty got up and repeatedly stomped his enemy's head until he was dead and brain matter covered Little Ty's boots.

"Take that, bitch!" he yelled at the dead Pirate. He smiled at me, laughed, and said, "Let's move on, kid. I'm ready for more!"

I nodded, and we ascended the partly destroyed stairs. There were two Pirates at the top of the stairs. I stopped my men. The two Pirates had not seen us yet, but were ready as soon as they did. I felt a need to test myself a little. I ran up the stairs and into sight of the two. The men showed surprise and fright, lifting their weapons to end me. Using my Uzi, I dispatched them without letting even one of them discharge his weapon. They were dead, and I summoned my team to come. We continued our assault.

Their death count was at 14 now. These fools were dropping like flies. We ourselves had only lost three. Just as I had believed, my first assault would go off without a hitch.

I was actually pretty good at this. We were moving quite quickly as well as killing the opposition with little to no issues. I felt so powerful at the head of this assault. No man could stand in my way. I was invincible. The Pirates would perish. Of this, I was certain.

After climbing the stairs, we made our way through many hallways and numerous rooms. Everywhere we had gone throughout the building, our foes had lain in wait. We worked as a team to dispatch these Pirates, and our force was astounding. Not one man on our side saw major injury as we traversed the second floor. Some men had been grazed by bullets or stricken by shrapnel, but every member could continue through the fight.

I split our forces into groups of five and sent them through halls and doors to seek out the enemy. Though they hid in the shadows, we had the upper hand. Our advantage was fear. We were so well-known in this city that even our rivals trembled at the sound of our footsteps. They fought, but they knew they would not win.

I was starting to understand their strategies more and more now. This "hide-and-wait" tactic was simply the diversion. They knew that we were most concerned with the life of their leader. He was hiding somewhere among them, and it would be a trial to find him. Though, I did not believe he would be so courageous to hide on the field of battle. Surely, he had planned an escape route and was somewhere in close proximity to it. We just had to reach him before he could run.

Continuing through the second floor, we came to the end of a hall where it took a ninety degree turn. I looked around the corner with a mirror I had found in one of the first rooms on the second floor. Seven men were at the ready. Mr. T stepped up to me. He pointed to his LMG. I nodded and backed up.

He inspected the weapon briefly and readied himself. Then, he passed the corner and slaughtered the seven Pirates. He continued spraying until the room was devoid of any life. I walked up and patted Mr. T on the shoulder.

Such bravery was in this old man. I had never once asked his age, but I knew it was upwards of sixty. Yet, here he was in the middle of an all-out war for possession of the city. From where did his strength and courage come?

A group of five came back through a door that was in the room.

"We killed five men," one of them said.

We had killed a total of 36 of the Pirates by this time. Victory was assured. With only about 4 men left, there was no way that they could match the force of our numbers.

I placed some of the C4 I was given in this room. From what I could tell, this room was in the dead center of the whole building. It seemed appropriate to place charges here.

We went up the stairs to the third floor. When we reached the top, I sent five men with Little Ty and five men with Mr. T. I took another five with me and the three groups split-up. The rest of the team was setting charges on the first and second floors.

I went down the hall with my team. We cleared out the rooms and killed a total of six people. This meant there were more than 40 because we had taken out 42.

We entered the last room. With caution, we searched the room and found nobody. Hopefully, we had finished the Pirates. I decided to wait here for Little Ty and Mr. T. Little did I know that I was not safe here.

I heard multiple shots from a pistol ring out from behind me. I spun around. My whole team was dead except for one, the one who had killed them.

"Oh, Beast of Flame, what shall you do now?" he said with an evil grin.

"What the hell is going on here, Jared?!" I yelled at him.

"The monstrosity said to the executioner. Don't play dumb with me. You know this fate has been waiting for you for too long. Now, drop the gun, Martin."

I threw down my Uzi and froze as Jared approached me with the gun with which he had murdered my team. This man had been my brother. This man had been trusted and accepted by us. We let our guard down before him, and he had taken advantage of that.

"You're finally getting what you deserve, you monster," he said as he put his gun to my head.

My instincts faster than his, I grabbed my tomahawk and put it into his side. His tool of murder went off in this moment, but I ducked away from death. I knocked the gun away from him and wrapped my hand around his throat.

"Who do you work for?!" I questioned him as he struggled for air.

"S...stop! I...can't...breathe!"

I loosened up on my choking and asked him again, "Who do you work for?!"

"You...you must know...who has sent me...Martin. You must... have known... they would... come for you... eventually," the traitor choked out.

"Just answer my question already! Who has sent you to kill me?"

"You...don't know...what I'm...talking...about? What...what has...happened to you...you killer?"

"Who are you? How do you know me?!"

"I...I...won't tell. Just...know....Martin...we will be...back for you."

"Fine! Have it your way!" I said, my grasp tightening firmly around his flimsy neck. I could feel the pulsing of the muscles fighting against my crushing force, but there was no escape for him now. His trachea was giving way to my rage.

He struggled for breath and said, "Can't breathe. Please! Stop, I…I…please...work…life."

"I don't care about your life, you monster!" I yelled at him.

He flailed desperately as I cut off all air from his lungs. His face darkened, and his eyes flooded with tears. I shoved the tomahawk deeper into his side, and he could not fight back. He stopped struggling and went limp. His life drained away from his body with a final exhale.

My team lay dead on the floor of the Pirate base. Their lives were over, too. It was my fault. These men were under my control, and I had failed them. I could not protect them from the traitor in their midst. Their blood was on my hands.

Little Ty came in from a door to my right.

"What happened here?!" he asked me, falling to his knees at the side of one of his brothers.

"He killed them," I said, pointing a shaking finger at the betrayer.

"A traitor?! Jared?! I can't believe it," he said, standing.

Little Ty stood and then kicked the dead body of the killer. He then turned away and took a few paces, only to return and angrily stomp on the corpse. Little Ty retreated to the other wall, and I pulled my tomahawk out of Jared's side. I wiped it off and put it away.

"We killed six men," I said to Little Ty.

"Ten," he said back to me shortly.

"So there were more men than we had thought. I was expecting 40."

"Yeah. More bastards stuffed in here than I could have guessed."

Mr. T walked in from behind.

"We killed six men, but we could not find the leader… What happened here?!"

"This traitor killed everyone on the kid's team," Little Ty said, kicking him again.

"Tristan, Thomas, Boris," Mr. T said, looking at the victims.

He fell from his high spirits, seeing his brothers dead on the floor. They were killed by one whom he had trusted. Mr. T shot the dead body of the killer.

"Damn you, Jared!" he yelled at him.

He had been his brother as well, but not anymore.

"Let's find the Pirates' boss already," he said gravely.

We searched the complex until we found a ladder and a hatch that led to the roof. Opening the hatch, the chopping of spinning blades overpowered all other noise. I climbed out on the roof. A news helicopter with graffiti all over it was just taking off.

Suddenly, a rocket whizzed by me, missing me by inches. I saw a man with a rocket launcher up in the helicopter. I could hear a voice on the helicopter screaming for the man to reload before I could shoot. My bullet reached the man's heart before he reloaded, and he fell to the building with a thud. The voice then screamed for the copter to leave as quickly as possible.

Mr. T climbed up onto the roof. He pulled out a nail bomb from his backpack and threw it with all his strength. Luckily, it landed in the helicopter. He grabbed the detonator and pushed the button. The helicopter burst into flames. Nails rained down from the flaming copter, but none struck us, for we were below the epicenter of the blast. The helicopter spun out of control. Beeping rang out urgently from the aircraft, but no one and nothing could calm the instruments.

Another of our soldiers got onto the roof and grabbed his RPG. He launched it at the helicopter. It was a direct hit, finishing off the destruction. The helicopter crashed down to the ground near the building. The Pirates' boss was dead, and so was the entire Pirate gang.

Death to an entire group. I thought about our gang and how close to dying many of us came as well. Death could have taken all of us, but we survived. I knew it was because of my superior power and leadership. My influence on these men guided them throughout the fight, and I led them to glorious victory. Without me, there would be no reward but the cold hand of death for my comrades. I killed all the Pirates. I was the conqueror.

The group searched the rest of the compound for any sign of Pirate life. Nothing was left here but their lifeless bodies, strewn about the building. As we headed for the door, one of my comrades handed me the detonator to the C4.

We walked out of the building, and everyone jumped in the cars. I pushed the button. In a brilliant display, flame and debris shot out from the Pirates' base in all directions. The walls crumbled, engulfed in smoke and flame, and the building went to the ground in a firestorm. Through the thick layer of dust floating in the air, I could still see the skeleton of the building, fire shining bright within. People would know that The Beast of Flame had been here.

I looked over at Mr. T, and Little Ty stuck his head down outside Mr. T's window. There was a joy on his face that was slowly overtaking my own.

"Mission complete."

Chapter 14
The Vaillancourt Incident

Horns honking and machine guns blasting, we sped home to Don Sanzano. We crowded the streets as we barreled through West City. Our victory over our rivals yielded an ecstatic response from all members. Some people threw grenades out the window to celebrate. The civilians that were still outside would run for cover at any sound. The gunners shot up garbage cans and mailboxes. Some people even blew up idle cars as we flew through the city.

I could not wait to share the good news with the don. This felt like a whole new kind of victory. I had to toss a few grenades out the window myself. Chaos abounded within celebration on the ride back from the mission.

Our car was the first to reach the mansion. I exited, as did Mr. T. Little Ty jumped off the roof with an crazy yell, almost pouncing on me. The three of us laughed, drunk on triumph, and walked up to the house, leaving the rest to wait with the vehicles. Keir greeted us as we approached the door.

"I can see it on your faces! It went good! How good was it?" he asked us.

I grinned at him and said, "We killed every single one of the Pirates along with their boss. We had only eight casualties, and we lost one car."

"Not bad, kid," he told me and patted me on my shoulder. "Not bad at all."

It may have been a successful operation, but surely it was not lacking in fault. If it had been my operation, I would not have accepted any casualties. This man looked past the death and saw the conquest. He saw his new city and his new power. His greed overcame his other emotions, and he was happy.

We walked inside with him.

"It sounds like the mission went off perfect...except for the casualties," my boss said, some disdain appearing on his countenance.

"Yes, they were very unexpected deaths," I said, provoking his continued interrogation.

"What do you mean?" he asked me, his eyebrows rising.

"The first three happened when we were driving to the Pirate base. One of the Pirates threw some C4 under their car and destroyed it along with them. The other ones happened when…" I started to say.

Mr. T interrupted me and said, "The other five were murdered by Jared."

"Jared?! But he was one of the most loyal of you guys. I had him watching all the other soldiers! I even let him do my accounting! That makes no sense. Why would he kill them?"

I stepped up again and said, "I think he was trying to sabotage the mission. Sir, I think he was one of them."

Keir glared at me fiercely.

"How dare you accuse me of letting such a thing happen! Why would you think that I would not run an extensive background check on every single one of my members?! He couldn't have possibly been a Pirate. I kept an eye on him like I did with all of you! He never had contact with any of the Pirates!" he yelled at me.

"I'm sorry, sir," I apologized to him.

"It doesn't matter," he said. "What I want to know is how the mission went. How many Pirates did you kill?"

I thought it mattered still, but my boss had asked something of me. I was to deliver.

"I think we killed about 60 men including the boss. We destroyed the base as well, so, if anyone was hiding in there, they would be dead, too," I answered him.

"Good, it sounds like the mission was a complete success."

He paused to clear the background thoughts running through his mind. I could see the betrayal from Jared was weighing on him, even if he did not want to address. I also saw that he was frustrated that he was not happier for our victory. His failing was bothering him. He turned away momentarily, and then his eyes met mine again.

"You know what? I think you guys deserve some kind of reward," he continued, his anger now subsiding. "I think I will take all of you to the Vaillancourt, and you can do whatever you guys want," he finished.

"That sounds awesome, sir," Mr. T said.

"Tell the others," the don ordered.

Little Ty and I went for the door, but Mr. T did not. He instead moved forward to the table positioned behind the don and set Mrs. T down. He then turned back to us.

"Don't want to carry her around everywhere I go," he laughed.

We laughed as well, and then we left the mansion.

We went outside to tell everyone about the don's idea. Everyone cheered when we were finished speaking, for they could have no other emotion but happiness in the aftermath of our victory. My brothers jumped back into the cars with huge smiles. Keir came out of his house, said something to a man I recognized as Grimey, and came over to our car. We all took the armored cars to the Vaillancourt.

Grimey was the consigliere. This title meant that he advised the boss about daily mafia activities. Plans to rob the bank and to attack the Pirates all probably originated from him. He directed most of our actions. He worked mostly in the shadows, for I had barely ever seen him in all the months I had been with the mafia and never up close.

"What did you say to Grimey?" I asked the don.

"Nothing important. I just want him to stay behind to guard the mansion. You never know if there could be one foolish man that comes back for vengeance."

"They're all dead. I think it will be safe, sir."

"Me too, kid. Me too."

Again, the drive was out of control. Destruction was made commonplace on our trip to the Vaillancourt. Looking back, I could see the much larger than usual evil grin on the don's face. He had it, his ultimate power.

We crashed through the parking lot and slammed into a spot. My brothers and I got out of the cars and ran into the hotel. Many of them jumped onto the couches and took a much deserved rest. Others jumped into the pool, first shooting into the air to scare everyone off. Everyone did as they pleased, such as going to the hotel's arcade or watching a fight at the Fight Arena. Everyone rejoiced with an almost childish happiness. The hotel was chaotic.

Miles came up to me as I observed what was going on with my comrades.

"Please, Martin, make them leave," he pleaded, a weight of defeat pulling all the muscles in his face downward.

"I no longer belong to you, remember? You wanted it that way. You are the one who made me this Beast of Flame," I said and ran off into the hotel. Miles, with a look of absolute despair, walked out of the hotel back to his house.

I stopped quickly at my room to unload my gear and change into my day-to-day mafia apparel. I dropped all the weapons to the ground and removed the worn clothes in which I had fought. I wore the suit once more and felt all the more powerful in it. There was a completeness in this suit now. Knowing we had taken over the city had put new authority in this suit. I stood a little taller when I looked at myself in the mirror. I left my room having completed this important task.

I went to the Fight Arena and destroyed the competition. There was not one who could stand against me in the ring. It felt fantastic! I came out of the ring and collected my $2,500, all in cash. Pulling a lighter from my jacket, I lit up the bills and dropped them at the gate to the cage.

"Don't you forget who you gave up on, bud. You didn't speak up for me, and you left me on that mat without a second thought. Now, live in fear of the Beast of Flame," I said to Creighton, patting him on the face before leaving the Fight Arena.

I had so much power and wealth. It made me feel amazing that I had finished off the Pirates. We now had the entire city. West City was controlled by my mafia. I was second in command of a city. I intended to be first someday.

I went up to my room and lounged about. Nothing could make me feel bad. I had it as well; absolute power was mine. I drifted off to sleep on my bed to finish a great day.

When I woke up, it was 11:48 am. I had slept in until about noon. I woke up with a feeling of refreshment. I went down and had breakfast and lunch at the hotel's buffet. I gorged myself with the unlimited amount of the finest food in the city. I ate about half my body weight, or at least that is what it felt like.

I then went to the lobby. A few of the mafia members were still asleep on the couches. I saw the don at one of the check-in desks. I walked up to see what was happening.

"You can't just check in to 42 rooms for free!" said the girl at the desk.

"I think I can," said the don, flashing his ring.

The girl looked startled for a second, and then she giggled.

"Oh gosh, I thought you were going to pull a gun on me because of your comment! Wow, you scared me! That's a very nice ring, by the way. But sir, you still can't check in to 42 rooms for free," she continued.

I thought she looked familiar, but I did not immediately know why.

"You're not from around here, are you?" he asked the woman angrily.

"No, actually I came from Alemande. You know where that is?" she asked, oblivious to the don's anger.

Then, I remembered where I had seen her. She was the woman who had checked Jonah's family and me into the Ale Inn about one year ago. Her name was Amber.

"I don't care where you are from! Just drop the stupid act!" he yelled as he pulled out his magnum.

She screamed and yelled, "He's got a gun!"

The don was about to execute her right there. I stepped between them.

"Whoa, sir, no need to kill her. She is not an enemy. She's just incredibly annoying. Just put the gun down," I pleaded with the don.

He growled at me and put his gun away.

"Get lost!" I yelled at Amber. She ran out the door. With that small problem solved, I said goodbye to the don and went off to the arcade.

There were six mafia members here, including Little Ty. "What's up, Ty?" I asked him with a smile.

"Just destroying in pinball, kid. 4215 was the old high score. The new high score, set by me, is 8416," he said proudly.

There it was again, an almost childlike joy. I analyzed the idea. It was true that these men were not children, but were they ever? Most were practically born into the mafia, and none had experienced a normal childhood. I had noticed this in myself in some ways as well. No childhood in my memory had left me yearning for one.

I looked at the pinball game. Even though I knew nothing of how pinball worked, my mind figured it out in about ten seconds.

"So, what exactly is the objective?" I asked him to confirm my hypothesis.

"Well, you want to hit all these things that give you points. And there are special things to hit that give you more points and even more balls. Like this!" he said as he launched the ball into a strange looking box thing.

"What's that?"

"It's the Miracle Box. This is War on Zorph pinball, so there are things from the movies. Of course, after the Miracle Box, things only get more difficult."

"War on Zorph?"

"Yeah…wait you don't know about the Zorph movies?"

"Why should I? We've never watched them at the mansion, and I don't really remember anything before I came to West City."

"Yeah, you've mentioned that before. Why is it again that you say you don't remember anything before coming here?"

"Well, I have amnesia. I lost my memory shortly before I came here."

Little Ty flipped around from his game. He checked my face to see if I was kidding and turned back to his game.

"What?! You never told me this! All I knew about you was that you were a tough guy! I didn't know you had amnesia!"

"Well, yeah, I don't even know why I am such a tough guy. It probably had something to do with my past. And I don't really like talking about my past."

"Multi-ball!!!" the machine shouted as about ten more balls flew out of secret slots. Tyler seemed a little preoccupied with me to notice at first, but snapped back to his game within a second.

"But dude, we've known each other for, like, a year now. I get not wanting to talk about the past, but come on! This is kinda a big thing to keep from people."

"I know, I know. I just didn't think it really mattered all that much. Who cares if I can't remember what makes me so special? It's not important to me anymore."

"Not important? Kid, trust me. It's important. You should probably try to figure out what happened back then that made you so tough," he said as sound effects from the game sounded throughout the arcade.

"I've tried that. All I found was that my fishing boat had been blown to pieces in the middle of the ocean. It was completely destroyed. The trail went cold."

"Blown to pieces? Well, couldn't that mean that you were a very dangerous tough guy like now before? And maybe somebody tried to assassinate you on that boat because of how you are. That would make sense to me."

"I never really thought about it that way," I said contemplatively. "The guy at the docks told me that the engine naturally exploded. Like, because it wasn't maintained correctly. He never said anything about explosives being used."

"Not maintained correctly? Kid, that makes no sense. I have a lot of explosives training, and I know that there would have to be a large explosion to blow a boat like that to pieces. Otherwise, it would just put a whole in the hull and sink to the bottom of the ocean. No, it would have to be C4 or Semtex or something like that to shatter a boat."

"But the guy at the docks said…" I began.

"The guy at the docks was a liar, and you were a fool. If that guy had any experience, he would know that, even if the engine is blown to pieces, it doesn't mean the whole boat would blow to pieces. You need huge amounts of explosives to see something like that."

Little Ty had opened my mind to this new option. I had not understood explosives enough to know I was being tricked at the docks. I had never thought that it was some kind of attempt to kill me. Why would someone want to kill me? The only reason was because of my super powers. In my mind, it seemed rational, but another problem came up. Why would someone want to kill a superhero when I could be such a benefit to society? Unless, I was some kind of super villain. I did not know what to think.

"I don't know where you would go to look for someone who blows up boats to kill super people, but maybe it was like an opposing gang like the Pirates."

I thought back to when Jared, the traitorous murderer, tried to kill me. He saved me for last so he could savor the kill. So he could confirm the kill. So he could make sure I was dead. He also aimed straight for my head and killed anybody that would try to stop him. I was his target, not the whole team.

Maybe the Pirates were the ones who blew up my boat. Knowing that they failed the first time, they found me in the mafia and sent a spy to kill me then. They got me into a position where their whole team was there to kill me. Jared was the spy for the Pirates, but his plan ended in his death instead of mine.

Another thing made no sense. Keir said he had done an extensive background check on him as well as watching him to make sure he did not try to contact the Pirates. There was never an answer to my questions. Nothing ever made sense. There was always another hole in my ideas.

"Did Don Sanzano really do background checks on Jared?" I asked Little Ty.

He took a second to answer because he was concentrating intensely on the pinball game.

"Yes, very extensive background checks on everyone. Even on people like you and me! There was no chance that Jared was a Pirate. That man is very precise in his background checks."

"When did Jared join the mafia?"

"He joined a little while after you did."

I did not know what to say. It seemed so perfect to say that Jared was an undercover Pirate that infiltrated to kill me, but I knew that could not be the case because of the don's extensive background checks. This mystery was getting frustrating. I just gave up and went to go swimming. I snuck away silently from Little Ty without saying goodbye. Little Ty did not bother to say goodbye either because he was still destroying in his pinball game.

Passing through the hotel's grand halls, I wondered what happened in the past. Was I born with these powers or did something give me them? Who blew up the boat, and why did they want me dead? I wondered like I had wondered before I joined the mafia. I walked back to my room, drenched in the wonder.

I thought that I should probably talk to the don about Jared. If anyone would have more information on him, it would be the don. I decided to detour to the lobby on my way to my room.

When I got to the lobby, I saw about six important-looking men in full suits walk in and talk to the man who had replaced Amber. The check-in man rang the bell, and a bellhop came running.

"Yes, sir?" he said, standing extremely straight.

"Carry these men's luggage in for them and up to their room, please," the clerk said to the bellhop.

"Yes, sir," he said and ran out to their car with a cart.

Both the bellhop and the clerk were two people who were completely new to me. The Vaillancourt Hotel must have had a high turnover rate. In fact, of all the people working the desks, I knew only one. I found it odd, but I did know Mr. Vaillancourt to be quite fire-happy. This instance had given me a little more knowledge for my analyzing mind, but these people had chosen a bad time to come here with our mafia here as well. Business stops for no circumstance, I guess.

I saw the don relaxing on the couch, and my idea of asking him about Jared faded away. I did not want to anger him once again. I would only get the same answer I had gotten before, anyway. I then trudged to my room in wonder.

I was curious about how long we were going to stay at the hotel. I did not know if the don was too satisfied with our performance and if he would forget about gathering the protection money. I hoped he did because I really needed some time off to think about my past. I thought that I decided that I would only care about my future and not my past, but now I was thrown into confusion by it once again.

I got into the elevator and pushed the button for the top floor. There was an old lady in there, and she was going to the third floor. I remembered seeing her leave the arcade with some children who I expected were her grandchildren when we came down there. I smiled at her, and she tried to manage a smile back. She must have known that I was in the mafia. In would have been a difficult detail to overlook, with my clothing and all.

I waited awkwardly with this lady in the elevator for a few seconds, when the doors opened and in walked the six men I had seen in the lobby checking-in. Every single one of them looked at me as they entered the elevator and not one of them looked at the old lady. They, too, must have known I was in the mafia.

I rode for a while longer in awkward silence with these passengers. I noticed a tremor in all of them. Even the men were intimidated of me. It made sense that the old lady feared me, but the men were near my stature and outnumbered me six to one. Perhaps they knew me as the one called the Beast of Flame.

We got to the third floor, and the old lady walked quickly out of the elevator, noticeably panicked. The men's tremors remained with them, and each snuck a look at me from behind their tinted glasses. I ignored them, for I was not the one being intimidated. Two floors up, the men exited the elevator. Alone again, I spent my time in wonder of the past.

When I reached my floor, I went to my door and swiped the card. It was a quick job I had to do in here, and so I did not waste my time with trivial manners. I grabbed my towel and swimming trunks and left my room to go check out the pool. The elevator ride was not as awkward this time because the people actually talked to each other. I recognized these people as a family I had seen in the lobby.

When I got to the pool floor, the family in the elevator ran out to get in the pool. I sighed at the thought of more people in the pool. When I got to the pool door, I saw the family walking back towards the elevator. The three kids were sad, and one was crying. I opened the door and walked in.

"Whoa, whoa, whoa! Show me your ring," said the mafia man who I recognized to be Brandon.

He had just stuck out his arm to stop me from entering. He was not looking at me. This was something Brandon did to seem more powerful. He refused to grant you the respect of his gaze. When he lifted his eyes to me, he immediately apologized to me as his boss and let me enter.

I was starting to get a bit closer with my fellow mafia members. Brandon was one person of whom I saw a lot. He arranged all of our weapon shipments. He was the guy who could get what you needed when you needed it. No one denied that his ability to procure whatever someone needed was of the highest caliber.

At first, I never really cared to learn their names. I was above them, why should I have need of a relationship with any of them? My analytical mind made me curious, though. I began to take interest, as I did with everything with enough time. Little progress had been made in my attempt to move closer to them so far, but I was starting to see some value in it.

The pool was full of only mafia members. Brandon must have been doing a great job. I jumped into the pool and enjoyed the rest of the day with my brothers. The water washed away the burdens of fighting and the past that were both still plaguing my mind. I stayed in the pool for quite a few hours before taking off.

When I finally got out of the pool, my hands looked like prunes. I took the stairs this time to avoid any unwanted socializing with elevator-goers. I got up to my room and swiped the card. I looked at myself. I was no longer a prune. My body had fixed my skin in the short walk up the stairs. This was a mystery that hung on me and would not let go.

I walked in and jumped onto the bed. When I looked at the clock, it was 8:23 pm. I had had a long day, and so I lay on the bed for a while and went to sleep.

I dreamt of my past and how the boat was blown up. I dreamt of who I was before the amnesia. I dreamt these things, but there were no answers within my dreams, and they only led me to more confusion and frustration. I woke up not much longer after having fallen asleep. My dreams felt like nightmares now. I did not feel good, so I went to go find Mr. T or Little Ty.

Leaving my room, I noticed Mr. T entering his not too far down the hall.

"Hey, T!" I yelled to him.

He turned his head to me, and a tired smile appeared.

"I'm about to fall asleep here, kid. I'll have to talk to you tomorrow," he said, tipping his hat to me.

"All right then. I'll catch you sometime in the morning. Sleep well."

"I have a feeling I won't get too much sleep tonight, but I'll try, kid. Thanks," he said and entered the room.

Mr. T was actually worn out from all the excitement. I did not think that that could happen to him. For all the time I knew him, he was always the one to be bursting with energy at 1 am, wanting to go out and do something crazy. He always had the most life out of all of us. I guess he deserved a rest sometimes. I made my way to the stairs so that I could continue a search for my brothers.

I walked down to the lobby and found Little Ty.

"What's up, Little Ty?" I asked him.

"Not much, kid," he answered, reclining eccentrically on one of the couches.

I had run out of topic matter. I looked around the room and saw the clock on the wall. It was 10:08 pm. "You wanna go catch a fight?" I asked him.

"Nah, that seems kinda boring. I'm really more about getting in a fight than watching one. We could go grab a beer if you wanted, though. I know a good place."

"Okay, let's do that!" I said.

Little Ty and I left the hotel. There was a bar two blocks from the Vaillancourt called the Black Hippo, a name that you could only appreciate when you were really drunk. We entered the bar and sat down at the counter.

"Get us the usual stuff, lady," Little Ty said, waving his ring.

The bartender ran to get us the beers. She grabbed two glasses, filled them to the brim, and set them before us like kings. I grabbed my beer and drank. This was exactly what I needed to get my mind off the past. Of course, things do not always work out for me.

"So...you been thinking much about your past, kid?" Little Ty asked me.

I took another large drink and said, "Yes, Ty. Yes, I have."

He nodded.

I glimpsed around the bar to check my surroundings. The bar was quite crowded, and I was curious as to why that was. I followed their collective gaze to a TV screen on which men ran back and forth, kicking a white and black ball. It was my hypothesis that this game had brought in the crowd. I, too, decided to watch the game. I had no idea how the game worked, but it was still entertaining.

"You know, kid, you miss out on a lot of cool things when you have amnesia."

"Tell me about it."

"I mean, I bet you have no idea what it is we are watching. You don't even know where these teams are from."

"You got that right, Ty."

"I bet you don't even remember ever having a beer at a bar before. Of course, you were probably too young before the amnesia."

"I'm pretty sure I'm still too young. What's the age limit?" I asked.

"Well, it's 21, of course. How old are you?"

"I'm about 18 or 19 or something."

"Haha! I guess that doesn't really matter since we are in the mafia, kid," he said and laughed.

I was about to say something about legality and right and wrong to him when I was almost thrown from my seat by a huge explosion that sent a shockwave through the entire bar. The TV fell from the wall, and everyone's drinks flew out of their hands.

I grabbed Little Ty and picked him up off the floor. "What just happened?!" I yelled, my ears still ringing.

He did not hear me. The blast caused his ears to ring as well. I repeated the question.

"What?!" I heard him yell.

My hearing had recovered by now, but Little Ty's ears were still ringing. I grabbed him close and yelled in his ear, "What happened?!"

"I don't know!" he yelled, bewildered as I.

Screams and gasps could be heard everywhere. I saw astonishment on the faces of those who had run outside. We both followed them out.

You could see it for miles. Right where the Vaillancourt Hotel used to be was a colossal pile of burning wreckage. I looked at Little Ty. The expression of horror and confusion was frozen on his face. I pulled him over to the burning hotel. This was where I would have been if Little Ty had not convinced me to go to the Black Hippo.

I then thought about Mr. T who was in that burning wreckage. If only I could have taken him with me before Little Ty and I had left! Keir, Mr. T, and all the rest of my brothers were dead. Only Little Ty remained. Tears fell from my face. Not only had I lost my best friends, but I had lost all my wealth and power. All my money was stored in my room. I had lost everything just as I had before.

I looked at Little Ty. Tears rolled down his cheeks, too.

"Whoever did this…they…they will die a horrible death! I'm gonna kill you! You hear me? I'm gonna kill you bastards!" he yelled at the hotel that was no more.

I completely agreed with him. The people who did this were still trying to kill me. I would not let them do this to me and my friends. I would avenge Mr. T and Keir and everyone else who had died this tragic day.

"NOOOOOOOOOOOO!!!!!!!" I heard from behind me.

I looked at the source of this scream. It was Miles Vaillancourt. He had just shown up. Apparently, he did not stay to announce the fight because of all the mafia members. He fell to his knees and pounded the ground.

"Why?! Why?! Why?! Why?!" was all he could say.

He lay there sobbing on the ground.

"Come on, Little Ty. Let's get out of here," I said. I knew there could be no survivors. It was time to leave this place of death.

We walked the streets back to the don's mansion. I thought back to my past. Seeing this burning wreckage of the hotel was just like seeing the debris of my fishing boat, but this wreckage was much more painful. I had lost my past when I had seen the boat, but, when I had seen the hotel, I had lost my friends and my future. My life was always going to be full of misery, and there was nothing that I could do. Some mistake that I or someone else had made in my past had trapped me in this living hell. Just when things got better, something horrible would happen to even it out. I wished that I could fix what was happening. I wished that this weight could be removed from my shoulders.

When we got to the mansion, another horrible surprise awaited us. The people who had blown up the hotel had set the don's mansion on fire as well. We had nowhere else to turn. All our security, everything familiar, was going up in flames.

I sat down on the don's lawn and stared at the burning mansion. Flame was taking all from me. An explosion obliterated the Vaillancourt, the place I considered home, and arsonists had taken a fancy to the destruction of my boss' home, too. I was the one who played with fire. I was the Beast of Flame. Finally, I had gotten burned, and many with me.

While I sat in despair, Little Ty ran into the burning building. I could not open my mouth against him, for my mind had lost control of it. This grief was overwhelming me. I did not know what Little Ty was doing, and I could not stop it. Fortunately, I did not need to do so. Seconds later, he exited, holding a shotgun, Mrs. T.

He dropped himself to the grass beside me. Little Ty sighed so painfully that my own pain was magnified. We both shook and stared. Neither of us spoke, but we did not need to speak to know what the other was thinking. Everything good was gone.

"What's next, kid?" he asked me.

He and I locked sorrowful eyes, and I gave him the best answer I could.

"I don't know."

Chapter 15
A Return to the Past

My mind slowly clearing and my body shaking less, acceptance of what had just happened was coming to me. Everything was lost. These simple familiarities that I had not fully appreciated were now gone. They had fallen to dust and ashes. I had to get to something familiar.

I had spent all of my remembered life with these people. My whole life was gone in a flash and a boom. So much time invested into a life that no longer existed. My entire life plan had switched in the blink of an eye, and it was the same for Little Ty. It would take days before the severity of what just happened fell fully upon us. I knew we had to move before that hit and incapacitated us.

The only thing I had left were my friends from Alemande. Jonah, Mia, Alyssa, Cody, and Donovan were the only people I knew in this world, and so I would return to them. Little Ty decided to go with me, for he was as lost as I and I was all he had left. Fortunately, we could keep each other as a sole link to the life we once had.

I only had 30 dollars with me, and Little Ty had 60. We had enough for a few meals and a subway ride to Alemande. Further planning would have to take place after we were already on our way. We took off from the don's burning mansion, afraid that the arsonists might come to kill us as they had our brothers.

I feared what forces might try to stop us on our way to Alemande. I was a known criminal, a very known criminal. Surely, my infamy had reached all over the region. I had no problem being a criminal in the past because of the mafia's power. Now that the mafia was gone, we had no power over the police or any other person. Every decision I made now had a consequence, but perhaps it had always been like this.

I did not know if my family, the closest thing I had to a family at least, would even take me in. I had left them so suddenly. Now, I came back almost a year later, hoping things could go back to the way they were? I did not know if the kids had grown to hate me. What would I do if they could not accept me? My only plan was to try to apologize for what I had done. I hoped that they would take me and my friend in and support us in this hard time.

In fear of capture by the police, Little Ty decided to put Mrs. T in a duffle bag that he found in the streets. He understood that the police were of some danger to us now.

We walked to the cafe at which I had eaten my second breakfast. It was also the cafe at which I had stopped to collect protection money many times. When we walked in, everyone moved to the chairs in the back. Little Ty and I walked up to the counter.

"Two cheeseburgers, please," I ordered. The man behind the counter confusedly took our order. We sat down and waited to be called. When our food was ready, we both got up, and I grabbed the meal.

"That will be $15.30," the man behind the counter said uneasily.

"I don't think so," Little Ty said as he flashed his ring.

I pushed his hand away and gave the man a twenty dollar bill. Little Ty and the man both looked confused when I let him keep the change.

We sat at a table and ate the burgers. Little Ty did not understand, but I was trying to teach him that he could not use his mafia powers anymore. If he did, there was a good chance it would fail, and there was also the possibility of us being caught by the police. Tactically, I wanted to get as much out of the ring as we could before it became useless, but he had to get used to the idea of actually paying for the things he took.

We finished the burgers and threw away the trash. I left the cafe without breaking anything or even raising my voice. I had to turn my back on that way of life.

When we got to the subway, Little Ty tried to cut in line. He still had no idea what he could and could not do. I pulled him to the back of the line, and we waited until our turn. I bought our tickets, and we entered the subway.

Again, Little Ty tried to use his mafia power.

He walked up to a full bench and said, "I'll take that bench, my friends."

I grabbed him and pulled him away again. "You can't keep doing that. That ring means nothing to them anymore. And you could get us arrested," I told Little Ty. He seemed reluctant to do what I said, but he pulled away from me and then chose to sit at a free bench that was a little ways away.

I sat next to him. "Ty, I'm sorry. What's wrong, man?"

"This ring will always mean something," he answered angrily, lifting his fist with the ring on it.

"It won't to them. With the mafia gone, it no longer holds anything against them."

"It may not mean anything to you, kid, but it means a lot to me!"

"That ring means a lot to me, too, Ty! You aren't the only one who lost your brothers in that explosion!" I yelled at him.

"I didn't just lose my brothers! I lost my way of life! I lost my entire life! I now have nothing! I can't do anything! I've never known anything but the mafia!" he yelled back.

People seemed startled around us and moved away. I made an effort to lower my voice.

"I guess it's kind of unfair to compare our situations."

He sighed and said, "I was born in the mafia. Keir's dad was my father's boss. I was raised into this life. I don't know how to do anything else. I don't know how to do anything normal. I can't even get a job or pay for things! I can't survive without the mafia! I don't think I can live without this ring, kid."

I did not know what to say to him. He did not have the fallback plan that I did. Where I had lived outside the mafia briefly and had seen what a normal life looked like, he had been shut up with criminals his whole life. This transition would be much harder for him than it would be for me.

"I can't say I really know how you feel," I said, putting my hand on his shoulder. "But when I woke up in the lifeboat, the one that brought me to the people we are going to now, I felt helpless. I felt like there was nothing I could do to find my memory. I felt like I could do nothing in this world because of my lost memory. I had no hope. But now, I was one of the top members in the mafia. I have experience and strength. I know I can do something with my life. I'm starting to see that there is always hope, even in darkness."

He looked somewhat inspired.

"Well, I just lost my way of life. But your amnesia took your memories, kid. I'll always have my memories, but you've lost them forever…but maybe not," he said, a new look present in his wide eyes.

Yes, he looked at me with something inside him that I had never seen before. Something had changed. Little Ty had realized something.

"Kid, we've both suffered a terrible fate, but I can see you've lost something more than me. What I've lost can't be restored, but I think what you have can. This life might be a tough one from here on out, but I believe we can take it down together. And I'm sticking with you, kid. I'm gonna help you find your memory if it is the last thing I do!"

I was tremendously happy to hear this. My friend was going to help me find the one thing that eluded me all my new life. I needed a partner in this fight.

His decision also meant that we were partnering together to move on from our life of crime. We would put it away together and find something better for the both of us. I was glad to turn over a new leaf with this man. We could now move forward in a whole new way.

A train pulled up, and we boarded it. This subway ride, I sat next to my trusted friend. Last time when I was on a train, I sat next to a man who wanted me dead. Instead of heading into the unknown, away from something familiar, I was going back home. There was a peacefulness in the antithetic nature of this ride from the last.

I noticed that some of the passengers would occasionally look at me or Little Ty and then talk to the person next to them. Obviously, they were talking about us.

"Little Ty, I think we have some people taking an interest in us." He looked at the people around us. He scoffed and shook his head.

"Screw them. I really don't care if they think I'm about to kill them," he said loud enough for everyone to hear.

Everyone looked away from us and did not look back throughout the rest of the ride. Perhaps a little bit of fear here and there would not get us caught by the authorities.

"You know, you don't really have to call me Little Ty anymore."

"Well, what should I call you? You haven't given me any other name."

"My name is Tyler Ishler. You can call me that."

"Okay then, Tyler, I shall call you that. I was hoping to get a real name out of you so I didn't have to call you Little Ty to my family. Thank you."

He smiled back at me, and the rest of the ride was spent in silence.

When we arrived in Alemande, it was very early in the morning. After exiting the train, we came out of the subway station. I remembered the smell of fish and the crowded streets. It was good to be back in Alemande.

"God! What's that smell?" Tyler asked, his face contorting because of the smell.

"It's the glorious smell of fish," I answered.

"Glorious?"

We continued down the streets of Alemande. Even in the dark of the very early morning, lots of people came up to Tyler to try to sell him something. Did these parasites sleep? Fortunately, I did not even have to tell him anything. He blew every one of them off. He was a natural.

Another one came up to Tyler. This one was carrying carpets, and they blocked the man's face.

"You wanna buy some quality carpets?" asked the man.

"Piss off!" was Tyler's response.

The salesman grumbled and walked off.

He turned, and I got a slight glimpse of his face. His face was recognizable somehow. His voice seemed familiar, too. A list of all the people I had known in Alemande scrolled through my brain. Suddenly, his pictured popped up. That man was no salesman. It was Liam the Mugger!

I ran up to him and grabbed him. He turned around, confused, and, within a second, he recognized me. He pushed his quality carpets in my face and ran for it. I caught up to him in no time. I tackled him in an alley. Tyler came up behind me.

"Well, don't beat him up, kid! He's just a salesman. I thought you said we were trying to lay low. You're gonna get us discovered."

"He's a little more than a salesman. Isn't that right, Liam the Mugger?" I asked the mugger. He refused to answer my question and squirmed to get away. "Let's make a detour to the police station," I said, and Liam squirmed even more.

"Wait, we can't go there! We're criminals! I even have a loaded shotgun here!" Tyler told me, which made Liam squirm even more.

"It will be okay, Tyler. I know the men at the station," I reassured him.

"Well, okay then. Just don't get me arrested. I'm not going to jail just because you want to have a little reunion with your cop buddies. We are on a team here!"

I remembered traveling with this man in my arms the first day of my memory. That time, he was knocked out and not even a problem, but, this time, he squirmed to get free, and the only thing keeping him from screaming for help was Tyler's hand over his mouth.

When we arrived at the police station, Tyler was still hesitant about going in.

"What if your guys don't care about the fact that you were friends? They will arrest us on the spot," he said.

"Uh, well, we weren't exactly friends before, anyway. I only really talked to them once or twice," I answered Tyler.

Tyler's jaw dropped, and he stared at me as if I were insane.

"But don't worry. I got this," I said, disregarding his expression. I then walked into the police station. I heard Tyler quietly mimicking my voice as the doors closed behind me.

When I entered, a different man was at the desk, but I knew him. It was the officer that had brought me to the police station in West City the day I joined the mafia.

"I got one for you guys," I said to him.

He looked up and asked, "What has he done wrong?"

I was confused. "Well, he's Liam the Mugger. He's a criminal."

"Whoa, whoa. I think you're making a mistake there, buddy. Liam was released last month on good behavior. The law doesn't want anything from this guy. He's not even a mugger anymore," the officer said.

I let go of Liam the Salesman, and he brushed himself off and mumbled to himself as he went out the door. I guess people can change. He had been redeemed. I was wrong to have assumed his guilt.

The officer looked at me more closely. Then, he jumped out of his chair and backed up against the wall.

"M-m-mafia!" he exclaimed.

I seized this opportunity to keep myself safe from the police. I got in his face and said, "If you let me go, this police station will stand for many days. If you don't let me go, it will be burnt down tomorrow. Understand?" He nodded and stayed against the wall.

I started to leave the station but then remembered something. I turned around and asked, "The officers who are usually here... Nick, Heath, and Chase... Where are they? And why are you here?"

He took a breath and answered slowly.

"Nick Turnbull and Heath and Chase Thompson were transferred to the regional station in West City because of the increase of crime. They put our team here to replace their vacancy."

"Well, if you see them again, tell them hello from Martin," I said. With my business finished, I left the station.

"How'd it go in there, kid?" Tyler asked, his foot nervously kicking the steps. "Your mugger guy just walked out the door. I assumed he was good to go."

"He's not even a mugger anymore. Anyway, this station is under new management."

An increase in crime. That was what had brought my old police buddies to West City. Now, they had a greater jurisdiction, covering over five cities in the area. Officer Turnbull had gotten what he wanted at last.

I remembered Officer Turnbull laughing at the thought of me going to clean up the streets. I now found it even funnier.

How things had changed since I had been here last! Nick, Heath, and Chase were replaced by incompetent officers. Liam was no longer a criminal. I had known very little my first time here, and now most of it had changed.

To think that a criminal so notorious that he received the name "Liam the Mugger" could change and contribute to society. He had been redeemed from his lifestyle of crime. If he could, could I? My time in the mafia had hardened me and made me uncaring to the way of the law. But Liam changed; he was a good man once more.

I resolved to finish this life of crime just as he had. When I came face to face with my friends, I would be as I was before. If Liam could, so could I.

We continued walking down the middle of the street. It was peaceful now, but would it stay peaceful? I hoped that I had gotten rid of the police by threatening the officer. I hoped that he had understood my message to leave us alone. I did not want to have to deal with the cops anymore.

"So, kid..." Tyler spoke up as we made our way to the docks.

"Yeah, what's up?"

"You said you didn't have much of a life before coming to West City. How long after your accident were you in Alemande?"

"It was about a day and a half. I first remember waking up in a lifeboat out in the ocean about an hour in that direction," I answered, pointing to the northwest. "My boat drifted to shore, and that's where I met Jonah and his family. They took me in and then brought me to Alemande because I thought that I might find the boat my lifeboat came from there."

"And then you left after only a day? Why was that?"

"Well, my boat, the *Annabelle*, was found blown up at sea. I decided that I should give up on searching for my past and find a better future for myself."

"I get that. But why not stay with your friends?"

"I guess I wanted to prove to myself that I could do it alone. My pride wouldn't let me stay with them. So I took off and got a job fighting for the Vaillancourt."

"That's right! I remember watching you fight!"

"You saw me fight?"

"Yeah, the don, Mr. T, and I went to watch your fights at the Vaillancourt. It's where we do... where we did, I mean, a lot of our recruiting. You did really well the first night, but that one guy beat the crap out of you the next."

"Weird. The don never told me about that. But anyway, you're all caught up now, right, Ty?"

"Uh... One last question, kid. Your friends, are they going to be cool with our past? Like, do you think they're gonna just forgive and forget?"

The sun was rising over the docks right about now. It was a glorious sight that reminded me of that first day. I remembered jumping into Jonah's car and seeing the beauty of my first sunrise. It was something that I had taken for granted then. Today, I took it as a sign that things were going to get better.

"You know, I'm hopeful. They were really wonderful people, Tyler. Luck is on our side at the very least. I can't be sure, but I'm hopeful."

We arrived at the docks, and I saw many familiar faces. Andrew was sitting on a barrel just as he had before. Many of the fishermen who had watched our debate and then fight were running around, preparing for a big day. I saw many familiar faces here, but the best one was the face of Jonah.

He was bringing in a bunch of fish to sell. I noticed that Donovan was also helping him. These two must have been working very late tonight, for it was quite early for them to be dropping off their catch of the day.

I ran up to these two friends, but I stopped myself before I got there. What if they did not want to see me? What if they no longer cared about my existence? What if they thought I had abandoned them? Could I face them knowing that they hated me?

Tyler caught up with me.

"Are those the people we are going to see?"

"Yeah, it's half of them at least."

"Why did you stop here then? Go see them."

I agreed and walked up to Jonah and Donovan.

They saw me when I was within a few yards of them. I made eye contact with Jonah. His face was stern and stoic. In the pit of my stomach, a lead weight dropped, awaiting hatred and rejection. Out of nowhere, tears began running down his face. He ran up to me and gave me a huge sailor hug.

"You're back!" he cried.

"Yes...I-I am," I said, surprised by this loving embrace by the man who I was convinced hated me. He held onto me and shook me back and

126

forth. His joy was undeniable. It burst from him and covered the dock. That joy covered me, too, for he had forgiven me.

Donovan smiled at me and waved. Jonah let go of me.

"I knew you would come home, Martin," he said. "The kids have been heartbroken ever since you left. I can't wait to get you back there."

"Good to see you back, Martin," Donovan said, coming up behind Jonah. "You wouldn't believe how much this guy has talked about you."

We laughed, and Jonah shrugged, somewhat embarrassed.

"I'm glad to be back, guys."

Tears of joy for me, for the one who came into and exited out of their lives in just over 24 hours. How could he have such emotion for me? Had I truly affected his life so much? How had I made such a strong bond so fast? My best guess was that bringing Jonah's family out of poverty and giving them hope had put me into a high place in their hearts. The way they helped me, I felt I had the very same bond.

Tyler approached us. "Jonah, Donovan, this is my friend Tyler," I said. Jonah offered his hand to Tyler. Tyler was cautious to take it, but he did. He never had shaken hands in the mafia, so this was new to him. He shook Donovan's hand, too, and they introduced themselves. Tyler was part of the family.

"Martin, I heard you were in the mafia," Jonah said.

"Yes, I was, but that is over now. Tyler is out as well, and he is going to help me find my past."

"Good, good. That's exactly what I wanted to hear," Jonah said.

"So...how's the new fishing business going, Jonah?" I asked.

"It's been great thanks to Donovan. He has given me the help that I have really needed and, as he had said, someone to talk to," he said, patting Donovan on the back.

"Yeah, my work with Jonah has been awesome. With the new money he's raking in, he built a new house and gave me a room," Donovan said.

Donovan's dirty appearance was no longer present. Even though they had been fishing, both of them looked much cleaner, happier, and more confident than when I had met them. They were in top condition now, and I could tell that they were thankful to me for that. I did not believe that they owed me anything, for they had helped me just the same.

"It seems as if everything's working out for you guys," I said.

"Of course, Martin! All thanks to you. Now, it's time to take you to see how things are working out over there," Jonah said, gesturing to the north where his home was.

"I would like that a lot."

I felt a huge hand land on my shoulder. I whipped around and was ready to attack. There was no need for that, of course. It was only my seafaring friend Andrew.

"Good to see some old muscle back in town."

"It's good to be back, Andrew."

"You would not believe how much Jonah talks about you, Martin. My god, some stranger walks into his life for a day, and he just won't be quiet about it! But he always knew you would come back. Wouldn't shut up about how you would come back someday."

I looked back at Jonah, and he smiled and nodded.

I turned back to Andrew and asked, "Do you know anything else about my past, guys?" They shook their heads.

"No, Martin, we haven't heard one thing about your boat since you left," Andrew said, solemnity taking over his face.

That news hit me hard. Nothing was here for me to learn. Then, I remembered Tyler's words about having to place a bomb on the boat for it to be destroyed as it was.

"Was there any news about how the boat exploded?"

"All that the one guy said was that it was a natural explosion due to a lack of maintenance. People around here have been getting their engines checked like hell this past year because of it, but I've never heard of such a thing happening," Jonah answered.

Tyler stepped up.

"I've had enough experience to know that, unless you place huge amounts of explosives on that ship, there is no way that that boat could have been blown up as it was. It would have been impossible without a bomb or something."

This was the first time Tyler had spoken to them.

"Really? But that one guy said that some regular engine failure could have caused it," Jonah said.

"We now believe that investigator was a liar," I replied. "He lied to throw us off the trail as to how the boat really exploded."

"Then, he is our only lead," Tyler said.

"You're right. He is the one we will need to look for."

"But guys, I think you can forget about that and go have a meal at my house first. Mia's probably got something good cooking," Jonah said.

"I think we can. I wouldn't want to miss out on Mia's cooking," I chuckled.

We helped Jonah and Donovan finish unloading the fish, and then we boarded the boat. The boat must have been fixed-up quite well because, before I left, it was unusable. Now, it was in great condition. This vessel was smaller than a usual fishing boat, but it was perfect for one or two men to fish on. I also noticed that my name was painted on the rear of the ship.

We pushed off and dropped the sails. They had fixed up the motor, but we could get by on the wind for now.

I was again on the open seas. It felt strange to be on a boat again as I had been when I woke up from my amnesia. Now, I was off to something familiar instead of everything being new to me.

I wondered what Mia, Cody, and Alyssa would think of me. Jonah had been very forgiving and greeted me with open arms, but would they be the same? I only said a few words to each of them and walked out without looking back. How could they take me back when I had left like that?

I asked Jonah about it. "How will they respond when we get there?"

"Martin, they will take you in like family. Just like the first time they met you. We are the forgiving type," he reassured me.

"And what about me?" asked Tyler

"Family of family is family to me, Tyler. They hold the same ideals. We'll take you in as well."

Tyler and I looked at each other and smiled. It was all working out. We had a home to go back to. At least for now, we could rest in assurance of some safety and security.

We pulled up to the docks of his home. I examined Jonah's new house. It was a two-story building that was pleasantly painted a bright white. It was a large house, and it was the antithesis of his old cottage. The road leading out of it was paved, and he had a nice new car parked on it.

"Wow! Nice house, Jonah," I told him.

"It's all thanks to you, Martin. You got me to Alemande."

"Heh, I'm glad I could help."

We got off the boat and jumped onto the docks. The group of us walked to the house. The whole way to the door behind which those whom I had left awaited, my heart was beating as fast as it was when I took a beating from Jack Lamb.

Jonah opened the door for us, and we all walked in.

"We're home!" Jonah called out to the house.

Mia was in the kitchen.

"How was your night, guys?" she asked Jonah and Donovan.

"Well, we got a pretty good load of fish. I even brought you something from Alemande," Jonah said.

Mia turned around. She froze. She had seen me. I just stood there like a statue. Then, she ran over to me and gave me an even bigger hug than Jonah had.

"I knew you would come home, Martin!" she cried.

"It's so good to be back," I said, happy to be forgiven.

"Kids! Dad's brought something that I think you should see!" she yelled to Cody and Alyssa.

"Is it my present?" I heard Cody say as they ran down the stairs.

Cody and Alyssa got to the bottom of the stairs and stopped. I gave them a great big smile, and, when their initial shock subsided, they returned a bigger one. They both ran up and gave me bigger hugs than either of their parents.

"Martin!!! You're back!!!" they cried with happiness.

"Yes, I am," I told them, finally home.

Chapter 16
Celebration

We sat down to a large fish breakfast. This was the same meal I had first eaten with the family, but its quantity had increased drastically. With his new fishing boat and supplies, Jonah was bringing in a lot more fish, but his success was not due to these factors alone. His dedication and work ethic had catapulted him higher than many could dream. They were lacking qualities in these days. I was glad to see my old friend so successful.

I had retaken my place at the end of the table, a much larger table today. Tyler was to my right, and the kids were to my left. Next to Tyler was Donovan, and Mia sat next to the kids across the table. Jonah sat opposite me at the other end of the table.

"Martin," Mia began. "What brings you back to Alemande. You've been gone in West City for a long time now."

Swallowing the food in my mouth, I responded, "I just needed to return to something familiar in life, and you guys were my true home from day one. I had hoped that coming back here would give me, and Tyler, a chance to start over. I'm not sure if you've heard, but things have fallen apart for us in West City."

There were looks of confusion around the table. They had not yet heard about the bombing at the Vaillancourt.

"What happened in West City, Martin?" Alyssa asked me.

"I...uh... I lost my job. Tyler, too. Our company went under," I answered, keeping in mind that the children probably had no idea I was a major criminal or that I had anything to do with the West City Mafia. I would be surprised if the kids knew much at all about the severity of crime in the city.

"Oh, I'm sorry, Martin. That's really hard. Sorry to you, too, Tyler," Alyssa said.

"Yeah, sorry, Martin and Tyler," Cody chimed in.

"Wait... Your company went under? You mean..." Donovan began.

"Yes, it's been ended. My... my fellow employees are all gone now," I said, some of the emotion rising in me, tears on the brim of falling.

"God, I'm really, really sorry, guys. That's so awful," Mia said, her empathetic soul feeling our same pain.

"I didn't know. I'm so sorry, you two. I can't believe it," Jonah said.

"Thank you, but we're moving on from it all. There are brighter things ahead," I reassured them, but I struggled to believe it.

"Yeah, we do appreciate your sympathy, though. Thank you. I think we needed to turn over a new leaf, so things are looking up in a way, I guess," Tyler added.

"That's good. Where are you guys planning on going from here?" Jonah asked.

"I believe we should track down the lead investigator of the *Annabelle* explosion. If he truly was lying and hiding something, which we believe he was, we'll find it out. He's the only person who might have some answers for us."

"When are you leaving, Martin?" Cody asked me.

"Tyler and I are going to go find the man who lied about the boat tomorrow," I said. Cody's levity fell. "Don't worry, though. I will visit a lot and will probably be back within a month."

"I was hoping you could stay for my birthday party… It's tomorrow," he said, looking down at his food.

"Your birthday's tomorrow? Well then, I guess we'll be leaving the day after tomorrow," I said, smiling at my faithful fan.

Cody jumped up and down with excitement.

"Thank you, thank you, thank you!" he shouted.

"I couldn't miss your birthday now, could I, Cody?" I said with a warm smile. Mia put her hand on Cody, and the boy's calm came soon after.

"Will you bring a present?" Cody asked.

"You bet I will," I answered. Cody was ecstatic again.

I was glad to celebrate someone's birthday since I could never celebrate my own. I did not know what to give to Cody, but I would make it a gift that would serve to hold great memories of me. Hopefully, I could find a good gift before the party.

After breakfast, Jonah and Donovan went fishing again. Mia was doing the housework inside while Tyler and I played soccer with the kids in their newly cut field.

A lot of improvements had been made to this house and property. The field was even painted to look like a smaller soccer field. I was very impressed with how far Jonah and his family had come this past year.

Playing soccer with the kids, the angles that I needed to kick for a good pass appeared like instinct to me. The strength I had to kick the ball to get it where I needed it was so natural to me. A thousand tricks to evade and score were up my sleeve. My performance was on par with that of a professional athlete. Knowing that not even Tyler could keep up with me, I passed to my partner, Cody. Although still ripe at age, this boy displayed an aptitude for the game above most older than he. Despite the age difference, he was better than his sister.

Tyler and Alyssa were on the opposite team. Even though they had Tyler and I only passed to Cody, they had no chance for victory. I would run down the field until I was close enough to kick it in myself. When the two came to guard me, I passed it to Cody, who shot it into the goal. When they had the ball, I would expertly take the ball from Tyler. I would never take the ball from Alyssa, but that is why I had Cody. They never scored, and our score was high up in the double digits.

Expertly learning soccer so quickly, was this part of my super abilities? After the game was explained, I continued to gather information and made myself increasingly better. It only took me about five minutes before I had mastered the game. This heightened mental ability had to come from somewhere in my past. I hoped that I would find the answers to my questions when Tyler and I went to search for my past.

The soccer game over, we came back to the house. Cody and Alyssa showed us their new rooms. They had separate rooms, which was much different since they had to share a room with their parents in their last house. The rooms were not huge, but were quite accommodating to the children's needs. The two kids were happy to host us in a space that was all their own.

Tyler was not used to this kind of thing. He had never really had contact with children, and this was the first time he ever really spent with them. Despite this, he did well with them and, in fact, flourished with them. It seemed as if he had longed for this type of interaction.

We soon went downstairs and talked to Mia.

"What happened after I left?" I asked her.

"Well, when you left to go to the subway, Jonah and Donovan came to the room not too long after. Jonah asked where you were, and I told him you had left."

"What did he do then?"

"He ran right out the door. He sprinted all the way to the subway, but he was not fast enough. You were already on the train and taking off. He contemplated catching the next train to West City, but he knew you had left for a good reason. He came back to the room, crushed that you were gone. He thought the only thing he could do was to fix that boat. He fixed it the next day. He and Donovan worked day and night to finish it. In your honor, he named the ship the *Martin.*"

"Wow, I never knew that I played such a big role in your family."

"You were like a beacon of hope for us. We were out of money and could not pay back the bank. We were down to the last dollar. Then, you came riding in on that boat, and you saved us. You convinced us to go to Alemande, where my husband had always wanted to work. You were a miracle in our life, and we wanted to help you, but you had other plans. You had to make a life for yourself. Don't think we resent that you left, Martin, because it was your choice to make. We're just glad you're back," she said with that calming smile.

I was very happy to hear how much of a difference I had made in their life. It made the fact that I had lost my memory bearable. When I finally uncovered the mystery of my amnesia, I would come back here. The people in this house were my greatest friends, and being separated from their presence once more felt unfavorable to me. However, Tyler had pledged to help me find my memory, so the decision was made for me. I would find my memory and come back to my family, for this was my true home.

Not long after I had spoken with Mia, the sun was beginning its downward trajectory in the sky. This time was also marked by the *Martin* returning to the dock outside this home. Jonah and Donovan came back in the door. In Jonah's hands was a large blue box with a bright red bow.

"My present!" Cody exclaimed.

"That's right, kiddo, but you can't open it until tomorrow," Jonah said, lifting the box away from Cody's reaching arms.

Cody heaved a sigh of disappointment and sat back down.

"Martin, when do I get to open your present?"

"Same time as your dad's: tomorrow," I said. He was still disappointed. Jonah went back to his room and hid the present.

"Man, am I hungry. When's dinner?" Donovan asked.

"It's only 4:42!" Mia said, astonished.

"I had a small lunch," Donovan replied confidently.

"Fine then, we will have dinner at…uh…5:30," Mia said, glancing up at the clock on the wall, estimating cooking times in her head.

"Do you need any help preparing the meal, Mia?" Tyler asked.

"Oh, don't worry about it! I've been doing this for years now. You guys go off and have fun with the kids. But thank you, Tyler. That's very sweet."

Donovan went off to his room, and Tyler and I went off with the kids.

The two kids showed us around the house. The whole time, I studied things around the house to try to find an exceptional gift. I had no idea what to give him. I no longer owned anything that I could give away. I thought that maybe I could give him the jumpsuit in which I had come to their house that first early morning. Perhaps they kept it, and I could give it to Cody.

But why would Cody want some old jumpsuit, anyway? That gift idea would not work. I thought back to all the things I had owned. I had owned a lot when I was rich and powerful, but they would mean nothing to Cody. This task would require careful thought. I would have to sleep on the idea.

We came back for dinner. Mia had cooked some steaks for everyone. It was surprising and delightful to have a meal other than fish in this home. Tyler and I ate a lot of food since we had not eaten lunch. The kids had kept us too busy to eat anything. The dinner was fantastic.

"You're an awesome cook, Mia."

"Thanks, Martin. You two deserve to have a good meal after what you've been through. But really, it's nothing," she said bashfully.

I had eaten steak many times when I was in the mafia, but it was never cooked like this. "Better than mafia steaks. Right, Tyler?" I said to him. He nodded his head and continued eating. I could tell he thought that they were delicious.

After dinner, Tyler and I went on the boat with Jonah and Donovan. They wanted to do one more sweep of fishing, and so we went with them to talk. Tyler and I just packed the fish, for we were not as experienced as Jonah and Donovan. We helped and conversed with the masters as we did.

"Did you figure out what you want to get for Cody, Martin? We could always stop in Alemande to pick something up for you if you would like," Jonah said.

"No, I have no idea what to give him. Do you know what I should give him?" I asked, hopeful of a solution to my problem.

"You should probably give him something that would remind him of you. Of course, he wouldn't really care about a picture or something. He would like something a little more sentimental. Maybe a bit more tangible," Jonah answered, staring off into the horizon.

That was exactly what I was thinking about getting him. What was it? What would I give him that would remind him of me? I had no clue! Why did this answer have to evade me as all other answers in my life had? After a few hours of fishing and talking, we went back home.

At Jonah's house, I lay in one of the guest room beds. I wondered what to give Cody that would make him happy. My concentration was broken by the loud snoring of Tyler in the bed adjacent to mine. I had never had to deal with this at the Vaillancourt since I had my own room. I attempted to block him out with a pillow and continued to wonder.

Cody was adventurous and wild. He would want something bold and dangerous. He would not care about something plain and dull like a picture. The answer was somewhere, but I could not see it. I thought about giving him something from my time in the mafia. One thing came to mind, and that was my tomahawk. Of course, it was not as sentimental as I would have liked, and I would have to go back to West City to find it in the wreckage of the hotel.

Suddenly, the answer came to me. I had the answer with me all along. It had helped me make a new life for myself when I was lost in West City. It was a symbol of reputation, and, even if Cody did not know mine fully, he knew me. My gift would not let him forget me. I had carried it with me for so long, I had forgotten it was mine to give away. Satisfied with my gift idea, I drifted off to sleep.

At the appearance of first light through my window, I snapped awake and jumped out of bed. I woke up Tyler, who had slept very well. We then snuck up to Cody's room. I stood above Cody and patted him on the shoulder. "Cody," I whispered. He woke up, but was a little groggy.

"Huh?" Cody mumbled.

"HAPPY BIRTHDAY!!!" Tyler and I both yelled while shaking him.

Cody was startled. He woke up in a second and let out a confused shout. Tyler and I both stood over him, laughing.

He got out of bed. Alyssa came in behind us. She giggled to see what we had done. Cody got up and smiled at our small celebration of his birthday.

"Thanks, guys," he said, wiping the sleep from his eyes.

He walked downstairs for breakfast. The three of us followed him.

I sat at the birthday breakfast for Cody and took in the wonderful scents that were filling the air. Before Cody sat a plate with three big waffles covered in strawberry syrup. This was his favorite breakfast, and one could see it from the light glimmering in his deep blue eyes. He, of course, did not mind sharing with the rest of us.

Cody turned his eyes from his food to me.

"When do I get to open your present?" he asked as he had yesterday.

"Soon enough," I said. I was going to wait until he had received all his other gifts.

"Okay," he sighed dramatically and fell back in his chair.

He finished his breakfast, and we went outside.

We played another game of soccer. To make the game more fair for Tyler and Alyssa's team, Mia decided to help them. It was two against three, but Cody had the Martin advantage. We played exactly as we did last time. I would get the ball to the goal, and then I passed it to Cody. He had a little more trouble because they had caught on to our plans and because there were more people to defend the goal. In the end, we were the victors once again, but we failed to shut out the other team this time. The score was 7-3, and it was a terrific game for Cody's birthday. Satisfied with the sport, we returned to the house.

Cody ate his birthday lunch after that. The lunch consisted of take-out pizza from a restaurant. I was happily surprised to find out it was from the pizza chain where I had eaten my first remembered slice. I gobbled up the food as exuberantly as Cody, while his sister, mother, and Tyler watched in amusement.

"Can I open my present now?" Cody asked me eagerly after he had finished.

"Soon enough," I said again. He was becoming more and more impatient.

"Okay…" he sighed once more.

We went up to Cody's room and played games with him. He had a Game Box, and we played games until his dad and Donovan came home. When he heard the door shut, he turned off the game immediately and ran downstairs.

When they got home, Donovan was carrying a box.

"Is that my present?" Cody asked excitedly.

"You bet," Donovan said with a smile, holding it above his head so Cody could not reach it, even if he jumped, which he did.

Cody was getting excited. Really excited.

We sat down for Cody's birthday dinner. Burgers had been grilled up for us by Jonah. Needless to say, the food was delicious. The medium rare, juicy half-pound burgers perfectly complemented the toasted buns and melted cheese with ketchup and mustard. No wonder Cody had picked this as his birthday dinner. I had three by myself.

As dinner concluded, out came the presents. Alyssa was first, and she gave Cody his present with a smile that had greater origins than simple filial obligation. He opened it as fast as he could. It was a new Game Box game. Cody thanked his sister with a hug, and then Donovan gave his present. Cody opened it with the same speed. It was a bunch of fishing tools and supplies. Naturally, Cody was quite fond of his father's profession. He thanked Donovan as Tyler was coming forth with a gift.

"Here you go, Cody," Tyler said, holding out a bag.

Opening his duffle bag, Tyler held out a shotgun to Cody. It was Mrs. T. With sudden realization, Tyler quickly broke the gun and unloaded the two live shells. He glanced around awkwardly before handing the harmless weapon to the boy.

"I just wanted to give this to you. It is very special to me, and, when you are old enough, I hope you use it a lot," Tyler said, scratching his head, for he was unsure if Cody would like the gift and was rather nervous.

Cody took it with gleaming eyes and thanked Tyler politely. Jonah came up and took the shotgun and laid it against the wall. Young boys should not have such dangerous weaponry laying idly near them, even unloaded.

Then, Mia gave Cody his present from Jonah and herself. Cody opened it with lightning speed. Inside the large box was a bow and a quiver full of arrows. Cody absolutely loved it. I saw the wheels turning in his head with all the possibilities that this gift afforded him. I could understand why he liked it. He was an adventurous kid, and bows and arrows seemed to symbolize battle and adventure. He thanked his parents a thousand times.

Last was my gift. Cody turned to me, anticipating great things. I stepped forward and knelt down to be on Cody's level. I then pulled the ring off my finger. "Happy birthday, Cody," I said and handed him my shining mafia ring. His eyes were huge as he took it. He studied the ring. It was a little too big for Cody at the time, but he would grow into it. He just stared at the ring. Eventually, he returned his gaze to me. Then, he practically tackled me with a hug.

"Thanks, Martin! It's so cool!" he yelled in my ear.

"I wanted you to have something to remember me by," I told my faithful admirer. Jonah smiled at me in the background. Cody loved my gift, and that was all I could want. I was so happy to have him in my life.

I went to sleep happy that night. I was somewhat downcast that I had to leave my family tomorrow, but I would do it so I could clear up all the confusion. With my identity finally mine in truth, I could return to them a full man.

It brought great joy to my heart that Cody loved my present. I did not need the mafia ring anymore, and I knew Cody did. I believed Tyler felt the same way. We both were done with that chapter in our life, but the tools of the trade could be passed on. They would hold an entirely different meaning to Cody than to us, and that was the point. We wanted him to go down a different path. It made us both very happy to give him his gifts.

It would be okay to leave tomorrow. I would go to Alemande and find out who that investigator who lied to us was. Following that trail, I would find my past. I would escape this confusion once and for all. I would know who I was, and the hidden past would no longer taunt me.

Chapter 17
True Criminals

When I woke up, Tyler, Donovan, Jonah, and I took the *Martin* to Alemande. We were going there to find the news station that had covered the boat explosion. We would there find more information about the investigator. We could then find him and question him about why he lied and about what he knew.

When we got to Alemande, Jonah and Donovan took off in the boat to fish. Tyler and I went to the Alemande News Center. The building was in the middle of the city, and we took our time getting there on foot. We kept out of sight for the most part, fearing the consequences that possible recognition would bring. The news on the Vaillancourt explosion would have spread to a lot of different places by now, and people would be on the lookout for remaining mafia members. We kept to the alleys and made our way to the news building.

We soon arrived at the Alemande News building. Unlike many of the surrounding buildings, this one's exterior was not composed of simple brick, but instead looked new and sophisticated. Yet, this new look was comparative. This building appeared as if it had not undergone any renovations for a long time. Still, it was impressive. It was one of the larger buildings in Alemande, but paled in comparison to the size of the buildings in West City.

Of course, all the characteristics that made this structure unique would soon make it commonplace. Since we had gotten back, I was noticing more and more construction around this town. Skyscrapers were threatening to replace the simple, two-story structures that made up the vast majority of this town. The economy was shifting here, and fish would no longer suffice. Bigger business was moving in.

All of this flowing throughout my mind, we walked in through the large glass doors.

Inside was a quaint set-up of a couple coffee tables covered in old magazines and some bench seating with cracks in the cushioning. This was the lobby of the building. We wanted to find the archives. I deduced that any one of the staff members would know where it was, and all we had to do was ask them. A woman was behind a counter at the far end of the room. We made our way there.

"Hello, how can I help you?" the woman at the counter asked kindly.

"We need to see the archives," I told her.

"That's against company policy. I can't let you into that area unless you are detectives or part of the news corporation. Sorry, gentlemen. Anything else I might be able to help you with?" she said to us.

Tyler stepped up.

"What's your name?" he asked.

He was employing one of the mafia's methods of intimidation.

"Priya," she said, pointing to her name tag.

"Listen, Pryuh," he said, horribly mispronouncing her name. "We need to see the archives now because someone lied about the boat explosion that happened about a year ago. So, it would be in your best interest to let us in. Okay?"

She rolled her eyes before answering Tyler.

"You listen, sir. We can't let you in unless you are a cop or a reporter. So, it would be in your best interest to just get out of here. Okay?" she said with an attitude that only angered Tyler.

"Let's get out of here," I said to Tyler. He was reluctant, but, after a grumble, he came with me. We threw open the large glass doors and stomped out of the building.

"Why did you give up like that, kid?" Tyler asked me, still angry.

"I did not give up. I found a better way to do it," I said, pointing to the fire escape on the side of the building.

"Oh. Heh heh, nice, kid. You know, your plans are always more fun, anyway," Tyler said with a chuckle.

We went to the side of the building. I grabbed a dumpster and pulled it over to the fire escape. Tyler got on top of it and tried to reach the escape.

"Still too far, kid," he said, attempting to jump and grab the hanging ladder.

Waving Tyler down, I walked over and grabbed another dumpster. I pushed it next to the other one. Then, I used all my strength and picked up the dumpster and put it on the other one. The top dumpster crushed the lid of the bottom, but it remained in its place and allowed us access to the ladder. Tyler looked at me in amazement.

"I still have no idea how you do that," he said, shaking his head and smiling giddily.

"That's what we're going to find out."

I climbed the dumpster staircase and jumped up to the fire escape. Tyler did the same. We climbed the fire escape stairs until we were five stories up, near the top of the building. I climbed into a window. To our good fortune, there was no one around. I waved Tyler in. We began the heist of intelligence.

We were in an empty studio. I went to the door and opened it slowly. People were walking around outside. They all had very nice clothing. Even though we were wearing the expensive clothing from our mafia days, there was no way we could blend in with them. Fortunately, another idea came to mind.

Tyler and I walked out of the room. A man in a suit immediately stopped us.

"What are you doing up here?" he asked, putting out his hand in front of our path.

"We got lost. We were supposed to do an interview about the mafia. You see, we were in the mafia and left right before the Vaillancourt Incident," I told the man. Tyler flashed his ring to give some validity to my statement.

"Okay, then. Who was the interview with?" he asked us, still suspicious.

"Uh…I think the name was something like…" I said, not able to think of a name.

"What was the name? You should know if you were going to do an interview," the man asked again, his face scrunching with suspicion.

My eyes desperately searching, I luckily found a board on which was listed the room numbers and uses of each room on this floor. One of the rooms was listed as "164: Special Report with Michael Wolfe".

"Uh…the name was Wolfe," I answered finally.

"Ah, well, Mike starts his show in about two hours. Why don't you guys go wait down in the lobby?" he suggested.

"Good idea," I said, and we took off for the elevator. We walked down the hall and took a right so that we could escape the sight of the suspicious man. Approaching the elevator, I saw a sign on the wall giving a description of the floors. Floor 3 was storage. I assumed that this included data storage. We entered the elevator, I pushed the 3 button, and we went to steal the info.

The doors opened, and we cautiously stepped out. No one was in here. We ventured through the halls filled with dusty stationary fans and boxes of camera parts until we came upon the room marked "Archives."

Entering, all was silent except the gentle hum of electronics. We went to a computer on a desk in the room. I clicked on the search bar and typed in "Boat explosion". There were 415 results. I turned to Tyler.

"When did I join the mafia?" I asked him.

"Uh…sometime in June," he said after a second of thought.

I typed in "June 2013 boat explosion". Four results popped up, but the first one was my boat.

I clicked on the link, and a video popped up. I clicked the play button. Tyler and I watched the reporter talking about the *Annabelle* and how it was destroyed. Then, the screen switched to a close-up of the investigator discussing their findings.

"We believe some internal flaw with the inner machinery of the engine caused by manufacturer error led to a slow leak of fuel. It is also our belief that the engine was routinely tossing sparks; that's due to lack of maintenance. Obviously, that makes a volatile environment that's just ready to go off. This is something that should have been caught earlier, and that's a lesson for any mechanics working on boats these days. This kind of accident is preventable. Very preventable. It's extremely tragic, but we need to be working to cut down on the number of this kind of incident," he spoke softly and calmly.

Pausing the video, I looked down to see that his name was Jeff Quackenbush.

"Hey! There's his name, kid!"

"Yeah, but that's nothing we couldn't have found on the internet. We're here for more than just a name."

I exited out of the link and went to the Alemande News Center database. The company was required to keep detailed information on everyone who went through their system, whether it be through interview or other contribution. This database had to have his contact info and, hopefully, his current location.

When it opened, a message popped up asking to reconfirm the password. I was close to attempting other means of getting this information, but Tyler stopped me. He ducked under the desk and searched around.

"Aha! Okay, the password is 'anc81615'," he said, appearing from under the desk with a sticky note.

Typing in the password and hitting enter, I gained access to the database. I typed in the name of our guy, Jeff Quackenbush. His file then came up, and we had all the info on him we could ever need.

The file reported that Jeff had been employed by the Regional Police Department of West City. He had been assigned to work the *Annabelle* case because of his experience with the nautical investigation branch of the Alemande Police Department. He, too, had been a transfer, just like Officer Turnbull.

Before I could look up his current location, an alarm went off. An error popped up on the screen informing us that there had been unauthorized use of the data storage system. Our time here was more limited than my plan had suggested.

"Crap! Ty, we've got to get out of here," I said, but it was already too late.

Two men from the news security team burst in. One of them grabbed me, and the other went for Tyler. I broke free and also broke the man's arm. Tyler's man, seeing what I did to my guy, dropped Tyler and tried to taze me. When he lunged at me, I dodged and shifted his momentum past me. When he came back at me, I repeated the move, and Tyler hit him with a metal garbage can as he passed me. With the man down, he kicked him in the face and knocked him out. I knocked my guy out right after he called for back-up.

"Hell, what do we do, kid?" Tyler asked in panic.

I ran out of the room, and Tyler followed. I could see a window at the end of the hall, opposite the elevator. I sprinted down the hall and threw myself through the glass and out into the sunlight. I landed on a one-story restaurant below.

Tyler looked down at me from the window.

"Come on, you big baby! Jump!" I yelled.

Being a daring and brave man, he trusted me to catch him and jumped. I caught him just as the back-ups came to the window. Tyler flipped them off, and we ran down into the restaurant.

We came through the kitchen and ran through the restaurant. Pushing past confused waiters and jumping over counter tops, Tyler and I managed to make our way out. We came out the door at the same moment the police pulled up to the news building. They saw us, and Tyler taunted them with a flash of his ring before we sprinted away.

Sirens blaring, a police car was hot on our tail. My legs carried me much faster than the vehicle, but Tyler's were not able. I would not let them catch him. I jumped in front of the car, braced myself, and took the blow. Like running full-speed into a brick wall, the sensation mimicked that of a brick wall running into me at full-speed. All my muscles tensed, and the crunching of metal and breaking of glass was all I could hear. Wobbling backwards, I fell on my back.

The front of the car was busted up quite a bit, and it definitely was not going anywhere. The officers were disabled by the collision, and their vehicle blocked the road and caused a traffic jam. My whole body was sore, but I rose and motioned to Tyler to run. We took off, and the other officers got out of their cars and chased us.

Tyler panting and I at full alert, we ran down the stairs into the subway. We had no problem with the cops since they were not as well-trained as the officers who used to be in this city. We jumped the turnstiles and ran to a train.

Boarding the train, I yelled to one of the passengers, "Where is this train headed?"

The shocked passenger answered, "Uh... we're going to Poplen."

"Good enough," I said, and we got on the train. Right when we were almost ready to take off, the officers finally caught up to us. I grabbed them and threw them off the train when they came to grab us. The doors closed, and we were free.

People gave us peculiar stares. They saw me push those police officers out the door when the train started up. They did not know what to think of us. We just sat there and waited until we came to Poplen. It was an awkward ride.

When the doors opened again and we stepped out, we did not know whether to wait for another train or to go into the city of Poplen. I never even knew about Poplen before now. All I had known was Alemande and West City. Not knowing anything about Poplen, I decided to go check it out. Besides, it was very possible that waiting here could result in the police finding us.

We came out of the subway to reveal only another huge city. Poplen was probably five times larger than West City. The streets were crowded with people, and we did not know where to go.

A new city full of new things. My brain once again started analyzing. I counted people, guessed population, approximated the time it would take the cops to get to us, and ran over the plans of escape for when they did come.

In a big city like this, it was not too hard to hide from the police. The best part was that we could hide in plain sight. The crowds were quite large here, and we could easily hide amongst them. We blended in with a crowd and followed it around. We would switch groups of people as the crowd slowly broke up. Luckily, we came to a hotel before our choice of crowds had begun to diminish. We entered only to find that this place was almost as crowded as the streets.

I walked up to the main desk.

"Hey, we need a room," I asked the woman behind the desk.

"Surely. We have two rooms available. One on the fifth floor and one on the third floor. They're both $120 a night. Your pick."

"We'll take the one on the third floor."

She rattled on the keyboard in front of her for a couple seconds, and then she turned back and grabbed a key card. Swiping it through the reader on the side of her monitor, she gave us access to our room. I took the card from her hand.

"Here you are, dear! My name is Tammy Shepard. If you gentlemen have any questions, come ask me."

"Thank you," I said, and we went to our room.

Another hotel room. This was where people like us were destined to stay most of our time. Always traveling and always on the run, we needed a safe and moderately secure place to stay. Hotel rooms gave that to us.

The room had two beds, one TV, one bathroom, some tables, some chairs, and a desk. Basic setup. They could not match up to the rooms at the Vaillancourt, but the price was less than a hundredth of the Vaillancourt as well. I lay on the bed in relief that we finally had rest.

"What are we going to do next?" Tyler asked, plopping down on the other bed.

"I guess we could go down to the lobby again and ask when a subway train is going to West City," I suggested.

"Why don't we just go to the subway station again and find out there?"

"We wouldn't be able to find it again. Anyway, the woman at the desk could tell us where it is. I think it would be better to not risk getting lost in the city and then found by the police."

"Fine, but we do it tomorrow. I need some rest, kid. Like, seriously."

I, too, needed some rest. We stayed in the room for a few hours and regained our energy. Drifting off to sleep much more quickly than expected, I concluded that I most definitely needed the rest.

Later, we got up and went to get some food. We went down to the buffet and ate until we were stuffed.

"Best lunch I ever had," Tyler said, patting his belly.

"Me, too, Ty," I said. "Except for the fact that I can only remember about a twentieth of the lunches you've had!" He laughed as did I, but only for about a second.

A police officer entered the buffet and positioned himself in the center of the room. Seeing this, Tyler and I darted under the table, which fortunately gave us some cover beneath the table cloth.

Holding up a piece of paper with picture of Tyler and me on it, he announced, "Attention! Two fugitives have escaped into the city, and we believe they might be hiding somewhere in this hotel. Here are pictures of the fugitives. If any of you have seen these men, we need your help. There is a $4000 reward on each of their heads. We're dealing with two very dangerous criminals, ladies and gentlemen. Your assistance in this search is absolutely vital to our success and safety. Once again, if you have any information, please come forward."

People immediately started coming forward. Tyler and I realized we had no time and got out from under the table. Attempting to sneak away, we walked nonchalantly towards the exit. A burly man blocked our path and called to the officer.

"They're right here!" he shouted.

Left with no other option, I decked him and we bolted. Out of the dining hall and into the lobby, we were going to run out the front doors, but officers were stationed there. We were out of luck.

"Hey! There they are!" one of them shouted as the officer from the dining hall reached the lobby.

"Come on, come on!" I yelled to Tyler, yanking him up the stairs to our room as the policemen drew their weapons on us and screams rang out.

We sprinted up to our room, the shouts from our pursuers not far behind. When we reached the room, I slid the card, and we raced inside. I latched the door, and Tyler and I went out the window. We were on the third floor. This problem would be easily solved with simple jumping. I landed on the balcony of the floor below. Tyler jumped, and I caught him and brought him in.

"Heh, heh. Kid, I still have no idea how you do that."

"We'll find out. You promised."

We jumped the last floor and then to the ground and took off running. We had made it away from the police for now. Sirens were blaring in the distance as back-up was surely already called. We had to get away from the hotel. Hell, we had to get out of the city!

Somehow, I remembered the route we had taken to get to the hotel quite vividly. It had been about 20 blocks, but I remembered exactly how to get back to the subway. Tyler and I made sure to blend in with the crowd as much as possible. We avoided all police stations and walked mostly through alleys. We made it back to the subway, but that was not the end of the trouble.

As we entered the subway station, a news report came on all the televisions.

"Watch out for two men. They were in the West City Mafia before it's fiery end last Tuesday night after the infamous Vaillancourt Bombing. One, only known by the alias of 'The Beast of Flame', is about 6' 4" with short brown hair. The other one, Tyler Ishler, AKA "Little Ty", has been in the mafia his whole life and is about 5' 5" with short red hair. These men were last sighted on a subway train going to Poplen. If you have any information, call 757-NO-CRIME," the man on TV said as our pictures were displayed on the screen.

We averted our faces to the crowd as best we could, and I sneakily stole some sunglasses from a vendor and put them on. We walked over to the ticket booth to get some tickets. Tyler paid for the tickets, and we entered the station. Luckily, it seemed as if no one had paid attention to the report. Nothing was going wrong, but that never seemed to last very long for me.

A train pulled up, and the first man to exit was Officer Heath Thompson. He must have come from West City to investigate the two criminals in Poplen, and we were the criminals. Tyler and I quickly ducked to the side and looked down at the floor. We must have looked suspicious, because he came right to us.

"Do either of you gentlemen have the time?" he asked.

"Um, no, officer, we do not," I said.

Heath looked at Tyler.

"No, that's wrong. I could have sworn I saw a watch on your wrist, sir," he said, gesturing for Tyler to prove him wrong.

"Nope, no watch here," Tyler said, lifting up his arm.

Heath quickly grabbed his arm, revealing Tyler's mafia ring.

"You may not have the time, but you have something much more important," he said, backed up, and pulled his gun.

Crowds in the subway screamed.

Tyler looked at him with aggravation.

"Nice try, but you are not going to kill me. And you're definitely not going to bring me in," Tyler said, standing straighter and more confidently.

"Why's that?" Heath asked, taking another step back.

"Because of this," Tyler said, reaching for his pocket.

As Heath focused on his pocket and got ready to shoot, I came in and punched him in the face. His gun went off, missing Tyler by inches. Screams echoed through the subway station. I kicked the gun out of his hands.

"Where is Jeff Quackenbush?!" I asked him.

I held Heath down and stared menacingly into his eyes. In those eyes, I saw realization appear. Heath blinked his eyes to confirm he was seeing what he was seeing.

"You! You're the guy that brought in Liam the Mugger so long ago!" he said as I held him down with my foot.

"Yes, I am. Now, where is Jeff Quackenbush?!" I said, even louder.

"You're Martin," Heath said, not interested in my interrogation.

"Yes, I'm Martin. Now, tell me where Jeff Quackenbush is! You work with him in the police department. I know you know where he is. Now, answer me!"

"I have no idea who that is. Martin, what are..." Heath was saying.

I slammed his head against the ground, knocking him out.

"Let's go. The other officers will be here in no time," I told Tyler.

Picking up Heath's gun, I nodded at Tyler, and we ran to the train.

We jumped on the train, and Tyler and I went to the front of it. The conductor was not ready to take off yet, but we made him ready. I held the gun to his head.

"Take us to West City now!" I yelled at him.

He nodded, and I led him over to the controls. He started the train, and we took off. He took us straight to West City and said nothing the whole ride. He only moved the controls on occasion and sat in his seat. As he did this, Tyler made sure to lock and barricade the door.

We arrived in West City soon after, and I thanked the conductor for his cooperation. I holstered the pistol, and we left the train. Upon exiting, we got an unhappy surprise. Officers Nick Turnbull and Chase Thomson were waiting for us.

"How's it going, guys?" I said uneasily.

Nick radioed for back-up, and we came off the train with our hands up.

"Any ideas, kid?" Tyler asked me.

"I'm fresh out this time, Ty. I have no clue."

"On your knees!" Chase yelled.

"Drop your weapon!" Nick yelled.

I set the gun on the ground slowly and slid it to them. We both got down and put our hands on our heads. The valiant officers handcuffed us and removed us from the station. The crowds in the subway clapped as they brought us out.

I could have easily broken the cuffs and taken down every one of the cops, but I worried for Tyler's sake. He could be shot in my escape attempt. I would not let anything happen to Tyler. I just cooperated with the police as they stuffed us into the car after reading us our rights. Tyler and I made sure not to talk, accepting the fact that we were caught and that anything we said could and would be used against us.

They took us to the police station where they locked us up. Tyler was in the cell across from me. I sat on the bed as did he. Here, all I could do was stare at the floor in disbelief. We both knew we were finally going to pay for our crimes.

"What do we do?" I asked him.

He just shook his head. It was over for us. We had been caught, and there was no way to escape with both of our lives. They would shoot Tyler on sight, mostly because of his reputation in the mafia. He was already most likely going to get life in prison. Life and death were such similar sentences.

Soon after, an officer came to our cells and began unlocking mine.

"What's going on?" I asked him.

"You're being released," the officer responded.

"What? Why?"

"We ran your prints, but they came up with nothing. Trying to dig deeper, we couldn't find a single trace of you. It's like you don't exist aside from your alias of The Beast of Flame."

"There are no records of me at all? Like, even a birth certificate or social..."

"Nothing," the officer said, opening my door. "We brought it up to our boss, and he brought it up to big shots in the government. They sent down orders to release you, so that's what we're doing."

I stepped out of the cage and glanced over and Tyler. He just shrugged. We both had no clue as to what was going on. I was free, but my friend still was imprisoned.

"I'm free to go then?" I asked.

"Yes. We need you to leave the premises now."

"What about Tyler?"

"We have no orders concerning that piece of human garbage, only you. Now, get the hell out of here, Martin."

I looked over to my friend who was sitting at the edge of his bed.

"You go, kid. You got a full life ahead of you. You know where I'll be waiting."

I nodded, understanding what he meant and what I had to do. The officer then escorted me out to the entrance of the building.

I stopped by the office before leaving the station. "I need some information on Jeff Quackenbush," I asked Officer Turnbull, who had been glaring at me every step I took towards him.

"Confidential, you scum!" Nick growled at me.

He knew I did it. He hated the fact that I was being released. Somebody above him was withholding the pleasure of his bringing me to justice, and he loathed that with all he was. The internal conflict of obeying the higher authorities, executing justice, and bringing safety to the streets was grinding within his gut.

"Don't think you've got me fooled. We have enough evidence to convict you, no question. Personally, I've got enough on you to suggest you're Martin Yellog, a former gang member that escaped our cells a few years ago. But they don't care what I think. Hell, even if you aren't Martin Yellog, you were the one with him, so it doesn't even matter. We've got a whole file of you and Little Ty in the mafia. We have proof!" Nick growled. "We will catch you, Martin. Just because the higher-ups say we can't touch you doesn't mean I won't be looking for you. You better watch out!" the police officer threatened me.

Martin Yellog. Was that my name? Had I found my last name at last? I wondered this, but could not be sure. I did not even know what this Martin Yellog looked like!

I left the station with neither my friend nor my information. I had lost even more in this attempt to find my past. Tyler was in a cell, and I had put him there. He only wanted to help me, but I had failed him. I would not let the police steal everything from me. I would rescue my friend and steal the information. Nothing was off limits this time. I would find my past, whatever I had to do.

Chapter 18
Everything Changes

Night came, and struggle came with it. My funds depleted, food and shelter were out of the question. Life was beating me down into my hole once again. No friends, no family, no plans for the future. I would need to rest before I figured out how to free Tyler. I went to my old box in the alley where I had spent my first night. This is where I slept.

I closed the box, but the rats still got inside. I was miserable the whole night. I had lost my best friend, and the police officers I had once respected greatly had turned their backs on me. The only lead I had for finding my identity was now gone. I fell into despair.

My mind wandered back to the words that were spoken to me in the jail cell. The officer spoke as if I never had an identity. How could I find something that had never existed? This would make the search many times harder. Even if I had no identity, there had to be something left for me in the past. The past was the only thing I could chase.

Hopeless and terribly fatigued, I fell into a deep sleep. My dreams played with what I thought I knew. I dreamt that Tyler and I confronted Jeff Quackenbush. I kicked in the door, and Tyler shot him with a beanbag round. Taking the round to the gut, Jeff fell to his knees, and I picked him up and slammed him into the wall.

"Jeff, we know you lied about what happened to the *Annabelle*. What's the truth? Why did you lie?" I yelled at him, my face inches from his.

"I don't know what you're talking about! I don't know the *Annabelle*. I'm not the guy you want!" he cowered.

Tyler hit him hard in the gut with the butt of Mrs. T.

"Jeff, you're gonna want to start helping us out here, or I'm going to shoot you again, and it might not be as pleasant as the first time," Tyler said, shifting his aim downward.

"Okay! Okay! Please, don't shoot! I know what you're talking about!"

"Then, talk!" I ordered and slammed him against the wall again.

He cleared his throat and took a deep breath before beginning.

"The explosion on the *Annabelle* was due to a malfunctioning trap set in the ocean to catch drug smugglers. West City had been experiencing a huge upward trend in heroin trafficking, and I was in charge of the unit tasked with stopping it. The trap was a prototype, and no one was supposed to be out in that area where we were going to test it. Your boat came within proximity and triggered the device. It was supposed to fire an EMP blast into the boat incapacitate it so we could board and apprehend the criminals. It didn't work, though, and it caused a huge explosion that wiped out the ship. Since it was a failed operation by the police, we had to cover it up. That's why I lied."

"What about me? Why are there no records of me?"

"You were born on the boat, Martin. It was an undocumented birth, and you went on to grow up mostly on the boat or in rural Alemande. There was never an occasion to have you documented. Because of that, you existed completely in secrecy to the outside world."

After he had given us the answers we were seeking, we handcuffed him and brought him to the police to be arrested. The whole incident was uncovered to the public. Finally, I knew the truth about my past. Everything was changing, finally for the good.

Then, a rat bit my arm and jolted me awake. The little beast darted out of the box, and my groggy daze quickly faded. My dream seemed so real. I would have given up anything for it to be real. More than anything, I needed this. Jeff held the truth, but, in order to find Jeff, I would have to break into the police station and steal the information and Tyler. This was the only way. No other decision was afforded me.

I left my box and kicked the rats away from me. While stretching, I glanced down at my pitiful shelter. It had been my thought that I was done living like this. Sleeping in that box was not comfortable in the slightest. Soon, though, my soreness faded, and my body was brought back into its proper alignment.

It was strange how my dream did not come up with an explanation about my strength and healing abilities. My dream only explained why I was not recorded in history. Fortunately, I did not need to rely on my brain to think up theories about who I used to be. All the answers would be found as soon as I found Jeff.

There was really no good way to steal from the police. This kind of behavior should not have even been in my plans. I wanted to live a life that was better than the one I was living now. The lifestyle of wounding, stealing, lying, and killing should have been put to death with the Vaillancourt Incident. When I left the mafia, I thought of it as a way of freeing me from the evil inside, but I still had not gotten rid of it. Violence and selfishness still plagued me. Without a proper way to end these qualities within myself, I would have to focus on my objective to find out the truth from Jeff. Could the truth free me from my wickedness? It was my only hope.

A daze overtook me as I walked through the streets. What was I going to do about my situation? Should I really go through with this? Freeing Tyler was of greatest importance to me, but I feared what I was becoming. Also, I could not chase down Jeff until I had the information from the police station. How would I solve this? My mind was quite hazy, but that did not last long.

A bloodcurdling scream pierced the haze and brought clarity to my troubled mind. I looked towards the noise. What I saw confused and startled me. Ahead, there was a woman cowering on the ground while a giant metal sphere levitated menacingly above her. Other people did not stop to save the woman, but they had enough time to save themselves. The machine shot fire from six holes in its shell spread equidistant from each other around the sphere. The scene was completely surreal. I took action and ran to save the woman.

I picked her up and ran from the machine. It levitated after us, but the machine moved slowly and could not catch us. Unfortunately, it did not have to catch us. In front of us was another machine, spitting fire like the last. The woman in my arms screamed and struggled out of my grasp. She ran into a building and locked the door.

All around me, people scattered into alleyways and buildings. Their fear was as mine: the fear of the unknown. What were these machines?

The machine locked onto me. I studied it, knowing that the best way to defeat it was to know what it was. Basically, this machine was a floating metal sphere, about five to seven feet in diameter and armed with six flamethrowers. My best guess was that it was controlled by multiple inertial-propulsion devices, even though there was no record of these devices ever having existed. Of course, there was no record of me, either. These devices produced greater thrust in one direction than the other, allowing the machines to defy gravity and giving them the ability to levitate. Inside the machine, I hypothesized, was a large tank of fuel. It did not fuel the devices, but instead fueled the six flamethrowers. Knowing this, all I had to do was destroy a few of the devices or set the inner tank of fuel on fire. These ideas would disable the machines.

The machine rotated itself and blasted fire at me. I dodged to the left, and it failed to follow me. The machine was most likely guided by multiple thermal cameras. When the fire came, it blocked out its view. Knowing this, I could dodge side to side, and it could not follow me.

Its fire stopped, and it relocated me. It fired again, desiring my cremation. Another dodge saved me from the flames. When it was lost in the blaze, I punched the machine with all my strength. It slammed into a wall, and the fire ceased.

However, it was not finished. It levitated again and resumed fire. I dodged and attacked again. My fist dented the side this time, and the beast of flame crashed into the wall. Once again, it levitated and came after me. Relentless, this machine would not stop until its purpose was completed.

I put some distance in between us. The machine tried to follow me, but it was now very unstable. The metal shell dented into one of the devices, its levitation path was not as clean as it was programmed to produce. It hit the ground and attempted to levitate again. Before it could, I slammed my fist back into it. The side dented inwardly and crippled another device.

I landed multiple blows to the machine's outer shell in rapid succession. The devices ceased to function, and the machine fell to the ground with a loud thud. I had won this battle with the fire-breather. It let out bursts of flame with little accuracy.

Approaching the machine that was not yet finished, I squeezed the tube where the fire exited. Doing this, my skin sizzled, but I found that it did not burn. I put distance between myself and the machine.

The fuel shot through the tube, but could not ignite at the end. The tube was clogged with fuel and finally ignited, but it had nowhere to go but inside. The flame arresters were most likely broken from the squeezing, and this allowed the flame to travel back through the tube. The main tank ignited, and the machine detonated. Pieces of the heavy metal shell exploded out from the epicenter. Its parts were scattered in the streets. I had conquered the death machine!

I moved on, thinking that I had saved the city from this menace, only to see that the whole city was covered in these machines. They burnt down buildings and chased after people. The police were fighting these monsters in vain. Their bullets bounced off the outer shells futilely. I watched the chaos, not knowing what to do. West City was burning to the ground.

There was no safe place from the machines. Even though people ran into buildings and locked the doors, the machines smashed their huge bodies into the doors and windows and gained access. Once inside, the building was burnt down within 15 minutes.

I counted over 50 machines. 50! Who had storage or ability to create these beautiful masterpieces and still keep them secret? It was outrageous what havoc they had wrought on the city. I knew that I could not defeat all of them. If only I could find the source!

Then, I noticed something. One building was untouched by the machines. Even though most of the machines were surrounding this building, not one bit of flame had graced its exterior. That had to be their origin. That building was the key to stopping the menace that was quickly overtaking the city.

I took off at a full sprint to the building. I helped as many people as I could on the way, but there were too many of them to save the city. The police were calling in back-up and trying to get away from the beasts. I ran with all my strength to the source of mayhem.

The machines were definitely coming from this building, which seemed to be an apartment complex of about eight stories. Not only that, but they were protecting it. A wall of steel and fire descended on me as soon as I neared the entrance. I tried to fight them, but I had no chance. I could only damage a few before I had to run away. After pushing past their defenses, I kicked in the doors. Unfortunately, the main floor had these machines inside as well. I ran past them, knowing that I had to get to the top. The machines were too large to fit inside the stairs, which provided an opportunity to escape and to ascend towards my objective.

I was lucky they could not follow me. As I climbed the many flights of stairs to the top, the view from the windows provided me with nothing but horror. This was the place I remembered most, and it was burning to the ground. Another item from my past destroyed with fire.

I climbed the last flight and saw the door. Who was behind it? Who had created such evil with such knowledge? Whoever this person was, I could not let them continue.

Standing at the door, I reached to open it, but then I noticed something scary at my feet. A microwave was rigged to blow if I opened the door. It would have taken a mastermind to figure out how to do all this. Who was behind it all?

Taking a closer look at the bomb, I realized what exactly the trigger was. The power cord was positioned to be unplugged if the door was opened, which would cut power to the microwave, forcing it to utilize its back-up battery. The back-up was connected to a wire that brought power to the main oven. Inside the oven was a gallon or two of what looked to be common household cleaners, mixed together to create an extremely volatile concoction. The door to the oven was glued shut, and I did not think it would be wise to try prying the bomb open.

All I had to do was keep power coming in to the microwave from its main source, not the back up. To get through the door, though, I would have to unplug the machine. Having no other alternative, I ripped the microwave from its place and tossed it down the stairs, racing behind the door as soon as it left my hands. The door did not fully close before the explosion rippled in the narrow stair column. The blast threw me to my face and deafened me temporarily. A sulfury smell drifted in through the open door leading back.

My ears stopped ringing, and I regained my feet. I was in a bare hallway, just a long corridor from one door to another, lacking any artwork or touch of color. There was sound coming from the other side of the door at the end of the hall. Behind me, the doorway was destroyed and blackened by the bomb. I walked over to the door at the end of the hallway and inspected it for explosives. Surprisingly, there were none to be found.

It was the moment of truth. I slowly turned the knob. The door was not even locked. Whoever was behind this obviously thought that nobody could get past his machines and the bomb. This villain was quite simply wrong.

I slowly opened the door. Inside, I saw a room full of monitors. It appeared that all the walls on this floor had been knocked down to create one large room. There was a balcony in the back of the room and a man in the center who was sitting on a stool and carefully watching the screens.

"Come in," I heard the man say, not even turning to look at me.

I was terrified to find out that he knew I was there. I came inside and closed the door behind me. Cautiously, I approached this villain to put a stop to his plans. Then, the man flipped around to reveal an abhorrent face I could never forget.

The man that was causing all this chaos in West City was right before me. A hatred in me came to the surface for a character I thought had finished playing his part in my life. It was the one man whom I despised more than anybody else. Jack Lamb, who had humiliated me at the fight in the Vaillancourt Fight Arena, sat there and smiled. He looked much older now, even though it had only been about a year.

"I pray you have not lost the memory of my face, Martin. Do you remember me?" he asked, a clever grin stuck on his face.

"Of course I do, Jack Lamb," I answered, stepping forward.

"I have counted the days since we last spoke. Ah, how long it has been! Terribly, I have longed for a chance to speak with you once again."

"Strange, I've wanted to talk with you for a long time, too, Jack."

"But Martin, you lack the knowledge of what I shall say to you. I know exactly what it is you desire to say to me," he said, grinning and standing up from his seat.

"Oh yeah? Then, what is it I want to say to you?" I asked, not believing he could know the answer.

"You wish to demand a rematch. Through many trials and much tribulation, you feel you have been remolded into an infinitely more powerful man, and you desire to prove that to me so that you can finally be free of your horrid self-doubt," he said, and he was completely correct on all accounts.

I slowly nodded in confirmation.

"I feel it only appropriate to give you fair warning, Martin... It would do no good. The means to defeat me you lack. I hold strength you cannot possess."

"We'll see about that! Did you know that I destroyed some of your machines down there? If I can kill them, then I can kill you," I said, determined to surprise him and wipe that horrible grin from his face, but he was not surprised in the least.

"Of course you can kill them, for you are as I. Simply stated, you just are not as good as I," he taunted.

"What the hell do you mean?!" I yelled, frustrated by this man's mind games.

"You remain a mystery to yourself. It is sad, truly. Retrograde amnesia is an abominable thief for men of great potential such as yourself. When the news reached me, I was completely distraught. Inconsolable!"

This confused me even more. How did this man know who I was? How did he know what had happened to me? More questions than ever entered my mind, but I knew the answers were close.

"Saddest all, Martin, is that you have been robbed of memory of myself."

"Why would I remember you?"

"Only a single friend was yours; I am he. I was the supplier of false hope, but this method was piteous treatment, not a cure to your affliction. Know that I have the deepest of apology for what has happened to you,

Martin. If you believe anything I say, it would be my choice for you to believe that."

"How do you know me?" I asked, finally realizing that this man was the key to my past.

"You know what? You can be of some assistance to me," he said. "But first, let me display to you that with which your purpose is fulfilled."

He led me over to the monitors. On the screens were images of the thermal outlines of people running for their lives. The screens would glow intensely red and white and then return to normal. I was correct about the machines' tracking systems.

"The eyes of the beasts. The videos displayed are provided by thermal cameras on the machines. My creations' activities can be observed through these eyes," he said, flipping through the feeds from the machines.

He led me over to the balcony. There was a machine there as well, but this one was different. It was not a complete sphere. The top had a platform on which one could stand. Instruments protruded from this place, and it appeared as if this was where one would pilot the machine.

"Martin, all valiant warriors require a steed. This will justly serve as your war horse. Similar to its counterparts but separated by its sole difference, it can be piloted. Its controls are not suited for the laymen, but you will learn quickly. You always learn quickly," he said, looking into my eyes.

"What exactly is it you want me to do?" I asked, still very confused.

"You will be terminating those inferior maggots who have made my life..." he paused and chuckled, "...hell."

"Who are they?" I asked.

He did not have time to respond. Men in body armor crashed through the door. They all carried assault rifles, and all meant business. Jack jumped out of the way of their bullets. I fell to the ground to avoid the fire. He boarded the flying machine and jetted away. I jumped to my feet and watched my past fly far away. Misfortune had taken its whip to me again!

The soldiers ran at me and knocked me to the floor. The others shot at Jack, but he was too far away. Jack Lamb had escaped me once again.

"Hands above your head!" a soldier yelled at me.

I got to my knees and put my hands on my head. I looked up at the emblem on his body armor. Clearly printed on his chest was "L.I.F.E."

"Dammit, he got away!" I heard somebody say.

My head was then pinned to the ground by a rifle, and I could not see who it was. I did not recognize the voice.

"Let him up," I heard him say.

The men around me backed up and motioned that I could get up. I took my hands off my head and got off the floor.

I analyzed the speaker. He looked much older than the other soldiers, and it was clear that he was the leader. He had a certain force that emanated from his presence. Behind his glasses, his eyes gleamed with excitement. He grinned as he walked up to me.

Putting his hand on my shoulder and with joy encompassing him, he said, "Welcome back, Agent Shepard."

Chapter 19
LIFE

I stared, speechless, at the men before me. Their eyes were steadily on me, unwilling to shift. Anticipation hung around us all, my response not yet given.

"What?" I barely choked out.

"I said, 'Welcome back,'" he repeated.

"But my name isn't Shepard. It's Martin. My name is Martin."

"No, it's not your first name, but your full name is Martin Christopher Shepard," he told me, slowly taking steps away from me with a huge grin on his face.

My gaze was fastened to him, and my mouth had no words to speak. The men under this leader's command lowered their rifles and stood at attention, paying to me a great deal of attention as well.

"Martin, you were an agent working for the Living Improvement and Fullness Enhancement Organization. That's L.I.F.E. for short. We at the L.I.F.E. Organization protect the lives of the people of the world to ensure a better life for all," he told me, turning back and giving me his full focus. "We came here because the man who has created these machines was threatening that quality of life that we so wish to defend. We destroyed most of his machines outside, then we quickly made our way here."

He could see that he was giving me too much information at once. I could not take in the fact that I had just found my past. After a long and fruitless chase, I had stumbled upon it. Not a single word left me. I was entirely frozen in my place, jaw hanging slightly ajar. Machines dropped out of the sky, attacked the city, and led me to the man who led me to my past. I was stunned. Here were the people who were going to tell me all about myself. The answers had come to find me!

"Agent Shepard, we understand your predicament, but, please, if you would come with us to our headquarters outside of Alemande," the leader said, gesturing that I would follow him and his men out of the room.

My mind recovered itself and allowed me to break my catatonic state. My eyes moved to meet the leader's. My head nodded to show my concurrence with what he had said. My body then snapped to attention and awoke me completely of this trance.

"Yes, I shall," I answered confidently and eagerly.

He signaled the team, and we made our way outside.

Outside the building was the destruction of the flying machines. The machines had wrecked the city a considerable amount, but now they lay on the ground, wrecked themselves. More L.I.F.E. agents were taking action, finishing off the rest. They used high-tech weaponry such as strange electric rifles and armor-piercing bullets to take out any machines that were lying broken on the ground. The functioning machines, now that their master was gone, flew away in the direction that Jack had flown. The agents did not follow, for they set their priority with saving me.

Confused citizens and even children wandered the burning streets. Even with all this going on, all the leader did was make gestures to his agents as he continued to lead his squad and myself. With the name of the organization, I assumed that the agents would soon step in to help the people of this city.

As we continued away from the building, I noticed that these agents were not even attempting to help the people of West City. They continued walking around, studying and disabling the machines without any care to be given to those who were frightened and alone. It seemed as if they were only concerned with the machines and me. I wondered if the agents had set their priorities correctly, but my true concern lay elsewhere.

In the distance, several blocks down, I saw a helicopter to which I guessed the leader was taking us. Closer than that, I saw some police officers trying to help citizens. One of the men was Officer Turnbull, who noticed me and looked upon me with disgust. He seemed as if he wanted to confront L.I.F.E. about me, but he was too busy helping his citizens to be concerned with me.

I found it so crazy how, only yesterday, I had been locked within the station in which this man was employed. My life once again seemed to be on the fast track. Life changing events would fly by in such short time. It amazed me how quickly these things were happening.

I boarded the helicopter with the leader. A portion of the team that escorted us there stayed behind to finish up the work that needed to be done. They saluted us as the helicopter rose from the ground and took off to the west.

I did not speak much on this ride. Instead, I took the time to evaluate my situation. All this time, I had searched for the past. Now, I had found it. I still did not know all the details, but they would come when we reached the headquarters. The precious answers would soon be mine.

They took me back to the L.I.F.E. headquarters outside of Alemande. I remembered passing this building the first day of my amnesia recovery. I had somehow recognized it and had wondered for what L.I.F.E. stood. The answers to those questions were now in my possession. This was the Living Improvement and Fullness Enhancement headquarters, and it was there to ensure the bettering of the lives of people everywhere. They used taxpayer dollars in their labs to create technologies that would benefit mankind. I had once worked in this building as Agent Shepard. This was where my past was all along.

The helicopter landed on one of many helipads on the roof. Stepping out of the helicopter, I started the analyzing process once again. I noticed many, many cameras and quite a few guards on the roof. Near the center of the roof seemed to be an elevator that led into the building. The leader continued his fast footsteps towards this.

After entering, he pushed the 5 button code, and we descended into the complex. Exiting from the elevator, we stepped into the building which had held its secrets from me for too long. I walked the halls in amazement. Looking down to the lower floors, I was impressed by the expansiveness of this place. People in professional-looking suits and lab coats dotted the halls, and, without fail, their eyes latched onto me as we passed by.

The leader's path brought us all to his office. He dismissed the other agents and motioned for me to enter as he held the door open for me. He then led me to a chair that was in front of his desk.

The leader's office was considerably sizable and had a huge floor-to-ceiling window that faced the road just outside the building. The floor was made up of large, three-by-three foot tiles of what seemed to be marble. His desk was made of fine mahogany, and high-tech monitors were all around the office. The leader sat down in his expensive and comfortable chair, and I took a seat in front of his desk.

"Shepard, it has come to our attention that you are suffering from retrograde amnesia. How much do you remember?" the leader asked me.

"I can't remember anything before the accident," I answered. He frowned and glimpsed away, then returned his gaze on his former employee.

"Do you remember your training?"

"Yes, but I don't fully understand it."

He nodded, looking down at his desk.

"My name is Zak Kurien, and I am the founder and commander of the L.I.F.E Organization. You used to work here, you know. We lost you in a mission around June of last year," he told me, a weak smile on his face.

"What was the mission and how did I escape the ship?" I asked, eager to know my past.

"The mission was to destroy a boat called the *Annabelle*, which was transporting illegal arms to a small militia outside of Alemande. We sent a zodiac over to the boat and took out the hostiles. It was your assignment to plant the explosives in the engine room. And what would you know, one of the hostiles was hiding down there, and he knocked the gun out of your hands and hit you in the head with something…we think."

"You don't know for sure?"

"No, we don't. But the hostiles were known to be savage brutes, and it is possible that this knocked you out as well as causing your loss of memory. Not wanting the rest of the our team to find you, that brute most likely threw you into the lifeboat and dropped it into the water. When you did not show up, the team searched for you and found the hostile. They killed him and planted the engine room charges in your stead. Not being able to find you and assuming that the hostiles had killed you, they left the boat and detonated the explosives. We had no solid evidence that you were alive until the confrontation with Jack Lamb today. Though, we did have agents tracking you at the end of your time in the West City Mafia. We received many reports about The Beast of Flame, and there were some agents reporting that it was you. Turns out it was."

I now knew what had happened aboard the *Annabelle*. This truth was beyond my ability to predict. I could not have hypothesized this revelation. Now, I was back with the L.I.F.E. Organization, and I had found where I belonged. I would have all the information I needed here.

Then, another question arose. "How did I get my super strength and fighting abilities?" I asked Zak, anxious to finally know the truth.

"Well, you were one of our top agents. You excelled in all of our advanced programs. That training makes you what you are today," he said, looking down at his desk.

"I know I was trained, but my strength and healing is superhuman."

"I don't know about that. But it is a fact that you are a gifted individual. Why do you think we hired you?" he said, still not answering my question.

"But, that is…" I started to say when he cut me off.

"Look, Shepard, you have had quite the day. Why don't you go to your room and rest for a while? I understand the stress that has been put on you in so short a time period. A rest will do you much good. Trust me," the commander instructed me.

I nodded reluctantly.

He led me to my room on the fourth floor. There was a panel beside the door that required a code to unlock the door. Zak motioned to the panel before addressing me.

"All right, Shepard, to open the door, type in '4815162342', and that's it," he said, pushing each number firmly and deliberately.

The door unlocked and slid open. Security must have been very tight since my door had a ten-digit code.

"Do what you wish, Agent Shepard. But do remember, we need to start tracking down Jack Lamb. The computer should have all you need. Enjoy," he said, and then he returned to his office.

I walked into the room and was happily surprised. The room was nearly as furnished as my room in the Vaillancourt was, and it was twice as big. I had a king-sized bed, a 60-inch flat-screen TV, a large bathroom, a computer that had access to the organization's records, and even a kitchen. I opened the curtains to see the breathtaking view of the ocean through my window. It was an awesome room.

On the bed, I found a new expensive suit as well as an I.D. badge. Taking my wallet from my pocket, I slipped the I.D. into the wallet and then changed into the suit that was the uniform of this agency. Wearing the suit, I felt powerful, and it looked good on me. Yes, I truly felt back in my proper place.

I walked over to the computer. There were multiple monitors feeding me tons of information. Its processing power was lightning fast, and it had extensive access to everything I might need to perform my duties.

A file was on my desktop, labeled, "New Assignment". I read up on my new mission. It said that I was to assist in locating Jack Lamb using the global satellite imaging system on the computer. After he had been found, his threat level would be assessed and reported to me. Then, a plan would be devised to capture and kill Jack Lamb, and we would carry it out as soon as possible. This was my mission.

I started by reading about Jack. I went to the computer's database and typed in his name. His file came up, and I clicked on it. A picture of him as well as his height, weight, and age were listed. Reading on, I found that Jack was once an agent for the L.I.F.E. Organization. About four years ago, he had gone rogue and attack the organization. Then, he escaped and could not be located until the incident with the flying fire machines. His location at the moment was unknown. I had been assigned to assist in finding him.

My rival was once in the L.I.F.E. Organization just as I was. Maybe this was what he meant when he referred to being my only friend. He had said something about false hope, and I still did not know what he meant. I would have to ask these questions to Jack Lamb himself before I took his life and my revenge.

I turned on the satellite globe scanner. Real-time pictures of the Earth appeared on my screen. It was fascinating the technology to which I now had access. I zoomed into West City, and I could see that L.I.F.E. had destroyed all the machines and that they were maintaining peace in the city now. Jack Lamb and the machines had taken a path straight south when he had fled. Following that direction led me to a city called Wallace.

Wallace was a city about the size of West City. Nothing unusual was happening in Wallace, but it was the place he most likely was hiding. I would have to wait until he showed his face again.

Scouring the globe, both for work but also for entertainment, for hours, I soon found myself worn out from looking at the screen for so long. I minimized the screen and went back into the database. I typed my name in. My picture popped up. It looked as if it had recently been updated. I could tell because the picture was one from the cameras that took surveillance pictures. They must have closed my file thinking that I was deceased. They had to reopen it when they found me again.

I read my description. Height: 6'4", weight: 229 pounds, age: 19 years. I no longer had to guess my age. I was 19, and now I knew for sure.

In the description, it talked about how I was believed to be dead, but was recently found and taken back into the agency. It said nothing about how I had lost my memory or how I had superhuman abilities. It talked about me as a regular agent. I would have to talk to Commander Zak once again about my unbelievable powers.

I looked at the clock on the wall of my room. It was 4:23 pm. I had skipped breakfast and lunch. I walked into the kitchen and grabbed some pizza out of the freezer. I put it in the oven and lay on my bed. After it was ready, I downed the feast and refilled my empty stomach.

Being quite full, I decided to walk around the L.I.F.E. complex. I typed in the code, and the door slid open. I found it strange that the code had to be entered even from the inside of the door.

Agents waved and nodded at me as I passed them. I knew none of them, but they knew me. This was an uncomfortable feeling for me. One of them stopped me.

"Hello, Agent Shepard. How are you doing, sir?" he asked me.

He addressed me as a sir. What made him do this? Was I of higher rank than he? I did not know if there was even a ranking system between us agents. Whatever the reason, this agent had respect for me.

"I've had some problems locating Jack Lamb, so I left my room for a break. By the way, and please excuse me for this question, who are you?" I responded with a friendly and semi-awkward smile.

"Oh! I'm Agent Turner. I was with you when we took out the *Annabelle*," he said.

"Ah, nice to see you again, Agent Turner," I said and shook his hand.

"It's such a pleasure to have you working here again. You are an incredible agent and a good man," Turner said.

"Thanks. That is very kind of you to say. And it's good to hear. I'm still putting together the pieces of who I was before I lost my memory."

"Well, you're welcome. Don't worry too much about diving back into work. Lots of us are working to find Jack Lamb right now, so it's not all on you. I'm actually on my way back to my room to put in some work."

"I'll let you get on with that then, Agent Turner," I said, and I moved on, as did Turner after a slight chuckle.

Agent Turner, I had known him before. To think that this man had destroyed my boat, I thought it to be quite funny. Surprising, though, that they let a kid handle terrific explosives. I was quite young, and Turner appeared to be only about 20 or so. He was barely older than I!

Yes, this was very strange. Why had they sent us? I had to be only about 18 back then, and they sent me to destroy an illegal arms boat? I was very young to be working for an organization like this. Maybe they had selected young agents because they could train them before they hit their prime, and then they would be huge assets when they grew up. I did not understand this, but I would probably ask Commander Zak later.

The complex was terribly big and had much to offer, but I decided to go to the rec room first. The room looked as if it were a crucial asset to the organization, for it appeared to have had a ton of money thrown at it. Several agents were sitting around watching a movie, and others were playing some military-based game. The game was called Firefight. I had remembered this game from when I was in the mafia and had played it in my room. Perhaps it was considered a training device for these agents who would find themselves in a firefight from time to time. It was most likely just there for entertainment and decompression, though. I took a seat next to the agents.

"Who's who?" I asked them, referring to who was each player in the game.

One of the agents responded, "I'm top left, she's top right, he's bottom left, and he's bottom right," she told me.

I watched them, eager to make some friends in this place. After the game ended, they all turned around to greet me. The agent who had talked to me introduced herself.

"I'm Agent Bestwick," she said, throwing me the controller.

"And I'm Agent Lowry," one of the guys said.

"Hey, I'm David Stafford...uh...I mean, Agent Stafford," the other guy said, suddenly embarrassed by his slip up.

"Rookie," the other girl said, shoving Agent Stafford. "I'm Agent Braae," she said. "Rebecca Braae," she teased David, shooting him a mocking smile.

"Okay, I'm pretty sure I can remember those names. I'm Martin Shepard... Ah, crap! I mean Agent Shepard," I said, teasing David.

He looked annoyed, but the rest of the group howled. I had made friends. These people were exactly what I needed in my life now that everything was changing so quickly. Some people to lean on from my past would help me adjust here.

They were also agents of my age. Not one of them could have been any older than 25 years old! I did not really understand many things about the world because of my amnesia, but I did know some things. I knew that it was strange to have so few agents in an organization be over the age of 30.

They started another round of Firefight, and I beat them all, quickly adapting to the controls. I knew they could not defeat me, even in this game, and it became too easy. I held back my skill to some level as to not frustrate my friends into giving up entirely, but I still beat them every round.

"Man, I'm hungry. We should get something to eat here," said Agent Lowry.

"Let's do it. You coming with, Shepard?" Agent Braae asked me.

"Sure. I can always eat."

We went down to the food court and had a dinner consisting of burgers and fries. Despite the food court's small appearance, I counted over twenty agents eating. Televisions on the walls blared with sports that many of the agents were all too eager to actively watch. We sat at a table in the center of the room. This presented us a little elbow room away from the rambunctiousness of the game's spectators.

It was strange meeting agents here that were about my age. I did not know why the agency would hire such young agents. I guessed now that they ranged from 19 to 22 years old, just slightly older than I was on average.

Not that there were not agents who were adults, but the younger ones outnumbered them easily. To have an even split of young to old would have been odd, but to have such a majority be young was something of which I took note. This organization got results, good ones, and I guessed that was the main goal. Their focus was on protecting and serving the masses. However they were achieving it must have been working for them.

Many agents came and went as they talked to me. I informed them on the what the leading theory to how I lost my memory was, my previous encounters with Jack Lamb, and what I would say to him when we found him. They were interested in the story, and I continued to tell them about how I had come back here. My story bounced around from the mafia to my family by the sea. I told them how I had broken into the Alemande News archives and how I had killed the three men in the subway.

Agent Lowry stiffened up at the mention of the three men in the subway.

"Do you know who they were?" Lowry asked, leaning towards me.

"One of the men introduced himself as Jimmy Hanson. I did not know the names of the other two," I said.

An aggravated look came across his face.

"You killed three men, and you didn't even know two of their names?" said Lowry, visibly upset.

Agent Bestwick put her hand on his shoulder. The look went away, and he loosened up. He then suggested that he go do some more research for his mission. He left the table and went back to his room. I was confused but said nothing.

"Agent Lowry is right. I should probably go get some more work done for my assignment," I said and got up. The other agents got up with me and said goodbye. They walked away, and I left to go back to my room.

On the way back to my room, I thought about Agent Lowry's response to my mentioning the three men in the subway. Being an agent, he should have been accustomed to hearing about death. One explanation was that he thought the men were innocent. As part of this organization, it was his job to deeply care about protecting the innocent. He probably thought that the men were police and mistook me for a criminal. Thinking that I was deadly, they used more force.

Why, then, would they pull a switchblade on me? They could not have been police, and Lowry should have caught on to that. I did not know who they were, but I would have to ask Commander Zak about it. Surely, he would not have all the answers I needed, but there was hope that he could clear up a few of the blurry details.

Lowry's judgment of me stuck in my mind, and I could not let it go. Another explanation was that he was disgusted by how quickly I moved to kill the men whose names I had not even asked. This man fought to save people daily, and it was obvious that he understood the value of life. He must have been judging my instinctual decision to kill my attackers instead of incapacitating them. This explanation made sense,   and I began to question whether or not I had made the right decision in killing the men. His judgment convicted me to my core.

It happened so fast. Jimmy tried to stab me, and I broke his arm without barely knowing what I was doing. I had dodged around the other one, and it ended in his broken neck. Had I known that was going to happen? When I punched the other attacker in the throat, did I know it was going to crush his trachea? I must have, but could I have stopped myself? These ponderings were beginning to upset me, too, so I put them away and turned my thoughts back to the L.I.F.E. complex.

I could have returned to my work at my room, but I decided to take a tour of more of the facilities within this building instead. My first stop was on the ground floor where the food court was located. I entered the weapons tech lab. Upon my entering, a woman looked up from her work. She appeared to be in her forties. In front of her was what looked to be one of the disassembled fire-breathing machines.

"What are you doing here, Agent Shepard?" the woman questioned, her hands restlessly continuing her work while her eyes were on me.

"I'm just taking a look around, trying to spark some semblance of a memory. What is it you're doing with that thing?" I said, moving closer to her and the machine.

"Me? I'm dissecting one of Jack Lamb's terrorist machines. If I do my job right, we could really do some good with this thing," she said, yanking a device from the beast.

"Good coming from a death machine? That sounds pretty contradictory to me."

"We…uh…just wanted part of it. Not the whole thing," she said, showing me the device she had pulled from the machine.

"Ah, those. They are inertial-propulsion devices, aren't they? I, too, am curious about how they work," I told her as she set the device into my open hands.

"Yes, yes, they're incredibly interesting. And their possible applications are astronomically more interesting. We wish to get this technology back to the world. It could revolutionize transportation as we know it!" she said excitedly as I held the device in the air and inspected it in awe.

"Sounds smart to me. By the way, what is your name?" I asked, handing the device back to her.

"My name? It's Ryan. Ryan Vicek," she said and set the device on the table so that she could shake my hand.

"It's very nice to meet you, Ryan. And you already know who I am. I'm going to continue my walk, but know that I am very interested in the work you are doing here and wish you the best with all you're doing. I will let you get back to it."

"Thank you! I hope to see you around…Agent Shepard," she said as I closed the door.

Inertial-propulsion technology, it sounded amazing. Here it was now, in a lab with talented hands to develop it and return it to where it should be. L.I.F.E. would take this technology and improve upon it, making it a proper gift back to society. To think that this organization was created simply to better mankind; I loved it. This was a government organization I could get behind!

My next stop was the medical labs. The talented men and women here worked on new medicines and techniques that would be implemented to save lives. The department was on the second floor. As I opened the door, I heard a slight commotion. When I looked in, a startled doctor slammed a door, locked it, and turned back to me.

"Ah! Martin…I-I mean Agent Shepard…what brings you here?" the frightened doctor asked me, almost guarding the door with his body.

"Is something wrong, Doctor?"

"No, nothing. I'm just testing a new drug. Hopefully, it will bring about all new cures for some of the world's worst diseases!"

"That sounds terrific! But what was with all the noise? What's behind the door?"

"My assistant is just working with the drug and must be left alone. I walked in the room and…heh heh, immediately turned back and locked the door. I don't want to contaminate anything, you know!" he answered, chuckling from the nervousness of his close call.

"I see. Well, I hope it works. You definitely have my support, Doctor. The world has too many diseases and not enough cures."

"We can only hope that it works, Martin. But I do need to get back to work here. You must excuse me," the doctor said.

"All right then, I will leave you to it. Good luck," I said and began to leave.

As I was leaving, the other door opened. Walking out, I heard the assistant ask for the doctor's help. His voice sounded urgent. I feared that the drug would not be successful.

I climbed the stairs after visiting a few more rooms. They had psychology departments and armories. They even had labs dedicated to understanding the potential of nuclear fusion. Many labs and departments crowded the first and second floors. The third and fourth floors were strictly for housing of the agents and other facility workers. The fifth floor had offices all around it, including Zak's. His was the largest and, obviously, the most well-furnished. In the center of the building was the elevator that led to the roof.

I remembered the general size and shape of the building from when I had observed it from the helicopter. It had a rectangular base that lasted three floors. The remaining two floors were in the shape of a square and were centered on the base. On the two roofs of the third floor were many helipads and helicopters, the same as the highest roof of the building, but with the addition of missile implements on the corners of the building. Its back was right at the cliff's edge. After the building, there was nothing but a drop into the glimmering ocean. In front of the building was the road on which I first traveled.

I thought of the location of the L.I.F.E. complex. It was positioned in an expansive forested area at the top of the highest cliff in the area between the town of Alemande and Jonah's house. It was right off the road but all the same mysterious. Why was it here? I supposed it was because this area was so open and out of the way. It could be easily guarded from anyone who meant harm. No one could sneak up on this place, and, with the technology inside, no one could stand a chance against the force of the L.I.F.E. Organization.

I got to the fourth floor of the building. Before going back to my room to do more research, I went to see Commander Zak in his office. I climbed another floor and went to the front of the building.

I entered the room. In front of Zak's desk was a man leaning forward in his chair, speaking in a loud voice.

"And that's what…" I heard the man say, but then he noticed me.

Zak saw me and made a gesture to the man.

"You are dismissed, Agent Grimes," he said.

The agent left the room and acknowledged me as he passed. I nodded back and came into the office. I felt as if I remembered this man.

"What is it you need, Agent Shepard?" my commander asked me.

"I need to know who the men in the subway were. The one's who tried to kill me."

He motioned for me to sit down, and I did. He thought for a second.

"I really don't know who those men were. Is there anybody who would want you dead, Agent Shepard? Anyone who I wouldn't know about in this organization?"

I thought for a second. The only people who aggressively tried to kill me were the Pirates. I never thought that these men had been Pirates, and I doubted they were. The tactics I had seen from either of them differed, as did their clothing, but I thought they were worth mentioning to my boss.

"There was a gang in West City called the Pirates. They could have wanted me dead," I said. He thought for a second. His eyes then lit up, and he leaned closer to me.

"Wait, the Pirates you say?" he asked in a hushed tone.

"Yeah, they were a rival gang when I was in the West City Mafia. We had several conflicts between us, and they held a section of the city that we wished to take. So we took them out," I answered him.

"The boat you helped destroy, the *Annabelle*, was carrying illegal arms to a group called the Pirates. We thought they were a small militia who set up around the coast, but it is possible that they were stationed in West City," he said, leaning back.

It made sense now. No wonder the Pirates had such expensive explosives and weapons. They were getting weapon shipments from the *Annabelle* for a while before it was destroyed. It was also most likely why they had the explosives that they used to blow up the Vaillancourt Hotel to take revenge on us. It all made sense.

"I think that clears things up a lot for me. Thank you for the information, sir."

"Anything else you need, Agent Shepard?"

I thought for a moment and remembered what I was going to ask him earlier.

"Commander, I need to know about how I got these powers."

He paused momentarily as if he did not know to what I was referring. Then an exaggerated look of revelation came over his face, and he leaned back before answering my question.

"Oh, your powers! Well…I wouldn't necessarily call them powers, but you definitely are special. Why do you think we hired you? With those kinds of powers…uh…strengths, I guess...why wouldn't we want you on the team?" he said with an uneasy smile.

"Yes, but how did I get these powers?" I asked again.

"Well…we do have a very strict training policy for our agents..." he said, repeating what he had said earlier.

"I did not get these powers from excessive training. Now, tell me how I got them," I told him, much more demandingly. As soon as the words left my mouth, I knew that I had made a mistake. I was commanding my boss to do as I said, and that was quite out of place on my part. The little cooperation I was getting from this man was now lost, but it did not matter, anyway. This man was not going to tell me what I wanted to hear.

He stood to his feet above me, breathing out anger heavily.

"I think you are forgetting your place, agent. Now, go back to your room and get back to work on finding Jack Lamb! That's an order!" he shouted.

Odium became me. This man was hiding something; he was withholding the truth! I gripped the armrests of my chair with a similar rage as my boss, but with more muscle behind it. If he was going to lie to me, then I would just have to find the truth for myself. I was the best there was at finding the truth.

I went back to my room and typed in the code. The door slid open, and I went in and lay on the bed. I was frustrated that I could not find out the source of my powers, but I soon fell asleep after this long day. I needed the rest desperately, and rage could not keep me from my sleep.

My dreams were haunted by Jack Lamb. He moved within them, impossible to catch. He truly was an opponent that would be a challenge for me. Fighting him that first day… I had no chance against him. I still did not completely understand what had occurred in that ring that day.

Jack Lamb was strong, smart, and experienced. I was strong and smart but not experienced. At least, not then. I now had much more fighting experience, a year of it. I knew I could find and kill this menace. He would not be better than I for too much longer. I would prove to him that I had what it took.

Waking up in the morning, I checked the computer. Nothing unusual presented itself on the screen. I searched around for a while, but the results were the same as when I had started. I got up, changed into my suit, and left the room.

The first thing I had to do was to attend a debriefing of all that had happened to me during my absence from the organization. I told them about Jonah's family, the mafia, and everything in between. I hid nothing from my interrogators, for they were on my side. We were finally done after my hour long story as well as many questions from the agents. They permitted me to leave and returned my agent status officially.

This day in the complex went the same as the last. I looked around the place, searching rooms for fragments of my past. I learned new things from my surroundings, but information on my past was not readily available at this time. Agents gave me short answers that never really answered my questions. Commander Zak was busy at meetings throughout the day, and so I was not able to discuss my previous employment with him. Even when I went to the daily agent briefing in the afternoon, Zak left before I asked a question. I made no advances in completing the recovery of my past this day.

Another two days went by in the same manner. Talking, searching, being ignored, and wandering aimlessly were my daily tasks. I felt as though I had already found everything about my past and that there was nothing left to discover. I could not give up hope. There had to be more to this story.

I returned to my bed after looking through maps for Jack Lamb. Fruitless was the word I used to describe the digital manhunt. Lying down on that bed, I felt my eyelids become heavy and I knew that escape from this mundane search would come soon. I fell asleep not too much later.

When I woke up, I heard a beeping nearby. I looked around. First, I noticed that it was 9 o'clock in the morning. Also, my computer screen was flashing. I ran over and checked it out. My real-time satellite map was still set on the city of Wallace. The beeping was a warning that the police had been sent to Wallace in mass amounts.

I looked at their position. A building was on fire, and the police surrounded it as well as firefighters. A police car exploded, and I zoomed in. The machines were surrounding the building and destroying the police's forces.

Before I could react to contact Zak, he popped up on my screen.

"Attention, agents! Good work completing your scout mission. You could have found him before he attacked another city, but nothing we can do about it now. Now, we must confront Jack and terminate him. We can show no mercy. I'm putting together a team of ten of you. You all will be heavily-armed, and you, Agent Shepard, will lead the team. There is no chance we can't capture Jack if you are with us, Agent Shepard."

Strangely, his words reminded me of Keir Sanzano's words. Keir was always confident that, with me, we could not lose. Zak was the same way.

It was time to kill the man who had ruined my chances of a normal life. The opportunity to knock him around as he had done to me was now mine. I would defeat him in front of the whole world. This was my rematch, and the victory was mine to seize. This man's life would be taken, and I would have saved the city. I would be a hero, and he would be out of my life. This was revenge, and it was time to take it.

Chapter 20
Vengeance

After donning the body-armor in the bottom drawer of my dresser, I hurried downstairs to the armory, where I met the rest of the team. There was everything from combat knives to rocket launchers in this one place, positioned artistically on the walls and also hanging commonly from the ceiling. The other nine agents were in here, and so was Commander Zak.

"Are you ready?" my boss asked me.

He had just asked me if I was ready to kill the man who had ruined a great part of my life. I nodded my head in obvious confirmation.

"Good. Now, the ACR over there and two of the auto pistols over there, you three can take that," he said, pointing as he spoke. "Now, Dutt, Bird, Long, and Shepard grab a grenade belt and a tactical vest," he continued.

The three other agents and I took what we had been ordered to take. The others did so with an almost bored demeanor. This was common for them. For me, this was exciting and new, but they practically were yawning at the prospect of our mission. I wrapped the belt around me after putting on the vest.

"And grab a gas mask and five of our combat knives," he said to us again, pointing still.

I put on the gas mask and put the knives in the holders of the tactical vest.

"Shepard, you take these as well," he said, handing me two large, shiny pistols. "Those can put gaping holes in Jack Lamb's machines. Use them well."

The guns had a different weight than what I had used before. I ejected the magazine and inspected the bullets. They were big, heavy, and made out of a strange material that I could not identify. These were unusual weapons, but, from what the Commander had said, they would prove most useful in this fight.

Zak turned back to the others.

"You three," he said. "Grab those RPGs."

They eagerly grabbed them and put the extra rockets in a backpack.

"You three," he said, turning to the other three agents. "Grab those light machine guns and guided rockets."

They put the gun on their back and held the rockets.

"And lastly, you, Shepard, grab that," he said, pointing.

Following his finger, I saw what appeared to be a gun. Its general shape seemed like that of a gun, but it looked much different. It was oddly oversized and had a lens at the end of the barrel. I grabbed the strange-looking weapon.

"That is our prototype laser blaster, the L-1000. It works like any other gun. Just point and shoot. It's incredibly powerful, so keep that in mind when you use it. And one more thing, Shepard. As soon as you see him, you are to fire this at Jack Lamb's head. No hesitation. Got it?" he said, looking over his glasses at me.

"Yes, sir," I responded.

He grinned and said, "Good to hear. Now, we're ready to move out. You know our target well, agents. This man is extremely dangerous, and you should have no hesitation in killing him. He won't have any for you. The chopper is on the roof."

There was a pause in his speech. He glanced around the room at the ten of us. His eyes landed lastly on me, where they rested momentarily. He saw something in me that he would not tell me. A smirk came from the the corner of his mouth.

"It's time. Let's make the world a better place, agents! Move out!"

We all saluted and marched out of the room.

The team then went to the elevator and took it to the top of the complex where a high-tech battle helicopter was waiting for us. On the large sliding door of the helicopter, L.I.F.E. was painted in the center. We piled in, and the helicopter took off.

I felt as I did when I was heading to take out the Pirates. I had just suited up and boarded a vehicle that would take me to the enemy. Only this time, my target was one man with an army of death machines. I had a smaller team, but we were better trained and better armed. Our mission was to execute a threat, and that was what we would do.

I looked at the equipment that covered all my body. I wore steel-toed boots, armored pants, an armored tactical vest, a gas mask, and a grenade belt wrapped around my waist. Holstered at my hips were the two high-powered pistols and ammunition for them was in my vest. On my back was the laser gun. I felt completely invincible with all this equipment. I knew Jack Lamb could not defeat me now.

I took the laser gun from my back to inspect it further. It amazed me what L.I.F.E. was able to create. The laser gun seemed to consist of multiple lenses, a core of many different magnets, and something liquid inside. I guessed the liquids were for a chemical reaction that would excite photons at an accelerated rate. The chemicals mixed, creating the reaction, the beam was directed through magnets which controlled the wavelength, and then the lenses shot the beam out of the gun. The technology was astounding.

I returned the laser gun to my back when I noticed that the agent next to me was leaning in closer.

"Are you the memory loss guy?" he asked, yelling over the noise of the helicopter.

"Yes, I am. Agent Shepard," I yelled back, shaking his hand.

"Agent Long, T.J. Long."

I paused for a second, noticing that he gave me his first name. "Aren't you not supposed to say your first name?"

"Hell, who cares if you know my first name? L.I.F.E. regulations state we're not to give our first names to those outside the organization; that's it. Zak isn't going to do a thing about me giving it to you. Anyway, if I hadn't told you my first name, you would have spent this whole ride thinking about what it might be instead of thinking about blowing Jack's head off."

That was quite true. I had wondered what the first names of Agents Bestwick, Lowry, and Turner were. I always felt a little better knowing the agents' first names. There was a better connection between us because of it.

T.J. sat back, and I studied the rest of the crew. I noticed that Agent Turner was here on this mission, too, only about five feet from me.

I leaned closer to him. "Agent Turner," I yelled. He turned to me.

"Yes? What do you need, Agent Shepard?" he asked.

"What is your first name? You didn't tell me when we spoke before." He stopped for a second. He looked around himself before answering.

"My name is Adam," he said, chuckling a little.

T.J. smiled at the thought that he had planted an idea in my head.

"What's your name?" I asked the woman next to Adam.

"My name's Deveyn Dutt," she said.

Already, I felt much better knowing their names. I asked the rest of the crew their names before we arrived in Wallace.

The city of Wallace soon came into sight. I saw the fiery terror swarming a building in the distance. Jack Lamb was there, down somewhere in that building. I clenched my laser rifle anxiously.

Zak said very clearly to shoot him in the head. A laser of this magnitude, you would think, would kill a man even if you shot him in the chest. Why would the Commander tell me to shoot him in the head? A shot like that would be complete overkill. Perhaps overkill was called for with a threat of this caliber.

If he could survive and defeat me in the ring, then he could probably take a bullet or two. The man was tough, smart, clever, and fast. Jack would be a hard target, but I would walk up to him, say a final remark, and shoot him in the head. I would end the miserable life of my rival without a second thought.

The helicopter approached the building. Screeching filled the air as it opened fire on the machines. Missiles flew and hit their targets. When a spot to land had been cleared, we dropped down near the ground. I was first to hit the ground and then opened fire on the beasts with my laser.

The laser was amazing. A single blast shattered the shell of the machine and took out the tank. Such monsters were destroyed almost instantly. These weapons were unfathomably powerful. I fired at them until one of the agents put a hand on me.

"Don't waste all your fire on the Spheres. Remember our primary target," she reminded me, pointing to the building.

I nodded and let them take out the rest. I assisted with my pistols instead. Obviously not as powerful, the pistols still worked wonders. When we had cleared the area well enough, we moved to the inside.

I planted a breaching charge on the door and backed away while the team took out the machines with guided missiles and machine guns. I blew the charge, and the entire door flew into the building. Machines and flames flooded out. The team took their attention away from the sky and aimed at the extruding Spheres.

I got out of their way and opened fire with my pistols. A Sphere fired back at me. A dodge got me out of the path of the flames. Within the second, another machine was positioned, ready to cook me alive. My reflexes took me to safety once again but only momentarily, for fire came at me from a third one to my side. I dodged, and Adam took it out for me.

There was no question about it. These beasts of flame were after me. Knowing that I was the secret weapon of L.I.F.E., Jack Lamb was trying to kill me. I would not let him, and neither would my team. No matter how hard Jack tried, he would not win the rematch. I was to be the victor today.

We moved on into the inside. As we climbed the inside of the building, many booby traps endangered our lives, but we moved carefully and stopped to disarm every one. With level heads and patient caution, no one was hurt. We proceeded slowly but safely.

The fire-breathing Spheres crashed through the halls as we made our ascent. We neutralized every one. They might have been too big for the halls, but that did not keep them from smashing through them. The team and I smashed back and fought through the building.

About halfway through the building, the rooms became too numerous for us to search them quickly. We split up into five groups of two. It was T.J. and I who searched for Jack at the top. The rest of the team took the lower floors.

I was glad to be paired with T.J., for he was an intelligent man and a skilled agent. Not one trap delayed us. Not one machine slowed us down. My partner was quite well-trained. Paired with me, he could not be stopped.

He led the charge through the few floors before the top, and I followed shortly behind him, watching our flank. I noticed something while looking at the back of T.J.'s head. They were hard to see, but he had faint scars that wrapped around his hairline by his ears. Given his profession, my guess would have been war wounds, but the lines were precise and symmetric, suggesting surgical scars. Had T.J. undergone some sort of brain surgery? In he midst of our fight, I had no time to ask him.

I grabbed my laser gun as we approached the door to the final room on the top floor. I took a breath before looking at T.J. to see if he was ready. He nodded, and I readied myself. Then, I kicked in the door.

Jack Lamb did not wait for us here. All that was here for us was a deadly surprise. Something pulled a tripwire, and gas filled the air. Suddenly, small metal balls flew through the air. I dodged to the side, but T.J. did not. Five balls struck his gas mask, rendering it useless. As holes were punctured in his mask, the gas entered. He took a breath, and that was all he needed. It filled his lungs, and his muscles seized. As if he had become inanimate in that instance, he collapsed to the floor, rigid. I ran to him and tried to help, but there was nothing I could do. His body then wildly contorted on the floor. It only took three seconds for him to die.

I stood up above the body of a man whose kindness was recently given to me, furious. Jack Lamb would pay. He had killed my new friend. He had ruined my life. He had made me look like an idiot in the ring. I would avenge T.J. and take my revenge. He had gone too far, and now there was nothing holding me back from shooting him in the head. But I would make him suffer. Oh, how I would make him suffer! He would die slowly for all that he had done. I would rightfully take revenge for everything this man had done to me. Vengeance would be mine!

I left T.J. there and entered the gas room. To the left of me were stairs that led to the roof. I climbed up them and opened the door to the roof. When I reached the top, I saw over twenty machines circling overhead. Before me, a horrid villain stood as well.

He stood, silently watching his creation. I watched with him as they took down the helicopter on which I had ridden to Wallace. Instruments blared, and the pilot jumped out, flames already consuming him. The burning helicopter death spiraled violently, plummeting to the ground. Jack was a cold-blooded killer, and I would not let him get away with it.

I stepped out of the doorway and closed the door behind me. Feeling rage flowing through me, I moved forward to confront Jack Lamb. With my laser gun pointed at his back, I yelled to him. He turned around very calmly.

"Are you enjoying the fireworks, dear Martin?" he asked with that cruel grin.

I fired at him. He stepped to the side, taunting me as the blast whizzed by him. Even though the laser blasts traveled at the speed of light, I could not hit him. I fired again and again, missing each time. He laughed at me knowing that, with his speed, I could not hit him. My aiming could not match his dodging.

Frustrated to my last nerve, I dropped the laser and threw the pistols. I ripped off my gas mask and threw my vest to the ground. Unburdened by what I no longer needed, I marched forward to my foe and punched him hard in the jaw. He let me, knowing that I could not really hurt him.

"That was for T.J.," I yelled at him.

"For T.J.? The name is not in my memory, and I have not the brilliant excuse that you do. Tell me; should I know this name? Or can you not recall one remarkable trait of the man whose name you bring to me? Should memory of his name be as worthless as the memory of my dinner three years ago?" Jack questioned, knowing it would only anger me further.

I held back my anger. I needed to ask him questions.

"Why did you want me to destroy the L.I.F.E. Organization?" I asked him.

He smiled and said, "Martin, you were never one for trivial means. You have limited your questions to only those of great importance."

He was complimenting me, but I said nothing.

"Yes, an important question it is, but I shall not answer it."

"Why not?"

"Why should a man be given a rod before being given the fish it provides? You need to find your own answers, Martin...and I know you to be beyond capable."

"Why do you say that?"

"As I have said it, you have no poor questions. Answers can be given to you, or they can be taken by you. Quality finds itself in the deed, not the reward. I say that I know your capability to be past adequate because you have made it this far. Of course, I never doubted to find you returned to my company."

"Jack, please answer me this. How do I find the truth?"

"You seek a horrible truth. It resides in the L.I.F.E. database."

I was confused. Obviously, he knew I would have already looked in there.

"What do you want me to look for?"

"Search for that for which you have always been searching. Search for you. Search for me. The information there pertaining to us is that truth which you have sought."

"I've already tried that. Why wouldn't I have?"

"My apologies to you, dear Martin. I have given credit to you past the point at which you are due. Know that you sleep among the greatest of deceivers. They have shown you only what they wanted you to see. They have given you a pleasant lie, not the horrible truth they hide. That lies deep within their archives, buried by the past. Buried, I say, because they could not bear to destroy such evidence. Yes, they would not risk losing the memory of what you are. A lesson that must not be forgotten."

His words twisted around me and brought more confusion than clarity. What I was? What did he mean? Why would he not tell me what was happening?

"Why are you doing this?" I asked.

"As I see it as obvious, none see as I see. My destruction is a magnet of strongest pull to the L.I.F.E. Organization. With its presence, I am given a beautiful opportunity to make those derisory agents drown in their blood."

"Why do you want to kill them if you were once one of them?"

"Shall I say it again? You sleep with liars!"

I sighed. "Thank you for the information."

"You are terribly welcome, Martin. Although my words may ring dull to your unrefined ear, I shall say that L.I.F.E. is…" he was saying, but I stopped him halfway with my combat knife.

I stabbed it through his chest repeatedly. His white shirt became dark red as the knife jumped through and retreated with such repetition. Then, I put it through his throat. The blade went through the jugular, and I ripped it back out viciously. Blood flooded out onto my hands. The red mist dampened my arms, legs, chest, and face. He backed away and fell on his back with a thud in which I heard nothing but victory.

"It appears I have won the rematch," I said pridefully, and I turned away from that loser. I had done it now. I was the triumphant one. It was so easy. He was mortal as I. Jack Lamb could never be better than I.

I started to pick up my gear, when I heard soft chuckling behind me. Horrified by this sound, I froze. Every hair on my body stood, and ferocious chills ran up my spine. I had to force myself to turn around and face the sound. Behind me stood Jack, still bleeding through his neck, standing at his full height. I watched as the blood went from a pouring to a drizzle to a complete stop. The skin separated by my knife stitched itself together. His laughing continued as he walked up to me again, my triumph no longer with me. His eyes were crazy with giddy joy. I gazed at him, truly terrified by what I was seeing.

"What makes us do that?" I asked in horror.

"My dear Martin, are you finally beginning to understand?" he asked me, reeking of his fluids and shaking in manic excitement. "You ask the most important question of all. But as I have said before, hear me again; I shall not answer it!"

The man threw back his head and let loose his insanity. His laughing echoed throughout the city of Wallace. Not one nook or cranny was safe from the oppressive blanket of despair that flowed through this man's mouth. I stood, motionless, too afraid to do anything but listen. His laughter burrowed into my soul. It was the laughter of a man who had lost everything, but more than that. It was the laughter of a man from whom everything had been stolen.

This man was a monstrosity. He had gone crazy with rage. His abilities were similar to mine, but he was so much more. He lived to kill as I did. He could heal within seconds and packed the punch of a semi. He was unstoppable and would not stop on his own. The only thing that could kill him was one who was the same. The duty fell on my shoulders.

"Answer this, you monster!" I yelled as I put the laser gun to his convulsing chin. Pulling the trigger, I ended the monster's life. His head exploded from the blast, and his body collapsed to the ground. I stood over the man who had ruined my life. He was dead and could not ruin me further.

I backed away from him. I heard footsteps behind me.

"Agent Shepard," I heard behind me. "Well done."

It was Adam. The rest of the team followed. I watched as the machines fell out of the sky. The team had disabled the main control system of the machines. They had no more controls and terminated. The whole ordeal was over.

Overwhelmed by the situation, I shut my eyes and slapped my hands over my ears. What was happening to me? What insanity was befalling my own life? Who was I really?

I opened my eyes and uncovered my ears. My fellow agents stood around the corpse of my former rival. He was dead by my hands. His chaos had died with him. This had been the task assigned to me. Now, it had been finished.

Words from my greatest friend echoed in my head.

"Mission complete."

Chapter 21
The Horrible Truth

L.I.F.E. sent another helicopter to pick up the team, and it arrived after a couple hours. During my wait, I sat away from the rest of my team and retreated into myself. I reflected on the deed I had done. I killed a man, a man who was possibly once an ally, and I killed him unfairly, taking a cheap shot when he was in the droves of madness. As the others rejoiced, I sat away and shook, terrified at what I was still. I was still a monster.

After the helicopter landed on Jack Lamb's roof, agents stepped off to document the death of our target. Pictures were taken of the body, and prints and blood samples were gathered. The kill had to be confirmed. They would not stop examining the body until they were assured that this was Jack Lamb and that he was gone forever. I had made this task difficult for them because they could not use facial recognition on him. They might have worried that it was not he, but I did not. I knew it was he because of the feeling of satisfaction I now had. Jack Lamb, my rival, was dead.

After all Jack Lamb had done to me, I was finally done with him. He was out of my life. All of him was gone. He could not stand in the way of my life any longer. Yet, to tell the truth, I felt as if I was going to miss Jack. Perhaps it was just the challenge he provided, but I knew my life was going to be different without him. Not that it mattered. Jack Lamb was gone for good.

Unfortunately, I had not fully rid myself of his influence on my life. Terrible guilt filled me for what I had done. These conflicting emotions felt as if they would rip me apart. I was so glad to have killed Jack Lamb, but I was also so disgusted. I knew he was a monster and the world would be better off without him, but I, too, had proven that I was of the same kind. Attempting to break away from the guilty happiness, I stood and boarded the helicopter. I just wanted to leave this place.

After Jack's body had been quite thoroughly inspected, we took off. I stared down next to the bag in which my deceased friend, T.J., was. It interested me that, in about an hour, this man had made himself a friend to me. The first time I had met him was in this helicopter about five hours ago.

Somehow, he had made me feel as if we had been friends for a much longer time. I wondered if the L.I.F.E. agents were trained for things like that. I wondered if we were trained to work ourselves into a person's life. That kind of training would be needed in an organization that was like this. It was odd to think I might have had a manufactured friendship with this man. The one thing I could say was that this man had made himself a friend to me.

The death made me think of a person whom I had forgotten in the chaos of my life. Just four days ago, Tyler was sent to jail while I was sent away free. I was going to save him, but when the machines attacked, I must have been distracted from him.

The thought was funny in my mind. It was funny that an intervention of fiery death machines was the only thing that would keep me from breaking into that jail and setting him free. I would save Tyler. I would not let him rot in jail because he would not do that to me. Tyler would be free, and he would be free soon.

As these thoughts went through my head, I was too distracted to notice that the agent who was sitting next to me, Abe as he had introduced himself, was reaching for my laser gun. I was too distracted thinking about T.J. and Tyler to defend myself from this thief.

Before I could react, Abe had the gun and pointed it at my head. Out of the corner of my eye, I saw this. My instincts kicked in, and I hit the gun away from my head. It went off and put a hole in the roof of the helicopter. That is not the best place for a laser to go off. It destroyed the rotor, and the helicopter dropped out of the sky.

Only one thought went through my head before I jumped. Why did this man attempt to kill me? I fell through the sky towards a building below.

My body hit the roof of a building, rolled, and flipped around. I watched as the helicopter slammed into the adjacent building. It burst into flames as it demolished itself in the collision. None survived. It was all because of a rogue agent. This man killed the rest of them even though he just wanted to kill me. The helicopter fell through the roof and into the building. He was a madman who did not get for what he bargained.

Then, another thought came into my head. What if the agent was one of the men who tried to kill me back on the subway? What if he was a Pirate? If he was, he would have definitely earned respect. He had infiltrated a top government agency and tried to kill its secret weapon. Instead, he killed the other agents. He had completed his mission even if his mission was to kill me. The agents in that helicopter were about as strong as me if you combined them all. He had done his final duty for the Pirates.

Of course, there were other possibilities. What if he was not a Pirate? What if he was indeed in the L.I.F.E. agency? What if the L.I.F.E. Organization wanted me dead? I remembered what Jack had advised me to do. He said to go to their archives and to find his file. He also wanted me to look at my file.

His words now made sense. I was sleeping with liars! These agents were pretending to be my friends so that they could get close enough to kill me. That was their real mission. They needed to kill anybody like Jack and me. They wanted to kill us, people with superpowers. I would not let them. I would stand against the L.I.F.E. Organization, and I would not back down.

My mission now was to get back to the L.I.F.E. headquarters and find out the truth. I would have to act like I had no idea what was happening. If I confronted them and let them know I knew what they were doing, they would try to kill me again, and my opportunity to get the truth would be lost. My return needed to be dramatic and threatening to put them on their toes. Obviously, no one would be pleased that they had been shot out of a helicopter. They would bring me inside and debrief me. When I got back to my room, I could sneak out. Then, I would know the truth.

I began to walk towards the subway to head back to Alemande, but then I remembered something. My friend was still in jail. I would have to make a detour before going back to the L.I.F.E. headquarters. I went to West City using the subway trains.

I got off the train and started for the police station. I was ready to extract Tyler. I still had my vest which I had snuck into the subway. I had hidden my pistols and a few knives in there. I had convinced the subway management to give me a free ride on the train by telling them I was a government agent. They allowed me passage upon seeing my L.I.F.E badge. Then, I just walked onto the train.

After leaving the train and the station, I walked through the West City streets, focused on the job I would have to do. I passed the ruins of the Vaillancourt Hotel. I had never thanked Tyler for getting me out of there before it exploded. My friend would greet freedom and my thanksgiving today.

As I approached the police station, I pulled out the pistols. I opened fire on the cars outside the station. Lobbing a grenade beneath one of the vehicles, I watched the parking lot light up. My steps took me through the blaze stoically, showing everyone the man whom they had feared and thought long gone, the Beast of Flame.

An officer came out of the building, spotting me as I moved through the wreckage.

"Stop! Freeze!" he yelled, but I was disobedient.

He shot at me in fear. His shots whizzed by me and left me unharmed. On his fourth try, a bullet struck my chest, bringing me to my knees. The officer ran to me. He came up with handcuffs, but he did not use them. Grabbing his legs, I dropped him. I got up, put my foot on his throat, took his handcuffs, cuffed him, and chucked him into the street. I grabbed his gun and tossed it away as well.

The officer yelled for help, and two more officers came out of the station. One of them was Heath Thompson. I shot out their legs from under them. They fell and dropped their weapons in pain.

"That was for earlier," I said to Heath, confidently walking past them.

I entered the station and threw my knife at the man at the desk. It entered his shoulder and knocked him to the floor. My path took me past the office and into the back of the station to where the jail cells were.

As I entered the hall with the cells, a bullet hit me in the chest once again. I fell and dropped a smoke grenade. The room filled with smoke, and the officer who had shot me could not find me. Using my advanced hearing, I tracked him down and put my foot in his face. He fell, and I took his gun and his keys.

As the smoke cleared, I saw my friend still in the cell. I unlocked and opened the cell, and out came Tyler. He gave me a big hug, cheering joyfully.

"All right, kid! Way to go! But I did expect you earlier," he said with a chuckle.

I laughed and said, "Something came up." He may have been in a jail cell when it happened, but, even in that cell, he had heard the news of an attack of flying machines that breathed fire.

Yells rang out from the other criminals imprisoned here. I may have freed one criminal, but I had no reason for more. Tyler gave a cocky bow to his former fellow prisoners, and we left them.

We walked out of the hall and into the main office. Stepping out into the main office, we found our path blocked by Officer Nick Turnbull. His gun was held solidly in both hands, and it was aimed right at us.

"I will not let you leave," he said, and he meant it.

Tyler and I stood there and stared at the officer who took his job incredibly serious. He pointed his pistol at Tyler's head.

"Either you both get into a cell, or I kill you and your little friend."

No excuse would get me out of this. Nothing I could say would change his mind. There was only one option. I pulled out my pistol, and, with a quick draw, I shot Officer Turnbull. At the same time, I pulled Tyler to the side. As the bullet entered his shoulder, his gun went off, and the bullet hit where Tyler's head was just milliseconds ago.

Nick tumbled to the floor, and I ran up and took the gun away from him. I put my pistol to his head and said, "If you follow us, I will be forced to shoot you again. I haven't killed anyone here, but some are very injured. I suggest you take them to the hospital...and make sure to get yourself there as well, Nick."

"You're gonna pay for this, Martin! I will never let you escape! You will rot in prison for the rest of your life!" Nick yelled at me as I turned away.

Tyler and I went out the door and walked through the burning wreckage outside. Tyler gave me a high-five. He was glad to be back on the team.

I could hear Nick shouting from the station. He would not forget this. Nothing would stop that man from hunting me down. I doubted that I could hide from him for long. His hunt for us would begin soon and perhaps never end.

On the way back to the L.I.F.E. Organization, I explained what had happened to me. A normal person would have thought I was kidding, but Tyler knew me too well and understood the seriousness of the situation. He believed every word I said and still offered his help. He pledged his support to me in attacking these people who wanted me dead. Tyler would do anything he could to assist me with this.

Tyler had always been there for me. His loyalty was beyond belief. He was selfless in all his actions, searching for the best outcome for me and not himself. I could not have asked for a better person to help me find my past. It was time for me to learn the truth, and I owed it all to my greatest friend, Tyler Ishler.

We took the subway to Alemande. Flashing my L.I.F.E. badge gave me complete control and free access to the subway. It was like my new mafia ring. Tyler was incredibly jealous and suggested that he, too, get one. He was kidding, of course. He knew the only way to receive one was to join the secretive L.I.F.E. Organization.

When I arrived at the L.I.F.E. headquarters, it was about 7 o'clock. It felt as if it had been forever since this morning. I stumbled up to the doorway as if I had traveled a long way after being shot out of a helicopter. I banged on the doors and demanded they be opened for me. Tyler was preparing my escape and was not with me.

The doors opened, and out walked the guard, his hand on his holstered pistol. He was very confused to see me. I showed him my I.D., and he took a long look at me and at it. He finally let me in.

I was led straight to Zak's office, complaining about what had happened all the way there. Halfway through being escorted to my commander's office, I broke away and led myself there, ignoring the authority of those whose job it was to take me there. I did not even knock when I got to his office.

I burst in on a meeting and yelled, "What the hell is happening around here?!" The look on his face was priceless. There was so much fear and confusion in his expression. Before this, he felt assured that his goon had killed me.

"A-Agent Shepard! Don't you know how to knock?" he stammered, rising from his desk, attempting to show anger instead of shock.

"Don't you know how to screen your employees?!" I yelled, really playing it up.

"W-what happened? You were due back here hours ago."

"I'll tell you what happened! One of your agents tried to kill me and brought down the whole helicopter! He died and killed the whole team!"

Commander Zak looked away from me and stared downward with terrified eyes. He was trying to absorb all that was happening. Or as I believed, he was trying to come up with a convincing lie. He then looked back to me.

"Which one, Shepard?" he asked.

"It was Agent Bird, sir. That traitor!" I shouted my answer.

He sighed and looked down at his papers, plopping back into his chair.

"Well, we're glad you made it out of there. It was reported back to me that Jack Lamb was killed, but the samples and his body were surely lost in the explosion. You were the one who fired the shot. Are you sure it was him, Shepard?" he asked with a much calmer tone, but he remained somewhat dazed.

"Yeah, let's just forget the fact that one of your agents murdered a whole team! A whole team!"

"Agent Shepard, remember your place and answer my question!" he yelled at me, losing the calm he was using to hide his fear.

Knowing that being too rebellious was not to my benefit, I dropped my act and talked to him like I should. "Yes, it was him. I'm sure of it."

He gave a sigh and nodded his head approvingly. Jack was dead, and that relieved some of the tension he was feeling. The other half of it stood before him, angered and beginning to believe his suspicions. Zak felt the need to separate himself from me.

"Okay, you're dismissed," he said, waving me off.

"But, sir!" I said, taking a step towards him.

"Let me figure it out, okay?!" he yelled, pushing back in his chair away from me.

I stepped back. With reluctance, I nodded and then saluted. He gestured for my departure once again, and I left him.

Before going back to my room, I made sure to yell at everybody about what had happened. I even went down to the gadgetry department, and, while yelling about what had happened, I snatched something important from a drawer. After I had made a convincing case for myself that I was not aware of the malevolence of this organization, I returned to my room.

Before I got there, two agents confronted me and took back my weapons as well as the armor I had worn. If I had any trouble, I would not be armed to face it. I changed back into the organization's suit and tie and then proceeded to my room.

I entered '4815162342' into the code panel, and the door opened. I walked in and locked the door by pushing the lock command on the panel on the inside of the room. I also pushed a desk and a few chairs in front of the door, just to be sure. I would not let anyone enter this room.

Sitting down in the desk, I began searching the computer for some way to enter the archives. Hooking up the decrypter I had snagged from the gadgetry department, I was able to expand the capacity of the computer to reach files that had been once been restricted. After decrypting several larger files and programs, I had access to the Top Secret Documents storage kept on the L.I.F.E. Organization's server.

When the screen popped up, a solitary search bar was in the top left corner while a long list of documents lined the rest of the screen. I typed 'Jack Lamb' in the search bar. After hitting the enter key, Jack Lamb's file came up, and I found out what he had wanted me to see.

The file included Jack's height, weight, and age at the top, but, reading further down into the file, I discovered an entry from a few years ago.

"07/16/2011

Jack Lamb (SSX-08) has escaped the L.I.F.E. Organization research compound and is currently at large. This man is more dangerous than he appears due to his highly advanced brain, providing him with increased mental and physical ability. Lamb should be treated as a Level Sigma 10 threat, and only personnel with such clearance are allowed to engage him. He is not be captured; terminate the subject with utmost prejudice on sight.

Lamb was the first to undergo phase two of 'Super Soldier' experimentation, and the experiment has proven to be extremely effective. It has increased his strength, speed, mental capabilities, and healing by approximately 15 times. A side effect given to that of the experiment has caused him to age approximately 15 times faster as well. Additional effects of the experiment have reworked his psychological makeup, increasing his killer instinct and heightening his malevolent behavior by unprecedented levels. Together, these qualities make him an extremely valuable weapon.

After learning that another subject had escaped the facility, he fled the compound and has waged war on the L.I.F.E. Organization. He is not the first to survive 'Super Soldier' experimentation. Another subject, Martin Shepard, who was given the experiment during phase one…"

I stopped reading. I was just given a horrible amount of information. Typing my own name into the search bar yielded similar results. I found an entry from around the same time period.

"07/04/2011

Martin Shepard (SSX-04) is a L.I.F.E. research experiment. He is the product of phase one of the Super Soldier experiment. Currently, he is being evaluated to test the full range of his abilities and the properties given to him by the experiment.

Shepard is the first to survive 'Super Soldier' experimentation and is showing great promise. This experiment has increased his strength, speed, mental capabilities, and healing by approximately 5 times. A side effect given to that of the experiment has caused him to age approximately 5 times faster. Additional effects of the experiment have reworked his psychological makeup, increasing his killer instinct and heightening his malevolent behavior by unprecedented levels. Together, these qualities make him an extremely valuable weapon.

At the end of his 18 month trial in four days, he is to be executed. Martin has exhibited signs of rebellion against the researchers and is becoming increasingly dangerous. It is believed that he has gained too much knowledge of our experiment, and he cannot be permitted to leave the facility. Knowledge of the program seems to have been given by another 'Super Soldier', Jack Lamb (SSX-08). Follow-up is needed on relations between Jack Lamb and Martin Shepard."

This was insane! The words were right there in front of me, but I was having difficulty grasping them. I scrolled down to find another entry that had been dated two years after the previous.

"06/23/2013

Martin Shepard (SSX-04) was a L.I.F.E. research experiment, and the product of phase one of the Super Soldier experiment. The subject has been terminated.

When Shepard was about to be executed by lethal injection at the end of his evaluation period, he fought back and escaped the compound. He fled to a fishing boat in the city of Alemande and had hidden there for about two years. L.I.F.E. agents were recently sent to the boat after locating him in an extensive search. Agents killed everyone on board and shot Martin Shepard in the head, exterminating him.

Shepard's body has been dumped in a lifeboat and sent adrift back to the mainland. When his body turns up on land in the next couple days, he will not be able to be identified, for he has no traceable identity. This incident should distract the media to hide our actions.

Further experimentation with the 'Super Soldier' program is needed to create a more obedient soldier. Recent discoveries serve to remind us..."

My eyes strayed back up to the top of the page where it listed my height, weight, and age. I saw something very strange there. My age was not listed as 19 years old. It said my age was 4 years old. I thought about what I had read and figured it out when I read the final entry.

"05/08/2014

Martin Shepard (SSX-04) is an escaped L.I.F.E. Organization research experiment. This man is more dangerous than he appears due to his highly advanced brain, providing him with increased mental and physical ability. Shepard should be treated as Level Sigma 3 threat, and only personnel with such clearance are allowed to engage him. Special privileges may be given to lower-class personnel on the basis specified in Plan Delta.

Shepard has been confirmed as alive and not dead. Previously reported, agents attempted to exterminate Shepard with a bullet to the brain. The bullet proved not to kill the subject, but it did erase his memories. He has aged enough to be able to take a bullet to the head. Basic weaponry is now known to be ineffective in eliminating 'Super Soldiers'. New weapons will have to be developed to destroy the brain of a 'Super Soldier' like Shepard.

Currently, Shepard is a high ranking member of the West City Mafia. Two of our agents have infiltrated the group and are working on the means to either kill or bring him in, the latter being more preferable. Under Plan Delta, Shepard would be manipulated to believe he was previously an agent for our organization. Our purpose for him will be to kill Jack Lamb (SSX-08), since we find ourselves at a great disadvantage to face him.

Should the plan backfire and he escapes, his appearance is in our favor. No one, not even his family, will recognize him because of his age. He looks as if he is approximately 22 years of age instead of his actual age of four and a half years. His brain's over-functioning has caused him to age five times faster than usual..."

My actual age was four years old when I looked to be 22. My life was a lie. I was an experiment, an experiment that was done on a baby. These heartless L.I.F.E. scientists did their experiments on babies! The "Super Soldier" experiment was done on me most likely the day after I was born. They stole me from my parents and ran experiments on me in a lab. I could barely fathom my own past.

My rage boiled over. I could have had a perfectly normal life if the L.I.F.E. Organization had not kidnapped me. They did not "enhance" my life; they had ruined it. These agents did not work for "improvement and fullness." They were cruel and heartless liars. I would have my revenge on them.

My thoughts were interrupted by a red message and a beeping from my computer. It said, "Illegal Access!" They knew that I knew the truth.

Banging came from outside the door.

"Shepard, open this door!" I heard Zak yell.

I would not let them in. I got up from the chair and walked over to the window, gazing out at my wonderful ocean view.

The banging continued. I ignored it and smashed my window with a chair. I looked down and backed away. Glancing back around the room, I knew I would return to this place.

The door to my room was forced open just after my exit out the window. I dove down into the beautiful ocean below.

Chapter 22
Running

Tyler gave me a hand onto Jonah's boat. I climbed aboard, dripping wet, and looked back at what I was leaving behind. I glared angrily up at the broken window from which I had jumped. They were still up there, plotting against me. Yes, my return would come, and it would bring an end to all their crimes.

We sailed away from the organization of liars. Tyler, Jonah, and Donovan were as shocked to learn the truth as I was upon hearing my story. They were struck speechless, clueless of how to comfort me. In bewildered silence, we sailed back to the house where my true friends were.

Our feet hit the dock as we departed the *Martin*. Jonah and Donovan took point, leading us back to the house. Tyler walked with me, his hand on my back pushing my reluctant body forward. It had become lethargic and apathetic while my mind was battling the new horrors that had been discovered. I did not want to move. I wished I could stop thinking.

This horrible truth had driven me into despair. I was nothing more than the result of an experiment to create Super Soldiers, a successful result. There was no joy to be had in this success, though. My life had been stolen from me. Everything that should have been mine stripped away for a life of extreme ups and downs, bursts of simple joy splattered conservatively among terrible heartbreak. All my skill and all my strength was due to this brain experiment. I was a monster created for evil.

That fact hit me hardest. My brain had been reworked to make me a killer. All I had done before, all the violence and destruction, it was due to this experiment. Some scientists in their lab had decided that I was going to be used for their twisted desires. They had etched their plans into my mind. Could I not escape this terrible destiny? Was I to be forced through life as a monster, fighting for a purpose that men in lab coats had put into me?

Almost everyone who had told me about my past was a liar. The L.I.F.E. agents acted as if they were my friends only to get me to feel safe so they could kill me. Zak told me that I was an agent in the past when I never was. He told me that the Pirates caused my memory loss when, instead, a bullet from an agent did. The Pirates had nothing to do with my past. I did not know anything about the Pirates until I had joined the mafia.

No wonder I had no identity. My death supposedly came the day after my birth. My parents lost me after only just having met me. I had no idea from where they had taken me, so I could not find where my parents were. Everything was clear now. This clarity was more of a burden than I ever thought it would be. There was a bliss to the ignorance of my past to which I wish I could have returned.

It was strange to think that I was really only 4 years old. My brain's over-functioning caused me to age five times faster than an ordinary human. I would be dead when I turned 20ish. This life kept getting better and better.

Jack Lamb must have gotten the procedure the same time as I. He aged 15 times faster than usual, and that made him about 50 when I first met him. According to what I had read, Jack had escaped after another subject had left the facility. Was I that subject? Had he escaped because I was no longer there with him?

Jack had been right when he had said that he was my only friend. In a world full of scientists and experiments, the one thing one could want is another person like himself in there. Jack was that person for me. He was always three times older than I. He was the perfect older brother to me. When they tried to kill me and I escaped, he decided to fight back against the organization. He was sticking up for his little brother.

I woke up from my daydreams to the calls of children. Cody and Alyssa ran out to greet us. I hugged them both and picked them up. Their laughter revived my spirit, and a smile returned to my face. I let them down, and they asked me more questions.

"Did ya find what you needed to?" Cody asked.

"I did," I answered solemnly.

"So...now, you can stay here?" Alyssa asked.

I thought about the question. I did not have a home and needed a place to stay, but I had to run from the L.I.F.E. Organization. Knowing that I knew what they were hiding from me, they would pursue me with everything they had. I could not stay here or everyone here would be in danger.

"I can't stay for long."

They were very disappointed, but I understood that I was making the right choice.

We went inside, and I ate a well-deserved meal. It was late at night, and the kids were put to bed. I thought it funny that I, too, should be going to bed since I was only four, but I kept it to myself.

Mia, Jonah, and Donovan asked me questions throughout the night. I told them how I was used in an experiment and how I only had one friend. In the end, that friend became my enemy. I told them how I aged five times faster because of my condition, but also how it gave me my powers. Many questions were asked, and I answered them all. It was a new feeling to have the answers.

One question went beyond my grasp. Where would I go next? With L.I.F.E. after me and my non-existent identity hindering me, I did not have a good place to go. It would be hard to get a long term job, and, even if I did, L.I.F.E. would find me in a day. Also, Tyler was a fugitive of the law. He had a record in the mafia and was a high-level target to the police, and I, his co-conspirator, was a target as well.

My only option would be to look my problem in the face and kill it, but I did not have the resources to fight the L.I.F.E. Organization. They were ruthless, and now I was on their kill-list just like Jack Lamb had been. The fight against L.I.F.E. was not one I could fight without either an army or weapons of mass destruction.

Perhaps the authorities could assist us, but why would they listen to two escaped criminals? Maybe I could go to a rival gang in West City, but they would kill us on sight for being part of the former West City Mafia. There was a possibility Jack's building in Wallace could be holding some valuable technology or weapons, but L.I.F.E. would surely be crawling all over there. Where could I go? Was no place safe for me?

"Did you learn anything about your parents, Martin?" asked Donovan.

I remembered looking through my file. In haste and confusion, I had not looked over the rest of the documents. I did not have much time to read since they had only taken about five minutes to find out I had hacked into their database. I had not learned anything about my parents. I did not even know from which hospital I was taken.

"No, I didn't have enough time. I didn't learn anything about them."

He looked disappointed for me, but he could not have been as disappointed as I. Even if I miraculously found my parents, they would not welcome me in as their son. I would be a stranger and would be told to leave if I told them the truth. I had no evidence to support me. I could not prove that I was their son at all. Only a DNA test could tell them that I was, but that would most likely cause me to be found by L.I.F.E. or the police, and I would be captured there. My parents would not even be a safe choice for me.

Where would I go? My strength was not enough to overcome the agents. Their resources were too great for me to defeat them. Tyler and I made a great team, and he was a trained killer like me, but we could not hold them off. We were terribly outnumbered. Our strength alone would not be enough to stand against the behemoth that had deemed us its prey.

I looked over at Tyler for an idea. Before he could supply me with one, I had another idea. Whatever happened to Tyler's family? He had told me that his dad was high up in the mafia, and maybe his family had support for us. They could be our only chance.

"Tyler, what about your family?" I asked. Sadness came over him.

"They're all dead, kid," he said. "They wouldn't help you, anyways."

Again, I had no idea where to turn. I also had no time to come up with an idea because L.I.F.E. would be here in no time. The clock was ticking, and I had nowhere to turn. The pressure was taking its toll on me.

"Fine then! We will go to Poplen," I announced, standing.

"What's there?" Tyler asked, standing with me.

"Nothing. They will not expect us to go there, but we must hurry," I said. Tyler grabbed a backpack full of food, supplies, money, and one gun. The family had made it for us. We also changed clothes as to not be spotted as easily. I thanked them for their help, and Tyler and I moved to leave.

Before I was fully out the door, the kids came down quickly to say goodbye. They both hugged me, and I hugged them back, squeezing them tightly.

"Will you be back soon, Martin?" Alyssa asked.

"I sure hope so," I said, kissing her on the head.

I noticed that Cody was wearing my ring. I patted him on the shoulder and said, "You always have that to remember me by."

"You hurry up and come back, Martin. You're my hero, and I'm gonna miss you," said the young boy with the deep blue eyes.

"Know that I love you both and that I shall do all I can to come back as soon as possible. But you are going to have to be strong. You're going to have to be patient. Just know, no matter how long it takes, no matter what happens, I shall see you again," I told my two faithful admirers.

They both nodded, and I said goodbye to everyone. Then, I turned my back and stepped out the door. I left the family behind and fled.

Tyler and I ran to Alemande. We stayed in areas that were well-covered in trees. As we darted through the woods, I could see flashlights that belonged to L.I.F.E. search parties. Icy rain pelted us, but we were too soaked in our fear to even realize it. Helicopters and trucks crossed over us many times, but we always somehow managed to not be seen. Tyler and I held our breath when they came close, but they never found us. We made the trip unseen.

When Tyler and I reached Alemande, it was quite past midnight. We were exhausted and needed rest, but there was little time for that. I leaned against a telephone pole, and Tyler lay on the street. No one was out at this time of night, and L.I.F.E. had not sent agents to look here yet. This brief period of time could be our only rest.

I looked at the pole on which I was leaning. On it was a poster with pictures of Tyler and me.

"Wanted: Criminals Tyler Ishler and Martin Yellog. Reward: $5000 each."

Officer Turnbull was looking for us. He would not let us get away from him. I showed it to Tyler, and he knew that we were not safe here. Nick would look for us anywhere from West City to Alemande to Poplen to anywhere else. He would not give up the search for us. This seeker would not stop until he found his justice.

"Kid, if we stay here much longer, somebody's going to find us. It's time to move. We need to leave this area," Tyler said.

"I know, but, Tyler, I can't just run away. L.I.F.E. will not stop its experiments. Those scientists will continue creating Super Soldiers out of innocent people."

"People like you?"

"And people like Jack. He would not have been a man who would wage war on humanity if they had not messed with his brain. He wouldn't have killed people just to get a chance at revenge if they hadn't."

Tyler understood why I had to take a stand against them.

"How do we stop them?" he asked.

I did not know. They were a super power. It was like trying to knock down a skyscraper with hammers. The only way we could knock them down was to get a bigger hammer. Where do you get the hammer? That was the big question for me. Even though I had unlocked the secret to my past, I still had big questions to answer.

My thoughts turned to a person who was many times stronger than I was, Jack Lamb. His approach was to attack L.I.F.E. with his own homemade weapons. He must have stolen most of his supplies and created the invention himself. In the end, though, the machines were destroyed. He had failed at his mission, and he had died. His death had come at my hands. My mental capabilities were nowhere near sufficient to create such machines. Jack was about three times smarter than I. His methods were not for us.

My thoughts then turned to a lost boss. Don Sanzano used team tactics. We went to the Pirates with a strong team, and we conquered them with ease. We lost barely anybody, and most casualties were caused by a traitor. Our team was killed in the end. A surprise attack had wiped them all out. A surprise attack on the L.I.F.E. Organization might work, but I could not even begin to contemplate such a plan because nobody would be on my team. I would not be able to bring a team together or use Keir's methods.

Tyler's question was the big question. How could we stop them? I could neither create a team nor bring one together. Tyler and I had no friends who could help us. Jonah's family could not help us. Tyler had no family to help him. Everyone else hated us and would not help us.

"We can't," I answered. I did not want to say it, but it was the right answer. "We can only hide from these monsters. We should get far away from here," I said. Tyler knew the pain it caused me to say that. I did not want to give up the fight against L.I.F.E., but I had no choice. We only had the option to hide from them. If we did not, we would be killed in no time.

"We should go," Tyler suggested.

He was right. We should go to Poplen. Nothing was in Poplen that would bring us there, so L.I.F.E. would not expect that choice from us. Perhaps we might survive in the city of Poplen. It was our final hope and only chance.

"How do we get there, Tyler?" I asked. "We can't take the subway because that's exactly where Officer Turnbull will be looking for us."

Tyler said nothing. He just pulled out a pistol that had been packed for us.

"I will not kill him. I will not kill any those officers. They are good men. They seek us justly. I won't spill any more blood onto my hands," I responded.

"You don't have to kill anyone. Officer Turnbull isn't even going to be there. Remember, you shot him in the shoulder today. And the rest of his men aren't going to stand up to you if you have a gun," he said.

Tyler was full of risky plans. If I actually went through with this, our location would easily be found by the agents. And what if the plan backfired? What if they got past my bluff? They would shoot us right there for the trouble we had caused. There had to be another way of getting to Poplen.

"What if we drive there, Tyler?"

"Kid, I'd never left West City before you came. I don't have a clue where it is. Do you know how to get to Poplen?"

I did not, but I still thought driving there was our best bet. "I don't, but I don't need to know how. Why don't we take a cab there?"

"That would be great, but we don't have any money."

I took out my L.I.F.E. badge. "I'll just use the new edition of the mafia ring," I said. Of course, the sole cab for the city did not usually run this late at night, so we would have to wait until tomorrow. That was our plan.

We needed a place to stay the night, so we decided to go to the Ale Inn. Also, this was where the taxi cab spent most of its time. In the morning, we could catch it, and then we would be on our way to Poplen.

When we entered, I remembered the face at the desk. It was Amber, back to work here in Alemande since fear of mafia members had driven her out of West City. Ironically, it sent her to the only place two more members would show up.

I walked up to the desk and told her we needed two rooms. She told us the price, and Tyler pretended to look through his pockets. Doing so, he put his hand on the counter and showed the big mafia ring on his hand.

Amber started shaking. Trembled words came out.

"Are…you guys from…West City?" she asked.

"What's it to you, lady?!" Tyler yelled at her in a booming voice.

She backed away from the counter.

"D-don't hurt me! I don't want any trouble. Please!" she whimpered.

"Just give us the room key, and nothing will happen to you," I told her.

Shakingly, she handed us a key. I forcefully grabbed the key from her hand, and she backed away from us. Tyler snatched a cookie off the counter before we left. We high-fived on the way to our room.

We were on the top floor. It had a great view of the road that stretched all the way to the docks, and that gave us the chance to watch for agents in search for us. I sat restlessly at the window, looking for a sign that they might know where I was. Tyler went to sleep immediately, not knowing what kind of danger we were facing.

He did not know of what they were capable. They had both created and killed Jack Lamb, who was many times stronger than I. Tyler had earlier argued that they used me to kill Jack, and now they could not use normal human strength to kill me. This was somewhat true, but a more horrible thought came to me.

Yes, they no longer had me to lead the team or to kill a super-powered man, but I feared that they could create another person that was just like Jack and I, but many times stronger than each of us combined. Certainly, they had not stopped attempting to create the perfect soldier. What if they had been holding something in reserve all this time, preparing for the perfect time to unleash it?

That thought kept me up through the night, looking out the window. L.I.F.E. had all the resources needed to find me, and it had a weapon that would end me. This reality was worse than any nightmare I could dream.

I remembered my fight with Jack in the Fight Arena at the Vaillancourt. I used many tactics to try to defeat him, but none of them worked. They failed because he saw every single one of them coming. Yes, it is true that you can defeat brawn with brains, but Jack had both, and there was no way I could overcome him because of that. I would not be able to kill the person they would send. There was no way I could find victory in a battle such as that.

I sat at that window with insomnia and despair. Again, my life felt impossible. Every time I dug into my past, the hole caved in, and I had more problems. Now, my life seemed the worst. I was wanted by the police. I was the top kill for a secret government organization. I learned that my life was an experiment with a deadly result. There was nowhere to go except Poplen, and I was only going there to hide. My life had fallen apart once again. A few days ago, I had obtained everything, as I had in my mafia job, but, by the end of the day, everything had turned upside-down once again.

I eventually fell asleep in the chair by the window and got my much needed rest. My dreams were not good, though. All night, I was chased by Commander Zak and Officer Turnbull. I watched as they shot down my family by the sea and Tyler. They would take everything from me. That is how they would weaken me. They would kill them, and I would have no help. I would be forced to submit, and their mission would be complete. All night, I ran from the inevitable.

When I woke up, the sun was high in the sky. I groggily walked over to the clock on the table. It was 12:20 pm. Tyler and I had slept in a lot longer than we had planned. Of course, we needed the sleep since we had stayed up until about three in the morning. I woke Tyler up and told him the time. He got up from bed, and both of us got ready to get a cab and go to Poplen.

We did not bother with food, even though I was very hungry. I could not risk the possibility of the agents finding us. We stayed out of sight in the lobby, and we took the stairs instead of the elevator. I dropped off the keys to our room at the desk. Luckily, Amber was still working there, so we did not get a bill.

Walking out of the inn, I was shakingly paranoid. I did not know who could be an agent in disguise. I made sure to locate and identify every person around us. My eyes buzzed through the crowd. I kept an eye on every person that came within 50 feet of us. Fortunately, the crowds were smaller due to the fact that it was the middle of the work day. Still, I kept looking through the crowds.

It did not take too long for the taxi to pass by the inn. Tyler and I waved it over, and, when it stopped for us, we got inside.

Climbing in, I heard the driver say, "Where to?"

"To Poplen," I said.

The man turned back and, with a confused look on his face, asked, "You do know how far that is, don't you?"

"Yes, of course. That is where we want to go. Is that going to be a problem?"

The driver shook his head and then started the meter.

"Also, we won't be paying," I said to him. He flipped around immediately.

"Then, get out!" he yelled.

I put my L.I.F.E. badge against the glass that separated us. "We're commandeering this cab. Now, take us to Poplen."

The driver was reluctant, but he did not think he had much of a choice. With two government agents in his cab, he had better do what they said. He drove us right out of the city and away from the men who would have had us killed.

Even though we were out of the city, I held onto my paranoia. The drive to Poplen was a few hours, and I watched the driver the whole time. I needed to know if this man had been sent to pick us up and then kill us. L.I.F.E. could have easily sent a taxi to every hotel in a large area. They knew that we would be in one of them and that we could not get to where we needed to go unless we had a taxi cab. If this were true, then we had just given them the information that they needed: where we were going.

My mind raced with ideas concerning this man. If he were an agent, he would not risk scaring us away by trying to kill us. He would wait to drop us off, and then the other agents would kill Tyler and me. This man was definitely a spy from L.I.F.E. who was sent to pick us up and find where we were going. I remembered how fast he accepted that we were from a government agency. He took one look at the card, turned around, and drove. It was only a matter of time before we would reach Poplen and be executed upon arrival.

Tyler sat there, looking bored, not knowing what I had discovered. He still seemed tired from the long night of yesterday. He had no concern in his mind. He was at total peace. I wondered why this was. My mind could not find an answer, but soon reminded me that I had to continue to watch the taxi driver.

The rest of the ride was spent like the beginning. I studied the driver and came up with thousands of possible explanations. I studied all of his moves. How he turned, how he scratched his nose, his reaction to the bad drivers in the streets. I tried to remember if I had ever seen him in the L.I.F.E. complex. Nothing came to mind. Was he really with the agents? I did not want to hurt an innocent man. I wanted to turn the page on my violence which had killed many people, but this man could not be trusted.

As we pulled over to the sidewalk in Poplen, Tyler woke up, and I stepped out of the car. I walked around the cab and knocked on the driver's window, clutching my pistol in my coat pocket. The driver rolled down his window.

"Yeah? What do you need now?" he asked me.

"What is your name?" I asked.

He took a second but then answered, "Uh, it's Josh Webb."

I did not believe him. I pulled out the pistol and put it to his throat. Tyler, seeing what I was doing, suddenly stepped in front of the people walking on the sidewalk so that they could not see what was happening.

"Now, tell me. What is your real name?" I asked. "Josh Webb" looked scared and did not know how to answer my question. I pressed the gun harder into his throat.

"J-Josh Webb, sir. Please, d-don't shoot," he said.

"Stop lying!" I yelled quietly to him.

He closed his eyes and turned away.

I did not know whether I should shoot the agent here or not. He was from L.I.F.E., and eventually I would kill him, anyway.

"Where are the rest of the agents?" I asked him.

"I don't know what you're talking about. Please, don't kill me," he pleaded again.

"If you don't want me to kill you, then you will answer my questions!" I yelled at him loudly.

This was foolish of me. I had announced to everyone around me that I was sticking up the cab driver. People turned and looked at me. Tyler did his best to cover the gun and me, but he could not cover all of it.

Not knowing what to do, I grabbed the driver's hand and put the gun in his hand. I jumped back and yelled, "Don't shoot!" I fell to the ground, and the crowd turned to the armed cab driver. Tyler assisted me.

"He's got a gun!" he yelled and ran away.

The pedestrians realized the danger in which they were, and all proceeded into panic. Their screams and fleeing provided me with confusion I could use to escape. I followed Tyler as the driver was reported to the cops, and he drove away in the same type of panic.

We ran many blocks from where we had been dropped off. I had not gotten anything out of "Josh Webb". That is when I started doubting myself. What if this man was not an agent? He would report us to the police if they bought his story of my giving him the gun. It would take no time at all for L.I.F.E. to find us now.

I had never heard the name "Webb" when I was at the facility. The driver could possibly not have been an agent, but what if he was? He would be freed from the police only to send the agents straight to us. There was no good ending to this.

"What happened back there? Why'd you do that, kid?" Tyler asked.

"I think that the driver was a L.I.F.E. agent. Now, they will surely find us. I'm so sorry, Ty," I responded, feeling defeated and foolish.

"How long do you think we have?" Tyler asked me, ignoring my fault. I shook my head. "We only have about 12 hours I would say."

"Are you sure he was an agent?"

"Yes, I am," I responded confidently.

Tyler nodded his head in agreement. He trusted my judgment.

Fearing what could happen next, we went to hide somewhere. We ran all around the city looking for somewhere to hide from the police. We stayed in the alleys and hid behind dumpsters if we heard sirens. Slowly, we made our way to a familiar place. It was the hotel in which we had hidden when the cops were looking for us after we had broke into the Alemande News Center. We hoped that we might be safe from the police here.

We entered the hotel and walked up to the main desk. The lobby was as crowded as it was the first time we came in here. We were greeted as we came up to get a room.

"I don't have money with me, but I do have this. I need a room for an assignment that we are on. I hope there will be no problem with this," I said, showing the woman behind the counter my badge. She took the card from me and looked at it. She got about halfway down the badge, and then she stopped and stared at the card. Something on the badge got her attention.

Fear struck me. What if she had seen my name and had been told by the police to keep a lookout for me? What if she thought the badge was a fake? What if she was a L.I.F.E. agent? I just stood there in fear that she would do something that I would not like.

"Assignment? What is your assignment?" she asked.

"It's a stakeout, and that's all that I can tell you," I said. She took one more look at the badge. She handed it back to me. She also handed me a key card.

"No, it will not be a problem, Agent Shepard. Enjoy your stay."

She seemed to be in some kind of daze. I took the key card, and Tyler and I went to our room. I was very glad to have escaped that dilemma.

We sat in our room, thinking about our next plans. I stared up at the ceiling. The ceiling itself was plain white, and it was dull to say the least. It was not giving me too much inspiration.

My thoughts strayed to what I had done this day. I thought about the cab driver and the woman behind the counter. Was it possible that they were with L.I.F.E.? If that was so, how many of their agents could there possibly be? They seemed to have all the power. They were everywhere.

I looked over at Tyler. He was lying on the bed, and he was thinking intently. It gave me deep pleasure to see him thinking about our situation rather than ignoring it as he had done before. Although he was deep in thought, I thought I should interrupt to ask a question.

"Tyler, where do we make our next move?" I asked. He glanced over at me.

"Only one thought has come to my mind," he said, sitting up to look at me.

He then stared deeply at the floor. He was considering whether or not his idea was worthy of suggesting to me. "What is it?" Looking up, he sighed. He then stood up and gave me his suggestion.

"We need money to buy weapons to fight these monsters. I think we need to steal it from somebody."

I thought about the idea. Stealing would only draw attention to us, and the agents would surely find us. Buying the weapons would also attract more attention to us. We would not be able to buy strong enough weapons to fight L.I.F.E., anyway. I knew there was some merit in Tyler's idea, but there were flaws, and I knew I could not take any chances. What we needed was a way to get the weapons and an army without purchasing them. I did not know how to do this.

I told my counter-thoughts to Tyler. He dropped back into the bed.

"Then, what do you want to do, kid?" he asked, frustrated.

His frustration aggravated mine. I felt an unnatural rage welling up in me, and I hated it. What they had done to my mind was making me angrier than I should have been. Remembering how horrible my life was filled me with more anger.

I grabbed my head in frustration. Nothing was going right for me. There was no solution in sight. My mind fought against me, and so did my life. Every idea I created was littered with flaws. It felt as if the whole world was against me and nothing was for me. Despair was eating at me, and rage was flooding my veins.

"What do we do, Tyler?!" I shouted at him. "How the hell are we supposed to defeat these savages?! They are everywhere we turn, and we are all they want! They will do anything to kill us, and they show no mercy! So what do we do, Tyler?! What am I supposed to do?!"

I slammed my fist into the wall, shaking the room and putting a huge hole in the wall. I fell into the bed and clung tightly to the bed sheets. My frustration was extreme. I could not control myself.

Tyler completely understood my anguish. These people had ruined my life, and now their only mission was to hunt me down and finish the job. Even with my advanced brain, I could not think of anything to escape the nightmare.

As I released my rage into these bed sheets, Tyler sat there with the same frustration. Tyler had one big difference, though: he was much calmer than I. I lay there, throwing a fit worthy of my four-year-old self, while he tried to think. Tyler's calmness was one of our huge advantages, even though I had no idea where he got it.

Tyler walked over to the bed where I was. He sat down next to where I lay, shoving my face into the deepest part of the bed.

"To tell you the truth, I don't know what to do, kid. But there is one thing I know. These agents aren't smart enough to beat people like us. We work as a team, and nothing keeps us down. Hell, I could be in jail and flying fire-breathers could attack the city, but I know you would come for me. You could be trapped in a heavily guarded government facility, but you jump out the window, and I will be there. We have destroyed whole gangs of dangerous men. We escaped the destruction of the Vaillancourt. And you know what? Even if the agents captured you and took you to there highest security base, I would come for you, and I know you would come for me."

My tension eased with his words of encouragement. I flipped over and turned to Tyler. His expression showed me the bond he had made with me.

"You are exactly right, Ty. Nothing would keep me from getting you back. Even if I lost my memory again, I would find you. But I wouldn't even let them take you. We are a team, and these government-funded monsters can't keep us down. I'm gonna put them in their place, and I know you'll do the same right beside me."

I stood up, and so did Tyler. I stuck my hand out to him. "Tyler, why would we ever be afraid? We're not going to be taken down. Nobody on this planet could even touch us because we are a team. We shall not fear these agents, and, instead, they will fear us. That is...if you are on my team."

Tyler had no hesitation. He reached out, took my hand, and shook it.

"I don't see anyone else I would rather be on a team with but you, kid."

Chapter 23
The Miracle

We departed our room with a feeling of renewed strength. Intense worry no longer hung on my back concerning the people who sought my life. I was no longer paranoid nor did I feel afraid of them. My fear was dead, and my hope was reborn. I had Tyler at my side, and, somehow, we would take down this organization. My purpose would be completed.

Now, I felt free. My hope was being renewed within me. The bond I had with my greatest friend was stronger than that of any foe who could come against me. Released from my fear, I found that my mind was clearer. Without the paranoia crowding my brain, a new clarity was available to me, and I was stronger because of it.

We decided to go down to the lobby. Perhaps we could get some information from the woman who always seemed to be at the desk. I also thought it would be smart to analyze the whole lobby in case any L.I.F.E. agents were here.

Arriving in the lobby, I noticed a couple of things. That woman behind the counter was still looking at me in some kind of daze. Also, there were three other employees who were staring at me, trying to see something. These three were scattered about the lobby, but each of them triggered something in my advanced brain that caused me to give them a second glance.

I gave an analytic eye to each of them as we entered. The first was a tall, hardened-looking man. He seemed to be about his mid-40s, and he had a full grown beard. I noticed that his black hair had an accompaniment of grayish hairs, not brought out by age but perhaps by stress. His hazel eyes were locked on me with a longing look, and he seemed to wish he could see something in me.

The next person I noticed was young enough to be the first man's son, and I believed this to be the case. He was somewhat tall for his age, which seemed to be about 10 years old. He had spiky blond hair and squinted at me, not at all hiding that he was looking at me. The boy was young, but he showed a sense of maturity. He most likely worked as some kind of bellhop for the hotel. His proficiencies most likely did not lie with checking people in or cleaning the rooms, so he was given a job of simple, monotonous labor. The boy looked away when he saw that I was looking at him.

The next was a girl. She seemed to be at the age at which she would just be finishing high school. She had long brown hair and leaned against a wall, only barely keeping me in sight. This girl was hiding her spying best among the three. Though, she did not seem to care much for looking at me, for she mostly watched the crowd in the lobby. She very rarely took a look at me, but still I knew her mind was on me.

I walked over to the counter where the woman sat. Tyler took lookout by sitting in the lobby and pretending to read a magazine.

"How's the stakeout going?" she just barely got out.

"We can't disclose any details to the public. Sorry about that." She nodded at my response. Her dazed stare persisted. "What is your name?" I asked her.

The question took a second to register in her mind.

"Uh…um, I'm Tammy Shepard. If there is anything you ever need, just call down here, and we would be glad to help."

My meaningless question was proving a suspicion I had. My brain was recognizing something within this woman and the three employees. Her deep gaze and slow responses showed that she, too, had some suspicions about me.

My eyes darted around the room quickly. I saw an employee cleaning the floors that was not any of the other three. This felt like a safe enough environment for me to test a hypothesis I was creating.

"Well, mine is Martin Shepard," I said while watching the man. He did not even flinch. Meanwhile, the other three all took a synchronized look at me.

"I hope I can help your investigation, Martin. If there are any questions that…" she began to say.

"There are a few questions I have," I interrupted.

"Sure."

I pointed at the three employees. "What are the names of those three employees? I need it for the report," I said, blowing the cover of the three who were still spying on me.

She seemed almost embarrassed by the question.

"Um, those employees are my husband, son, and daughter," she said, waving each of them over.

The three family members walked over to the counter, rather confused.

"This is my husband, Ron Shepard," she said, pointing to the man I saw first. "This is my daughter, Anna," she said, pointing to the girl I had seen that had just stepped in front of the young boy. "And this is my son, Collin," she finished, putting her hand on the young boy's shoulder.

My theory was quite farfetched, but it originated from an advanced brain. I thought of this family's last name…and how it was identical to mine. I thought about how she looked shocked when she read my name on the card. I took into consideration the longing looks from the members of this family of spies. My conclusion was farfetched, but I could not hold back my thoughts. I was too desperate. I had to know if it was true.

"Mrs. Shepard, have you ever lost a child?" I questioned. At this remark, Tyler quickly turned around in his chair, which was a ways off in the lobby. Tammy, as well as the rest of her family, seemed shocked by the question. Ron drew closer to his wife, his posture much more defensive than a second ago.

"Once…about four years ago. Why?"

Her response gave me hope. "What was his name?" I asked again.

"Why do you care?" she responded, exhibiting insult.

"Why are you asking these questions?" the father spoke up, stepping in between us.

"Was his name Martin Christopher Shepard?" I asked them.

"How do you know this?!" she asked, more confused than ever.

"What do you know about our son?" the father asked me, showing a frustrated curiosity.

The kids looked afraid and confused, and their parents were more so afflicted in the same manner. I cleared my throat for what I had to say. I knew the truth; I knew that it had to be true! No matter how crazy it seemed to me, I was not going to let my fear keep me from saying what I knew to be true.

"I am Martin Christopher Shepard, and I am your son."

After a few hours, I had explained myself. With Tyler backing my story up, they were eventually pushed to believing me. I told them about my search for some kind of truth and the horrible discovery when I had finally found it. I told them how I learned my name and what I had learned about my past. It all led me to believing that I had found my true family. Out of the blue, here they were: my stolen family. It was miraculous.

The family, my family, did not know how to respond. They were disbelieving at first, but after my story and an hour of listing the facts, they had come to trust me somewhat. I had told them enough that their only choice was to believe me. And more than that, there was a void within them that demanded to be filled and an unnatural sense that our blood was the same. I cannot describe it, but they knew just as I knew that I was theirs.

My mother, Tammy, from the very first time she had seen me, had hope that, somehow, I was her son. Upon the completion of my story, she lunged at me with a hug. I accepted it gratefully, for this was for what I was searching all along. My dad, Ron, joined in, and I finally felt at home. For the first time in my life, I was home.

Life finally felt complete. Real truth was mine, and my family was found. My thoughts no longer strayed to L.I.F.E. or the police. I was the opposite of paranoid. They would not find me here. They would not look for me. I was convinced that everything was complete and all worries were gone for good.

Then, everyone had questions. I asked about their lives, and they asked about mine. I explained my story once again, now adding in much more. Tyler helped me out with commentary at the end of every part.

"And the whole time he's doing this, I'm in jail!" he would say.

There was an immediate bond between the family and me. They laughed whole heartily, as did I. Our family had been made whole. I did not understand it, but I understood that we were happy, truly happy.

I learned much about my family in this time. This hotel, Shepards and Sheep, was their business that they had started. The whole family worked here as employees and had kept it going. The small, non-commercial feeling of the hotel kept its guests happy with their service. The kids took no pay, for their parents' happiness was their pay.

The kids, Collin and Anna, had many questions themselves.

"So you were the one who stopped the machines that were on the news?" Collin asked with gleaming excitement.

"You were in the mafia and a government agency?" Anna asked with skepticism.

"If you're four years old, why are you so tall?" Collin asked.

Their questions came from disbelief that I was related to them, but I was happy to answer all of their questions and to talk with my siblings. There was an incredible joy that filled me as I was given the opportunity to have this fragment of a normal life.

214

The rest of the day was spent with my family. They told me what it was like to lose me and how great it was to have me back. Of course, they were somewhat confused by my mature looks for my age and my amazing strength and intelligence. I thanked them for everything, but they were just so thankful for my return. The entire family came to the room Tyler and I had rented from them, and we talked for the entire five hours left in the day.

When they left to go to sleep, I lay in my bed with a huge smile across my face. Tyler, too, was very happy for me. He had done as he had promised. He had helped me find my past, and, on top of that, he had returned me to my family. In his mind, though, the mission was not over.

"Now, the only thing left to do is to finish off those L.I.F.E. agents."

I looked at him with confusion. "No, Tyler, there's no need for that."

His look back at me was filled with even more confusion.

"What?! Why would you say that?! We can't just turn our backs on L.I.F.E. or they will find us, and they will kill us."

I was non-believing. Meeting my family had thrown me into a euphoric trance that made me believe I was safe. "There is no need to finish them, Tyler. They won't find us. They can't find us. You know they would never expect us to come here. We could be anywhere in the country. No way they'll check here for us."

Tyler could not believe it.

"What about revenge? What about helping all the people they have turned into experiments like you? They can't continue to do the things they are doing. We can't let them!"

"Tyler, the mission's over."

He gave it up. He knew he could not do it without me, and he also knew there was no swaying me. He lay back in the bed. He felt it was his responsibility to help the people being turned into experiments, including me. He had to get revenge on the menace, but I did not need that anymore.

I stared back at the ceiling. Peace was mine. My family was found, and my own mission was complete. I was not paranoid. I was happy.

Chapter 24
One Little Game

Waking up, instant joy greeted me at the foot of my bed with a childish smile. My siblings had silently entered our room, only managing to wake me up. They could not wait to spend the day with their new brother.

"What's up, Martin?" Anna asked.

"Not much," was my response; I did not have another.

Tyler woke upon hearing us speak. He smiled at them.

"What are you guys doing in here?" he asked, rubbing the sleep from his eyes.

"Waiting for you guys," Collin said, taking a step closer to Tyler's bed.

Anna pushed Collin in annoyance. She apparently did not want us to know that she was waiting for us. She must have wanted it to seem like a simple prank, not a desire to spend time with me.

"How'd you break into our room?" Tyler asked groggily.

"Dude, our parents own the hotel. We've got a master key card. We can get into any room in the hotel we want," Anna bragged, holding up the coveted card.

Tyler got up from the bed and threw on a shirt, already wearing pants fortunately.

"Not bad," he said to Anna. "Might want to get me one of those... Like this one!" he said and snatched the card from my sister's hand.

When Anna grabbed for the card, Tyler held it high above his head, but, because of his short stature, it was to no avail. She snatched back the card, and we all shared a collective chuckle at the failed scheme.

I got up from the bed and threw on a shirt as well. I stood and stretched, letting out a yawn. "So...what do you guys want to do, anyway?" I asked.

"How about we play hide-and-seek?" Collin suggested.

Anna rejected the idea, but I thought it was a good game for a hotel. "All right, all right. Sounds good to me. How about you, Anna, and Tyler can go hide, and I'll seek. Shouldn't take me too long to find all of you."

Collin jumped in excitement, "Awesome!"

All of them left me in the room as they went to hide. I stayed here and once again pondered my ever-changing life. This life I had was absolutely fascinating. While running from my problems, I had stumbled onto my family by sheer luck. I did not know what to think.

I left the room after a few minutes and began the search. I started in the lobby. I quickly went around the room, checking through the crowds and behind the counter. Finding that they were not here, my search moved on to the kitchen.

I took my time here, wanting to be thorough because this was a great potential hiding spot. I checked behind the different rows of shelves and cooking appliances. Attempting to not disturb the kitchen staff, I ducked and dodged around moving employees, startling them into almost dropping their dishes. My search was not in vain, though. When I reached the final row, there was Anna, hiding behind a large bag of flour.

"There you are!" I said, and she came out from her spot.

"Not bad, but even Collin could have found me there."

"Well, I am younger than Collin. You've got to cut me some slack for that," I said. She laughed at the joke, and then I continued my search.

Noticing a laundry chute in the kitchen, I decided to check the laundry room in the basement. Feeling a little adventurous, I decided to take the fastest way there. Leaving Anna, I jumped down the chute.

I fell down the chute, banging against the sides as I fell. The landing was not as bad. A huge pile of clothes waited at the bottom for me. I rolled off the pile and came face to face with Tyler, who had been sitting against the wall, his hiding place quite out in the open. He did not think I would check down here.

"Oh, come on!" he exclaimed, feeling this turn of events was most unfair.

The last one was Collin.

"You know where Collin is?" I asked Tyler.

"Of course, but it would be cheating to tell you, wouldn't it?"

Agreeing, I decided to move on.

Searching the lobby once more, I confirmed for certain that it was not his hiding spot. I then checked the kitchen again and the whole basement. He was nowhere to be found. Without anywhere else to search, I concluded that he must be on the roof, so I hustled my way up there to find my young brother.

On the roof, Collin was sitting on the very edge of the building. I came up behind him and said, "Not a bad hiding spot." It shocked him so much that I had found him that he almost fell. I quickly grabbed him and pulled him off the edge and into safety.

"How'd you find me?" he asked.

"This was the only spot left," I responded.

"Yeah, but no one ever checks up here. Not even my sister would look for me up here. Oh... I guess she is your sister, too," he said.

"Yeah... I can't tell you how good it feels to be reunited with you, with my family. I've longed for this for so long. I didn't even know how badly I wanted it."

I climbed onto the edge of the building and sat, prompting Collin to return to where he had been sitting. He then scooted over slightly to be closer to me.

"It's strange to think of you as my brother," Collin said. "Mom had sometimes talked about you about when she had lost you in the hospital and how nobody knew where you had gone. I kinda thought she was just joking. Obviously, she wasn't," he laughed slightly.

"What did she say about it?" I asked, curious to know my mother's thoughts on my disappearance.

"Well, she would cry sometimes when she told it, and she would always say how upset she was and how angry she was with the hospital."

My mom had done what was expected in that moment. Anger was to be expected when you lost a son, especially like how it had happened with me. No wonder she had looked so longingly and had accepted that I was her son so quickly. She needed something to fill the void I had left.

With Collin sitting with me on the edge of the hotel, the beautiful view captivated and comforted me. This day was my first real experience with these people I now knew as my family. Playing hide-and-seek with them had taken a lot of the day away.

While we were playing, I had noticed that even Tyler had thought of my family as his. Truly, he was correct. Tyler had been all the family for which I could have asked when both of our lives had fallen apart. He was as much family as my true family was. There was a connection between us that was so much thicker than blood.

Good emotions were coming back to me for the first time in a while sitting up there. Here, I was at a pinnacle of happiness. As I looked out into the distance, I did not fear what I would see. I found a unique and special joy in the beauty of the horizon. I did not just feel happy; I felt normal. Normality was something for which I longed greatly.

Anna and Tyler walked up behind us. Anna pulled Collin off the edge and told me to get off the edge as well. I had no problem with that. I climbed off the edge and smiled at my family, glad to do whatever was asked of me.

"I see you found him," she said.

"You wouldn't believe how long it took me," I responded.

"Oh, I'm pretty sure I understand how long you looked for him. I have played this with him many times."

"How did you know to look for both of us up here?" I asked Anna and Tyler.

"Your dad said he saw you headed up this way," answered Tyler.

"You're pretty smart to look up here for him. Wouldn't have thought of it myself. Not bad, bro," said my sister with a smirk.

My happiness and normality increased. That was not the peak of my day. When we went back down to the lobby, lunch was waiting. We were happily accepted and ate the food quickly. After that, my parents took us out for ice cream. I could feel my heart filling more and more with positivity as the days went on with my family.

My time with my family was almost like my time with the mafia. I was heavily waited on, and I was always enjoying myself in one way or another. Of course, it was many times better than my time in the mafia could ever be. I had no jobs to do, except my occasional chores with the hotel. My time was much more rewarding because I was spending it with people I loved deeply. Also, a weight of great guilt was not on my shoulders, for my efforts were not spent on criminal matters. Time with this wonderful family was some of the best on memory.

Every day, I was with them. Never did a day go by when we were separated. There was no way I could get away from them, anyway. I loved them too much to ever leave them, and they loved me so much that they never left me. Games like hide-and-seek were played with my siblings every day. Tyler always was there with me, too. This would be the best time in my life.

One day, my mother came up to my room where I was once again thinking.

"What are you thinking about, kiddo?" she asked, taking a seat beside me.

"I just don't understand how all of this is possible. The way everything has gone...I just don't understand," I confided.

"God has a plan for everyone, Martin. Yours must be incredibly special," she said to me with a warming smile.

This concept of God had eluded me all my life. I had only been to church a couple times and barely had a grasp on the subject. It definitely needed a lot of faith, which my brain had a hard time comprehending. My family had taken me to church, and I knew they fully believed. I trusted them, and some part of me believed as well. Somehow, I knew that I was not being lied to. There was some deeper truth to all this.

Church became a place of relief and redemption for Tyler and me, since we had always struggled with the sin of our lives. Instead of hearing each week how awful and sinful we were, we heard a message of hope and forgiveness. All the guilt and shame we felt for our lives of killing, crime, and destruction began to be lifted. There was something more to this place.

We were called to a higher purpose, to live better than we had. But this life had plagued me unfairly with strife and suffering. I hoped that, given my circumstance, I was still doing the right thing. Was what I did back then still wrong, even after I was forced to face? I was not sure, but I would try harder to do what was right. I had to do better with my life.

When my mother brought up God's plan for me, I did not know what to think. How could God use me? I had killed so many without remorse. I had stolen and imposed fear on many people. I was the epitome of wickedness. How could He use me?

I knew He existed, and I knew He was guiding me, but why? A person such as I deserved the suffering I received so often. Was I just being made to suffer, or was my way of thinking being made to change? I felt that the evildoers did not deserve another chance, yet here I was being given one. And not just one chance, but many. I did not know where I was being guided, but I would trust and follow.

In following this call, I discovered a Savior, someone to remove all my shame. More than this, He walked beside me in the trials and through them. Jesus was not concerned with the crimes of my past, only with where I was going. He was leading me into something better. The path had not been revealed yet, but I knew it would lead somewhere better. I trusted that He could save me from any force that came against me.

Tyler, too, was feeling this call, but his was different from mine, just like how my parents and siblings had a call all their own as well. When I would speak to him about it, he would tell me about freedom from fear and being able to be his real self. I shared with him how I was experiencing freedom from shame and redemption from my darkness that

I thought I never could escape. We were both on different journeys, yet we were journeying alongside one another.

With all of this changing inside of me, I vowed to live a different life. This meant more to me than when I had wanted to change in the past. Now, I had a partner backing me up in the fight, and his name was Jesus Christ. Even though scientists had put malevolence within my brain, trying to bind me to the life of a killer, I would fight back against my own mind with Him by my side. I could accomplish anything while He was with me.

My mother would share stories of her own redemption with me when I would share mine with her. Even though she grew up as a Christian, there was much darkness within her, too. Together, she and her Savior had conquered over these trials, and she was the woman she was today because of them.

My mother once told me about one of her greatest trials: losing me.

"When the nurse came in, she had that look. That look that tells you that something horrible has happened. Your dad was at my side when she came in. I remember his rage, but, even more, I remember mine. I just did not understand why something like that would happen. Why would that happen to us? We filed a lawsuit against the hospital, and we made enough money to build this hotel, but I could never get you back. I've never stopped looking for you until now."

She stopped for a second, and I saw a tear on her cheek.

"It was a miracle to get you back, Martin. When you came in and I saw your badge, I knew it was you. I knew you were my son. I didn't understand it, but somehow I knew. I'm so glad you're back, Martin."

Many stories were told to me, but this one stuck with me. My family truly did love me and never gave up hope in seeing me again, either in this life or the next. They did not expect me to show up as I did, but they knew they were going to see me again.

After a few weeks with my family, I had learned so much. I, along with Tyler a lot of the time, spent a majority of my time with my father. He taught me everything he knew, and I absorbed all of it. From him, I learned new morals and new ways to look at the world. My father taught me so much. He crafted me into a new man.

Time rolled on. In that time, I had learned to entirely forget about L.I.F.E. and the agents who could be searching for me. I never thought about running into Officer Nick Turnbull when I went into the city. People like Jonah and his family drifted out of my mind. I would sometimes think about visiting them and having them meet my family, but something always came up. I never took the opportunity. Somehow, I was forgetting from where I had come. This time, it was without amnesia.

My family often asked questions about my past life, and I always answered them with large stories of grandiose proportions. They loved each story I told and often asked to hear them again or for me to tell them to the guests at the hotel.

I would tell them stories such as "My Great Fight with the Undefeatable Jack Lamb", "How I Destroyed the Flying, Fiery Machines of the Sky", and "Running from the Law". Everybody loved the stories, but only my family believed them. The guests, almost always people from far away traveling through, laughed and commented on my amazing imagination. I did not mind because, if they had believed, they might have attracted Officer Turnbull or Commander Zak to the hotel. The guests believed that they, too, were made up by me.

As the days went on, my daily rituals became more endeared to my heart. Days were spent playing with my siblings or working in the hotel. It was an easy life, one of joy and peace. Tyler often showed a lack of excitement, a desire for some action,so we all went out and did something fun each day.

Tyler was only looking for a little excitement, not being accustomed to never having any. Our games of hide-and-seek would become great chases across the hotel with Tyler. He almost would have liked it if we were being chased by L.I.F.E., even if the chase was for our lives.

One day, Tyler was no longer looking for action. A game of hide-and-seek was all it was. As my family hid, I waited in the room.

After about three minutes of waiting, I was going to go look for them. Before I could, there was a knock at the door. I walked over and answered the door, thinking that it was either my dad or mom. His actual identity differed greatly from either of them.

The result of my opening the door was a pistol pointed at my head. Instinct suddenly kicked in, and I dodged the bullet that was shot only a centimeter from my ear. Instinct also made me put my fist straight into the man's ribs. He fell, and all that was left was a kick to his head, snapping his neck and killing him in the process.

The shot put almost into my head had deafened me. If it had not, I would have heard the shouts from his partners.

One thing I noticed before the bullets came whizzing at me was that the man I had just killed dropped a badge with the L.I.F.E. logo on it. That was all I had time to notice.

The bullets flew into my chest, legs, and arms. Six shots taken from pistols brought me down to my knees, but not before I had grabbed the downed agent's gun. I, too, fired shots into the enemy, but my shots killed.

Suffering from the loss of hearing and the bullet holes in me, I crawled over to the laundry chute. I managed to throw myself into it before more came.

As I fell, bullets dropped out of me, and so did blood. I angrily contemplated my obvious stupidity. Why did I let my guard down? Only about two months after I had escaped, they had found me, and I was not prepared. Thoughts of regret tumbled out with the blood and bullets.

I hit the pile of clothes, leaving a huge dark red stain upon all of them. I rolled off and cried in agony. Even with the superhuman strength, I could not withstand these wounds. I gasped for air, for even the fall had knocked all of it out of me.

Then, an even greater pain hit me. What of my siblings? What of Tyler? I lay there with the greatest pain I had ever experienced. It was the pain that accompanies fear of loss. Loss of loved ones.

My pain was somewhat relieved by the footsteps of my young brother slowly approaching me.

"Martin?" he said, afraid.

"Collin! Please, go hide!" I yelled to him.

"What happened? I heard screams," he asked, terrified.

"Just hide here until I say so!" I commanded.

Gunshots sounded throughout the hotel. Collin flinched at the sound, and terror consumed him.

"Collin! Go hide now!" I commanded again. Collin did as he was told and retook his hiding spot.

I pushed myself back up and tried to recover my strength. Grabbing the dirty laundry, I proceeded to wrap it around my wounds. Just as they had when a surprise attack hit me at the Pirates' base, my wounds closed and stopped bleeding. My strength slowly came back. As this happened, I could hear the screams of the guests and the yells of the agents trying to find me. I checked the bullets in my weapon and then proceeded to the stairs.

I left the basement and continued through the hotel, shooting the agents in vengeance. As I did this, I searched for my family in vain. Making my way to the lobby, I heard the call to retreat. This made me run to the lobby, eager to kill whoever was left.

I entered the lobby and saw the agents running out the door. I shot at them, missing the targets as they sprinted away. Before pursuing them, I checked behind the counter. There was my mother, hiding under the counter.

"Mom, stay here! Don't let them find you! I'll be right back!" I said. She nodded. I turned and ran out the door. I had to end this here and now.

Luckily, this attack had not been planned very well. I had not seen even a single agent with a laser rifle. I wondered why that was. It was all in my favor…or so I thought.

I could see the car to which they were running. I was faster than they. Putting bullets into the backs of those running from me, I killed all but one. Then, I shot out the legs from the last man with the last of my bullets. I sprinted and came upon him. He tried to find his gun, but it was a fruitless endeavor, for I found it first. Savoring the moment before the kill, I paused and breathed heavily over my soon-to-be victim. Then, I put the bullet straight between his eyes and heaved a manic and euphoric sigh.

I turned to go back to the hotel and search for anyone remaining, but then I heard a ringing. I turned back to the executed agent. The ringing came again. I reached into his pocket and found his phone.

The caller's name was displayed on the phone's screen. "Zak Kurien" it read. It was the Commander calling. The phone rang again, and then I answered.

"Hello?" I answered the phone confidently, speaking to my abhorred adversary.

"Hello, Shepard," I heard him say.

"Hello, Zak."

I heard him chuckle in an evil manner.

"They're dead. Your agents are all dead," I told him, but his chuckle was not stopped by that.

Instead, he said, "Do you remember the Vaillancourt?"

I was confused. "What?!" I asked, panic beginning to fill me.

"Do you remember the Vaillancourt?"

As I realized what he had said, an explosion rippled through the city. I turned as my home exploded. The building burst into flames the next second. I did remember the Vaillancourt. Oh, how I remembered the Vaillancourt!

I dropped the phone and ran to the hotel. Tears flew from my face as I came to the hotel. How ironic my words to my family were! I had told them to stay within the hotel to keep them safe, but I had condemned them to death with such a command.

Dead bodies lay scattered across the pavement of the former hotel. I cried at what had happened. Again, L.I.F.E. had destroyed all my friends in an explosion that even searched for the death of civilians.

I fell to the ground and wept uncontrollably. I remembered Tyler's words to keep fighting these monsters. If only I had listened!

I stared at the dead bodies in despair. Sirens were wailing in the distance. They were coming for me. The smell of smoke was heavy in the air. The air had once been so clean here. This place had once been so active, so alive. Now, it was as still as the death that covered this area.

With this death, the most horrid sorrow I had ever experienced encompassed me. On my knees before the tomb of my so beloved family, I could not control my eyes as a flood of agonizing tears poured out. My father, my mother, my sister, my brother, my friend. Ron, Tammy, Anna, Collin, Tyler! They were dead! I vomited when the next wave of this most hideous sorrow hit me. I was sad beyond myself. I was so overtaken that I no longer felt human. All I was now was the epitome of grief, of despair.

Now, I truly could see the horrible pattern of my life. Up and down it went, more and more severe each time. Things would get better only to get worse. Even though the good got better, the bad was the most hideous thing of which I could think. This was my life, and it disgusted me.

While I convulsed in terrible sadness, the air around me was motionless. Then, an object broke the dead stillness. I quickly got up and pointed my pistol, hoping to kill another agent in sweet vengeance. It was a good thing that I did not fire upon the man.

Tyler limped towards me. I ran up to him with a hug instead of a bullet.

"They can't kill me," he said, weakly chuckling.

I laughed as tears rolled down my face. We both laughed and cried with horribly mixed emotions.

"I found your mom," Tyler began. "And she said you were outside. I ran to join you, and I was right at the doors when it happened. The place blew and tossed me a good dozen yards or so. I don't feel 100 percent, but I can make it."

"Tyler, we cannot be taken down. Nobody could do that to us. Do you know why?" I asked him, looking intently into his eyes.

"Because we're a team. And I sure don't see anyone here that I would rather be on a team with but you, kid," he said as he looked upon the dead bodies surrounding us.

Chapter 25
The One

Was my life always to be like this, a rollercoaster of triumph and tragedy? From blissful high to sorrowful low, this life's repeating pattern was becoming stronger with each repetition. When I was accepted by an amazingly kind family who pledged their support to helping me find my memory, my hope of finding it blew up in the sea. When I had an actual job and a room built for a king, I lost a fight and broke the deal of a lifetime. When I joined the mafia and unlimited power was in my hands, an explosion killed all who kept it possible. When I joined an organization and thought I had found the truth, that organization turned on me, and I found the horrible truth. Finally, when I had found my biological family and had true inner peace, the agents returned and destroyed it.

The burning shell of the hotel lay before me, smoke rising steadily from it. I felt it to be too much like the Vaillancourt. In a singular horrible event, both had been destroyed in an attempt to kill me or, at least, kill those whom I loved. Both hotels had been occupied by those without whom I felt incomplete. Zak was correct in asking if I remembered the Vaillancourt. He had recreated it right before me.

The wailing of sirens continued in the background. They would be here within two minutes. With the police would come endless trouble for us.

Tyler gravely took in what he had lost just as I did. He understood how much more of a loss it was for me, and I understood that it, too, was a loss for him. In the presence of intense pain, we each realized the toll it would take on the other. He realized something else as well.

"We must retaliate," he said, tears still wetting his cheeks.

I understood him, but I still did not have any way of retaliating. "How?" I questioned. Tyler was again stumped by the question. It begged for an answer, but we could not supply it with one.

As the question was still in his mind, three police cars raced up behind us and came to a screeching halt. With them were four ambulances, two fire trucks, and many cars of those who came to see what was happening. The first one out of the vehicles was a man with his arm in a sling. I recognized him.

"Freeze!!! Get your hands above your heads!!!" yelled Officer Turnbull.

I only stared at him silently in despair.

"Get your hands above your heads now!!!" he commanded.

I could see the satisfaction of finding us was overwhelming for him.

"How's the shoulder doing? Does it hurt? I'm sure it does, but it can't possibly hurt as I hurt now. Does it hurt, Nick?" I asked him.

He shot his pistol at the ground right before my feet.

"Do what I say! Get your hands above your heads!"

"Why?" I asked, for I was overly aggravated over what I had just lost. I began to approach him with wrath in my eyes and my fists clenched.

"Do it now! Now!" he yelled, backing up a few steps.

"Do you even know what just happened here?" Tyler asked.

"It looks like you guys just blew up a hotel and killed hundreds of innocent people. That's why we're here. Now, get your hands above your heads and get down on the ground! Now! I said now!"

I continued to approach him without my hands above my eyes, revenge clearly my intent.

"Freeze!" he commanded.

I did not stop. He took the shot and put it straight in the center of my chest. I knew the bullet had hit me, but I was numb to the pain. I fell before him, and Tyler put his hands above his head and fell to his knees.

Nick smiled uneasily at what he had accomplished. He had finally taken me down. His mission was over. He looked down at my body while he stood above me. Two other officers ran over to cuff Tyler. The moment was perfect for Nick Turnbull. The only thing that could ruin it was a hand grabbing on to his leg.

As I grabbed Nick's leg and threw him onto his police car, Tyler took out the two cops who came to cuff him. I took Nick's gun as I threw him and shot it straight at the fire truck. Hitting the main water tank, my shot caused water to cover my pursuers at terrific velocities. I placed another shot into the foot of the second officer with whom Tyler was struggling.

We took off, having subdued our enemy. I turned my back on the past once again and ran for my safety. It was time to start a new chapter of life.

The city was filled with cars of people who had stopped to look at what had just happened to the hotel. This made our escape so much easier. We darted through the crowds of cars and people and made our way out of the city.

Fueled by grief and fear, we ran for the rest of the day. I had decided that it was best to return to something familiar. This is why we headed for Alemande, planning to return to Jonah's home outside the town. L.I.F.E. had found us, and there was no real hiding now, only running.

Even though we started quite early in the day, we could not make it back all the way to Jonah's home within the day. We had refused to use the subways and never picked up a cab. I had remembered the way back to West City well enough from the cab ride. This brought us to West City just as night had fallen.

We decided to hide in my old spot. I slept in the large refrigerator box which still had not been picked up after all this time. Tyler compiled many other boxes and made a fort in which he slept. The night was long, and I barely slept.

My insomnia was not brought on by the fact that I was to sleep in a box, for I had gotten very used to sleeping in such places. It was brought on by the death of even more people I loved. These people were my family. Now, they were gone. Gone. All night, I remembered the precious memories I had shared with them. My inner peace had forsaken me. I wept until I slept.

They remained in my dreams. How they danced through my mind all that night! It was not pleasant, but more of a constant and seemingly endless reminder of what I had lost. Nothing I could do would let me escape the depression. Everything I loved was torn away. Never did the happiness remain. Goodbyes attacked me violently whenever they could. Then, they tormented me afterward. I suffered my dreams that night. It was a suffering beyond describing, beyond what words can convey.

When I awoke, I found Tyler looking in from the front of the box. As much as I contemplated giving up and not leaving the box, I came out and stretched my tired bones.

"Where to next, kid?" Tyler asked me.

The answer was easy in my mind; we should return to my family by the sea. Wishing to be cautious as to not make any further mistakes, though, I thought about it for a second. Upon thinking about it, I came up with a better solution.

"Tyler, you stay here and find some food. I'll run over to Jonah's house, and there I will decide the best course of action. Then, I'll come back, hopefully with more food, and tell you the plan," I suggested.

"Why can't I come?" he asked.

"It's in case L.I.F.E. has anyone stationed in the area. I can avoid them better than you," I answered.

He scowled but accepted my idea.

"Give me some money," he said. I gave him all the money I had, 42 dollars, and he took off.

Before he was too far away, he yelled, "Kid, if you take too long, don't expect me to not come looking for you."

I affirmed what he had said with a nod, and he ran from sight.

The run from West City to Jonah's home was a long one. It took me two hours running full speed before I came to the woods outside Jonah's home. I took my time from there and caught my breath. I sat on a stump and breathed hard. Having run full speed for two hours had left me fatigued to say the least. I yawned from my exhaustion and rolled off the stump. There was no way to prevent it; I fell asleep.

In my dreams, I cried out to God concerning the loss of my family.

"Why?! Why have you taken them from me?!" I screamed, but there was no answer. "I can't keep losing them, everyone I love. Why must they all die? Why are you letting this happen to me?!"

No answer. This was torture, losing them systematically to my screwed up life. There was so much pain! I was nearing the breaking point, the place of no turning back. Soon, I would give it all up. This life was not worth suffering for anymore.

"Fight, Martin. It's what you were made for," a voice called out from behind me.

Flipping around, I was faced by the Jonah.

"Jonah? What are you doing here?"

"You've gotta fight, Martin. You've got a huge battle ahead of you, and you can't give up now. People are relying on you to fight," he said, stepping closer to me.

"I...I can't. I can't keep fighting! It's too much! I can't take another blow!"

"Yes, you can, Martin. You're so much stronger than you know. I know it hurts, but you can do it. All the pieces are coming together perfectly, just as they're supposed to. Don't give up! Keep fighting!"

"Why? Why am I fighting? What am I suffering for?"

"Only you can save them. L.I.F.E. cannot continue to manipulate, kill, and destroy. You're the only one who can stop them."

"I don't know. Am I even strong enough? Can L.I.F.E. truly be stopped?"

"You have all the strength you need by your side. I will never leave you, Martin. Now, go! It's time for you to wake up."

Instantly, I snapped awake. Dazed, I glanced around at the thick trees surrounding me. I then remembered what I was doing. How long had I been asleep? I quickly got up and made my way to Jonah's home.

As I came out from the trees, I saw what I never could have suspected. Like so many structures I had seen before, Jonah's house was blackened and collapsed.

Trembling, I ran to the house. I thought that there must be some way out of this nightmare. Touching the burnt wood, again I became emotionally unstable. I cried as I thought of Cody, Alyssa, Jonah, Mia, and Donovan. They were all gone. They had been taken from me like everyone else.

I entered what would have been the living room. Nothing lived here, nothing. The charred boards resembled the skeleton of a corpse picked by the vultures. It was so empty. No longer did compassion warm these walls. No pictures, no furniture, no distinguishing characteristics…and no family.

Standing in the middle of true desolation, I contemplated giving up once again. When all my foundation was shattered beneath me, I no longer believed I could stand. My tears fell quietly to the ashes at my feet. Hope was dead.

I heard a crash behind me. I flipped quickly around to see a man about a foot taller than I and probably four times as muscular. The man grinned as I looked upon him.

"Martin Shepard, I have found you in desolation. Zak Kurien informed me of the great likelihood of your return to Alemande. Using my own calculations, this corpse of a home is the place to which you would most likely come," the man said in a deep voice.

"Who are you?" I asked, wiping the wetness from my eyes.

"I am as you are, Martin Shepard. I am a superior being."

This man who stood in the ruins of my life was a Super Soldier just as I was. He looked to be maybe 30 years old, but, of course, he was not this age. It was possible he was only one year old, and the experiment had done the rest.

"Yes, it is true that I am only one year old, but I must assure you that I am the finest that L.I.F.E. has ever produced. My presence here instead of an army of well-equipped agents should be fine evidence to that fact. Ah, Martin Shepard, please do grant me your pardon. An introduction I have not given you out of my superior intellect, but yours is lacking and pitiful. I am The One. At least, I have been deemed as such by my creators."

It was alarming how he had just seemed to read my mind. I knew he had not because I could do the same thing on a lesser level. He simply deduced that what he said would lead to me thinking what I thought. On this occasion, he got it right.

"But I speak of a lack in comparison to myself. You do not lack intellect, Martin Shepard, for you are correct. It is not mind reading in truth, but, surely, it could be considered its equal. My abilities more than rival any psychic powers one might fictionally possess. I must mend your flaw in this one detail, though. Your abilities are, in no way, on a lesser level to mine. They are infinitely less. Your comparison is between a mite and the brilliant sun," The One chuckled, mocking me.

Again, I was shocked. The intelligence it took to guess such dialogue so quickly…it was astonishing!

"I extend my gratitude to you, Martin Shepard, but flattery is but the handsaw of the weak. I say lay down your tools and retrieve enlightenment freely from me."

"Did you kill the people in this house?" I asked, barely understanding his previous comment.

"No," he said and gave me hope. "Their death was procured at the hands of one quite less than I," he completed and crushed all of my hope.

He then tossed something to me. It was the mafia ring I had given to Cody. They really were gone. They, along with my biological family, truly were the people who cared about me the most, and now they all were dead. Their lives would no longer accompany mine in this difficult journey. My eyes filling with more tears, I slid the ring back onto my own finger.

"Standing outside, I much enjoyed the grand sight of the flames engulfing this less than humble abode. It would have been my wish that those within were not without their voice so that their screams could have been my joy as well. They were undeniably the kindest souls I have ever encountered. Of course, the mite would pride itself against the sun once more! I have known only L.I.F.E.! But I do not diminish them in such humor. Traitors to you they were not. Playing hypocrites, their masks declared no knowledge of your name, Martin Shepard. They were devoted in their scheme until I ripped your jewelry from the foolish boy's digit! I would take shame to not inform you that their faith in you was unwavering until the final breath exhaled. They hid away their cooperation behind a thousand locks and the equivalent amount of keys. The young fool, the boy, even ran for a gun! A shotgun! A true fighting spirit was in him, and one with a justified cause."

"How could you?! They had nothing to do with this! You had no reason to kill them!" I yelled, furious.

"Your question is quite flawed, Martin Shepard. The weak ones formerly housed here had everything to do with this. Amnesiac, you are no whore with your affections. Were it to be your choice, you would lock them away with yourself forever, never to be lacking their presence. Your mind desperately desires familiarities. With nothing familiar left in this world, to what do you cling? You cling to L.I.F.E., and then you cling to death!"

Poetic as it was, I refused to accept it. "I would never go back to L.I.F.E.! You have already taken everything, and I know that is the last place I would ever go!"

"One remains yours even now, Martin Shepard. Patience… A whole world of loss awaits you!"

Now, I was terrified, and my panic was overtaking me. I needed to act soon or I would freeze up and be dead for sure.

"So it will be, Martin Shepard. Let us finish this tiresome game. I shall not allow the air of my world to be wasted on the unmeritorious."

When he said this, my mind went crazy. Somehow, I had to come up with an idea to kill this colossus. My mind scrambled for an answer, but there were none.

First, I thought that maybe I could just run, but to where? Also, there was no way I could outrun him. He had to be about six times faster than I. There was no way I could run. Second was the thought of fighting him. How could I fight this beast? His powers were six times more than mine. He could probably kill me with one punch. I could not fight him.

As I started thinking about the third, his punch connected with my chest, and I flew through the burnt wall. Broken wood falling with me, I grabbed a board quickly and tried to attack him. He grabbed it, and then kicked me away, expending nothing on me.

When I was on the floor, I saw a nail and grabbed it. Lunging at The One, I tried to put it in his eye. A push from him knocked me away, and I dropped the nail. He picked it up. He then stabbed it into his own eye.

"Naught availeth, Martin Shepard," he said as the nail was pushed out of his eye and then strange liquids flooded his eye.

The eye repaired itself almost within seconds. It was beautiful, yet terrifying. His power was so undeniably greater than any power I had ever witnessed. L.I.F.E. had created such wonder. Seeing this man inspired humility in me.

I lay on the ground in horror. I could not win. He was so powerful that he could heal himself in seconds. Even if I hit him in the heart, he would probably regenerate it before anything happened. Nothing I could do would hurt him.

I fled. Getting outside was an accomplishment itself, but he got out as well. He was there in a millisecond and grabbed me at the same time. I was lifted up high in the air, and, in a desperate attempt, I flailed and squirmed to escape.

"Futility, thine name is Martin Shepard. You have shocked even me in your attempts at battle. Did you even think? Is cerebration an impossibility for you? Credit I gave you a plethora in excess. You are without hope in this endeavor, Martin Shepard. And as it is with me, it is with L.I.F.E., I must inform you. Escape from them: impossible. Victory against them: inconceivable."

I spit in his eye.

He wiped out his eye and said, "All other pleasures in existence will not, even combined, reach the sum of this, Martin Shepard. Your death is my joy eternal."

I laughed at him. It was my last insult to the L.I.F.E. Organization. If I could have, I would have spit in all the L.I.F.E. agents' eyes.

"In conclusion, nothing were you but a failed experiment. You fool, you fought your strongest of desires. You set yourself as your foe, and weak you became. I give you my apology for only…" he said, but stopped, let go of me, and collapsed.

I saw the blood shoot out the back of his head as the bullet entered his skull. He now lay there, knocked out. His head wound healed, and the blood stopped coming.

I sat on the grassy ground in awe. Then, I saw Tyler running up from the distance. He ran up to me to see what he had just done. He looked down at The One. Setting down his sniper rifle, he grabbed a grenade out of his pocket. He stuffed it deep into the colossus's mouth and pulled the pin.

We backed away from The One before his head exploded, finishing him off. A bullet to the brain might not have killed him. In fact, it might have only made him lose his memories, but the grenade made sure to fully destroy the brain.

"What happened to you, kid? What was that thing?" Tyler asked me.

"That man was with L.I.F.E., one of their Super Soldiers like me. Luckily, you are never too far off. He was about to kill me."

"Well, you know me, always wanting to help," Tyler said with a cocky smile.

I gave him a chuckle, finally feeling a bit of relief. Then, I put my hand on his shoulder and looked him in the eyes.

"Now, what happened to you?"

Chapter 26
Assemble

With his sniper rifle carried on one shoulder and his backpack of weaponry on the other, Tyler led me to the car in which he had driven here from West City. As we got into the fancy SUV, he told me all that had happened to him.

"So... I went to find some food, like you told me to. And so, I was walking, and guess who I saw?" he said, starting up the car.

I shrugged my shoulders.

"Ol' Miles Vaillancourt! Anyway, I walk up to him, you know, and he recognizes me. He takes off running, and I'm, like, right behind him. I catch him right as he gets to his house, and I grab him. Practically tackle him to the ground! He wants to know what I want, so I tell him that I'm here to mug him. You know, just for fun. He then takes me inside, and I take a look around the place. Well, I go down to the basement and find a whole cache of weapons. I mean, RPGs, shotguns, explosives, and all kinds of crap!" he told me, gesturing wildly.

"What?! Why did Miles have all the weapons?" I asked, suddenly very interested.

"Well, it turns out that, after his hotel blew up, he no longer had any kind of business because he put all his assets into the hotel. Not knowing what to do, he got into some shady business with some rival gang of ours."

"The Pirates?"

"Exactly! And these Pirates want to become the alpha gang again, right? They need weapons to do that, and they don't have any cash. Vaillancourt does, though. They then force him to buy weapons with his remaining cash that he got from his relatives. But, Miles being a smart one, before he gives them the weapons, he kills them using the high-tech weapons..."

"Wait," I interrupted. "Miles killed them?"

"Yeah, I was pretty shocked! But when you take everything from someone, I think you know what happens, kid," Tyler said.

After he said this, I remembered The One's words. He said they would take everything, and then I would come back to them. Miles was not returning to the Pirates, for he never knew them, but he was returning to that hostile mindset that got him his hotel. The One was quite wise for a one-year-old.

"Now, he has no way to get rid of the weapons without somebody being able to trace them. They've been in the basement since," Tyler said, finishing up his story by drumming on the steering wheel as he drove.

We had found weapons, lots of weapons. High-tech weapons that were almost equal to that of the L.I.F.E. Organization's weapons. These weapons could bring the destruction of L.I.F.E.! The one thing we needed now was an army.

"Wait, Ty. How can we be sure that, when we get back there, he won't be ready to kill us with those very weapons?" I asked.

"You're just gonna have to trust me, kid," Tyler said, and we continued to Miles Vaillancourt's home.

We soon entered West City, and Tyler drove me to Miles Vaillancourt's house. I was anxious to see what Tyler had done with my former boss. With Miles in an unstable state of mind, I did not think it was best to have him in the house filled with highly dangerous weaponry. Whatever Tyler had done, I had to trust him.

We pulled up along the street and left the car. Tyler led me right up the stairs and into the house. We entered, and Miles was sitting there, not knowing what to do. His former employee and then boss had just entered the room.

"What's up, Miles?" I asked, looking down at the man.

"Oh, you know. I've just been sitting here, holding this grenade," he said, and I saw that he was holding the lever down on a grenade with his hands zip-tied together and his legs zip-tied to the legs of the chair.

Tyler smiled at me, and now I knew how he had kept him in here.

Tyler locked the door.

"Now, Mr. Vaillancourt, you better not throw that grenade or you will have a lot of damage to your house. And hell, you wouldn't want the police getting involved, would you? With their new zero-tolerance policies and increased sentences, that would be really bad. Understand?" Tyler said.

Miles nodded grumpily, and we made our way down to the basement.

Down in the basement, there were hundreds of weapons. The place looked like the armory in the L.I.F.E. facility. All kinds of digitally equipped weapons resided here. Heat-seekers and satellite-guided rockets were lying down in my former boss's basement.

"What do you think we'll need, kid?" Tyler asked me.

"We will need all of it, but the real question is who will use them? We can't storm the castle ourselves."

"This is true, but what if I was on a boat in the water outside the facility and fired the rockets from there? I mean, it would totally catch them off guard, and then you could go and kill everybody inside."

Tyler's idea just might work. The one thing we needed was a boat. If the agents could not get Tyler, he would be able to shoot them before they had a chance. There was the chance, though, that Tyler would take a missile to his boat. If this happened, he would be done for, and the probability of that happening was high, especially with the missile implements on top of the building. The idea was risky, but it was the only one we had now.

"I think that might work. We should go to Alemande to get a boat from their docks," I said. Tyler agreed with that idea.

Walking back up the stairs from the basement, a feeling of uneasiness was creeping up on me. I knew we had to go down to the docks at Alemande to figure out what to do, but I just could not feel safe with Miles, who had been driven crazy with all that had happened to him because of me, holding the lever down on a grenade in the house with the weapons. I feared that he would try to throw the grenade down the stairs to the basement filled with weapons, but I hoped that he had not progressed to that state of insanity.

We then left Miles in the house, clutching the grenade. I looked him in the eyes, and my eyes made sure to tell him not to try anything. His eyes said back that he would not do anything and that he had just given up. I felt a little bit safer now.

It was a sad sight to see that look in Mr. Vaillancourt's eyes. He was defeated. This was the man who was a defeater himself. He had conquered West City with the most luxurious hotel in the country, but then he had lost it all. Now, he was nothing. All he had left was despair.

The call to not give up myself from my dream rang within me again. I had to keep fighting. People needed me to do this. I could not let L.I.F.E. go on as it had. They must be stopped, and I was the only one who could stop them. It fell on my shoulders, so I would not give up the fight, not until I was dead.

We then went to Alemande, driving very cautiously. I felt as paranoid as I had before I had found my family. This time, I had good reason to be paranoid. The agents could find us at any moment. If they did, there was no way we could run from them. They could dispatch a whole army and find us in no time.

Finally, after hours of stealthy driving, we made our way to the Alemande docks. As I looked through the crowds that usually consisted of mainly fishermen, I noticed a few men in black suits. The agents were here.

The black suits were a statement. The agents had no fear; why should they? They were supported by one of the strongest and best armed forces in the world. By wearing the suits everywhere, they proudly exhibited their connections, and no one dared to stop them. It was all part of their manipulation, their ability to control.

We kept low and tried to blend in with the crowd as much as possible. By studying our environment, I found that there were only five agents in this general area. After locating all of them, I kept both Tyler and myself the greatest distance from them. I also made sure we always had a good amount of people between us and the agents surrounding us.

Tyler and I hid behind some large crates, far out of sight. Taking a second to rest, we heard some conversation from some of the fishermen by us.

"Can you believe those nasty suits?! There goes our taxes right there!" one said, throwing an object he had been holding to the ground angrily.

"I know, I know… How can they continue with these crazy stunts that they keep somehow doing? I mean, they think that they are helping us! They think that they are 'enhancing our life's fullness!' What a load of bullshit!" another said, and then he took a long swig from his bottle.

"Have you seen what they did to the cities like West City and Wallace? It's ridiculous! Why do they spend all our stupid money on full-scale assaults on a bunch of machines and one man?! And have you seen their facility?! All our hard-earned money right there! Unbelievable!" the last one said.

I knew to whom they were referring. They referred to the L.I.F.E. Organization. Even they knew how evil this group was. They must have spoken to the agents in West City when they were cleaning up the city. Rumors were also most likely spread.

"You know what probably the most expensive and unnecessary thing they do is?" the first one asked, visibly showing more outrage by the minute.

"Wasting our money on high-tech weapons?" the second one said, somewhat irritated now and gripping his bottle tightly.

"I heard that they do crazy experiments in their labs. Crazy, very expensive experiments! And even more disgusting, they are probably doing those experiments on children! That's what Chris told me," the first one said.

"And now they are patrolling even here because something they did caused even more problems. I just wish the government would just cut them off! With all the money they'd save, maybe we wouldn't be so deep in debt!" the third one said, chuckling slightly with his frustration.

Their outrage was quite clear. These men were angry and for good reason. Surely, they hated the evil that L.I.F.E. was. These were good men who did not want to sit back and watch everything go to hell. It was my time to step in.

"You know, you guys are right," I said as I came out from behind the crates. They seemed very surprised that anyone could be eavesdropping on their loud conversation. "I would really like it if they were put in their place. Do some experiments on them like they did to me."

"They did experiments on you? You've been in their labs? Hell, I didn't even think Kevin was telling the truth," the second one said referring to the first one.

"I have, and I know what they're capable of. They are liars, smart liars, who want nothing more than to create and control. They created me, and, when they couldn't control me, they tried to kill me. That is why they are here now," I told them, gesturing discreetly at one of the nearby agents.

"Listen, we would love to help you put those scum in their place, but we don't have any way of doing it. I mean, they are a government organization, and how can we put up a fight against that?" the third one said.

"I have the resources, and all I need is the manpower to back it up. I was hoping that you and your friends here could help me out. It's a lot to ask; I know. But please, I truly need your help. Desperately."

The three then thought about what I had said. These men were good-spirited, honest men, and they hated the thought of people experimenting on other people, especially babies. Even if they did not understand the full gravity of L.I.F.E.'s operations, the men knew that what they were doing was wrong.

When I told them that all they had to do was sign up and they could destroy the organization, many thoughts went through their heads. Is it really the right thing to go in and stop this organization by force? Can we really do this? Is this man lying to us? They also felt the need to help a fellow fisherman out. In the end, the conclusion was that the L.I.F.E. Organization had gone on long enough.

"You know what...yeah. We're in," Kevin said and shook my hand.

"I can't let these scum continue to do the evil they're doing," the second one said, setting down his bottle on a crate and shaking my hand as well.

"I once saw a child run from that building. The things that kid said were disturbing. I'll never let them treat children like that," the third one said, and he, too, shook my hand.

The sincerity of all three could not be in doubt.

We then snuck over to where Andrew sat upon a barrel like he always did. We told him our plan, and he, too, wanted in. He then went through the crowds of fishermen, pulled them aside, and told them as well. He had recruited most of the docks without the agents stationed there even knowing.

The team with which Andrew set us up had about 60 people in it. With that team, we snuck back to the Vaillancourt house. We all left at different times as to not cause any suspicion.

When we arrived, Tyler took the grenade from Miles and locked him in the closet. Tyler then took the pin out of his pocket and put it back in the grenade. He set the grenade down on the counter and went into the living room.

We met the 60 fishermen in the large living room of the house. There, Tyler and I explained what was going to happen.

"In the basement of this house are many, many weapons. These are what we will attack the L.I.F.E. facility with. I am hoping to have about ten boats in the water outside the facility. The people there will be set up with the high-tech missile systems. I think that we should have about four people per boat, leaving about 20 of you to help Martin and I storm the place. Those 20 will be armed with everything they can carry because the L.I.F.E. agents will be armed the same way.

When we have breached the facility, I will place numerous charges of T4 within the building. The T4 charges are many times stronger than C4 charges and will hopefully have the power to destroy the whole facility. If we're lucky, that hell-hole will be completely obliterated, reduced to nothing but ashes. Since I will have to hold all of the T4 charges, I won't be able to protect myself as well, so you guys will have to. Luckily, Martin will be the diversion so that they do not see me placing the charges. After they are set, all of you will be alerted to leave the facility.

Make a full retreat, and, in two minutes after the warning, Martin will have the detonator and set off the charges. Any questions?" Tyler said, addressing the whole team.

A younger man raised his hand.

"How can we fight? I don't know how to use missiles. I barely know how to use a gun!" the young man said.

Uproar started in the living room. Voices did not seem to venture to a lower decibel level, but instead remained much louder than needed. Andrew then stood up and demanded the attention of everyone with his booming voice.

"Quiet! Quiet, everyone! Many of us have never seen the battlefield, but I know I have. I have been trained with all kinds of weapons in Iraq, and I can train you. Just give me some time! I can help to make this happen!" Andrew spoke up.

A glimmer of hope for the team appeared.

"Yes, Andrew, please do train them. We can do this with your help. And I am sure there are other militarily trained people in this room. Step up and train these common fishermen for a better cause! Without your help, how can we triumph over these monsters?" I said to the crowd.

Murmurs vibrated through the room.

After about fifteen seconds, a man spoke up, "I can help."

More and more raised their hands and pledged their knowledge and experience to the cause. I smiled upon the scene.

"Thank you," I said. "We will need all the help we can get."

We then assigned the teams. Andrew stood in the front of the room and made the decisions. He addressed the many members and told them who would stay with me and who would go on the boats.

Andrew had known these men for a long time. He knew them well enough to tell me which ones should steer a boat and which ones could shoot down the agents. These men were Andrew's greatest friends over the years, but two among them were missing. Jonah and Donovan were gone. No wonder he worked so hard and fast to get this group together. He saw his opportunity to avenge those whose lives were so unfairly taken.

After we had figured out all of this, one problem still remained. How would we transport all of these weapons? With L.I.F.E. searching for us everywhere, it would not help to drive down the street with huge missiles on the back of our cars. There had to be another, more disguisable way. I thought of the answer as I heard Miles banging on the closet door, trying to escape.

The next day, two moving trucks were driven to the house. Miles sat outside and supervised as the fishermen disguised as Andrew's Moving Company's workers hauled huge boxes out the door and onto the truck. Miles never once tried to run, for he did not want the package of C4 on his back to explode.

Once the weapons were all on the trucks, they were driven to the docks in Alemande. There, they were loaded into the fish storage building. The fish were unloaded back into the sea. The shocked and disturbed faces of the fishermen watching their hard work be reversed, gave me some pause, but I knew we needed the space more.

Training began that day. Andrew, along with about ten others, spoke to small groups and discussed what they would need to know. Everyone was learning quickly, and the fishermen started to become troops. I could see everything coming together. We could win this fight.

After a long day of training, the majority of the troops went home to get a good rest before the most important day of their lives. Others remained to continue familiarizing themselves with the weaponry. The sun had set on our efforts today, and I was ready to allow myself to rest as well.

With the weapons stored, the plans known, the boats ready for morning, and the troops asleep at their houses, I was ready for tomorrow. This was for what I was waiting through all my troubles. When I lost my boat, when I lost my friends, when they lied to me, when my family died, when Jonah's family died, I knew what I had to do the whole time. L.I.F.E. had caused it all, and, finally, I would stop them.

The rest of the day was spent in that fish storage building. Many of my soldiers came up to talk to me. One was particularly helpful to me.

"Sir, are you Martin Shepard?" a man came up to me and asked.

"Yes, I am. Thank you for supporting us in this cause. What's your name, sir?"

"I'm Mike. I wanted to tell you that my brother was killed on your boat."

"You know about the *Annabelle*?" I asked, leaning forward eagerly.

"Yes, I do. If you don't mind, I have a lot to tell you."

We sat down, and Mike began his story.

"My brother, Duke, always told me so much about you. He was the captain of the boat, you see, and he was so fascinated by you. He first met you when you were just a little kid. You tried to get onto his boat unnoticed. You just wanted to be a stowaway, just wanted to hide for a bit. But Duke found you. He asked you why you were trying to stowaway. You told him about L.I.F.E. and about how they were chasing you. He didn't really believe you, thought that maybe you saw the building and were just playing some kind of game. So he asked you where your parents were. You then asked him what parents were… That's when Duke knew that he had to help you. He saw what horrible people the L.I.F.E. Organization members were."

I found it strange that I did not know what parents were then. Thinking it through, it made sense. I would not have ever met my parents, and, if no one ever told me what parents were, I would never have heard about them. It is possible for a genius to not know what dogs are, having never been introduced to one or never being told.

"Well, you stayed on the boat quite a while," Mike continued. "You helped with the little tasks, just because you were a kid. But you showed a lot of interest, and Duke always taught you new things. He taught you what parents were and just a lot about basic things in the world. He really educated you on all that L.I.F.E. never cared to tell you."

Now, things made more sense. With my amnesia, only my memories were erased. I still knew a lot of different things about the world. These things had been taught to me by Duke. I owed this man a lot, and I was grateful for what he had done for me.

"Time went by, and you always wanted to learn more. You started helping with the fishing. Duke talked about how much strength you had for just a kid that looked to be about seven years old. A little kid was working alongside men!" Mike laughed.

I laughed, too. No wonder Duke talked so much about me.

"Your main teacher was not Duke, though. He just taught you about different common knowledge things. Your real teacher was a woman named Olivia Taylen. She was the wife of one of the fishermen aboard the boat. Chris was his name. She was fired from her teaching job and desired to continue teaching. She taught you about math, history, science, and grammar. She said a lot about your amazing ability to grasp such complicated topics. She said you were really a very bright child."

Mike took a second to reflect upon the past. I could see that he really missed his brother. I had the same feeling about mine.

"And then Duke noticed something else," he began again. "You came aboard the boat looking like a seven-year-old. Not a year later, you were like a teenager. Duke was so confused. He asked you about it, about all that had happened to you in that lab. You told him. You told him all the horrible secrets about L.I.F.E. and about the one person who made it all bearable," Mike said.

"Jack Lamb," I said. Mike nodded.

"When Duke knew all of this, his hatred of L.I.F.E. grew. All fishermen don't like L.I.F.E. because they take away a huge amount of our state tax dollars. Alemande's infrastructure has been suffering for some time now, and they believe the money would much better be used on that."

I, too, agreed with this. If the city suffered, the citizens suffered. Money should have been set aside for such projects in Alemande instead of being thrown away on the evil organization. I would have much preferred a new road over an organization of liars and manipulators that sought total control in all aspects of life.

"Duke always spoke so badly about L.I.F.E. that all the fishermen no longer held back their dislike of the organization. They would vandalize the building and yell at people leaving it. L.I.F.E. turned its eye to the docks. Duke also talked so much about you, Martin, that so many people knew your name."

I remembered talking to Andrew the first time. When he had said I was kind of a legend, I did not know what he meant. He had apparently overheard some of the talk about my amazing abilities. I was a legend to these fishermen.

"The day the boat was attacked, I said good luck to my brother for the last time. I had been disabled in my construction job and had been living with him. He had been taking care of me for the time. He left that day, and I was already worried. It was a stormy day. Like, a really terrible storm. One that means a little more than just bad weather. I worried about him so much. When he did not come back, I thought maybe he was just delayed. Then, the next day..." Mike paused, frozen by the painful memory, "...the debris washes up. I've never known a harder day to keep on going than that one. Never."

It was a hard day for me, too. All hope for finding my past had been lost that day. I had not lost my only brother, though. I had lost much family as well, and I understood this man's pain.

I thanked Mike for talking to me, and he left. "You're a good guy, Mike," I said as he walked away. A weak smile appeared on his face.

"Thank you, Martin. I'll see you tomorrow," he said and left.

He had just given me so much more information. Unlike the information concerning my past that I had received before, this information made me a little happier. I left to go to sleep.

Tyler and I slept in the fish storage building, guarding the weapons. I could not fall asleep with all the excitement. Insomnia was also brought on by the information I had just received. I had wanted to know that part of my life for so long. It was so good to get to hear that part. It was one of the better ones.

I climbed to the top of one of the big refrigerators and made a bed.

I stared at the ceiling and thought about all the events that would unfold tomorrow. Mainly, my thoughts dwelled on what I would say to Zak Kurien when I found him, when he knew it was all over. I would have finally conquered him and his organization. L.I.F.E. would be ended.

This fight was not for revenge. I would not kill him because of what he did to me. I would not kill him because of all he had taken from me. I would not kill this man and his creation with my rage. I would destroy them because it was the right thing to do, and I would never let them hurt anyone ever again. Tomorrow, the pain of L.I.F.E. would be brought to an end.

"God, I trust You," I prayed. "You have made me new and led me to this point for a reason. If this is Your will, let me carry it out. May You give us safety and protection tomorrow as we fight for this justified cause. Give me the strength to fight this battle. I know that you will never leave me. Amen."

Chapter 27
To the End of LIFE

In the morning, we set off. The boat team loaded the rockets and their respective launchers onto the boats. The ground team grabbed their weapons and got into their cars. The boats sailed off, and the cars drove away. We were all going to the same place: the end of L.I.F.E.

Riding in the car, I suddenly felt guilt as I looked upon the overly confident fishermen in the car. In their minds, we were storming an embassy or some other low-security government facility, but that was not it at all. They were not prepared for the highly-trained soldiers inside or the weapons that the outside world had never seen. I felt guilt because I was sending these troops to their deaths.

Slapping each other on the back and psyching each other up, these fishermen exuded terrible confidence. They had no clue what was going to happen. Had I not either? Was I so set on revenge that I had risked all these lives to attain it? It was too late to turn back now. We could only give all we had, and all we would surely give.

Our vehicles came upon the facility, and the line of the cars was repositioned to block all traffic coming either way on the singular road. As my car pulled up, I saw the large letters that spelled out LIFE on the front of the building. All of a sudden, I became very anxious. We got out, and everybody hid behind the curved line of cars that blocked us from the building. Two agents came out with weapons aimed at us.

"Throw down your weapons and come out with your hands up!" an agent yelled.

"Surrender! This is not a fight you can win! Fire upon us, and you will die!" the other yelled, his threat valid.

I grabbed the radio from my vest. I looked to Tyler, and he nodded. I turned on the radio and said, "Fire."

Missiles screeched through the air and collided with their targets on the backside of the building. The facility shook, and I heard the damage that was caused. I saw as windows shattered from the shockwave and screams could be heard from the other side of the building. Even the giant "F" from the front of the building fell from the effects of shockwave, crushing the two agents. I smirked at the new spelling.

I jumped from the other side of the car, and so did the rest of the fishermen. Guns blazed as we charged into the facility. Confused agents ran as my bullets raced past and through them. When we had cleared the entrance, we all split up throughout the facility.

Everything went so fast as I ran through the halls. Whenever I saw an agent, I put bullets into him. These agents, I recognized their faces as I put them down. As Agent Stafford popped out in front of me, I slashed his throat with my knife. There was no hesitation in it. All the agents who had made themselves my friends I now was killing. I felt it was wrong to kill these people, but I knew the evil of which they were capable. This evil had to be put to an end.

It was strange how I killed these people who had, in some sense, been my friends in the past. Now, we tried desperately to kill each other. It did not matter with whom I had been on a mission or with whom I had played Firefight; I placed bullets within them all. No one could be spared for our mission to be complete.

There was a surreal nature in attacking this organization. I thought it funny that my true killer instinct was used only on the people who had given it to me. They never thought that they were the real enemy. Commander Zak had made a mistake in turning me into a Super Soldier. I now used all of that to destroy what he had developed.

More and more rockets flew into the facility. The men on the boats only stopped when they had run out. Then, large artillery shells flew into the building. Obviously, the attack by sea plan was working perfectly.

As I killed even more agents, I saw Tyler run by and place a charge on a pillar. He quickly saluted me and ran off. This was the second of the five floors. Tyler had covered the first and almost the second floor with the T4 charges. I had to give him more time to plant the rest.

I sprinted down the halls, following Tyler as explosions went off and bullets collided quite near him. I made sure to kill or, at least, maim the agents who sought to take his life. My fellow fishermen killed the agents as well. They quickly formed a team and surrounded Tyler. Feeling relief and knowing that Tyler was safe, I went back to finding and killing other agents in the building.

Soon, the deadly lasers of L.I.F.E. were reintroduced into the fight. Laser blasts flew by me as I slayed my foes. I either dodged the blasts or made sure to throw an agent in front of me before they hit. The agents exploded as the blasts hit them. The horrifying scene quickly made me distracted, and I was soon hit myself. My side blew open, and I fell through a hole in the floor.

Falling, I felt numb. Was this the work of my advanced mind? When I was in the fray, all pain and contemplation left me. My vision narrowed, and I could only focus on murdering the enemy. Yes, they had made quite the soldier out of me. I would repay them by taking their lives with the tools they had given me.

My body hit the ground a floor below, and I immediately pulled out my pistols. I aimed them at the hole above me. After intensely staring up for several seconds, nothing came. I had this one minute of peace to myself.

The hole in my side poured blood. Out of the fight and now able to focus on it, I felt the pain it was causing me. I chose to specifically focus on the wound and its pain, and my brain decided to tell my body to do something about it. Slowly, the wound started to heal. I got up, not willing to wait for it to heal completely. I looked around the room. What I found was disturbing to say the least.

I was in the lab. Right behind me was a table where a baby under anesthesia was strapped down. Its head was cut open, and the brain was revealed. The operation was only half completed because the scientists had run out after the explosions. They had left a perfect example of what had happened to me.

"I need some help in here, Doctor," I had remembered hearing when I had come into this medical lab previously. This was why he needed help. In this back room, the Super Soldier experimentation was taking place. With a complicated operation like this, I doubted that many made it through the procedure. That last one had died, and now this one would.

I had spent a large part of my life in these labs. As a quickly developing child, I had lived here. Oddly, this abominable lab was my birthplace and my former home. Jack and I had found the evil that was here. Jack himself had tried to finish the experiments; I had come to do the same.

Not wishing to linger here, I regained my senses and ran to go help my troops, but not before placing a T4 charge that Tyler had told me to place wherever I wanted. Anticipating this lab's absolute destruction, I could move on.

Arriving back at the second floor, I saw my troops fall. Without me, they did not have enough strength to fight back against the monsters. I ran to their aid, but I could not save them all. I watched in horror as the friends I had brought were gunned down by the liars who sought all our lives.

From a distance too far for me to react, I saw an agent knock Andrew to the floor with an electric-powered mace. Her name was Agent Bennett, and I had spoken to her only once during my stay in this complex. My friend crippled and twinging on the floor, she drew her pistol and put it to his head. Even running full-speed, I was not fast enough to get there before she executed Andrew. Arriving onto the scene, I relieved her of her mace, and then I swung the weapon as hard as I could at her head. She fell, dead, but my highly respected friend would not be avenged until we had finished the job. I would not let Andrew die in vain for this.

This fight was taking all I had left. Every ounce of might and will within me was devoted to this cause. The agents swarmed me as I tried ineffectively to kill them all. Grenades went off by me, and bullets went into me. Losing all of my strength, it became apparent that I could not fight them forever. I abandoned the fight, fearing for my safety.

I climbed the stairs, trying to find a place where they were not. But such a place did not seem to exist. How many people could have signed up for such an evil organization? How many had been manipulated into fighting for one man's evil agenda? Perhaps I would never understand why organizations like this one thrived, but all I needed to know was that I had to end it. I continued to fight for some sort of escape.

Then, it came to me all of a sudden. My old room was on the fourth floor, and it offered a brief sanctuary from this violent battle. I dialed in the code and ran inside. My hand slapped the lock command, and I collapsed to the floor. The wounds in my sides began to stitch themselves back together, and I elected to remain on the floor until I was healed. Afterward, I struggled to my feet and wandered to the window.

I looked outside and witnessed another soul-crushing sight. Missiles flew outside, but they were going the wrong way. They collided with each boat with my comrades in it. It disturbed me to the core, but even worse was the guilt that fell in the pit of my stomach. I had led them to their deaths. My crazy idea had done this.

Without warning, the door's lock blew off, and more of the monsters swarmed in. I aimed and fired at the menace that I could not defeat. They fell, but more started to come. Before they entered, an explosion knocked them all off their feet and eliminated all of the threat. The monsters fell in death, and I had been saved.

Looking beyond the blown up agents, I saw my greatest friend.

"They can't take us down, kid!" he yelled to me with a cocky grin.

"No one can! We're a team!" I yelled back as he ran off to plant the last charges.

I ran out of the room and again continued to fight off the agents. My weapons clicked with the lack of ammo, and I was forced into my desperate measures. I dropped a smoke grenade and hid within the shroud. Gunfire sounded outside my smoke covering, and bullets flew inside, failing to hit their mark. Using their fire, I then located all of the targets and threw my knives perfectly into each one's throat. They dropped, and I regained the ammo they had dropped.

Just as I had killed all of the agents around me, my radio gave me the message for which I had been waiting.

"The charges are set. Get out of here!" I heard Tyler say over the radio.

I did not choose to leave the facility. There was one more stop I had to make. I then took off for Commander Zak's office.

Arriving at his door, I kicked it in, even though he had dead-bolted it and blocked it with furniture. I entered, and, seeing a claymore on the floor, I jumped over it. The explosive meant to take my life in last resort missed. I walked into the large, open office of Commander Zak Kurien.

He aimed his magnum at my head. I, too, aimed at his head with my pistol. I knew that, with his shot, he could not kill me, but, with mine, I could kill him.

"Hello, Shepard. Not a bad try, but it ends here," Zak said, breathing a bit more heavily with anxiety and fear flooding his system.

"You know that you can't stop me, Zak. I hold the cards this time," I told him confidently, stepping closer to him.

"You may think you do, but, unfortunately for you, you forgot one of the cards," he said as he turned on a monitor with a remote in his other hand. "Look at this, Shepard."

On the screen was Tyler. He was on his knees and was surrounded by agents with guns pointed at his head. His hair was redder than usual due to a massive gash in his head. Tyler was not one to let the enemy capture him without a fight.

"You see, Shepard, I hold a very important card, your best friend. Actually, I think he is your only friend," he said as the grin appeared on his face once again.

I tried to fool him in a desperate attempt. "He is not my friend. He is one of the common fishermen whom I picked up at the docks."

Zak shook his head.

"You know, we have quite the file on Mr. Ishler, so there really isn't any way you can trick me," he said as he pulled out a folder from his suit.

He then slid it across the floor. I picked it up and looked at it. It was the entirety of the file they had on Tyler. Every little tidbit of information on him was in here. I saw pictures of Tyler and me at various locations. L.I.F.E. had proven itself to be excessively knowledgeable. There was no way I could bluff to save Tyler's life here.

"Now, drop the gun or I will send your little friend to Santidigo Island," Zak said.

"Santidigo Island?" I asked.

"That's where our new base is. We are testing a new experiment that can start the Super Soldier development even at an adult's age. And that's what's going to happen to your little friend if you don't do what I say. Now, drop the gun, Shepard."

I looked at the screen.

Tyler looked up at the camera and said, "Just complete the mission, kid! Don't worry about me!"

He was then hit with the back of a rifle from an agent.

I would take his advice. "I shall come for you, Tyler. Never forget that."

"I said drop the gun, Shepard!" Zak yelled.

"No."

"Do it," Zak said to the intercom on his desk.

The agents then stabbed a needle into Tyler's neck, and, after a weak gasp, he collapsed. The agents picked him up and carried him away.

"Your stubbornness will be the death of you, Shepard. As I said, they're now taking him to Santidigo Island," Zak said, a manic look in his eyes as he stared down the one who would end his life.

In the background, I heard the helicopter taking off. They were taking him to another base where they would experiment on him as they did with me. But not if I could help it.

I grabbed the first page of Tyler's file and looked down at his picture. This was a picture of Little Ty back in his mafia days. I remembered them well and how much more than a friend he was to me. He was my family, my brother who I could count on in any storm. I would not let them experiment on him. This facility would meet its fiery end, and then I would find Tyler. Nothing could stop me from saving him.

I dropped my gun and quickly pulled out my detonator. Putting my finger on the button, I locked eyes with Zak Kurien.

"You are the one who has caused it all. You did this to me, Zak. You stole me and experimented on me. You tried to kill me. You destroyed every good thing in my life. My friends, my family... You've taken everything, and now you've taken my greatest friend! But you will not die for all that. You will die because you are evil and because I cannot let you hurt anyone else. I won't let you make anyone else suffer. It started with me, and it ends with me. It is finished!"

My eyes turned to the detonator. I slammed my thumb down on the button, and time slowed to a crawl for my advanced brain. Turning back, I saw the explosion engulfing the room. I also saw the bullet launch from Zak's revolver.

As it raced towards my head, I remembered everything that I had learned. I remembered my family by the sea, my parents and siblings, the fishermen who gave their lives for a good cause, the officers who sought justice with all they were, everyone else I had met on this journey, and I remembered Tyler.

Then, I forgot…everything.

Chapter 28
Begin Again

My eyes opened to a darkened sky above me. The suffocating smell of smoke encompassed everything. Behind me was a line of cars. This line blocked off much of the road that was behind it. In front of me was a huge collapsed structure that smoldered from some kind of explosion. Little light shined through the blackness and quantity of ash that was falling.

My gaze fell upon myself. I could see my blackened skin through the holes in my completely burned clothes. What seemed to be bullet holes were all over my clothing as well. Gaping holes accompanied them. The holes were many and made it hard to tell, but I believed that the clothes were made of an armor-like material. Though the skin was blackened with soot, it did not seem to have retained any damage. What had happened to me?

In my right hand was some kind of device. I looked it over as I lay on the ground. It only had one button, and I concluded that its purpose was to set off some other device remotely. I set aside the device and looked in my other hand.

In my left hand was a piece of paper. I studied it with great interest. The picture appeared to be taken from some kind of security camera, for the man in the picture did not seem aware of his photo shoot. He was dressed in expensive clothing and appeared as if he were in some kind of organized group. The man was somewhat short and held a rifle in his right hand. I also noticed a very expensive ring on his right hand.

Looking back at my right hand, I noticed that I had the same ring. Had I known this man? Were we once friends?

Again, I analyzed the ring. It was made of silver and had gold around a ruby in the middle of the ring. I saw the name "Martin" inscribed on the top part of the gold on the ring. Was this my name? Was I Martin? If so, how did I know the man in the picture? How did I lose this memory? Questions began flooding my mind.

I looked back at the paper. At the bottom of the page was information about the man. His name was Tyler Ishler, and he was 5 feet and 5 inches tall. Hair color was red. He was 24 years old, and his occupation was criminal.

All these stats were just general information. Nothing told me who he was or why I should have known him. My only theory was that I was possibly in some kind of organized crime group with him. I still did not have much information.

I folded the paper up and stuffed it into my partially destroyed back pocket. I got off the ground and looked around me. The scenery still confused me. Why was I here? Did I destroy this building? With all the destruction before me, I wondered why I was not injured myself.

Was I in some kind of gang that had attacked this building and destroyed it? What purpose might such a gang have in destroying this structure? Was Tyler Ishler in this gang, too? Where was Tyler now? Why did I have this piece of paper that described Tyler? Where was I? Questions were entering my mind at an alarming rate.

Strangely, this feeling of confusion was so familiar. I felt that my whole life before this had been filled with the same confusion. Had I had so many questions even before my amnesia?

Before my next thought came, police cars swarmed the area behind me. Fire trucks and ambulances came right behind them. The vehicles maneuvered around the line of cars and came straight up to me and the building. The fire trucks quickly began their job, but not before the police.

The first one out of the vehicles was an officer whose eyes burned with both fury and satisfaction. He seemed overwhelmed with the scene in front of him.

"Get on the ground!" the officer yelled.

I fell to my knees and put my hands above my head. Another four officers swarmed me and cuffed me as quick as possible. I was then pushed towards the police car and stuffed into the back seat.

"We finally got you, Martin. It's all over now," the first officer said.

He confirmed that my name was truly Martin, and, at the same time, I looked at his name tag pinned on his jacket. This man was Officer Nick Turnbull.

I asked no questions when they told me something about remaining silent. The door was closed, and I was locked in the back of the police car. Officer Turnbull started the car, and another officer climbed in the other seat.

"Martin, I'm glad you were finally brought to justice. No longer will you terrorize the citizens of this state. I'll be very happy to see you behind bars," the other officer said.

"Isn't that right, Chase? Another criminal bagged! And this one means a lot more to me than all the others. We finally got him!" I heard Officer Turnbull say.

I was more important to the officer than any other criminal. I guessed that perhaps I was the leader of the criminal organization. That would give reason to Officer Turnbull's desire to bring me to justice. Even knowing what he had said, I did not believe that I could have been a criminal. In my heart, I knew that was not what I wanted for my life. I desired more for myself than the life of a criminal.

As I was being brought to the police station, I thought again about the man in the picture. Tyler Ishler, how did I know him? My best guess was that he was a partner in crime. He was perhaps one of many that followed under my leadership. I was arrested here because he and I had destroyed this building. I wondered if he had escaped, and I hoped that somehow he had.

Struggling with the handcuffs, I managed to slowly pull the paper out of my pocket. I laid it on the seat next to me. I unfolded it behind my back and then turned back to the paper.

I stared into the picture, memorizing every detail of this Tyler as well as the information printed below. There was a deep feeling in my gut that said he was important. I had a feeling that he would be able to clear up a lot about what was happening to me. The man in this picture was the key to finding my memory. Above all else, I needed to find Tyler Ishler.

This man, Tyler Ishler, was essential to finding my past. Against all reason, an unkillable hope lived within me that said he was still alive. If he was alive, nothing would stand in my way of finding him. Somehow, I knew it for sure. He and I had been a team, and nothing could take us down.

The End

About the Author

Alec Managhan

Growing up outside rural Alberton, Montana, Alec's youth was spent in the mountains and woods, dreaming up new adventures. Pair that with the rugged individualism of a Montanan and the self-inquiring soul of an introvert, and you will have the makings of the mind behind *The LIFE of Martin* and its sequel, *Monstrosities of LIFE*.

Alec has spent the vast majority of his life delving into the complexities and truths art can offer us about our human condition and the unsearchable realities of our world. Whether through film-making, writing, acting, storytelling, or philosophy, this author loves exploring the creative heart, anchoring this pursuit with his studies of Business Management at the University of Montana. Becoming a self-published author at the ripe age of 16, Alec wears his desire to share his experience of encountering life and truth on his sleeve.

www.ingramcontent.com/pod-product-compliance
Lightning Source LLC
Chambersburg PA
CBHW072212170626
46813CB00003B/901